BAD NAME

A.J. SCUDIERE

GRIFFYN INK

1

She stepped out onto the small front porch, into the circle of yellow light created by the old bare bulb. Finally alone, both kids in bed and asleep. The dishes were done, the kitchen counters cleaned and sanitized. She fished in the pocket of her big sweater for her crumpled pack of cigarettes. It should have been perfect.

There was still just a little bite at night at the beginning of the summer. Pulling out the pack without making it crinkle—as if the kids could hear that from upstairs—she fished out the lighter she'd shoved down in.

The kids didn't know she smoked. Her mama didn't know she smoked. As far as Kara knew, no one knew she smoked. Her gaze narrowed to the flick of the wheel and the burst of one tiny flame at the end of her lighter. It was all she needed.

Holding the cigarette up, she took that first drag, letting the nicotine hit her lungs. It flowed through her body, providing a relaxation she was no longer able to achieve on her own.

Taking a second long inhale and feeling her shoulders sink further, she looked up beyond the porch light at the stars hanging in the sky. She saw Orion's belt, and the North Star. So much dark cut only by the dim yellow bulb she should have replaced a while ago.

Movement caught the corner of her eye and she saw him then. A man hunched over, walking up her driveway, his fists shoved down into the pockets of his jacket.

He was already halfway up the drive. Had she not seen him turn in at the street? But the street was dark, too. The light was a few houses away. His head was down, the hood obscuring his face. He seemed almost mad about something.

"Hey!" Kara called out, "real late for a visit."

She knew him though. . . Kara took another drag on the cigarette. Whatever he wanted, he needed to work it out, maybe not with her. She would send him on his way, promise to help tomorrow. Out here, neighbors helped.

He was close by the time he tipped his head back, the hood sliding just enough for her to see his face. She did know him. *But did she?*

Somehow, she hadn't seen this before. There was something almost feral in his gaze tonight.

She would have called him a friend if asked—a new one, but a friend. Now when she took another drag on the cigarette, she didn't inhale quite so deeply. She stepped backwards, uneasy. Her heel hit the concrete of the stair and she took another step up, hoping to become just a little bit taller than him.

"Give me one of those cigarettes," he said.

"Please," she replied automatically, maternal instincts kicking in. She was reacting too harshly to being demanded of yet again. This time from someone who wasn't her own child.

Her normally mild-mannered acquaintance stared her hard in the eyes, not repeating any of it. Again, the unease grabbed her. It was enough that she figured maybe if she gave him a cigarette, he would state his purpose and go away.

For the first time Kara realized how dark her yard was, how

far back the house sat from the street. And how infrequent the streetlights were. If something happened to her here on her own front porch . . . She looked left and right. No, the neighbors wouldn't see.

She didn't fight it. Just handed over the one cigarette and the lighter, but he didn't take the lighter. Leaning forward, filter already tucked between his lips, he motioned for her to light it for him.

Something was wrong here. Very wrong.

She thrust the lighter at him, moving up the last two steps onto the landing. "You take it, I'm going inside."

Dropping her cigarette directly by her side, she ground it out. She wasn't even halfway done, but she wasn't thinking about the waste. "Have a good night."

It was such an odd interaction, but she didn't quite know how to leave. She couldn't open her own front door normally without turning away. She didn't want to take her eyes off him. Backing up would show him that she was, for the first time, scared of him.

"Are you worried about your two brats?" he asked.

"They're good kids," she replied almost rotely, but she was searching her mind, frantically wondering when she had told him that she had children. That she had two of them. That they were young enough that he might have referred to them as *brats* on purpose.

He grinned and his eyes gleamed. What she had thought was feral before now looked positively evil.

"I know about them," he said as he stepped up on the lowest step.

Could she get through the door and lock it fast enough? Would it keep him out? This house wasn't designed to be a panic room. It was a small country home—one she could afford on her salary. A big yard for her kids to play in. Neighbors that she smiled at as she drove by or when she was standing at the end of the street, putting the kids on the bus.

She stepped out here to smoke every night. No one knew that. Not unless . . .

She didn't have time to react. His hand shot out. He'd lit the cigarette and it was now a weapon. Feeling it sear into her skin. Kara almost cried out, but his hand was too fast. Pressed over her mouth, it was gloved and muffled her scream.

Kara panicked and fought.

CINDY BOLTED UP RIGHT in her bed, breath sucking in, hands clenching the covers. But there was nothing she could do.

2

The night had gotten dark quickly, too quickly. Georgia Dunham was losing hope.

The neighborhood was only passably lit and she wasn't stupid; that pretty places like this often only looked good on the surface. Basements could hide terrors; darkened corners could hide predators. She honestly wasn't sure quite what was lurking in her own heart. Still, she was determined.

Climbing the three short steps up to the small landing she knocked on the door. The car sat in the driveway just to her right. Lights were on in the back of the house and some faint noise she couldn't place was playing from somewhere.

Someone was home.

She waited a few impatient minutes, but nothing happened.

Hitting the door again, she told herself this wasn't her last chance to find her mother. Even if Jesse Nash couldn't do it, there had to be someone else. *Right?*

Georgia didn't want to admit that she'd exhausted the long list of every "someone else" she could get to. Some simply said they were too busy. The few who initially agreed to help backed out quickly when they figured out who her mother was. And maybe, by extension, who she was.

She knocked again, pounding on the door this time. She leaned in close, putting her ear to the panel to listen.

The sound was a television. Someone was home and simply refusing to answer her. Glancing over her shoulder, she made sure no one was watching.

Then, quickly, she grabbed the knob and twisted it as though she belonged there. It yielded under her touch—not locked at all.

"Jesse?" she called out. "I'm looking for Jesse Nash."

The sound and light pulled her toward a room at the back. Georgia kept calling out because her usual stealth could scare a person. The last thing she needed was Jesse Nash facing her down with a gun.

But, as she arrived in the back room, she realized Jesse Nash was absolutely not going to lift a gun at her.

Georgia felt her lips press together as disgust settled in her chest. But more than that—and it bothered her so much that she even felt it—was the disappointment.

3

As Jesse sat up, everything assaulted her at once: the light, the noise, the pounding of her own pulse inside her skull. She had a fleeting thought of *not again,* before she had to acknowledge to herself that *yes, she had in fact done it again.*

Then, she saw the woman sitting across from her on the couch.

Yelping, Jesse scrambled back, as if pushing herself deeper into the cushions would protect her. Despite the throbbing pain in her head, and the thickness in her throat, she growled out, "Who are you? What are you doing here? Why are you in my living room?"

The woman—who on second inspection, looked much younger than Jesse had originally assessed—raised one eyebrow. "I've been sitting here for eight hours. I've used your bathroom twice and had four glasses of water, with ice, from your fridge. *Now* you want to know what I'm doing here?"

Jesse felt her eyes fly wide. What the hell had she done last night? The woman must be lying.

Either she'd said it out loud, or it was clear on her face.

Sharp blue eyes bored into her as if looking at her very soul and finding her quite wanting. Brown hair fell just past her shoulder, shiny and clean, it had a bit of a wave. It emphasized a straight nose, high cheekbones, and lips that might have been rounder if they weren't pressed together.

Jesse managed to push herself just a little further back into the cushions. She felt every joint, every beat of her heart pulsing in her neck and her head. Her next move involved only a flick of her eyes. Glancing at the coffee table she saw the bottle of Blanton's Black Label lying there and she was pretty certain it had been full yesterday.

Gene deserved for her to drink his most expensive bottle of whiskey, but she'd deserved to enjoy it and she didn't even remember it. The bottom now held only enough to run laboratory tests that would prove that yes, it had been the real deal. Two glasses sat next to it. One upright, the other on its side though thankfully not shattered. It had dribbled a little whiskey across the coffee table. She figured for a moment there was at least a couple bucks worth in the drops.

Breathing in through her nose, Jesse realized it was a mistake. Her stomach rolled. It didn't matter though. She wouldn't vomit. She'd feel better if she barfed up everything that she had done the night before.

The woman stood up, black jeans and white tank top in contrast with what looked like a high-end blazer, cut to fit. Half thug, half businesswoman? Jesse wished her brain was working better.

When the woman returned, she set a glass of ice water on top of the coffee table just across from Jesse, clearly indicating that it was for her.

The sound of the glass tapping made her ears feel as if they were shattering. She had no one to blame but herself. When Jesse didn't move, the woman made a harsh gesture indicating she should drink it.

Jesse couldn't stop her eyes from widening. She might be hung-the-fuck-over, but she knew a predator when she saw one. There was something in the roll of the wrist, the angle and way the fingers lay together in the motion, that let her know this woman was highly trained.

Reaching out, Jesse wrapped her fingers around the cold glass and took a gulp. Only too late did she think *maybe it had been drugged?* Though why anyone would want to drug her when she was doing such a damn good job of it herself was a mystery.

She hated that she had put herself here, so far away from her own A game. And her A game was good. She drank another slug of the cold water wishing it would actually help, instead it just felt good.

Cradling the glass between her hands, she assessed the woman again and hoped that she did it with more clarity. "Who are you? And why are you here?"

"My name is Georgia Dunham and I was hoping—" her hand waved up and down indicating all that Jesse had become. Her lips pressed together one more time just in case Jesse had missed the obvious disappointment, "—that you could help me find my mother."

"Birth mother?" Jesse asked, trying for all she was worth to be something of a professional.

Georgia tipped her head back and forth. Jesse was proud of herself for having held on to the name.

"Yes, but she's actually been missing."

"For how long?"

"A year."

Jesse almost barked out a laugh at that but reminded herself that she did not want to fuck with this woman. *A year and she was only just now seeking help?* There had to be an expression on her face that said just how ridiculous she thought this was. Though she tried to rein it in, there was no way she was succeeding. "And where did you last see her?"

"I didn't," Georgia told her. "I haven't seen her in three years."

Damn, better and better, Jesse thought.

"This is her last known location." Georgia pulled a folded page from her back pocket, producing it seemingly out of nowhere. Unfolding it, she laid it out on the table facing Jesse. An article.

Gingerly, Jesse picked it up. The headline alone was enough to make her eyes fly wide.

4
————

She had to get her shit together. Jesse felt her tongue swell in her mouth. Once again, her pulse pounded behind her ears and at the back of her skull, which surely she had cracked somewhere along the way.

"There are no women in this story." She pointed to the page and handed it back. Georgia wouldn't take it.

There were only two men with a list of crimes tacked to their chests with a throwing star. A big red bow tied the two together.

"My mother is the one only briefly mentioned."

So Georgia Dunham thought her mother was the killer. *Holy shit.*

More things Jesse did not need on a morning like the one after last night.

"You want my help finding her?" Jesse asked even as she considered asking *what's in it for me?* Usually, she was paid to do jobs. Though lately that had been shit-all.

It would have taken a certain kind of predator to accomplish what was in the article. She added a brief thought about Georgia Dunham's clean, precise movements that only offered a threat if you knew what you were looking for. Unfortunately, Jesse did.

She'd learned to spot a predator at far too young an age.

Jesse wasn't taking the job, but she asked, "Why are you starting to look for her now?"

"I've been looking for a handful of months," Georgia replied smoothly.

A lie, Jesse saw, grateful that skill remained through the haze that pushed at her from every corner. "Well, maybe I can help if she's still missing in a few months, but I'm in the middle of a murder case."

On either side of the tipped over bottle of Black Label were printed papers, notes and a tablet. The screen had gone black, and she suspected the battery had died.

"It looks like a missing person, not a murder, and what you're in the middle of is a bottle of Jack," Georgia said with such disgust that Jesse realized it wasn't just about her.

She couldn't deny it, though that sure as hell wasn't Jack. So she simply tipped her head as if to say, *well, what are you going to do about it?*

"If you sober up, can you help me? Was this a one time deal?"

Jesse looked away and took another drink of water. She knew she couldn't cover her own lies very well. She opted instead to not tell them.

Georgia looked around pointedly. "The house is nice. The carpet is clean. You've either cleaned it yourself recently— which means you're better than this—" She pointed at the bottle this time, "—or you have a maid who hasn't left you for failing to pay. There's food in the fridge, although not that much. So someone went shopping recently, but you're overdue for the next trip."

Georgia wasn't so bad at investigating. She could probably find her mother herself. "Look, I'm sorry you're struggling to find your birth mother, but I'm in the middle of a murder case. I think you should go."

With one last look, eyes narrowing in a way that Jesse couldn't quite calculate, Georgia Dunham simply said, "Okay."

She put her hands on her knees, palms pressing down as though she were older and had to push herself upward. Jesse wondered if it was calculated to make her appear less dangerous than she was.

Following Georgia to the door, Jesse felt the bottoms of her feet. They reacted angrily to the weight she was putting on them and her hips were mad about how long she'd been on the couch. With a, "Goodbye and good luck," she promptly bolted the door behind her, fixing a mistake she made last night before sinking onto the couch and into the whiskey.

It took a moment to realize she should watch out the window and be sure Georgia Dunham actually left. Her acquiescence had been far too easy. But when she watched the car pull away, Jesse turned around and surveyed the landscape in front of her.

She could see through to the back of the house. To the messy coffee table and tipped whiskey. Had she damaged some of the files? She wondered. Many of the papers were irreplaceable and necessary. Spilling whiskey on them would be disastrous.

Had Georgia noticed the gruesome images?

Of course she had. Georgia had already proven herself far too observant.

With her hands flat on the door, Jesse braced herself so she didn't sway. *Was there alcohol still in her system?* Surely she couldn't be this hung over and drunk at the same time.

To her left, the dining room table still held two sheets of paper. Halfway worked with fourth grade math, they'd been sitting there for a month. Jesse didn't consider moving them.

She thought by now it would have run its course and her daughter would have come home, but that hadn't happened.

Veering into the kitchen, she opened the top cabinet and found only one half of a bottle of red wine. *Fuck.* She'd gone through all the good whiskey.

Georgia's words burrowed in deep and bit at her insides.

It hadn't been a one-time thing, but it had to be *the last time.* She had to accept that her daughter wasn't coming back.

Water, she thought, then, *orange juice.* She was pleased to open the fridge and find she had a little bit left. Chugging it right from the bottle, she let the sugar hit her veins.

Better. Not her best, but better.

The investigation work she picked up for the FBI here and there wasn't enough to pay the bills. So now she headed back to the coffee table. First cleared the glasses and the empty bottle, she then wiped the table dry before she spread the papers out one more time, pointedly ignoring the one Georgia Dunham had left behind.

Jesse reminded herself that Hannalyn Burkhardt's murder wasn't going to solve itself.

5

"**Y**ou need sun," Carter told her in a brusque tone that declared intent.

Cindy was grateful he knew her well enough not to just yank open the curtains. He didn't even move toward the window anymore with the threat of it. *Good, he'd learned.*

"I'm good," Cindy told him. They both knew it was a lie.

"You can't stay in here forever," he replied. Another thing he'd said far too often and was saying more often lately.

Oh, but she could.

"What triggered this episode?" His brusque tone demanded answers.

He was the only one who could push her like this. Hell, he was the only one who could even come into the room and speak to her at times like this. He called them her "episodes."

"An article," she confessed.

"This one has gone on for far too long."

He didn't know the half of it.

He didn't know that the article had been *good*. He didn't know that the police were reporting that they caught a man responsible for two rapes and two additional rapes that had turned to murder. What the police didn't know—and Cindy did just from touching the article—was that those four were nowhere near the extent of the damage this man had done. She told herself to be grateful he was in prison, and that he couldn't do any more harm.

Though she wanted to tell Carter, she hadn't been able to get those particular words out.

"You've been dealing with this since we were twelve," he said as if she didn't know that. But this time, he sat down across from her, taking her hands.

His were the only hands she could touch for months on end. The connection between them had always been there. She'd never asked if he could see what she saw. Just assumed that since he didn't shudder in revulsion, or yank back in fear, that he didn't see it.

"It was awful," he told her again. "It was terrifying for me, and I know it was a thousand times worse for you."

She nodded. She'd been kidnapped while walking home from school one afternoon. It was exactly the kind of kidnapping that parents were afraid of, but she now knew statistically didn't happen much at all. They lived in a decent neighborhood and the car had simply pulled up next to her and her best friend as they meandered along the sidewalk.

A man had jumped out of the backseat and grabbed Cindy, lifting her off her feet before she could even react. She was tossed like trash into the trunk of the car. The lid had popped open for him which she now understood had been a planned and concerted effort. But he slammed it down, shutting her into utter darkness as tires squealed beneath her.

She could still hear Annie screaming on the street. The sound had quickly faded as the car peeled away. Reaching out, Cindy screamed herself hoarse as she tested her environment, palms against the rough carpet in the trunk. That was the first time she had felt it.

When she touched the sides, she instantly connected to every other young girl who had been there before her. She saw their grisly fates.

With a squeeze of her hands, Carter seemed to pull her back to the present. "You need therapy. I'll find someone who can come to the house."

He'd told her this before, too. She used the same argument. "They're going to lock me up. Who would even believe it?"

"Let me see what I can find."

Only this time did she actually react as he tried to slip away. Before he could go make his phone calls, she lunged forward, grabbing him. Her hand slapped onto his and didn't let go. She squeezed tightly enough to break bones. "Don't you dare! Just asking around will alert people. A therapist will lock me up, and I do not want to touch the walls in the hospital!"

Getting thrown into a psych hospital was a threat she had used against him before. At least it was effective in stopping him.

But she couldn't trust that was enough. "Even just asking around will bring people here."

He didn't live here with her because it was his ideal life. He lived here because she desperately needed him and couldn't manage things on her own. This time, he said, "Okay, but tomorrow you have to get out of this room."

Not quite confident she was fully sober, Jesse pushed aside the article Georgia Dunham left behind and moved the remaining paperwork around on the tabletop.

She'd been staring at the case notes for a while now, knowing she had to find something. She was getting paid to investigate. She would still get the money even if she didn't turn up anything, but she doubted she'd get the next job if she didn't get somewhere.

Hannalyn Burkhardt was last seen just over a decade earlier, leaving a club with a man no one could identify. Hannalyn's mother was pushing the investigation forward though the police had closed it some time ago, declaring it a cold case.

Mrs. Burkhardt held out hope that her daughter would be found alive. Jesse didn't believe that for a hot second. Hannalyn was dead and had been for a decade.

Jesse had had a serious heart-to-heart with the woman before she said yes. But instead of knocking the woman up against the cold, harsh truth, she'd tried to frame some questions that might lead her that way. What if they found Hannalyn, but what they found was her body? What if they found concrete evidence that Hannalyn was dead, even if they didn't find her? What would Mrs. Burkhardt do then?

"At least we'll be able to offer her a proper burial and mourn her," the woman had replied calmly, surprising Jesse. The mother had espoused a firm belief that Hannalyn was alive somewhere and simply just not bothering to contact her family . . . for a reason none of them could fathom.

That was a possibility, Jesse knew. People sometimes disappeared on purpose. But usually not from nightclubs.

Flipping through the pages, she searched for anything she'd missed before. While there were security cameras on the gas station across the street there had been none at the entry to the club. Inside the building, cameras were mounted in the hallway leading to the bathrooms. Those had caught Hannalyn with the friend she'd come with earlier in the evening. There was no photographic evidence of the man she'd left with.

The young woman had not used her credit cards or her cell phone after eleven that night, and the phone had traveled a short distance away then promptly turned off. The police had done crap-all looking for the phone which was only slightly worse than they'd done looking for Hannalyn herself.

The parents had filed a missing persons report at 4p.m. the following day. At which point the police had agreed to file it. Before that they said things like "legal adult" and "probably walked away on her own." Jesse knew that song and dance.

Once she'd located a runaway teenager who did not want to be found. She was proud of herself for bargaining that part up front with the parents. She'd told them that plausibly all she would be able to say was "your child is safe." In the end, that was what she told them—and collected her final check.

She looked at Hannalyn's information again. Usually, Jesse didn't take a case unless there was something more than what previous investigators had already covered. Witnesses that hadn't been interviewed. A plausible tip that the police simply hadn't followed up on. Evidence that hadn't been processed.

That happened more often than people thought. The police were overburdened and undermanned. Sometimes they just simply didn't think something was credible, so they wrote it off. They dealt with preconceived ideas, pressure to close cases, and limitations of hours in the day.

The problem here wasn't that the Police hadn't followed up —though they hadn't. It was that there simply wasn't much to follow up on. Tapping on the tablet, she pulled up images of Hannalyn's bank accounts and phone records. Her parents could have had her declared legally dead a few years ago, but they'd refused.

The list of witnesses was short: those who'd seen her that night, her roommate, an ex-boyfriend. No one had much of anything to offer.

Jesse had been too desperate to say no. Honestly, she hadn't had to take this case for the money, though. Her bills had dropped considerably without Ciara around. Without summer camp or school supplies, she paid her bills and got groceries and ate out too often.

What she was desperate for was something to fill the time —something other than that half bottle of wine still sitting up in the cabinet. She thought about Georgia Dunham's ill-timed visit last night and her request to solve yet another case with very few threads to pull.

Jesse flipped over the witness list again, reading through it and the short, concise police notes. Suddenly, she knew what she needed to do.

Georgia planted herself at the local library. She could hear the quirky inflections of someone reading and asking questions, then children talking over each other as they tried to answer. It was in direct opposition to the articles she was reading.

She'd needed to get out of that hotel room. Her mother had called and woken her—*her real mother, Annika Dunham*—and asked how the hunt was going.

Georgia hadn't wanted to say that *it wasn't*. Her parents would be footing the bill for this search, and she didn't want to let them down. Her parents could afford Jesse Nash, but it wasn't throwaway money for them. They were as worried about her birth mother as she was.

Georgia's eyes glazed over as she stared into nothing, thinking about her birth mother. The three Dunham girls had seen her occasionally. Aunt Sin would turn up in town, stop by with a pizza, or take them to a movie.

Though it had only been recently that her father and mother had sat her down, and given her the truth about her birth, Annika had slowly been feeding Georgia clues her whole life.

Though she'd never just *asked* if she was adopted, Georgia always wondered. Her parents' names appeared on her birth certificate. There were pictures of her mother pregnant with her. Yet, in some space between a tragedy and a last-minute trade conducted in secret, here she was.

Owen and Annika were her real parents, she knew that in her heart. But "Aunt Sin" could be the thing that got them all killed. She had to find her.

Even as Georgia left to find Sin, both her parents had issued warnings that, just by looking, she could be putting a target on her own back. They'd raised her as their own because they wanted a baby, they knew Sin couldn't keep her, and because it would keep Georgia herself much safer.

Recently, however, little things had started to hint that the net of safety all three had woven around her wouldn't stay safe much longer.

Shaking her head, she scrolled further before giving up on finding any reports involving victims tied in red bows. There was nothing even mentioning throwing stars or mafia assassinations.

Aiming her focus in a slightly different direction, she thought about the case on Jesse Nash's coffee table. In the library so as not to record the history on any of her own devices, Georgia once again loaded Jesse's lone page of a website. It listed her as working with the FBI. It linked to several cases she had closed and far more articles than Georgia could count. Clicking on the last one, she saw the date was recent.

Functional alcoholics could do that, she knew. It took a lot to put away an entire bottle. Jesse hadn't taken any medication, not that Georgia saw. Though she had clearly been in pain, the woman didn't cringe or put her hands to her head. She had simply stayed rigid and had a calm, logical conversation.

Reassuring herself that the real Jesse was likely a better choice than the woman she'd appeared to be last night, Georgia went with her curiosity and typed in: Hannalyn Burkhardt.

The missing college student disappeared a decade ago but had only been a year younger than Georgia was now. There wasn't much else.

Annual reports showed the family asking the police department to reopen the case. Like victims who had to show up to parole hearings repeatedly, the family suffered the disappointment as the request was denied each time.

As Georgia scrolled through the list the search engine had returned, she could see that Mrs. Burkhardt managed to get a few interviews along the way. She would beg for anyone who knew anything related to Hannalyn to come forward. She offered forgiveness—both personal and legal—if they would just let her know where Hannalyn was.

Georgia closed the window. Jesse certainly had more information than what could be dug up here. Lord knew, Georgia had read all of it last night when she'd gotten bored as hell waiting for Jesse to wake up.

Before she stood up, Georgia cleared the history from the browser and pulled everything off the desk. She kept her head low and turned her face casually away from the camera at the front door.

A short while later, she pulled up in front of Jesse Nash's house again only to find that this time the car was gone.

8

———————

J esse struggled to fit her key in the front door lock. Plastic bags of groceries were cutting into her skin where she'd lined them up her forearm, because *of course she could carry it all in one trip.*

"Here, let me help you."

Startled, Jesse jolted backwards, almost losing her footing at the edge of the tiny front porch. She wasn't a fan of this house. It had been Eugene's house. She'd married him back in his better days.

Jesse would have moved, but it was her stepdaughter Ciara's home. She'd just lost her father, brutally. Now Ciara was gone, too. Jesse stayed in the house anyway, as though the girl might show up one day. And she might.

Her heart beating faster now, she could feel through her sneaker that one foot was still hanging halfway off the edge of the porch. Flimsy plastic bag handles still cut into her arm. She watched almost helplessly as Georgia Dunham plucked the keys from her hand and easily opened the door. She gestured for Jesse to go through as if this were her own home.

Though it took effort and the grocery bags swayed, trying to tug her off balance, Jesse snatched the keys back. "What are you doing here?"

"Waiting for you," Georgia said it evenly as though that wasn't creepy at all. "I knew you were out because your car was gone."

Jesse stepped inside, irritated but not surprised when Georgia followed her. Despite what she read as Georgia's ability, she didn't quite perceive the woman as a threat to anything other than her own desire to get out of town quickly. "What if I parked it in the garage?"

"You don't. Your garage is full." Georgia stated it with utter clarity.

Jesse narrowed her eyes, rapidly rethinking her decision that Georgia wasn't dangerous to her.

Then Georgia added, "I've been here far longer than just yesterday evening. You came out of the garage door ducking under it just a couple of days ago and I saw that it was full. This is why your car is always in the driveway."

Jesse narrowed her eyes again, wondering how she could get rid of the young woman.

"See? I'm a good investigator, too."

"Then *you* find your birth mother," Jesse said, thinking the best way to get Georgia to move on was to refuse all requests. Setting the bags on the kitchen counter, she made a shooing motion at the young woman as if that would work.

Georgia, not surprisingly, stayed put. "If I could, I would have found her already. I need help."

"I understand that," Jesse didn't look up this time. Just tried to keep on about getting ready. "But I don't even know her name. And I don't have time to help."

"Cynthia Beller."

With the groceries laid down now, red marks across her arms, Jesse simply raised her hands out in a huge shrug. She didn't want the case.

Georgia seemed to catch on and made a major swing in subject. "Was last night an aberration?"

Ignoring her again, Jesse began laying things out and organizing them across the countertop.

Georgia stepped slightly closer. "I need to know."

"You're not hiring me, so you *don't* need to know."

"So it was a one time thing."

Once again, Jesse didn't really answer. Maybe she should be oddly grateful. Georgia Dunham breaking into—or more likely *walking right into*—her home and sitting on the couch across from her all night had been a serious wake up call.

Jesse had been raking through all the evidence the Burkhardts had turned over. She'd been doing the work and gathering anything they didn't already have. She knew when nothing came to her, she had to go to the case.

Instead of doing that, she had gone to the liquor cabinet, feeling sad and sorry for herself. Today, she still felt sad and sorry for herself. She missed Ciara more than anything, but there was nothing she could do about it.

Something had snapped, some kind of determination had set in around 10a.m. this morning. She couldn't bring Ciara home, but maybe she could find closure for the Burkhardts.

"It looks like you're going on a trip." Georgia swung the topic yet again.

Because she was. At the store, Jesse had picked up a cheap amusement park rain poncho and flashlights—one of the packages clearly advertised that it had not only infrared, but blue light, and several other options.

She had snacks and sodas. A small cooler and even carrot sticks. She almost muttered out, "Great job, Sherlock," but it would be stupid to admit to somebody who'd already pushed her way into the house that she was leaving for a few days. Maybe longer.

"You need to go interview the people on the case."

"I'm not taking your case," Jesse ground out through closed teeth.

"No. In Hannalyn Burkhardt's case." Reaching into her back pocket, Georgia Dunham produced another slip of paper. As she pushed it along the countertop, Jesse read *Sun City Library* across the top.

"I found out where the college roommate and the friend who was out that night with Hannalyn live now."

"So did I," Jesse sighed.

"Why haven't you interviewed them?" Georgia had both hands on the counter, now leaning forward as if she'd been invited into this conversation, let alone this case.

"Where the hell do you think I'm going?"

"Great!" Georgia replied. "I'll trade you. We work on finding my mother while we find Hannalyn Burkhardt."

Taking a deep breath as if that could steady this whirlwind, Jesse tried to figure out how to shut down this "we" Georgia mentioned. But before she could say anything, Georgia replied to herself, as if it were clear as day, "I'm going with you."

9

J esse was going to murder Georgia Dunham.

Maybe she could "disappear" the young woman, keep the body in her trunk while she helped everyone look for the missing girl.

She'd said *No*, three times, clearly. But here was Georgia in the passenger seat, snacking on a can of chips and crunching in the most obnoxious way. Honestly, Georgia was probably eating like a perfectly normal person, but Jesse was used to car trips on her own. She was listening to an audiobook which she didn't need Georgia adding a soundtrack to or interrupting with questions.

After the three *no's*, Jesse had actually agreed to this. She was regretting her choices.

Georgia had begun her assault while Jesse was still organizing her purchases for the trip. Tall and lean, she looked like she wouldn't get much done. Jesse had quickly learned, Georgia was a steamroller.

"Do you have protection?"

Jesse had snarkily replied, "Yes, I carry condoms all the time."

"Like a gun," Georgia had immediately protested.

"Yes, also like a gun." Jesse had emphasized each word, hopefully letting Georgia know that she meant *no* in no uncertain terms. This was her trip and her case.

"But do you know how to use it?" Georgia had casually leaned on the counter, one hand on her hip, eyebrows up, as if confident that Jesse would just say no to this as she had to everything else.

It had been tempting to just tell her *yes*. But Jesse could already tell that would make the indomitable Georgia Dunham ask *more* questions. Instead, she replied, "I guess your research on me wasn't as thorough as you thought."

It was intended to be a conversation ender. Jesse would throw everything in a suitcase and hit the road. Instead, Georgia talked her into letting her buy lunch, where she'd been given a full rundown on why she shouldn't be alone on this trip.

Jesse had been tempted to say no again. There were articles out there about how Jesse Nash could face down the worst of the worst. That Georgia had missed those was a point against her, and Jesse was definitely looking for points. On the other hand, she was willing to let Georgia pay for lunch. Hopefully it would be a good way to shake her loose.

Jesse decided to bill Georgia for the most expensive local burger she could, even though it would take a bit longer. Leaving her things on the counter—mostly afraid Georgia would follow her into the bedroom while she packed—she ushered them out the front door. And even made Georgia drive her own car.

Not unexpectedly, Georgia had interrupted her first bite. "You need backup. Chances are high that one of the people you interview will be the person who murdered this young woman. For a decade they've thought they've gotten away with it."

It was easier to just agree. "Yes."

"I can get places you can't." Georgia added.

"Like what?"

"I can pick a lock and get through most any security system. I was raised by an FBI agent. He trained all us girls to watch for details, to pay attention to our surroundings, and that the best predators come with the cleanest credentials."

"All of that is lovely," Jesse replied. Still hoping to enjoy the meal, she took another bite of her burger, lifted a big fat fry and dunked it in truffle ketchup. "But those are all things I can do for myself."

The last part was a lie. She couldn't pick her way through most security systems, and she wouldn't. She didn't need to do time for breaking and entering.

"You can't be two people," Georgia responded as if that were her ace. "You can't be in two places at once . . . And I can help keep you sober."

Fuck her. The burger suddenly went tasteless in her mouth. Jesse chewed, swallowed, and set the angry thoughts aside. She should have lied and said no when Georgia had first asked if it was a one-time thing.

Instead of addressing the painful bullshit, Jesse said only, "You cost too much."

"I pay my own way."

"Do you have Daddy's credit card?" Jesse knew her mocking tone was a slap back and she shouldn't do it, but it was too late.

It stilled the younger woman for a moment. She lost the disapproving expression. Her lips had pressed slightly and for a moment Jesse had thought *she would lie.* Instead, she calmly took a bite of her own burger, finally and said, "I do. They know my birth mother and my parents are very worried about her too."

Fuck this. Jesse was tired of this argument, she wanted to travel by herself and do this on her own! She tried a different tack, no longer working toward the impossible task of shaking

Georgia Dunham loose but asking out of sheer curiosity. "Why did you even come to my door? Why didn't you just email me?"

"*I. Did.* Five different times!" Georgia smacked her own fry down for emphasis. Jesse was just glad there hadn't been ketchup on it, or it would have stained both of their shirts in a way that far too closely resembled blood spatter.

Then Georgia had gone oddly silent.

She'd ignored an email request that came five times? She wasn't as upright as she'd thought. *Fuck all of it.*

No matter how much she didn't want to admit it, two was often better than one. Maybe she could let Georgia get arrested for breaking and entering if they needed it. Jesse paced the whole thing out in her head, able to do so now that Georgia was finally being quiet.

Jesse was far closer in age to what Hannalyn Burkhardt would be today had she lived. But Georgia was closer to the age she was when she disappeared. She might have insights.

She didn't need a sober companion, but it had been a month since she'd lost Ciara and she'd stumbled more than once. Now, as she rolled down the road, listening to the audiobook, Georgia snacking in the passenger seat, Jesse realized she desperately wanted a drink.

10

Cindy threw short sleeve shirts and jeans into her suitcase. She had too many t-shirts and nothing nice. When had she become that woman who hung out in her t-shirts and sweats all day?

Well, she could pinpoint a number of days that had led her here.

To be honest, she wasn't quite sure if the jeans even fit anymore. Too tight or too loose, she didn't even know which direction it might go. How long had she been sitting in that room, watching the sun go up and then fade at the end of the day?

She'd been trying to close out the world and it hadn't worked.

Underwear, she thought and grabbed fistfuls of it out of the drawer. Not knowing how long she would be gone, she tried to estimate packing an extra pair for every day.

Carter startled her when he spoke. She hadn't heard him— or even felt him—come in. "I don't know what you're doing, but it looks like you intend to shit your pants each day that you're doing it."

Turning around, she raised one irritated eyebrow at him. "I'm getting out, like you wanted."

Okay, this wasn't what he wanted, but it was what she needed. "I'm just going away for a while."

Carter tipped his head toward the open suitcase. There was enough underwear for far more than *a while*.

"Fine," she conceded dramatically to his lack of a demand.

"Where are you going?"

She was going to get in the car and just drive. He wouldn't like that. "I'll call when I get there."

Maybe she could rent a little house in the mountains. Maybe she could be where she could touch things and it wouldn't trigger yet another memory that wasn't her own. Once they were there, she was unable to shake them loose, living and reliving people's worst tragedies over and over.

She was going to go clinically insane.

Why couldn't she pick up people's wedding days? Or the birth of their first child? Why couldn't she be there when a family adopted a new puppy or put the keys into the door of their own home for the first time? No. She got murders, abductions, torture.

Somehow, when she was twelve, her own kidnapping had unlocked a key to even more of them. Now she was past desperate to find something to close that open door and seal it for good.

Offering a quiet penance, she zipped the suitcase and turned to Carter, hoping her concession would pave a smooth path out the front door for her. "When I get back, I'll see a therapist."

"I can find someone?" His tone was tentative. Of course it was, she usually raved at him when he suggested it.

"Yes. However, please be very discreet."

"I know. I'm not going to get you locked up." The relief in his voice smacked her with the realization that he needed things too, and she'd been sorely neglectful. "I know what that would do to you."

He didn't. Though he came the closest anyone could to understanding, no one truly knew what it would do to her. Still, she couldn't go on like this.

Cindy thought about advice she'd been given once years ago when she was at a job that she hated. Back when she still held a job, back when the images were much fewer and further between, when she saw them but didn't live them. The advice had been that no one would leave until the pain of staying was greater than the pain of leaving.

She picked up the suitcase off the bed, surprised at its weight, and headed off as if she knew what she was doing. She was praying that her car keys were still in the dish by the door where she'd left them. When? A month ago? Two months ago?

Her phone was already in her back pocket. She had a car charger—she would be okay. Turning back at the doorway, grateful for the key fob in her hand, she looked at Carter. "I have to."

The pain of staying had become greater than the pain of leaving.

"When do we look for my mother?" Georgia steeled herself to ask it, and she wasn't confident about the answer.

At least she was on the trip. She'd somehow talked Jesse into letting her come along. She had told her parents, but in the message, she might have made it sound like the research was a fifty/fifty split.

Jesse was busy with the current case, but if Georgia took some of the work off her hands, they could investigate both. Right? She hadn't lied to her parents, but it was absolutely not what Jesse had said.

"I don't know," Jesse replied.

Honestly, it was the best answer that Georgia could have expected. Pulling back the covers, Georgia looked around the chain motel they had checked into just outside Magnolia, Arkansas. They were close to Shreveport and would head into town tomorrow to check out the location and hunt down anyone who could remember anything about Hannalyn.

Jesse had suggested that they stay in cheaper chains as she didn't want to spend more than she could recoup. Georgia had sighed her agreement though she was actually grateful. She might be putting it on daddy's credit card, but keeping the tab low would help. Jesse wasn't the only one who would have to account for her expenses.

Georgia picked up the tab the first night as a solid gesture. Jesse could get tomorrow. They were also staying in one room to save money. Or so Jesse had said. Maybe it was so Jesse could keep an eye on her, but she wasn't going clubbing or buying coke on the street corner or anything.

She'd been all bluster, pushing her way into this trip with bold comments she wasn't sure she could back up. In the tank top and shorts she usually slept in, she slid between the cool sheets of the queen bed. She felt smaller now and the chill calmed her, though the too-puffy pillow made her more aware this wasn't home.

Georgia had convinced her folks that if she could just talk to Jesse, she could convince her to take the case. She'd pushed because she couldn't fail. But now? Failure was definitely an option.

And Aunt Sin was a master at not being found.

When she'd asked about the trip, Georgia had watched her parents have an entire conversation without words. Then her dad handed over the credit card. "Four days." There had been other demands. "Check in at least twice a day. Check in every time you stay somewhere new."

Georgia easily agreed. She wasn't in any shape to cover this herself. Everyone in her family wanted to find Aunt Sin, but she was the only one who could pick up and leave.

It all felt odd. She'd missed her own college graduation for this. She'd graduated pre-law. She was supposed to sit for the LSAT this summer. She'd left her study materials in her car in Jesse's driveway. Only now admitting that it wasn't going to happen.

She would have struck out to find Jesse sooner, but she'd

had to finish her senior year. She'd handed in her thesis, waited for approval, and bolted. Her folks had wanted to see her walk. Hell, she'd wanted to.

But they'd all waited longer than they should—hoping something would turn up, something that would show Sin had just been lying low. Georgia's dad still had friends at the Bureau, ready to feed him info if anything popped. Nothing had.

This week was the first time they had admitted to the very real possibility that Aunt Sin was already dead and had been for a while. Just the idea of it hurt. It was Georgia's job to find out.

The things Sin did could get her dead very easily. Any normal mortal would have been gone long before now. But, for all the risks that she took, there seemed to be some fated element keeping her alive.

It had been Owen, as he handed over the credit card, looking Georgia in the eyes with an expression that reminded her, no matter her blood or her line, she was his daughter. *And wasn't she?* Economics, philosophy, business classes, headed toward a law degree. She couldn't be his daughter more if she tried.

But the look had been meant to remind her—now that she knew the whole story—that her birth father had died saving Sin. He, too, had escaped more scrapes than any one person should. Yet they had eventually caught up to him.

Georgia knew his name now: Lee Maxwell.

But here was Georgia Dunham—the least Dunham by blood, but somehow the *most Dunham* of any of the three girls.

Charlotte, the oldest, was a concert violinist. She liked to say she was never going to be Yo Yo Ma. However, Charlotte had played backup orchestration on more than one song that had hit the top 100 charts and had bought herself a very nice house with the proceeds.

Virginia, the middle child, who'd been quiet and soft until she wanted something, had gotten an engineering degree. Then she freaked the crap out of everyone by enlisting in the Marines. She was now an attaché in a foreign country. When they asked what she did, she jokingly answered, *I could tell you, but I'd have to kill you.*

Georgia, the youngest, had her humanities degree in hand, stitched together with bits and pieces of all the things she'd wanted to study. She had forged her own sword at a summer camp one year. She had a black belt, like every family member, but she ate popcorn and watched horror movies and grew to be the tallest of them.

She secretly went through her father's stash of newspaper clippings that, over the years, had turned to digital printouts—the ones he kept in the false bottom of his office drawer. So now, she used all the things she'd cobbled together. Because, if nothing else, she had to help Jesse Nash find Hannalyn Burkhardt, so she could then force the journalist's hand and make her help find Aunt Sin.

She had to piece together a trail to follow, marked by victims tied with big red bows.

12

"Everything looks different in the harsh light of day." Georgia muttered the words as she looked at the front of the rundown building. Though a few neon signs indicated it would be open later, this was not a club she'd be caught at.

"It looks a lot worse a decade later," Jesse told her.

They stood across the street, arms folded. Staring at the building, they looked like the worst kind of tourists. Jesse had a tablet and she tapped at it for a moment before biting her lip and looking up and around as if she could see the Wi Fi signal she wasn't getting.

Georgia was so not prepared. She did however, have a tablet. As soon as they stopped back by the motel it would be in her hand every time they went out. She would not be the weak link.

"Dammit." Jesse tried to connect again while Georgia scanned the area.

To the left of the club sat a gas station. It looked like it had been completely shut down. Another mutter came from Jesse.

Whatever she was doing, she wasn't sharing with Georgia. Mostly, it looked like she was just being frustrated.

To the right of the club, there was a strip mall with four storefronts. The first was a sushi place. The next space sat empty, rental signs taped into the big windows. Then, an old dry cleaner. Underneath the main sign—in old-school letters—it said "alterations" and then "cobbler." The last place was a bounce house playground, and Georgia was getting judgy because she really thought the ceilings could not be high enough.

When Jesse still didn't move, Georgia paced through how Hannalyn and her friend Becky would have driven here from Magnolia. She and Jesse had traveled in on the same roads, trying to mimic what the two friends had done on Hannalyn's last night.

Georgia had pulled out her phone and checked that, yes, these roads had been here ten years ago, and they'd been in good enough repair that this was likely the same path. She made a mental note to check the GPS records from Hannalyn's phone. *Would there even have been GPS on her phone back then?* At least, Georgia remembered seeing a record of cell towers the phone had pinged.

Looking to the right and holding her hand up to shield her eyes against the insane summer sun, Georgia tried to make a brilliant deduction. It was not happening. Mostly she was starting to sweat a little.

The only upside of the heat was that they were approaching the ten-year anniversary of Hannalyn's disappearance. So this was likely close to the weather she had when she was here—if that made a difference.

The club was on the outskirts of Shreveport. Closer to Princeton, and where state road 371 merged in. The girls had driven over an hour to get here. That meant they had intended to party.

"I'm not getting a good enough connection." Jesse finally gave up.

"I think we talk to the dry cleaner." Georgia pointed across the street.

"Why?" Jesse asked, though the tone wasn't bad, merely curious.

"It says *cobbler* and the sign is old. I think—of the things in the strip mall—it's the most likely to have people who were here back when Hannalyn disappeared."

"Good. You just want to go right in and ask them?"

"Maybe politely?" Georgia suggested, because that had been her intention.

"Okay," Jesse said, shockingly agreeable given her irritation with the tablet and the completely closed club. "Do me a favor and follow my lead?"

Georgia nodded and found herself looking both ways before crossing the street, though only two cars had passed the whole time they'd been standing here. Still, they darted across the four lanes and past the handful of cars in the parking lot. As they entered, they found two people waiting in line.

Jesse seemed pleased by this. Georgia pretended that she was, too. If nothing else, they needed to present a unified front. And Jesse wanted her to follow along, whatever that meant.

As they stood patiently, Jesse waved the new person who'd stepped inside in front of them. Were they ever going to speak to anyone, or was Jesse just investigating how an old dry cleaners worked? When the last one cleared out, the young woman at the counter looked up at them, a frown knitting dark eyebrows together.

"Hello," Jesse said with a smile, "thank you for being patient with us."

Interesting, at no point had any of these people been patient with them. It was a lie, but Jesse started with graciousness. Georgia filed that away.

Jesse had a business card in her hand already, and she presented it. "My name is Jesse Nash and this is my associate Georgia Dunham."

Georgia offered only a polite smile and a nod like she truly was an associate. It was disturbing how good it felt to be called that.

"We're investigating a cold case and I'm hoping that you can help." Jesse was all smiles and sweet tones. No hint of the earlier irritation.

The young woman still looked confused. Jesse hadn't even asked for her name.

"Was this store here ten years ago?"

She nodded. "My family has owned it for thirty years."

Spot on, Georgia hid her grin at being right.

"Did you work here ten years ago?" Jesse pressed.

It was a ridiculous question. Georgia thought the young woman looked barely any older than her if that. If she was working here ten years ago, child labor laws were being massively violated.

"No, but my father was. Would you like to speak to him?"

Yesss. That's what Jesse had been going for. She hadn't actually expected the young girl to be working here. But by asking her first, the girl had volunteered her father and unless he was willing to be openly rude, he was stuck answering their questions.

Georgia compiled all of it.

They waited with soft smiles and no hint of impatience as it took more than a moment for the man to come to the front counter. Down at her side, Jesse made a flat signal with her hand, as if telling Georgia to put the brakes on. *Put the brakes on what?* She'd done absolutely nothing. Maybe it just meant stay quiet.

The man approached, his frown already in place. His daughter must have given him some idea what this was about.

This time Jesse leaned forward on the counter and pled with him. "I'm hoping you can help. I'm here investigating a cold case. The family of this young woman so desperately wants to find her."

Georgia watched the master at work. Jesse was playing this guy radically differently. Maybe because he was older, or maybe because he might be the person they wanted. She would have to ask later.

In fact, Jesse even pulled out the eight-by-ten of Hannalyn Burkhardt that had been used on all her missing posters. She slid it across the counter to the man, her smile still in place.

Georgia watched as he visibly recoiled.

J esse didn't miss the way his eyes squinted or his mouth pulled back.

"Yes, I remember," he said without looking up. She watched as his fingers slowly reached out to touch the picture. "It was next door. It was terrible."

Interesting words. Was it terrible? Though Jesse was confident the young woman was long since murdered, Hannalyn was only listed as *missing*. There was still the option that she had simply run off. Adults apparently just disappeared all the time . . . Though not in Jesse's experience. Not without some warning.

She had to remind herself every time she interviewed someone that she was plausibly speaking to a killer. Hell, even the man's daughter was a suspect. While she'd probably been too young at the time to carry Hannalyn off, people could be baited into doing all kinds of things, and a child was excellent bait.

"What do you remember about what happened?" Jesse asked.

Instead, he changed the subject. "Why are you investigating this now? It's been years."

Jesse nodded along. *Always agree when possible.* "Almost a decade. You're right, it's a cold case. The police have closed it, but the family never found their daughter, and no one has any answers. If a cold case like this gets solved, it's usually because a family member has kept things alive. Made the police investigate again and again."

"What else can you possibly learn?" he asked, his tone sad as he turned away to pick up a stack of tags. He seemed to sort them, but Jesse suspected he just needed something to do with his hands. But why did a decade old missing woman bother him so?

Beside her, Georgia smiled blandly and looked innocuous. *Good girl.* Jesse wondered if having a partner would make people more or less likely to answer her. She'd have to pay attention and see if Georgia was help or hindrance.

"If we re-open cold cases, we often find new information. We interview people again and we hear something new." Jesse offered it with a smile, but she didn't want to tell him the whole truth. That sometimes it took a decade of living with the guilt for someone to crack. It might just be time that they were able to tell the truth of what happened.

Jesse added a little more, hoping it would get him to open up. Her gut said he wasn't a killer, but her gut hadn't always been right—*look who she'd married*. Mr. Wang was invested for some reason.

"Mostly, new technology comes along. We have evidence at the time, and we save it. We've cracked a lot of cases with DNA samples that couldn't be tested when the case was live, but now we can." She listed off the options as though she were just casually thinking of these things. But it was a very pointed piece of information she was handing out and she watched carefully for his reaction. He seemed intrigued and not alarmed.

"As long as I don't have customers, I'll answer your questions." But he shrugged and shook his head. "Not sure how much help I'll be."

It was a common disclaimer people liked to add. People often didn't know that they knew something important.

"I really appreciate it. I'm just trying to put the pieces back together." She offered a bigger smile then. "Is it okay if I have Georgia take notes?"

He nodded, as if to say of course, seeming less and less like a killer with every answer. His sense of defense had turned into curiosity and now to eagerness.

"I wasn't working that night," he started.

"The next day?" she asked.

"No, it was two days later. Sunday, I think. That's when the police began looking, started asking around. She disappeared on a Friday night, right?"

Jesse nodded. She didn't want to say yes, she hated feeding information.

"I think it took them that long to take the family seriously."

That matched what Jesse had heard from multiple sources —including the police investigation notes.

"They came around here. They asked us questions, a lot like you're doing. There were police cars all over the gas station. It was still open at the time."

"What kind of questions did they ask?" Jesse pushed. Next to her Georgia scribbled copious notes on a paper notepad Jesse had pushed on her in the car.

"They asked if we had been working that night. Had we seen Hannalyn either before or after Friday night."

That explained why he remembered it was a Friday. He had been asked about it a lot.

Jesse led him through a few more rounds.

"They told me she was wearing a sequined tank top, pale pink sequins everywhere." He made a motion down the front of his own body. "And a short black skirt with long fringe at the bottom."

For a moment the details struck her as odd—as the kind of thing a predator would remember. But next to her she saw Georgia's eyes roving and realized, of course. A predator would remember a victim's clothes, but so would a dry cleaner.

The man *worked* with clothing. And they didn't just clean it, they altered it. Sequins and fringe were probably a bitch; it was a detail that a tailor would hold onto.

"They said she had on black high heeled shoes and that she had painted the bottom red, like Loubitons." He even pronounced it right.

Cobbler. Mr. Yang remembered these details and understood that Hannalyn had been faking having expensive shoes.

"It was Sunday afternoon, the officer was standing right there—" He pointed where Jesse was standing on the customer side of the counter. "—when he got a call that they had found the one shoe in the field."

—————

14

The day was getting hot, and it was still in the early stages. Jesse left her business card at the dry cleaners, happy that Mr. Gregory Yang had put it in his pocket. Maybe he did intend to call her if he remembered anything.

Cold cases were difficult in general. They had to dig up all the information, nothing was breaking as she worked. No one handed her anything to weave into the braid of the story. She would need help to get her to the very tail on this one. Without Georgia, she would have to go back and dig up all the spare pieces herself. But with Georgia, she had promised to help find the missing birth mother, too.

Jesse still wasn't sure about any of it: having a partner, owing someone, or even getting involved with the elusive Sin.

But she was here now, and Georgia was sitting in the passenger seat as Jesse cranked the engine and waited for the AC to kick in. She asked, "Slushie?"

She was replied to with only a small but confident nod. Whether that meant the young woman was already tired of this or was simply taking things in, she couldn't quite tell.

Memories of her daughter assaulted her right then for

some reason. Jesse never intended to be a mother, yet there was Ciara. Her step-daughter had been expressive and bold and stubborn. Jesse had been reminded many times to try to see the positive. Her daughter's stubbornness was awful when used against her, but it would serve her well in the future. The sharp tongue when she was angry could slice deep, but it was good to know that Ciara could stand up for herself.

Jesse tried not to cry as she thought about the girl. She'd agreed to two more weeks, and she shouldn't have! Forcing her thoughts to something she could work with, she applied the practice of looking in the positive light now with Georgia. Not being able to read Georgia's expression would be good in an interview. The person wouldn't be able to get a read off her partner.

Georgia was not her partner, Jesse corrected herself. Georgia had barely managed to talk herself into coming along on this trip and likely would not be here for the whole case—not unless they solved it damn fast. Jesse had certainly warned the Burkhardts that it could take months. If nothing else, requisitioning the evidence took time.

They pulled into an open convenience store along the way and Jesse cringed as Georgia mixed a blue raspberry and cherry slushy together creating a disturbing shade of purple. But as she pulled the Mountain Dew version, she realized she didn't really have a leg to stand on. Paying for both drinks, she headed back out to the car and the AC.

"Alright, drink these down." She slid in and reached her Styrofoam cup across the way, tapping it against Georgia's in a poor facsimile of a toast. "We need to finish quickly. We're on our way to the police station. Shreveport handled this, so it's a little bit of a drive into the center of town. But we can't take these in with us."

"What are we doing there?" Georgia followed instructions

and drained the slushie faster than Jesse believed humanly possible.

"I put in requisitions for the footage from the club from the night she disappeared."

"That still exists?" Georgia seemed surprised.

"Yes." Jesse took a long sip and let the extreme sugar and caffeine hit her system. This was not the best move. She should have found real food. She should have brought her carrot sticks and little packs of hummus. But she sucked down the mountain dew slushie anyway. "It exists only because the police requisitioned it from the club. Because they took their time realizing Hannalyn was really missing, they almost missed it. Even then, they only did the basics because the family pushed hard. But they got lucky and a few days later, the tape had *not* been recorded over."

"Tape?"

"Oh, yes. It's VHS." Jesse tipped her cup, using her straw for emphasis.

"People were still using VHS?" Georgia seemed incredulous.

"Did you see that club?" Jesse replied.

"Touché." Georgia gave in. It was the kind of place that was not keeping up with the latest in security systems.

"But because it was entered as evidence, it does still exist. Not only can we watch it, we can use the department's VHS recorder."

"I feel special," Georgia replied in a tone indicating her sarcasm.

"Don't feel too special. We're not allowed to take the VHS for ourselves. But we will be welcomed by one of the officers who is assigned to cold cases. He was very happy to see us. We're taking some of the work off his plate. Some of the other officers though, they're not going to be happy."

"Why not?" Georgia asked as though she honestly had no clue.

"They don't want us coming in and scrutinizing their work. Our job is to—at best—solve what they couldn't. At worst, they'll get indicted for handling the case poorly. They do not want us there."

"Then why does the cold case guy like us?"

"Because he's new." Jesse took the next turn. She wasn't close enough to the bottom of her slushie. She needed the sugar; she had no idea how long they'd be in there. "He wasn't on the original case. There's not much that we can say or do that's going to rub him the wrong way."

Jesse had learned lessons from previous cases. So she'd looked up who she should contact and how long they'd been with the precinct and who'd been assigned to Hannalyn's case all before she even requested the tape.

Sucking down the last of her slushie too fast and gasping at the cold in her chest, she pulled into the police station lot. As she reached for the door handle, she had the ridiculously stupid thought to look at her tongue. Her lips were okay. Her teeth however, were a very mild shade of green. *Fuck.* And her tongue was damn near neon. *Not very professional.*

She turned and looked at Georgia. *Blue.* She rolled her eyes at her own stupidity. On Georgia, the blue was even seeping into the tiny feathered lines of her lips.

"Do you have any lipstick?" She said it too harshly.

"Why would I have lipstick?" Georgia asked.

Jesse shook her head. They weren't that far apart in age, but that answer sure felt like a generation gap. Pulling a liquid version one out of her purse, she used it first. When she handed it across to Georgia the young woman held up a hand in protest.

"You're not supposed to share makeup."

"You're not supposed to go into the police station trying to act like a professional with blue lips."

She watched as Georgia frantically flipped down the visor and checked herself. Her tongue and teeth were bright. "Oh crap." She frowned but accepted her fate. Reaching out, she took the lipstick and used the tiny wand before asking a question without touching her lips together. "Ho-lee shit. Duss thisss evver dryyy?"

"In one minute. It's nontransferable," Jesse said as though this were her triumph for the day.

Heading inside, they projected more confidence than two women fueled up on neon slushies had a right to. It took almost thirty minutes to go through all the checks. They showed their IDs and went through extra paperwork for Georgia because Jesse had originally requested the information be released to her.

Then they waited while the VHS tape was pulled from evidence. Finally, they were shown to a little room with a VHS player where officer Vallieres gave them instructions on how to use it—as if Jesse had never seen a VHS before. They began relentlessly rewinding and rewatching video that Jesse thought might be the poorest quality she'd ever seen.

After five minutes, Georgia pulled a pair of glasses from her purse. She slid them on, looking almost studious and surprising Jesse that she even needed them.

Forty-five minutes later, Georgia pointed at the screen. "Stop. Go back . . . There."

15

The hike had been beautiful—mostly fresh air and no people. Cindy had studiously avoided the few she'd seen in the parking lot at the base of the trail.

She wasn't really dressed for hiking, but she did own some knee-length spandex and sneakers. She got out her biggest t shirt and made it work. She wasn't going fast, and the trail was wide and well-maintained.

It had been seven hours of driving before she got the urge to stop for the night. The feeling alone made her want to keep driving. But, if there was one thing she'd learned, it was that she couldn't fight the pull.

She could have gone past the place her gut was telling her to stop for the night. If she did, she would come back eventually. And it would haunt her until she did.

In fact, though she hadn't said so to Carter, the urge was exactly why she had made the trip. It didn't always work, but she had to try. Sometimes hitting things and working her way through them could shake them loose.

She'd stayed in a hotel and slept soundly for the first time in weeks. Maybe the urge had been telling her she needed self-care. Nothing had haunted her. This morning, she'd found the "things to do in the area" list and decided to try hiking.

The trail was kept neat and clean, for which she was grateful. There were smaller paths leading off it. A good place to get lost. Cindy was not a skilled enough hiker to take any of them. The loop she was on was already seven miles—the high end for a woman who'd been in her room for weeks.

Breathing deeply, she tried to clear her mind and look out for small creatures. Then, for whatever reason, when the next little path veered off to the right, her body turned. Her feet stepped methodically. This path was not as well kept. She tripped on a root, going down. Her hands caught in the broken twigs and leaves that littered the ground.

Jarred at the sudden fall, her eyes opened slowly. Dirt pressed into the side of her face, fuzz covered her tongue. Things were blurry. Her legs didn't want to move. Pressing against the ground she tried to get up, but her arms couldn't lift her. Her shoulders ached.

Behind her a voice said, "Don't worry. I'll give you time."

She knew that voice. She couldn't place it, but she'd heard it before. Her blood instantly turned to ice as she realized what was happening. Blinking faster, she made out little bits of light. She was in the middle of the woods, and it was deep night.

Vague memories pushed at the back of her brain, none of them good.

For a moment, the thought flashed through her brain that he'd ruined her favorite top. Silky and covered in bright polka dots, it wrapped from one side to the other, and it made her look so good. She'd finally found a skirt that fell to the right point on her thighs to make her legs look long. She wiggled her toes. Her shoes were gone.

There was a stitch in her side and the more she thought about it the more it hurt. This time when she tried to lift her hand, it worked. She touched the spot on her torso. Though she was still lying on the forest floor, barely moving, just that light pressure sent a lightning bolt of pain through her. She tried to hide it from him.

She yanked her fingers back, as though she were the problem. The stickiness that came away told her more than she wanted to know. She didn't need to look, but she did anyway. Blinking in the dim light, she saw in only black and white from the glow of the moon. She could see the darkness that clung to her fingertips. She couldn't see that it was red, but she could smell that it was blood. *Hers.*

They stayed that way for a long time: Her lying on the ground, trying to think of a way out of this; him sitting behind her making noises as if he were whittling something.

She didn't dare turn her head and look. He seemed to be waiting. So she waited, too. Far too soon, he seemed to get tired of it.

"Come on . . . It's past time . . . I think you're faking it . . ." There were pauses between each time he tried to goad her, but the pauses were getting shorter and shorter.

He kicked her in her thigh. Hard enough to bruise, but she managed not to yelp out. Still, the point of what must be a boot made her flinch.

"Told you," he said. She could hear the grin in his voice. "All right. I'm counting to ten."

"What are we doing?" she asked, hating the way her voice shook.

"Nine. You run. I catch you."

"If I get away?" She was trying to buy time. She wiggled her toes again, wishing she had shoes.

"If you get away, you live." He said it like it was a joke, then he added, "Eight."

He was right. She had been faking. With one deep breath, she sprang to her feet and ran.

J esse tapped on the keys on her laptop. The small table was uncomfortable but she tried not to show it. Across the cramped motel room, Georgia did the same, legs crossed, sitting on the bed, spare pillow across her lap as a desk.

Georgia headed to the front desk immediately upon arrival to request extra pillows. Jesse had thought her new partner was being young, foolish, whatever. Now she saw the wisdom in it. She should admit defeat and climb onto her own bed and try the same.

Checking the time, Jesse realized Georgia hadn't asked a question in a while. Though she wanted to check in, Jesse held back. Her attention was pulled in multiple directions.

Her phone dinged periodically, and Jesse looked each time as if it would be something important. Usually, it was just a social media post or an email trying to advertise to her. This time, she tapped out a message to her house cleaner, making sure the woman was still coming the next day, since the place desperately needed it. And to water the plants, which needed it worse than the house.

If she'd done anything for her window petunias, she'd most likely offered them the Jack she wouldn't drink. That couldn't have been good. But when the messages were squared away, she tried again to focus on the case in front of her. She was out here wasting money every minute that she didn't spend working on this case. Every penny saved from expenses was another that went in her pocket.

She hadn't discussed how much she was paying Georgia Dunham. They'd agreed she would help look for the young woman's mother. Jesse was hoping that that would be payment enough.

Tired of poring through all the police documents and finding nothing, she turned around and looked across the short space. "What do you have?"

"Nothing," Georgia said, but didn't look up. "I can't find any new articles. I've contacted my dad—"

"About Hannalyn?" The FBI had not handled the case. It had all been Shreveport PD and the family. They'd even hired a private investigator before Jesse, about a year after the case had gone cold. But he hadn't come up with anything. The Feds had never been involved.

"No, about my Mom," Georgia said, still tapping furiously on the keys.

Spurts of irrational anger grabbed Jesse. Georgia was focused, but not on the case. "We're supposed to be working on this!" She pointed to her laptop, as if that symbolized everything they had agreed to.

"We're supposed to be working on *both!*" Georgia finally looked up, her eyes wary.

Fuck, Jesse thought. She tried to backpedal. "We solve Hannalyn's case then we work on your mother's."

Georgia didn't budge. "We do both at the same time."

"Not if you don't have any leads." Her irritation was irrational, but Jesse found she was scared of what she'd agreed to, scared of finding Sin. What little she'd found had made it clear this was not a woman to be trifled with.

"It's our job to *find them*." Georgia's own irritation was hitting the back of her throat, traveling across the room, and almost smacking Jesse.

This was good enough reason not to have a partner. What Jesse wanted right now was a really good bourbon. Eugene had always rewarded himself with the cheap stuff, but once in a while, he got drunk enough to buy something really expensive. He often passed out before he finished it and Jesse had gathered those bottles and hoarded them away. Eugene had never known.

Now they were all gone. She didn't think she could afford the tastes that stupid, drunk Eugene had given her. Her flicker of irritation at Georgia turned to acceptance then. One of the things Georgia had suggested was that she would help keep Jesse sober. Jesse was mad that it was working.

"I'll trade you," she offered. Maybe she could focus on that, because she was mostly frustrated that she couldn't make her brain focus on Hannalyn.

For a moment, she thought the young woman would just stand up and offer her laptop. But that didn't make sense. She needed to put it into her own search engine with her own history and her own terms. Doing something slightly different could be the thing to make something pop.

Part of being a journalist was knowing what to investigate and how to make people crack. How to tell the story, but also how to get the right fucking terms in the search bar.

She was just sitting down when an alarm went off. "What is that?"

"Timer." Georgia said it as though it was nothing. It had made Jesse jump.

"What in God's name are we timing?" There was nothing

baking, no one waiting on them, nothing in this forsaken little motel room but them and the need to find something.

"We stop work each hour and take a ten-minute break."

Jesse almost rolled her eyes, but Georgia seemed to catch it before it happened. "Well, how is *your* focus?"

It was complete shit. But she didn't admit it.

"You'll be better after ten minutes of no screen. Let's go get a snack. Food is good, too."

Jesse wasn't sure what was in the vending machine was food. The night creatures chirped at them from beyond the yellow puddles of light. But the drinks were cold and the little plastic bag held crackers that were ungodly orange.

Fuck it, but Georgia was right. Her focus was better. Though half an hour later, she was drawing a blank. At least she knew she'd done good work. "I've gotten nothing."

"What did you check?" Georgia asked, once again having built a pillow fort desk.

"Crime scenes. Anything that would make sense given the MO. You told me that she used big red bows. I checked for *Ninja*."

Georgia smiled at that one.

"—and anything related to the Kurev crime family."

"Anything under the last one?" Georgia's attention sharpened with that. *Interesting.*

"All kinds of things but, as far as I could trace it, they all managed to live through the last week."

Georgia tipped her head. She knew what that meant. The Kurevs tended not to in Sin's presence.

Then Jesse realized that meant it was another week without proof of life for Sin. Fuck. "We'll look again."

The woman nodded, seeming to know there was nothing more to do, not from here.

Changing the subject, Jesse headed over toward the bed

bringing her own laptop with her. "Tell me what you found on Hannalyn."

"So, I used these—" Georgia pointed to her screen where she was popping up images they had downloaded from the grainy VHS earlier that day. "I matched them up with driver's license photos from the people the police interviewed. I've got four of the seven."

It took a few minutes for Jesse to look over the young woman's shoulder and see where she'd matched them. She almost argued about two of them, but then she listened as Georgia pointed out eyes, nose, and the fact that one of them had frosted the tips of his hair, utterly changing his immediate impression.

In the end, Jesse concluded Georgia was right.

"It leaves three unknowns." Georgia added.

"No," Jesse told her. "Just because the police ruled out the others doesn't mean we do." Whatever the PD had done, it wasn't enough. They'd completely missed something, ruled out someone they shouldn't have. Jesse and Georgia would have to be much more thorough.

"I'm not ruling them out for that." Georgia kept proving herself. "I ruled them out because, according to the bar records that night, these men had credit cards that they ran through multiple times for multiple drinks."

"How does that rule them out?" Jesse asked. She agreed, but she was curious about Georgia's reasoning.

"It doesn't entirely," Georgia told her, finally looking at her, her eyes excited at the hunt. "But if you were going to a bar to kill someone, would you use a credit card with your name on it?"

"You have to show your ID to get into the club," Jesse pointed out.

"Sure. But all I need is a good enough fake one," Georgia countered, "and it's not like the bouncer remembers the names of everyone who comes through and every driver's license that passes through his hands. He's just checking to make sure it's legit."

So far, so good, Jesse thought. "How many cash accounts were there that night?"

"Way too many. Too many *transactions*." Georgia seemed to understand that someone had to usually leave their card—at least digital information—with the bartender to keep an open tab. Georgia flipped the screen around to face Jesse. She was looking at a spreadsheet the bar had handed over from that night.

Each cash exchange was an individual transaction. A beer here, three or four beers there, a couple of margaritas. Depending on the time between them, any of them could be the same person coming back to the bar and getting more drinks or just one person who got a beer and then didn't pay for anything else.

"I would guess this was somebody there by themselves. Which means probably one drink ordered at a time. But cash." Georgia looked to her as if to ask if that was a reasonable assumption.

"Totally fair. But there are a bunch of transactions here for just one drink."

Georgia looked at her as if to say *how would we even sort that out?* Jesse didn't have any idea. She closed the laptop and leaned her head back against a very uncomfortable headboard that wasn't attached to the bed but to the wall.

"Now what?" Georgia asked.

"We need to talk to Harper." Hannalyn's little sister. "We need to talk to the parents. We need to talk to Becky."

"We do," Georgia agreed, "But first I think we need to go see where her phone last pinged and we need to go out and see where the shoe was found."

"Do you actually think we're going to find more evidence?"

It had been ten years. The likelihood that anything could be found now was low. That anything found could be identified correctly was almost ridiculous.

17

Georgia stood on the side of a small, two lane freeway, pressing herself against the hot guardrail as a car whizzed past. The driver didn't even have the basics to get into the other lane and make space for the two women.

Never mind that they really shouldn't have been on the side of the road, but some common decency could happen. She rolled her eyes, reached up, and wiped at her forehead. Louisiana was known for being hot and humid.

Luckily, she had packed for Florida, expecting to talk Jesse into finding Sin and then heading home. Instead, she'd managed to get so very involved in Hannalyn's case.

Jesse was holding her phone into the air as if that would help. Then again, maybe it did.

"All right . . . here . . ." Jesse read out the coordinates.

"She was pinging off that cell tower." Georgia pointed to one that was painted to look like a faux tree.

Jesse shook her head. "I'm pretty sure that cell tower wasn't there ten years ago."

Georgia hadn't even considered that. They couldn't simply look at what was here, they had to look at what *had been* here.

"Her phone would have been pinging off of *that* tower." Jesse pointed into the distance. While Georgia couldn't see it, it was, apparently, old enough that it had been there when Hannalyn disappeared.

Georgia was a little surprised when Jesse pulled the phone down, looked at the screen one more time and turn to Georgia. "What are you thinking?"

"What are *you* thinking?" Georgia pushed back. It was almost too hot to be thinking anything.

"This was your idea. We pushed off interviews with family and friends to come out here and see where her cell phone last checked in," Jesse said.

"Before she was—" But Georgia jumped back, interrupted by another car whizzing by. Pressing into the guardrail again, she was glad that she'd worn her lightweight cargo pants, so she wasn't burning images of a guardrail into the backs of her damn thighs. She hadn't looked at Jesse's bare legs yet.

She did regret the choice of black. *Crap*, she thought, she was going to have to get khakis just to reflect the light. But as the car whizzed off into the distance, the sounds of the motor fading, Georgia turned around and motioned to the water beyond the guardrail. "What about this?"

It wasn't a bridge, just a strip of raised land, as if the water had known people would want to drive across it. "This was all here ten years ago, right?"

"Pretty much." Jesse nodded as she turned to look for whatever Georgia was suggesting.

How did she do it? Jesse seemed to easily be able to access maps and locations of things from a decade—or even decades —earlier. Georgia blurted, "I think her cell phone went in the water."

She saw as Jesse slowly took in the idea. The water hadn't been on the map. Maybe because there were a decent number of trees in it this close to the road, but just a little bit away, it was open. There was flowing water a good handful of feet down and out from where they stood.

Hands on the guardrail as though she were standing on a plantation balcony, Jesse surveyed the space and then turned, her black bob swinging with the movement. She looked at Georgia. "It's believed Hannalyn went willingly."

Georgia had read that, so she nodded. "Which means it was someone she knew. Or at least someone she felt comfortable with."

"Possible. The other option is that someone pulled her in close and put a gun to her side—or issued some other threat to keep her quiet and compliant—and ushered her out the front door, or the back, and nobody noticed."

Georgia turned both scenarios over in her head. Hannalyn's purse had disappeared, leaving Becky at the table nursing her own drink and carefully guarding Hannalyn's half-finished cosmopolitan. In the police report, Becky had commented that she didn't feel safe leaving the drinks at the table. So she'd waited too long to go find her friend.

By the time she went looking, Hannalyn could have been anywhere.

Georgia tried to imagine this road in the dark. Tried to picture it ten years earlier. She'd been barely a teenager herself. She'd never paid attention to roads. She hadn't been to Shreveport. It was a difficult task.

Turning around, she looked both ways and left Jesse at the guardrail as she stepped onto the asphalt. There was only the thinnest shoulder, so there wasn't much protection. Checking for traffic, and grateful to see none, she stepped into the lane and tried to stand in the road where a driver would have passed over.

Jesse looked at her like she was nuts.

Georgia explained. "If I roll down the passenger side window, could I chuck a phone into the water?"

Eyes narrowing, Jesse looked at her, then walked up to join her on the asphalt. They played with the options for a few minutes, ultimately getting back in the car and trying to locate things that were about the size and weight of a cell phone. They tossed them out the window several times before turning around and trying it again.

"We're littering, you know," she told Jesse.

"But it's for justice." The other woman said it as she leaned across Georgia, clutching the heavily folded paper they'd bound with duct tape from Jesse's trunk.

The first time, they'd tried just chucking the thing. Not good. It also told them their duct tape model wasn't quite heavy enough. They'd added some coins to this one. This time, Jesse threw it with a flick of her wrist, like a playing card.

"Holy shit," Georgia said and watched as it sailed fifteen feet out into the water.

Grinning, Georgia watched as it sent a splash into the air. But as she turned back, having caught Jesse's motion for a high five, she stalled out before putting her hand up. A truck was barreling down the road, riding the center line like it owned the whole pavement, and Jesse was looking at *her*.

"*Look out!*" Georgia screamed.

18

"I can't believe I'm out here doing this." Officer Vallieres looked over the handle of the metal garden rake that he was using at Jesse. As if he were accusing her of making Louisiana so hot and muggy.

She shrugged at him. "You could have hired a dive team. Like I suggested."

"*In this economy?*" he shot back quickly enough to make her laugh.

Even that movement made the water press and swish at her sides. He was in water just at his pelvis. She and Georgia were up to their waists.

Neither of them was used to wearing waders. She and Georgia both had theirs up under their armpits, the straps tightened down enough that they looked like ridiculous cartoon caricatures. It was still better than standing in this mucky water.

The three of them had started several hours ago, having spent the better part of yesterday getting this set up.

Vallieres had told them what to wear and what to bring. Then, he'd surprised her by launching them out onto this little patch of water from a nearby dock. He provided a metal skiff and a cooler with ice, sodas, and snacks.

This was better though. If Hannalyn's phone was found, Officer Vallieres could enter it into evidence with an exact geolocation.

So far, they'd found seven cell phones. And, after using their gloves to wipe away the muck, discovered none of them were the make and model of Hannalyn's missing electronics.

They'd found fishing gear, two sets of keys, and more beer cans than Jesse thought possible. Using wide tooth metal rakes, they slowly and carefully combed through the muck and plant life at the bottom until they felt it catch on something. Then they had the job of bringing up the mysterious thing without stirring the silt.

Jesse was unearthing rocks half the time, but she was determined. Ignoring the sweat at her temples, she leaned over for another slow pull of the rake.

"Got one," Georgia called out. She'd made the mistake of reaching a little too far the first time, and water had flooded in through the back of her glove. The expression on her face had told Jesse that, no, the cool water was not comforting on a hot Louisiana day.

She was grateful—if Georgia hadn't done it first, she certainly would have. She watched as the younger woman carefully lifted the rake up out of the water. The way she used the weight and balance of it told Jesse that her unknown object balanced on the tines.

At first, they'd all looked on excitedly each time someone found something, but now Jesse just kept working. She told herself that the little flame of hope that burned inside her was unnecessary. They'd once again put off interviews with Mr. and Mrs. Burkhardt, with Becky, with Harper, all in hopes of finding the phone.

Jesse desperately wanted new evidence to present to the

Burkhardts. She was out here in a ball cap that she had purchased the day before and her only consolation was that Georgia looked just as stupid as she did. Georgia's hair was at least long enough to make a nice ponytail that flipped through the back of the cap.

Until someone got close enough to see the perfectly winged eyeliner, Georgia managed to look like she might belong here. Jesse swore under her breath, feeling the tines catch on something too big and heavy to be a cell phone. She unearthed it anyway.

"Rock" she declared, holding it up in her thickly gloved hand looking like she was doing some industrial load of dishes. They'd agreed the rocks would be held back under the water and allowed to sink gently to the bottom so as not to stir up too much silt.

Ten feet away, Vallieres slowly waded his way over to Georgia. Holding his rake above the water, he made sure he didn't disturb anything underneath as Georgia pushed the muck off the phone she had discovered.

"No." She shook her head, telling all of them it still wasn't the right one. But he bagged it. Pulling out his own phone in its waterproof case, he logged the coordinates, and hoped that it might be essential evidence in another case.

Jesse unearthed two more rocks before she found something else. Working at it for a few moments, she tried to move slowly and not stir the muck. It was caught in whatever sea life had grown down here.

Slowly lifting the rake, Jesse brought up her mystery object. Unable to quite distinguish the color of it, she peered closer. It was just slimy and gross and made her grateful for the thick gloves.

She knew the drill. Don't move. Stay where she was so that when Officer Vallieres came over, he could hold up his phone and get the exact coordinates of where it had been found.

He was already on his way over. She planted her feet and brushed at the muck. A wallet.

It wasn't the bulky kind of thing that someone would carry around with all their cards, but a slim dainty piece. She undid the zipper on it, trying to dig in with the thick heavy gloves and realizing she was going to have to take them off.

She glanced inside seeing several pieces of plastic, coins, and what was likely disintegrated paper. Still holding the wallet in one hand, she used her pinky and ring finger to pinch the glove and slowly worked her hand out as Vallieres waded slowly her way.

Jesse was closer to the guardrail and was growing more disturbed. People could have lost cell phones while fishing out here. Wallets were a lot less likely. This was probably something tossed or lost from a car much the way that she and Georgia had considered yesterday.

With her finger now bare, Jesse squinted at the feel of the muck still in the wallet. The tip of her finger slid past the teeth of the zipper as she gingerly grabbed the plastic, assuming that that would be the most useful.

She pulled out a credit card and wiped it, the muck already making her regret her choice to touch things directly. The card looked colorful and brightly designed. Stuck behind it was a driver's license.

In for a penny in for a pound of coccidia, she thought as she wiped it again with her bare fingertip. Pressing more forcefully this time, she revealed the name and the picture on the driver's license.

She almost dropped it.

"Holy shit, guys!"

19

Georgia pushed a smile on her face and felt the tug in her cheeks and across the bridge of her nose. Despite the ever-so-stunning ball caps that Jesse had provided the day before, she'd still managed to get burned.

She'd pushed her way into this investigation and seen herself as a tagalong, but Georgia was starting to think that Jesse Nash could actually find Hannalyn Burkhardt.

Like Jesse, she was starting to believe that when they did find their missing person, it was not going to be alive. And it was not going to be pretty.

This was not going to be the case of *she wandered out of the club and got swept away in the river or lost in the cold and died quickly and happily on the side of the road*. No. Something bad had happened to Hannalyn, possibly something horrific.

Mrs. Burkhardt, Harriet, sat in the family's too-nice living room with a coffee table like a barrier against herself and Jesse. Though her words were open, her hands clutched in her lap. Next to her, the husband leaned back. But even Georgia could tell it was just to make it seem as though he was relaxed when he wasn't. The more she analyzed what he said, the more it sounded like this had hit him the worst.

Both mom Harriet and younger sister Harper had expressed confusion during previous phone conversations that Georgia had listened in on. They were still bewildered, ten years later, to how something like this could have happened. Jefferson Burkhardt managed to internalize the whole thing, as if it were somehow all his fault.

"We found this yesterday." Jesse held out her tablet to the couple. The pictures were clear, taken with Jesse's high resolution camera but the image itself was difficult to follow. "Is this Hannalyn's wallet?"

Georgia saw that the picture did not show the driver's license or credit card. And she didn't say anything about it. Not now, anyway. Later, she would ask Jesse why she had done it like that.

"I think so." Harriet nodded and handed the tablet to her husband as if he could identify the muddy, mucky bit of leather. "We looked through her room later and we found her everyday purse and her usual wallet. She was very neat and organized." Harriet sucked in a breath. "There was one empty slot and her driver's license was missing. If there was any cash or anything else going on, I couldn't tell. But yes, I think that's hers."

"I know it's difficult to tell," Jesse said. "It's been there for ten years."

Georgia was opening her mouth to add "in the water" when Jesse stepped right in. At the same moment, her leg slid so slightly, bumping Georgia. Jesse was controlling the conversation. She did not want her junior detective jumping in. Georgia covered it with a nod.

"It's not easy to see the color or any detail anymore. So I understand if you're not confident."

Harriet did her best, Jefferson couldn't say, but he handed the tablet back. They would likely also ask Harper.

"Where did you find it?" Harriet seemed to catch on.

Even Georgia wasn't comfortable giving up the exact information. Jesse only offered a non-committal, "Along the path where her phone last pinged the cell tower."

"Does it help?" Harriet leaned forward, needing to know. "Does it prove that Hannalyn didn't leave on her own?"

"It doesn't *prove* anything," Jesse said as gently as she likely could, "but it very, very strongly suggests it."

Smart wording, Georgia thought again, absorbing all of it—as if one day she might be the private investigator. *But no.* She was just doing her part to get Jesse to work on finding Sin.

It was an excellent education for a pre-law student. Because once she found Sin, and reported back to her mom and dad, she would get right back to it and start studying for the LSATs. She would lose a year, but Sin had given up nine months of her life to carry her and deliver her safely. From the story she was told, it had been a nearly insurmountable task.

The last time she'd seen Sin, her aunt had promised to tell her nieces the story of what had happened to her husband Lee. At the time, Georgia had only suspected that Sin might be her birth mother. She was putting together clues and seeing that Sin's hair color looked like her own, though Georgia's had some curl to it. Georgia's coloring was close but didn't quite match her own family.

Now she needed to *know*. She hadn't asked her mom and dad if they knew the story. She kept telling herself she would find Sin and get it straight from her. It would feel like failure to have to ask her parents. It would be an admission that Sin was gone. Her aunt had survived too many close calls so far for Georgia to believe it. Not yet.

"Don't you agree Georgia?" Jesse asked, turning and looking

at her with a soft smile but eyes that said, "pay some fucking attention."

Damn! Her mind had wandered. While she always managed to believe that Jesse should be putting more effort into finding Sin, she also understood that so far, they had no leads to follow. She needed to be present.

"I do." She said it confidently. Again, offering the same sterile half smile. The tightness of her skin where she'd covered the red with makeup held her facial expressions in check at least.

"I know you've told everyone these same things before. You and I have even talked about it on the phone. But since we're here in person, and I have both of you together, and my colleague is here now, I would love if you can tell me again what you know. About Hannalyn, about that summer, about the weekend she went missing."

"What do you want to know?" Jefferson asked, still leaned back on the couch, one ankle resting on the other knee, arm across the back. Still not covering his anxiety.

Harriet didn't need any prompting. "Hannalyn was the best child."

Georgia wondered if the woman said that in front of her other daughter. Jesse was purposefully interviewing the parents and the sister separately.

"She was a good girl, bright in math and sciences. She ran track in high school, and we felt really good about that. I think . . ." Her smile faltered. Her eye twitched. "I think Jefferson and I even had that conversation a couple of times . . . That at least nobody would be able to get her because she was so fast."

Georgia offered a sad expression and nodded as she watched Jesse make an almost identical movement. Oops, that did not look good. But, no, there wasn't much that would protect someone if a predator wanted them. Her father had taught her that.

"Hannalyn went off to college—to ASU."

Georgia noted she wasn't called *hanna-baby* or *nana*. Or even *sweetie* or *Puffin* or some odd nickname. She'd never heard either parent say anything other than "Hannalyn."

"She got into the University of Arizona on an engineering scholarship." Harriet was still proud. Even Jefferson beamed at that one. "She was home for the summer. Two years before graduation—it's a five-year program."

Harriet sighed, her shoulders still back, her spine straight. "I don't even know what she was doing at that club. It wasn't the kind of thing that Hannalyn did. Becky must have talked her into it. Hannalyn was a straight A student."

Georgia felt herself leaning forward as her mouth opened. This time Jesse turned to her as if to say *go ahead.* "Were there any drugs involved? Did she drink heavily? Was she meeting someone—a boyfriend?"

She'd seen the answers to all these questions before. But she understood now why Jesse so desperately wanted to ask them again. As the newbie, Georgia could ask without coming across like she just didn't believe them.

The way the Burkhardts answered was as important as the words. This was why they'd left Harper out of the conversation —though Georgia admitted it had taken her too long to put two and two together on that one.

"Never!" Harriet denied it, all of it, sharply and firmly. "Hannalyn was a good girl. She didn't even drink!"

Hannalyn did have a math scholarship at a university that Georgia herself knew was known for having a competitive engineering program.

"She didn't have a boyfriend either. She was too focused on her studies. That's why this was all so strange." Harriet just couldn't put the pieces together. She really believed there was no reason that Hannalyn would have been at the club by her own decision.

She went on, clearly irritated by it all. "Even the things they said she was wearing! That Becky must have given those clothes to her. Surely, she wouldn't have owned anything like that. It just wasn't *like her*." Harriet emphasized the last syllables and Georgia realized what Jesse had likely known all along: the Burkhardts didn't know their daughter at all.

20

J esse had lined up all the interviews like dominoes. So far, they were tipping in a timely manner. Right now, she and Georgia sat at a small table in the corner of a diner. Though it was lunchtime, their area was empty.

She was proud of herself, and Jesse watched as Georgia scanned the restaurant, watching for Harper Burkhardt to come through the door.

Jesse had never met her, but she'd seen pictures. She checked out Harper's schedule and had Georgia scrub her social media for any public information before setting up this interview.

Harper was three years younger than her sister. Having just finished her senior year of high school, she was headed off to UCLA when her sister disappeared. She'd probably been partying her way through her last summer with her friends before her life changed.

Jesse remembered her own senior summer and, given the way the Burkhardt parents held a beautiful, sunny, picture-perfect memory of Hannalyn, she suspected Harper could tell a different, more accurate accounting.

Leaving her back to the front door on purpose, Jesse set Georgia to the task of watching. She'd specifically set them on opposite sides of the square table. She wasn't going to make the young girl choose who to sit next to, but she also didn't want the two investigators sitting on one side together, making her nervous.

It was easy to see when Georgia's eyes widened, so Jesse opted for a smile. But then she saw what had made Georgia's expression change. The quick burst of surprise had been quickly covered with a welcoming smile.

Georgia had skills that Jesse had not anticipated. They couldn't have missed Harper Burkhardt anywhere. Blond-haired and blue-eyed, she looked *exactly* how Jesse imagined Hannalyn would have looked had she lived. She wondered how Mr. And Mrs. Burkhardt dealt with it.

She waved to get the woman's attention. While she'd had a good idea what Harper looked like, in person, the resemblance was stunning. Harper had no idea what she and Georgia looked like other than that Jesse had told her they both had dark hair.

It took a moment for Harper to motion to the hostess and walk her way over to the small table. She pulled out the closest chair sitting between the two of them.

"Thank you so much," she said with a soft sigh.

Not the greeting Jesse had expected at all. Putting her hand out across the table surface, almost as if she were going to clasp Harper's, she didn't quite. She said only, "Of course. We're going to do everything we can."

It hit Jesse for the first time: She'd only seen this young woman as a witness, a source of information. While she was sliding through the papers, she'd been reading from police reports when they had interrogated and maybe even badgered Harper. She was only seventeen at the time, a terrible, awful age to have your family go through any kind of upheaval—divorce, death—but a missing sister had to be too much.

Harper had put off her acceptance to UCLA for a year. In the sad eyes and forced smile, Jesse saw for the first time that attending the university must have felt like a failure. Because she'd gone and Hannalyn still hadn't been found.

"Do anything you can. It'll mean the world to my parents and I."

The corners of her mouth turned down and her smile cracked. Beside her, Jesse saw a server step up to offer them drinks. But she made a quick motion with her hand behind Harper's back and luckily the server stepped quickly away.

Jesse leaned forward to hear as Harper pressed her lips together, sucked in on her cheeks and fought the tears that threatened. "I know she's not alive. And I suspect that whatever happened to her was horrible."

Jesse and Georgia stayed silent, probably both wondering what Harper was going to offer. "My parents believe that finding her is going to put an end to the nightmare. I think it's just going to start a new one."

Fuck. Jesse thought. Harper had her finger on the pulse far better than either of her parents did. Jesse also knew that Harper had gotten a communications degree and worked for a few years at a local paper. She had to wonder if maybe that hadn't been the result of her sister's disappearance. But recently, Harper had headed back to school, this time a master's program on her way to a degree in clinical psychology and abnormal behavior.

Harper Burkhardt was clicking together like an easily solvable puzzle.

The woman sucked in a breath through her nose, her eyes her bright and wet, darting between the two of them. "You think I'm right, don't you?"

Georgia pressed her own lips together, albeit more softly and without the same emotion, but she said, "Yes, we do."

"Well, then," Harper declared, her voice stronger as she

picked up the silverware roll, peeled the napkin and used it to dab at her eyes. She sniffled once, then twice, and slapped it back onto the table.

"This is going to be awful," she said, "but fuck it. Let's find my sister."

21

Her eyes opened slowly. A sharp headache stabbed at the back of her head.

She felt dirt and leaves, small twigs and rocks pressing into her side. She grimaced and felt them rub against the fragile skin of her face.

Was she lying on the ground?

As she blinked her eyes open, she saw the day fading around her. Groggy, she pressed her hands into the leaves, and pushed herself upright.

Son of a fucking bitch.

That hurt. Everything creaked, she was not made for this. How long had she been out?

There were no mirrors, but she looked herself up and down. Absolutely atrocious. Leaves and twigs clung all down one side of her. As she brushed them off, she saw more along her lower legs and arms where they pressed into her skin, making little indentations she couldn't get rid of. Grabbing the stem of one leaf, she peeled it away. No, she could not hide that.

Ugh.

Had no one come by and seen her?

Looking around, she noted once again that the trail she walked on was narrow. Just a patch of slightly more worn dirt than the dirt around her. Not really a trail at all.

People had likely walked right on by because she wasn't on the marked path. She wasn't supposed to be here. She'd come in the early afternoon, right? Even in her own thoughts, the words were angry. This could have been dangerous.

Fuck, she looked down. Had she been lying in poison ivy? It was a park. They cleared the trails, but this was probably part of the reason they told people not to go off the trails. Obviously, people *did*, because there was a bit of a path here. But luckily, no poison ivy.

She breathed a sigh of relief. It was an unfortunate bit of botany that she'd learned to ID all the "poisons" while doing much the same thing in the past. *Fuckers sure did like the woods.*

She looked up. The daylight was disappearing, and Cindy was mad at herself. She should have brought Carter along. She needed time to herself, surely, but she obviously couldn't do it safely. When she stayed by herself, something like this could happen.

Checking both directions, she was grateful when she recognized the large tree she had passed on the way in. Heading back along the little slip of a path, Cindy picked her way along. She held back a few branches that had grown across her way. She touched each one gingerly, remembering that at least one of them had thorns.

Another sigh of relief huffed out when she saw the same spiky plant. The pinpoint of pain on the pad of her thumb remembered it, too.

With the tree canopy overhead, the light would drop to full dark quickly. She had on good sneakers and for that Cindy was grateful. It wasn't smart to try to move too fast, but it was equally not smart to be out in the state park at night.

Hell, it was probably already closed. Somebody could have

walked the trail calling out for stragglers, checking to see if anyone was lost, and she wouldn't have said shit because she was out cold, face down in the damn leaves.

She had to force herself to stay calm. Predators liked these woods and she knew better than most that anyone could be taken, anywhere, anytime. She shouldn't be roaming the hunting grounds alone.

Another deep breath helped to clear the disturbing thoughts that eased their way in with the falling night. The deep breaths turned to sighs of relief as she saw the main trail in the distance. The ground looked different where they had graded it.

Good. She'd taken a right onto this path, and she would take a left back onto the trail. First, she covered the last few feet and thought, it would be okay. Even if it got dark, this was an easy trail. She could follow along. She would likely see the lights from the parking lot soon enough. She would be okay.

But she had to stop.

She had to figure out where this point was. *She had to mark it mentally.*

Because this was where it started. Cindy had foolishly believed she was coming for a walk to clear her head. But it only worked that way sometimes, didn't it? *Sometimes she was stupid.* What she'd thought was nothing, just her following along some internal urge, had led her right into the heart of the beast.

Cindy Baker had seen some beasts.

As of yet, none of them seemed to know that she followed them. That she could see them. She hadn't seen his face, but she'd heard his voice.

Even now, just thinking about it sent chills down her spine. She fought the shudder that wanted to overtake her and looked around for other people. Damnit, she'd picked this trail because it was empty, and no one would bother her. She hadn't had the energy for even casual hellos as she passed someone.

Or had she picked it for another reason, one she hadn't even known at the time?

Still, she turned and looked, memorized the tall trees and the patterns in the bark. She would have to come back tomorrow. She didn't know how far the young woman had managed to run, but she had given her all. In the end, she hadn't won the game. Cindy knew.

Which meant, somewhere beyond where she'd turned off the trail, somewhere no one had yet found it, was a body.

22

B ecky laced her fingers together, clenching her hands into one fist. She put that between her knees and pressed them together. As if all the squeezing could make the pain go away.

Georgia didn't doubt that this interview was painful. Every memory of Hannalyn clearly hurt her. Like Mr. Burkhardt, Becky felt personally responsible. Unlike him, she'd actually been there, and she'd actually played a role in Hannalyn's disappearance, even if it wasn't one of responsibility.

After a deep breath, she started. "We were friends in high school. Kind of. We ran in the same circle. We both finally made cheer our senior year, but we weren't really tight. At least, not until we wound up at ASU. We had dorms on the same hall and we both had crappy roommates. The school was so much more impersonal than we were ready for. Suddenly, we were inseparable."

"Were you an engineering major, too?" Georgia asked, not sure why she thought that might be important. Also, she knew it could help get them talking to ask something easy.

"No. I was in Education. I thought it would be simple. That was a mistake."

Georgia couldn't hide her smile. She had several friends who'd thought the same. It struck her then that Becky—and even Harper—were just a fistful of years older than she was. Odd, it seemed, because Hannalyn was perpetually just shy of twenty one.

Her jaw clenched, and Becky looked away before she turned back to them, offering a wry smile. "Mr. Burkhardt says it was all my fault, right?"

Georgia didn't know how to answer. Though she tried to let Jesse lead, Jesse stayed quiet.

"It's okay," Becky filled the silence. "I know. My dad thinks everything was Hannalyn's fault. Once we were in college together, we would come back home here during the summer. We just kind of made an agreement—though we never said it out loud—but we always blamed the other one to our parents. We just always said it was the other one's idea. I know the Burkhardts think it's all me."

Jesse leaned slightly forward then, resting her arm across the end of the sofa as though she was having a casual conversation in the lovely little home. Becky—now Rebecca—lived with her husband and their toddler. Jesse had pushed for mid-afternoon when the toddler was asleep... but also because the husband was at work.

Now Jesse asked calmly, "When you spoke to the police back then and even to the private investigator a year later, did you sugarcoat things?"

Becky tipped her head back, the water pooling at the edge of her eyes. When she focused again, she looked directly at Jesse. Georgia was an outsider now in this exchange.

The first tear fell. "Of course, I did."

"Why?" Georgia asked, trying to keep her voice soft and create a safe place for Becky to confess.

Becky turned then, her smile clear even if her eyes weren't. She still looked sad though and Georgia wondered now why the young woman hadn't made the cheer squad before her senior year. She had the wattage for it.

"I guess you don't have parents like mine and Hannalyn's."

"Strict?" Georgia asked. Beside her she could see that Jesse hadn't planned for Georgia to interrupt and alter the conversation.

Georgia should apologize, but that would be about the worst thing she could do in front of Becky. Jesse seemed to be willing to let her run with it. So she did.

"It's not that they're strict," Becky tried to explain. "It's that they see you as this perfect little girl. Things go much better in your life as long as they get to continue to see you that way."

"You're an adult." Georgia was struggling to grasp it. It made sense while they were in high school. But both girls were cleanly above the legal age by then.

"I wasn't really an adult, and neither was Hannalyn. Not then. We were in college. We had to go home during the summers and live in our parents' houses again. Scholarships and financial aid didn't cover everything. Our parents were paying for school and honestly, I don't know if they would have if they knew what we did when we went out on the weekends."

"It's understandable that you didn't tell investigators everything." Jesse had jumped back in, her tone comforting, even to Georgia. "Honestly, it's normal. And it's why we have a chance of cracking the case now. Now that you're out from under your parents' home, you have your own place, I'm hoping you can open up to us more."

Becky nodded. The tears were starting to fall again. Georgia remembered Jesse saying that only about one percent of cold cases were ever solved. The ones that were almost always had at least one family member keeping constant pressure on the investigators. Sometimes for twenty, thirty or even forty-plus years. Georgia couldn't imagine it.

What had happened? Why would they lie at the beginning stages of an investigation when everything was so important? Because right now, that's where she herself was. What if somebody asked her about Sin and she said the wrong thing?

What if *she* was the reason no one could find her mother?

23

"I lied." Becky let the words tumble out like a confession. Even in just those two short syllables, her voice managed to break. "I just lied!"

"Of course, you did," Jesse comforted her. They weren't close enough for her to put her hand on the woman's arm or she would have done it. Instead, she used her best sincere expression. No matter how mad it made her that Becky had *lied,* Jesse tamped it down.

Cases went unsolved because people were covering their own asses. Not realizing the importance of truthfulness in their answers probably killed some victims that could have been saved but, *hey, as long as Becky had gotten off okay.*

Jesse took a slow deep breath and tried desperately to keep those thoughts from showing. She managed to stay sympathetic—or at least she hoped she pulled it off.

Becky rolled her lips in and fought tears before she started again. "I thought she was going to be found! I thought maybe she'd run off with somebody, at least that's what I told myself. Then she would turn up in a couple of days and be glad I hadn't told her parents what we'd been doing. So when they asked, I covered for me and for her."

Jesse had seen the videos of Becky's interviews with the police. It had been made very clear to her that Hannalyn's life was likely in danger, and she'd still *lied*.

"Why had you gone to this particular club?" She tried to think sympathetic thoughts. Becky had been a kid herself.

"We'd heard about it through friends in Shreveport. Well, people online. It had a hot new DJ, we saw posts from there. We wanted to be in Shreveport, not Magnolia. We were going to meet up with a couple of our friends. They called and bailed before we even got there." She shook her head as if she were still mad about getting bailed on a decade ago. "It's not like there's anything like that in Magnolia. And Magnolia people would recognize us! We couldn't do—" She cut off her own sentence.

"Do what?" Jesse wasn't willing to let that go. There was no room for self-censorship, not anymore.

"We didn't do anything that night!"

"Drugs?" Jesse asked. Becky had already admitted that they'd been drinking underage. They'd removed the under-twenty-one wristbands so the bartender would serve them. That alone might have been a good reason to go to the club.

When Becky didn't answer, Jesse tried to push gently. "Did you normally do drugs? Meet up with guys?"

"We tried acid once at school," Becky said with only an offhand shrug, "Neither of us liked it too much. We've done our fair share of Molly out at clubs, though. It was one of the things we'd heard about, though we didn't plan on doing more than scoping the place out and drinking that night."

"The police report said you were watching the drinks and that's why you didn't go after her." Georgia had jumped in again. Jesse wished she would stay silent. Her questions weren't bad, they just weren't the ones Jesse wanted asked.

"Well, yeah," Becky looked at Georgia as if she were foolish. "I don't want to get roofied. Molly's not the same. If I'm taking something I have every right to choose what it is."

Valid. Jesse thought, though when Becky told the story about watching their drinks, and covering for Hannalyn while she went to the restroom, it made it sound as though the girls regularly limited themselves to just alcohol. Jesse pressed on that.

Becky was forthcoming but with information Jesse had heard before, but now it explained why they hadn't been high as kites. "My family was having a big barbecue the next day. So no, we didn't do anything that night. If we'd showed up hungover or high, they would have known something was up."

"What about men?" Jesse asked before Georgia could get her next question in.

"Our friends—the ones who were supposed to meet us—were bringing some guys." She looked around the house, as though her new husband might be listening.

"Did you hook up sometimes?" Jesse asked.

"Who didn't?"

Also something that had been left out of the earlier reports. According to everything back then—and even a year later, when clearly Hannalyn was missing—Becky had covered her own ass. By all accounts then, both girls had been virginal.

The way it had been told ten years ago, both by Becky and Hannalyn's parents, made it seem as if the girls were squeaky clean. Becky hadn't even confessed to removing the wristbands and drinking alcohol until the bartender pulled up Hannalyn's credit card and showed what they'd ordered.

It had all struck Jesse as a little too whitewashed. She wasn't surprised at all now to find out it wasn't true. "The wristbands and the guy you met who cut them off—that part was true."

Becky smiled and had a sincere laugh at the memory, though she did it through tears that still leaked at the edges of her eyes. "There's always a workaround. See? Hannalyn was a shitty liar. We had to make it so that if anything happened, she could tell *a* truth to her parents. So when this guy started talking to us, we just said wouldn't it be funny if he cut our wristbands off? So we could get drinks at the bar. And he did."

The truth, Jesse thought, but not the way it had been told. The girls were much more savvy than Becky had initially told anyone. And certainly not the children their parents believed them to be.

"What happened at the barbecue the next day? It sounded like you thought Hannalyn was going to be there."

"I did!" Becky still sounded like she was covering her own ass. "She was supposed to be my moral support. This is my family's big annual barbecue. I had aunts and uncles and cousins coming. Lots of my dad's business associates were in from around town."

"Did you go?" Jesse had already read that Becky had attended as though it was normal. As though driving herself back to Magnolia alone and not being able to locate Hannalyn had been the original plan.

"I told my dad Hannalyn was missing and I wanted to look for her. But it all bit me in the ass." Becky said crying in earnest now. "*All the times I told them everything was Hannalyn's fault.* Daddy said she'd probably just run off and abandoned me, because didn't we know *how that Hannalyn was*?"

Becky sniffed. "Whatever had happened was clearly her fault. But it was my fault, too!" She couldn't hold back any of her tears now. "I'm the one who suggested that club that night. I'm the one who told her we could do it and still make the barbecue the next day. So while her family was out looking for her, I was stuck serving up hotdogs and being nice to daddy's coworkers. Now I don't know if she was still alive by then or not."

"You said when you talked to investigators, that you thought she would turn up." Jesse wondered if Becky had noticed they had information from her initial interviews.

It didn't seem to register. She was crying hard enough to offer only a sniffle. "That's what I told myself. That's how I stayed upright. I couldn't admit that she was gone. But, as much as we partied, and sometimes we left with other men . . . we did watch our drinks, and we watched out for each other. And Hannalyn sure wouldn't have left without telling me."

There was a long pause while Jesse and Georgia let Becky pull herself together. She was righteously upset about a friend she'd let die a probably horrible death without doing what was right.

"When you find her," Becky said just as a small cry interrupted through the monitor. No one had to say *he's awake*. Becky looked over at the device and started to get up without even excusing herself.

Jesse understood interviews like this were hard. Not only was it difficult to tell the story, it was always hard on those who had to admit that they'd covered their own asses, maybe at the expense of their friend's life.

So as Becky stood, Jesse offered what she could. "None of what happened to her was your fault. No one should be punished for being a typical college kid. Certainly not like that."

She could see the thanks in Becky's eyes. She could also see that Becky didn't believe one fucking word of it. She absolutely blamed herself. Her jaw set. "When you find the asshole who did this, I hope you nail him to the wall."

With that, Becky headed out of the room, up the stairs to the toddler, now crying in earnest.

"We'll let ourselves out," Jesse said. "Thank you for everything."

She didn't mention that she would likely be in touch. She hadn't told Becky that they'd found Hannalyn's wallet. She and

Georgia stepped out the front door, pulling it shut behind them.

Georgia made it only one step down before she had to open her mouth again. "Becky also thinks Hannalyn was murdered."

Jesse was still too busy processing all her thoughts from the interview to open her mouth and speak, but she nodded.

Everyone who actually knew Hannalyn was confident that she had not just walked away. Jesse knew that the deeper they dug, what they would find was going to be ugly as hell.

24

G eorgia helped make Jesse's bed, smoothing out the comforter to spread out all their notes on top. Tablets, laptops, papers, a spiral bound notebook that Jesse used.

Though Georgia hadn't fully understood the need for an eight-by-ten glossy of each image, Jesse told her the pictures would bring out details. The details could be what cracked the case.

They couldn't do this inside a restaurant or a library, because someone might hear. Jesse had quickly nixed the idea of sitting outside. What if something blew away?

So they were here, stuck in the motel room, A/C chugging in the corner, occasionally spitting or crackling as they spread everything out across the bed. Once everything was in front of them, they looked at the materials from several angles and dove in.

"Harper and Becky's stories line up almost perfectly." Georgia had noticed that the day before. Harper wasn't at the bar, but what she told of her sister absolutely matched Becky's version and not her parents'.

Jesse nodded but moreso seemed genuinely surprised that it had shocked Georgia. "That's normal?"

Jesse shrugged. "If I had a dollar for every time somebody told me about their perfect daughter, and then we find out that she was partying all the time, sleeping around, and lying to her parents, I'd be wealthy."

"Is it the same with their sons?" Georgia asked, just out of curiosity.

"Not really. They tend to acknowledge when the boys do it. To be fair," Jesse waved her hand at the bed, "I want to say it's just sexism and it is, but not necessarily on the parents' part. It may be more of a reaction to the sexism of the world. Because when their sons do those same things, this isn't how it ends."

That one hit Georgia square in the chest.

"How about you do a recap?" Jesse asked, as though she were training Georgia to be her apprentice.

Georgia reminded herself she was here to help, but for the purpose of finding Aunt Sin. She'd checked in with her dad again, let him know they were staying in the same motel. She told him that they were working on both cases, though there was far more work on Hannalyn's case simply because there was something to be done. Nothing had popped on her birth mother.

Swallowing down the lump in her throat and pushing aside the fear that another day had gone by with no word, Georgia made herself answer.

"Becky drove by Hannalyn's and picked her up. They told their parents they were going out for the evening, but they were in sundresses when they left the Burkhardts'." She'd known girls who did that, mostly in high school. They'd get dropped off in one set of clothing then change into another radically different outfit and re-do all their makeup in the bathroom.

Georgia motioned to a picture of the sundress in evidence.

"Becky at least admitted that at the time, they'd stopped and changed in a gas station as they'd gotten closer to Shreveport."

"She'd been forced to admit that though, because everybody at the club said Hannalyn was wearing the sequined top and the black skirt with the fringe." Jesse filled in.

Georgia nodded. In Becky's initial interview, she told the officers Hannalyn had been wearing the yellow sundress. Only later, when others told the police what Hannalyn was really wearing did she say they'd changed. She'd handed over the sundress into evidence, all those years ago.

"By that point—when they changed—they had already heard that their friends weren't coming. They decided to go anyway. They got in the front door with their actual IDs—" Georgia pointed to police files that had printouts of the girls' pictures and copies of each IDs, "—getting the wristbands, which were then cut off. After that, they ordered drinks at the bar. Hannalyn pays. They chatted with a bunch of different people and considered hooking up."

"According to Becky, only if it could be done quickly." Jesse added in, and Georgia shook her head, disbelieving.

She'd done her own share of partying in college, but she must have been closer to the actual good girls. Maybe because her father was an FBI agent, and all three of his daughters knew the consequences of leaving a club with someone they didn't fully know. Hell, they knew the consequences could be just as dire even if it was someone they did know.

"Around eleven-thirty they get their second round of drinks, Becky pays with cash." This was the hard part, Georgia thought. Somewhere in these few hours it all went wrong. "At about twelve-fifteen Hannalyn goes to the bathroom and leaves Becky at the table guarding their drinks—"

"Becky wasn't clear on that time, but the bar security footage from the camera in the bathroom hall shows that's when she went," Jesse added, and Georgia nodded along but kept going.

"Then Becky realizes she's been at the table alone for too long. Hannalyn doesn't come back from the restroom. Becky wonders if maybe her friend is sick—which is the first version from ten years ago. Now she says she thought maybe Hannalyn hooked up with someone. Though we can see from the video that Hannalyn did leave the restroom a short time after she went in."

Jesse jumped in, "Becky said then—and now—that she wondered if somehow she did get slipped some kind of drug—"

"That doesn't make any sense." Georgia cut in. "They got the drinks at the bar, they watched them—"

"It wouldn't be the first time the bartender was slipping drugs into the drinks." Jesse shrugged, but Georgia shuddered at the thought.

"But why just one of their drinks? Becky didn't notice her friend acting weird, she would have reported that. It would have been the perfect cover for losing Hannalyn."

"Good point. Go on."

"Becky waits longer." Georgia couldn't help it, her heart broke for Becky. The woman wasn't much in the sympathy generating department—she'd done all the wrong things, but she'd been a kid. And she clearly felt very responsible for the time that she had decided to wait for her friend thinking that maybe she was in one of the bathroom stalls getting her rocks off.

"She hoped Hannalyn would simply turn up in a little bit. But that was likely the time when Hannalyn had been taken and was getting further and further away." Every minute Becky waited, Hannalyn's chances got worse, and the evidence got more scarce. "When we put the timeline together, we can see Hannalyn's phone was shut off just before one a.m. If Becky's correct, then before Becky left the drinks to go to the restroom and check, Hannalyn was already down the street."

Georgia had to suck in a breath, but Jesse seemed to remain perfectly logical. She couldn't. Hannalyn was possibly dead before Becky even noticed her friend was missing.

She and Jesse had not pointed that out. The woman carried that guilt for a damn decade. It helped no one to add to it.

They talked through it a little more, lining up pieces. Talking about how Hannalyn's wallet was likely somewhere near her phone. Though they hadn't found the phone, it probably was there—or it had been. Officer Vallieres had called them off before they found it, though they had looked for several more hours.

"So we know where Hannalyn was and where she wasn't. But how do we use this to find out who took her?" Georgia had now completely abandoned the idea that Hannalyn had walked off on her own.

While it was easy to believe that Harriet and Jefferson Burkhardt had no clue who their daughter really was, Harper *knew* her sister. Becky knew her best friend, too, and when they said Hannalyn wouldn't walk away, Georgia believed it.

It still felt like a brick wall to her.

"What's next?" she asked Jesse, needing some way to move forward.

"Tomorrow we're going to go find out about that shoe."

The one lone high heel with the hand painted red sole. It was already entered into evidence.

Georgia wanted to ask what exactly they would find. The shoe wasn't there anymore. All testing had been done, but Jesse was lifting herself up off the bed and heading toward the door.

Grabbing her cell phone off the bed, she started tapping at it. She didn't even look back at Georgia, just said over her shoulder, "I'll be back in a little bit."

The room was too small for Georgia to protest. Then Jesse

was gone and the silence in the room settled in her stomach in an uneasy twist.

It was dark outside. Though they had drawn the polyester curtains closed, she could see that there were only lights from the walkway out front. The motel itself was in a reasonably populated area, but that didn't mean anything. Hannalyn Burkhardt had disappeared under the noses of hundreds of club goers. And Jesse had just walked out the door.

Georgia knew better than most that women disappeared on the Louisiana streets at night.

25

Jesse kept her hands on the steering wheel, gripping it and ready for the turn off. If they could find it.

She was tired. She'd stayed out late and, even though they slept in a little bit, she still hadn't quite caught up. Georgia hadn't either.

Jesse hadn't expected the young woman to wait up for her. But she'd been sitting up in bed with the pillow on her legs, laptop open, looking as if she might be about to nod off. As soon as Jesse came in, she folded it all up and crawled under the covers, as if she couldn't sleep until Jesse was in.

That had been startling. Before she married Eugene, she was her own woman, owing nothing to anyone. It had been a bit of culture shock to have a boyfriend, then husband, who worried. Then she'd worried about Ciara—the girl was still in elementary school, so that had seemed natural. This last month, she'd been beholden to no one again . . . and this time it showed.

When she'd headed out the night before, she hadn't thought of Georgia. It had taken her a decent walk to gather her thoughts. She'd wanted to simply roam and think. She couldn't though; she was in a strange town on a dark street relatively late at night. She'd gone only as far as the lights had allowed, which was barely a block in each direction. She'd made the trip back and forth several times as her thoughts rolled over each other.

Normally, she wouldn't have gone outside. She would have simply paced the hotel room, but Georgia was there. While the evening was much cooler than the day, the air was still muggy. It felt as if Louisiana itself were pushing her to solve this case.

She tried not to think about Ciara as she drove now. She tried not to count down the days. One more week, and it would be six weeks.

"Are you okay?" Georgia asked.

Jesse shook off the thoughts and reminded herself that Ciara wasn't really her daughter—which was the reason for this whole mess in the first place.

"We have to be close. We just need to find a good turnoff where we can park. We're just going to need to get out and walk it on foot."

"Are we trespassing?" Georgia sounded wary.

Jesse didn't help. "Probably, but I'm not seeing any signs, so I'm willing to risk it."

Once again, they were in old sneakers, willing to walk through anything to have a chance at cracking the case. Jesse wore her usual shorts and Georgia was in lightweight cargo pants again. However, she'd bought a few new pairs in khaki. She'd traded the black shirt, too, for a loose-fitting, almost neon pink. If the shirt had been just a little paler in color, she'd be stepping foot into preppy territory. Jesse didn't mention that.

She had no idea if khaki and bright pink was just another facet of who Georgia Dunham was or if it was merely an effort to stave off the heat.

"There!" Georgia pointed at a gap in the weeds and occasional fences that edged the properties. "There's a little gravel road coming up."

"We'll take it." Jesse figured the worst case was that she had to turn around and try a different one. Slowing as best as she could, she barely made the turn onto the gravel drive. Not only was it not paved, it was rutted and bumpy.

They bounced their way back a little bit further than she wanted before she could find a spot that was safe enough to pull the car off the side of the road. There was no shoulder, and no room for cars to pass. They were definitely blocking things, but since she didn't see anyone, she shoved the gear into park.

Georgia was already climbing out, though on her side of the car the ground dipped down a good bit. She almost dropped out of view, but she reached up and swung the door back shut, calling out, "You've got the GPS, right?"

Jesse did. The police reports had marked the exact location where the shoe had been found. The red painted sole identified it as Hannalyn's right from the start. Though she wasn't the only one who'd ever faked the expensive, it wasn't a common thing to find in a field. Her parents hadn't been able to identify it, but Becky had—instantly.

Then, later, the two drops of dried blood on the side had been the only things ever found of Hannalyn Burkhardt.

With her GPS held out in front of her, Jesse moved around until they found the right coordinates. "This is it."

Stopping, Jesse stood as close as she could get to the exact position and turned a full three-sixty, looking out over the land. When she came back around to her original point, she caught Georgia looking at her oddly and it took a moment to figure out that the woman wanted her to step out of the way so she could try it.

At the end of her turn, Georgia proclaimed, "There's nothing here."

"It's not about now. It's about what was here ten years ago."

Georgia nodded, as though once again she hadn't quite put that together. "What was here ten years ago, *less* than nothing?"

"The road over there," Jesse pointed into the distance where they watched a small car move like a rapid ant toward their left. "It wasn't there. That was all fallow field."

"The oil derricks?" Georgia asked, pointing into the distance in the other direction.

"Nope," Jesse replied.

"What was out here then?"

"Farmland."

"they were farming *this*?" Georgia stomped on the ground as if she could feel with the heel of her sneaker whether the earth had been tilled. "These were just open? All tall grass?"

That one Jesse wasn't sure about. "I don't think so." Flipping through her phone she pulled up the picture of the shoe from evidence. "Looks like it had been cut."

"Or it was just dead." The grass was pale. "Is that how they found it?"

Once again, Jesse wasn't able to pull it exactly from memory. She'd have to look at other photos later. "I think somebody just drove by and saw the red of the sole and reported it."

It seemed Hannalyn painting the sole of her shoe had somehow managed to provide the only piece of evidence they had. She couldn't have known when she was doing it that she was making a beacon that would lead the police to her own blood.

Jesse watched as Georgia did a slow three-sixty again. She looked like she was trying to imagine what it must have been like that day. She didn't have to imagine the heat or the oppressive air. She pointed to the road next to them. "This was here?"

"Yes," Jesse replied. Just then a car drove by.

"And the gravel one?" Georgia asked.

Jesse looked at the phone again, pulling up the picture and zooming in. "Looks like it was here then."

She turned the phone toward Georgia, but the other woman didn't look. Her eyes were staring off into the open space around them. "It's not even anywhere near where the wallet was found."

"I know," Jesse replied. She hadn't quite put the three points together. It created a triangle—the phone's last ping of the cell tower, the club itself and this point. It didn't look like someone had driven off and discarded Hannalyn's things along the way.

"Did the police triangulate it?" Georgia asked. "Figure out who lived in the middle of all three points?"

"They did."

"And nothing," Georgia guessed.

"Got it in one." Jesse hated that. She'd really hoped something would click while they were out here.

As Georgia moved away, she stared down at the ground, as if she might find the other shoe. Jesse stepped back into the spot and turned again to look at the road. "We're missing something."

When Georgia didn't speak, Jesse filled in. "There are only two options."

This time Georgia looked up.

"One, he's uncatchable—"

"What does that mean?"

"It means he left no evidence, that—no matter how good we are or how good forensics gets in the future—we're never going to find him. Or two . . ."

Georgia was looking at her intently. Jesse knew this was the far more likely option. "We're missing something, and it's something big."

26

Georgia wasn't grasping what Jesse was saying. *They had to be missing something . . .* "But we've read and looked at everything there is, *multiple times.*"

"No," Jesse said, still standing in the field, hands now on her hips. "I mean the police didn't find anything because they're looking in the wrong direction."

Georgia would swear they'd looked every direction. Literally, they'd stood in the spot and turned to face every direction. But figuratively? Jesse was as painstaking as anyone could be.

"Let's go backwards," Jesse suggested as she now crossed her arms and ignored the field around her, her brain almost visibly working.

Georgia needed to get on board wherever that train was going.

"What are some assumptions that we've made here?" Jesse pushed. "Things we don't actually have any evidence for but believe about this case."

This she could do. Georgia sucked in a deep breath through her nose and immediately wished she hadn't. Not that there was any other air to breathe. It was heavy, almost like a hot mist. "We're assuming Hannalyn's killer is a man."

"Good one." Jesse said. "We keep saying *he*. Statistically it will be a man, but truly we have no idea who killed her. More?"

"We're assuming she's dead," Georgia offered. As soon as Jesse had talked through the first part, the second part seemed more obvious.

"True. Though we do have some evidence for that."

There was a wealth of evidence, Georgia thought. Hannalyn's phone quit operating before Becky even started looking for her. That was probably because it went in the water. Probably, *but not guaranteed*. Georgia added, "It's possible she just turned it off."

She also hadn't used any credit cards or called any family members or friends or taken any money from her bank ever again. She hadn't logged into a single social media account or checked her email. There was absolutely no digital activity for Hannalyn Burkhardt after that night.

"We're assuming Becky's telling the truth," Georgia added. That one made Jesse's eyes go a little bit wide. It let Georgia know that Jesse had already figured out the first two assumptions herself—always a step or two ahead. Jesse no longer sounded quite like a proud teacher, but more like she was having to mull that one over.

"And if she's not?"

Georgia took a deep breath, still bothered by the events of that night. If Becky wasn't telling the truth, which part was she lying about or leaving out? "So according to Becky—and corroborated by the workers at the club that night—at about one a.m. Becky claims she had looked everywhere herself, so she then asked the staff to help her find her friend."

Jesse nodded. That was all entered into evidence, Georgia knew. "The club staff encouraged her not to call the police because it would reflect badly on the club and likely shut them down for the night. They insisted that Hannalyn had hooked up or left early. They were happy to help look, but they would not report *anything*."

That was the part that churned Georgia's gut. A young woman was missing, and the staff encouraged their friend *not to* report it. That probably gave Becky an out, too. "She followed the club staff's advice."

Georgia sucked in another breath, the late morning air flowing warm into her lungs. It was heavy enough to make her limbs feel a little slow. Maybe she could talk Jesse into a nap. But she kept talking through what they knew . . . or at least what had been reported.

"Later on, Becky drove an hour home without her friend." Another crank in her gut.

Jesse nodded. "But we know she did do that. There's evidence from Becky's cell phone, towers she pinged along the way, and her mother remembers the door opening and closing that night."

"And Hannalyn's parents didn't think anything of her being out because they thought she was staying with Becky," Georgia added, thinking about how her father had always waited up. No matter how late they got in, no matter that he told them they didn't have a curfew, he waited.

Charlotte, her oldest sister, had had some wild times in high school and when she came back from summers while she was at Julliard—because, of course, she went to Juilliard—their dad had never been able to sleep until everyone was back under the roof. Charlotte hadn't done it too often after they all watched their father, bleary-eyed the next morning, never say anything. He never asked her to come home earlier. Just ate his toast and drank his coffee and headed out the door on not enough sleep.

Virginia and Georgia had seen it and had never had the balls to pull it off themselves. Now Georgia saw what happened if no one looked when they should have. "So, the Berkhardts don't realize Hannalyn is missing until late the next morning. It's not until several hours later when they can't get her on her cell phone, and they call Becky's house. Becky says she thought Hannalyn went home on her own the night before that. They finally report it to the police."

"That's at least one lie," Jesse pointed out, then added, "That Becky said she thought Hannalyn had gone home the night before. She was pretty confident that her friend had disappeared."

"Right." *And Hannalyn was likely dead by then.* Georgia thought, but then she shut that off. Jesse was right. They were making assumptions that they couldn't back up.

"What would it look like if she isn't dead?" Georgia asked.

Jesse shrugged. "She disappeared of her own volition leaving her best friend behind. She manages to completely shut down and enacts strict protocols. She never again touches any digital account or any of her money. *Or . . .*" Jesse said, crossing her arms, clearly thinking it through. "She had money saved up somewhere else that no one knows about. She traded out her identification and decided to disappear."

"Why would she do that?" Georgia was confused. By all accounts she and Becky were thick as thieves.

"Yeah, I can't put a reason on it either. Abusive boyfriends, threats from the mafia . . ." Jesse threw out a handful of other ideas, but Georgia couldn't make them fit the Hannalyn Burkhardt situation.

"The Burkhardts have a far too rosy picture of their daughter," Georgia added. "But they didn't seem abusive. Harper didn't say anything bad about her parents, other than they just preferred to believe that the girls were saints. That life was easier when the girls pretended the same."

Jesse agreed. "It's an assumption that she's dead, but I have a hard time making it fly that she's alive and hasn't gotten in touch with Becky or Harper in all this time."

"Unless she can't. Maybe she's alive and she was trafficked." Georgia hated the thought. "That could stop her from contacting anyone."

"I'm not sure that's *alive*." Jesse muttered it under her breath but didn't look at Georgia.

It hit her then that Jesse wasn't as immune as she appeared. She might have a thicker skin than Georgia did, but it wasn't impenetrable.

This time when Jesse took a deep breath, she looked Georgia right in the eyes and said, "One assumption we've made is that what happened to Hannalyn happened *because* she was Hannalyn."

"I don't follow."

"What if it wasn't about her? It wasn't somebody she knew. Not someone who thought that Hannalyn was going to have sex with them and then got mad when she didn't and killed her. Not someone who drugged her and baited her away because they wanted her. *What if it wasn't about her at all?*"

"Do you mean the transient theory?" Georgia asked. It had been listed as an option in the police notes. Jesse had explained there was always a "transient theory" in these cases. If there wasn't hard evidence pointing at someone particular, then the idea was always floated that some random person had simply come through and committed this heinous crime against someone they didn't know at all.

Georgia was a little surprised when Jesse said yes. And then added, "But bigger."

27

This time, Cindy wore long pants and long sleeves. She knew she was going off the trail. She already had enough scratches.

Looking around at the trailhead, she was glad she didn't see anyone. *Good.*

Her small backpack was full of granola bars, water bottles she'd frozen overnight, crackers, and two little clamshell containers of cut fruit from the grocery store this morning. A flashlight had already sunk down into the bottom of the pack, stuffed with brand new batteries. It was a super high wattage LED. She was not going to get stuck without again.

With one last look around, she headed up the trail. It took more than she expected to make herself put one foot in front of the other today. Yesterday, she'd thought she was going for a pleasant walk. Today . . . she knew.

After she got well out of site of the parking lot, she stopped and checked again. *No one around . . .* Pulling the backpack off, she swung it forward, unzipped it, and pulled out the roll of duct tape. She taped her pants legs down right around her socks, just in case there was poison-something out here or ticks. There were probably ticks.

Putting the duct tape back in her backpack, Cindy zipped it shut and slung it back over her shoulder. Even as she did it, she debated whether she should have taken out one of the packs of crackers. But she was good.

She double checked her pockets. There were knit winter-type gloves in there as well as some of the blue non-latex ones that she pulled out of the box. Before her thoughts wandered any further, she shut down and started walking, the ball of dread in her lower gut growing.

This time, she didn't meander. Getting lost in her thoughts could be dangerous. Instead, she headed forward, looking out for the tree with the odd bark. When she saw it, she found the second tree and stopped, staring at the space between them. The little off-trail path was not difficult to find.

Though she couldn't tell if the broken branches and bent vines were from her passage yesterday or if someone else had been here in the meantime. She hoped it wasn't someone else, but that was a chance she was going to have to take.

With yet another furtive glance around, Cindy ducked her head and stepped off the trail. She was looking for familiar landmarks, the first of which was a thorny branch that swung right in front of her. She held the sharp spines out of the way, gingerly pinching the vine until she was well clear of it before letting it snap back into place.

It was much earlier in the day today. She had plenty of time and reminded herself to slow down. Cindy passed another point that she remembered and then another. Ducking under branches, stepping up and over a slim fallen tree, she kept pushing forward until she was back where she had stopped yesterday.

If it happened here, there had been a reason. She couldn't read his thoughts and for that she was grateful, but she could see there was a slight clearing, a small space with fewer bushes. Looking around again, she hated how the memories seemed to seep in through her skin, as if she breathed them in with the air.

This time at least, she didn't re-live it. Cindy had been on all sides, and she still couldn't quite tell if she was better off being a third party observer or being in the woman's skin as she had been the first time.

If it was brutal and exhausting being her, then watching and not knowing how she felt was tense and Cindy felt helpless. Either way, it haunted her when she closed her eyes. Even now, she could hear his voice from where it had lodged deep in her conscious. He was once again counting down from ten. The chuckle he offered as the woman bolted was a sound Cindy knew she would never shake.

She also knew if she ever met him in real life, she would recognize his voice.

She was supremely grateful that she'd never met any of them face to face. It was part of why she closed herself off so much.

As she stepped into the spot where he'd stood, the chuckle reverberated through her again. He was confident in his ability as a hunter.

Why didn't she go back to the trail? Cindy wondered. Then remembered. The woman didn't know where she was when she woke up. *Cindy* was the one who knew that they were just off the trail.

Now, she once again pushed forward, trying to keep to the woman's footsteps, not his. She was terrified—though whether it was her own terror at what she might find or if she was simply picking up the traces the woman had left behind, Cindy couldn't tell. Her heart was pounding, her lungs soughing, unable to get enough air.

No one could have won the game. It was rigged.

He was a dead empty space. His glee was in her pain, her terror. He had no sympathy and no remorse for any of it.

Being in the woman made Cindy scared. It stirred other bad memories. But being in him? That made her feel *unclean.* She tried to plant her feet where the bare feet had hit the ground, twigs poking into the tender sole, sharp rocks cutting skin. If the woman noticed, she didn't care.

Cindy stopped several times. She drank a bottle of water and ate a pack of crackers. The woman had run far. On the one hand, Cindy was so proud—her effort had been phenomenal. On the other hand, it had only made him happier to have a hunt that challenged him.

Cindy could feel it as she got closer—the pain as her hair was yanked. It brought her to a halt and ripped at her scalp. There was a white-hot pain at her side. A cut like a lightning strike as the knife sank in, though the woman only registered the pain, not how it was happening.

It was right around here, Cindy thought as she started to scan the area.

This was where it had happened. Where she would find it.

She searched for a few moments. He wouldn't have carried her far . . . but Cindy wasn't willing—not yet—to step into his footprint and pick up his thoughts. She turned away, her gaze on the ground, looking for any sign of the woman when, right behind her, a twig cracked.

28

J esse slid into the booth seat of a little chain restaurant they'd found. She wished there was somewhere less *vinyl* to sit but still the air conditioning felt good. It had been too hot, and they had definitely been out for too long.

"I'll bring y'all some ice waters first." The server appeared at the edge of the table with her too-red hair and almost too-thick accent.

Georgia heaved a heavy sigh and said, "God bless you," to the woman. Jesse couldn't tell if it was snarky or sincere or somehow both.

It was early afternoon still. Being overheated, Jesse first calculated how fast she could suck down a glass of ice water and if that would have any negative effects.

The two women sat in silence, just breathing in the cool filtered air as they waited. When the server came back with the waters, Jesse grabbed hers and swallowed about half of it while Georgia politely ordered a sweet tea. When she could breathe again, Jesse asked for a diet Coke. The woman headed off and

Jesse wondered how fast she could get a refill, because she needed about ten of them.

The field had been interesting. It seemed like a big, flat square of nothing. It had a lot of dead summer grass and they had examined the decade-old picture more closely as they stood in the sun. It wasn't that the grass had been mowed, it was just dead. Which was why the passing driver had been able to spot the pop of red against the pale bleached grass.

After pacing off the distance, Georgia proposed that the shoe could also have been thrown from a moving vehicle. Jesse was still turning that one over in her thoughts. The police had always made the assumption—and Jesse had a little bit, too—that Hannalyn had been in that field. Maybe she had even been killed there.

But, despite the two drops of blood on the shoe, there was no other local evidence. They figured she'd just lost the shoe somewhere in the process. Maybe as she ran through the field. They assumed the other had to be nearby and they had just never found it.

Georgia's idea would change all of that.

As the second round of drinks arrived, Georgia shook her head and held out her phone with the image. "That grass is dead now, too. It's the same time of year. Look."

Jesse frowned. Georgia was pointing out the footprints in the grass. "So?"

"I think you can read the footprints. I could easily read ours this morning. No one had gone traipsing through there for a while."

Jesse agreed. She leaned back to think, and instantly regretted touching the vinyl. Leaning forward again, she tried to have as little actual contact with the booth as possible. She rotated the phone, glad to be inside. Even looking at the picture made her hot again.

She was more than willing to talk in low tones about the

case when there was no one around them. She just wasn't willing to spread out all the papers in public. She couldn't run the risk of losing either a piece of crucial evidence or letting someone see something that had been entrusted to her.

She and Georgia grew quiet and Jesse turned the phone away as the server came back. "That Diet Coke is almost gone. Can I get you another one or something else?"

Jesse so desperately wanted to say *Jack and Coke*. But instead said, "another diet, please," for a number of reasons. If she took even one drink in front of Georgia, the girl would think she was truly an alcoholic and couldn't be trusted. Also, because the last thing she needed in this heat was alcohol even if she was finally getting cooled off. And, three, because she told herself that she wasn't addicted. The sheer number of times in these past several days when she'd craved it were all just a fluke and didn't mean anything.

"I got you, honey." The server smiled and turned to Georgia. "Should I just bring you another tea?"

"Yes please," Georgia replied with the kind of weary sigh that said the server was her hero.

"We will order food," Jesse offered, "We just need to get our body temperatures down first."

"I hear you." She was Alice by the name on her tag. "This summer is going to be horrific."

When she left, Jesse flipped the phone back up again.

Georgia leaned over. "See? There are no footprints in any of the photos from the shoe."

"There are plenty of prints." Jesse didn't see what Georgia did.

"There are a few around it, but there were no footprints that were a triangle with a dot."

Jesse caught on. That would be a high heeled shoe. So not Hannalyn.

If she ran through the field, she hadn't done it with the heels on. She would have run through barefoot ... but ...

Jesse picked her tablet up off the seat beside her and pulled up the same photo. It was almost five times bigger here. Georgia reached out instantly touching the screen and zooming in.

"See? These all look like investigator shoe prints. They're certainly not anything leading away from the shoe as if Hannalyn ran."

"Nothing looks like bare feet either," Jesse added.

This made it look like Georgia was right—the shoe had likely been thrown. While they were there, they tried the same thing they'd done with the wallet. Hitting up a nearby clothing store, they'd bought a few pairs of cheap heels and then thrown them out the window as hard as they could.

They'd gotten a couple near where Hannalyn's shoe was found. Georgia had pointed out, "Neither of us has a decent throwing arm. Anyone who could chuck a shoe could easily get it to where it's at."

Then Georgia had been irritated that Jesse had made them go back and pick up all the shoes. Jesse had told her, "We can't leave a field of high heeled shoes out here. The police would get very nervous."

"I guess I should be glad nobody drove by while we were doing it," Georgia said.

It would have looked suspicious.

Now Georgia leaned forward as they waited for their extra drinks. "So they missed that the shoe was tossed into the field."

"Again, that she left it there herself was another assumption, but one they didn't really look into."

"If he tossed it, then *why*?" Georgia mused. "Still assuming it's a *he*. It's possible that he just wanted to put the shoe somewhere that it could be found."

"You think he wanted to get caught?" Jesse felt it then—the

tumbling and clicking in her brain. "There are two kinds of killers."

She paused and kept going when Georgia tilted her head.

"The first acted in a way they maybe hadn't intended. In a fit of rage or anger they lost control and killed someone. Almost always someone they know. Definitely someone they interacted with. And they do not want to get caught." Sometimes they felt guilty and a lot of times they didn't. But they lied, and they burned and buried bodies, and did everything they could to get away with it.

"What usually catches those people is the occasional bragging when they're too drunk or too stupid. Sometimes they just think they're in a crowd that would appreciate what they've done."

But it had been ten years, and no one had bragged about killing Hannalyn.

Georgia was thinking the same. "How would we know if someone bragged about it?"

"Lots of times, these people wind up in prison for something else. Or someone else is in trouble and they'll tell you about the confession they heard as a bargaining chip. In exchange they get early release or get out of a death penalty."

Georgia nodded along. "That makes sense. So, what's the other kind of killer?"

29

J ust as Georgia asked Jesse what the other kind of killer was, the server came back. Georgia was not grateful for the interruption, but the liquid was welcome. Even the ice clinking inside the glass made Georgia think it looked like heaven. She was clearly still overheated despite the cool air and having downed an entire tea and half a glass of water already.

The server was looking at her expectantly, so Georgia asked for a salad.

"That's a good idea." Jesse immediately changed her order to a different salad and handed back her menu as if they weren't just discussing the different kinds of killers.

Salads could be incredibly high calorie, Georgia knew. But given all the sweating and walking around and probably trespassing in strange fields—she could probably use the extra calories.

"So tell me." She leaned forward and asked quietly when the server stepped away. "What's the kind that wants to get caught?"

"They don't want to get caught either."

Georgia felt a pang of disappointment as if she'd been misled. But then Jesse added, "They do like to let people know that they've done it—just to brag a little bit. They don't believe they *can* get caught."

Jesse was looking at Georgia in a way that suggested she wanted something to click. Georgia thought for a moment but didn't quite get the meaning. "Everyone brags sometimes. You just said it."

"But these killers like to tell people what they have done. It's not about finding the opportunity to brag because the situation calls for it. That's the first kind. A lot of times a cold case can break, not because an investigator did anything, but because new information pops up. So sometimes the family pushes and the case gets assigned to a new team that reopens it. They check DNA. Sometimes a new test is available that wasn't when the case originally occurred."

Georgia nodded along. That made sense. It even sounded like some of the things she'd seen on TV. Though she wasn't the kind to watch the murder shows as part of her regular viewing, she'd seen a few episodes. She didn't need to watch more, once she knew Sin was alive and safe, she'd head on to law school. A year later but a lot less worried.

Jesse was still going. "A lot of times the case cracks because prosecutors will be trying something else—even in another state—and an inmate or a defendant will volunteer that they know information about another case and use it to get themselves off the hook or, at least, a reduced sentence."

Georgia nodded. Jesse made sense. "So those investigators contact the other investigators on the other case? They work out a deal?"

With a nod, Jesse went on. "Usually, the person has to prove that the story they are telling is *useful.* Either they have enough to make the first person confess, or they know where the bodies are buried."

Georgia put those pieces together now. "No one around the whole country has volunteered information about Hannalyn. Is that the norm? Or is it more normal to have somebody volunteer information?"

"That's the problem." Jesse took another gulp of her water, then drained a good inch from her soda. "There is no normal. It may feel like people confess or narc on others a lot. It's a big deal when it does happen because it solves a case that's gone very cold. But the number I know is that only about one percent of cold cases are ever solved. Which means there can't be that many people just volunteering information."

Georgia absorbed all of that. "So you're saying that it's possible her killer just managed to keep their mouth shut?"

"I think we have to work that way. He managed to not brag to anyone who's turned him in. He sure didn't leave enough evidence to lead us to him. So it's not really an *assumption*." Jesse waved one hand as if her word was gospel.

"Except for the shoe," Georgia threw in.

"Right. And that shoe sure manages to be an excellent tease." Jesse was leaning forward again. Prompting Georgia, even if she wasn't getting it.

"Who would want to tease the investigators? And even Hannalyn's family?"

That was when Georgia caught on.

30

"You think Hannalyn was taken by a serial killer?" Georgia was incredulous. It didn't make any sense at all.

She hadn't been kidnapped off the side of the road. Her body hadn't been left posed oddly or dressed like a doll or have any initials carved in it. Her body hadn't been left at all. It seemed like somebody worked too hard to get rid of her for it to be that.

Georgia thought they were better off looking into Hannalyn disappearing of her own accord before they considered something like a serial killer. But Jesse just stared at her softly.

"She hasn't been found in ten years. Her body is just gone." Jesse said it as though they were discussing the weather. "Your average boyfriend in a rage doesn't have the kind of skill to make that happen."

Georgia let that roll through her head for a few moments. Jesse did have a point. Assuming someone had gotten rid of Hannalyn, they'd left no evidence, except for one shoe. Georgia, after this morning, was a firm believer the shoe had been tossed there.

"What if they threw the shoe into the field just because they were getting rid of it?"

Jesse shrugged at her, "But it doesn't make any sense."

Georgia felt her mouth running far ahead of her thoughts, but she couldn't stop it. The first question had been stupid. Was this one stupider? "Does it always have to make sense?"

Jesse grinned and looked up to the side, letting Georgia know that the grin might be for her, but it was also to let her know that their salads had arrived.

Alice took one look at them and said, "More drinks or more water or both?"

"Water," Jesse declared, and Georgia followed suit knowing it was the smart choice.

Even before Alice had fully turned away, Jesse dug her fork into the salad.

Taking her own bite, Georgia felt the sugar of the salad dressing hit almost as if she could absorb it directly into her bloodstream like alcohol. Shit. She hadn't realized how hungry she was. She was trying to mainline a salad.

"They don't always make sense," Jesse finally agreed, "But most of the time—once you figure it out—it does."

Georgia took another bite, hoping that by shoving food into her mouth she could stop her face from asking stupid questions. Luckily, Jesse kept going.

"Let's assume he threw the shoe out the window. One—why just the one shoe?"

"He doesn't have both." Georgia figured that was the obvious answer.

Jesse pushed. "Why not?"

Georgia thought for a while. Was the other shoe still with the body? But why would that be?

Jesse added, "Two—why throw it into a field where the grass was dead and low? It's not hidden at all. And with that red sole—"

"—It was going to be found quickly." Georgia got that one. It wasn't like their killer could possibly miss the bright red paint on the bottom. It wasn't like anyone would think that shoe could sit out there unnoticed.

"In fact, a couple people had said they had driven by just the evening before and no one had seen it then."

"So he not only tossed it into the field, he did it after Saturday evening." Georgia hated what that made her think: almost a full day after Hannalyn had gone missing.

"Lastly—there are two drops of blood on that shoe. They're not hidden." Jesse leaned forward, her fork full again, letting Georgia know she wasn't the only one who needed fuel. "Imagine you've killed someone, and you've got something with their blood on it. The thing is bright red, and you throw it into a place where it's easy to spot."

"You'd have to be stupid to do that accidentally." Georgia replied between bites.

"Exactly. And if he was that stupid—"

"We would have already found Hannalyn's body," Georgia filled in. She could now follow Jesse's train of thought. Thus, the killer wasn't stupid. The killer knew what they were doing when they put the shoe in the field.

She ate a few more bites and would have appreciated the silence, but she heard the crunching of the lettuce and croutons inside her head. She couldn't remember the last time she'd been so enthusiastic to put a salad in her face.

"Okay, let's say that's right. What if it is a serial killer?" Now she wondered if this wasn't yet another stupid question. "How do we figure that out?"

"We have to cast a much wider net. You've seen the paperwork from the police now, all of it."

Something about the last phrase indicated that Georgia hadn't seen all of it at one point. If it was a slip, Jesse didn't seem to notice. She kept going.

"They think it's someone Hannalyn knew, and they also floated the transient theory. They didn't entertain this possibility."

"I thought serial killers left their bodies in the open. That they wanted people to find them. You said they tease people." Georgia stabbed her fork back into her salad again, shutting her mouth by putting food in it.

"Some do," Jesse said, too calmly for the words she was spewing. "Some of the literature says there's approximately thirty-two serial killers operating inside the US borders at any given time."

Georgia paused, mid-bite. "Seriously?" If she had been asked, she would have guessed one, maybe three. "*Thirty-two?*"

"On average." Jesse nodded. "The ones that leave the bodies out in the open, they're few and far between. Most of them continue to operate because they're good at hiding it."

"So assuming that whoever got Hannalyn is a serial killer," Georgia put the pieces together once more, disliking—as Jesse had taught her to—the idea of the assumption. But she had to start from somewhere. "Then he's really good at hiding the bodies. It's been a decade, and no one has found her."

Jesse didn't say anything. Because Georgia was right. And Jesse's idea was starting to settle in. She'd said, *it usually makes sense once you figure it out*. And this was making sense.

So she asked. "How do we find her? How do we find him?"

31

Cindy sucked in a breath and looked in the direction where the twig had cracked, but there was nothing there.

She let out the breath. Probably a skunk or porcupine. Did they even have porcupines here? No, it was an acorn falling to the ground and cracking against a root or rock or something.

She'd just convinced herself it was nothing—no one— when another twig snapped. She froze.

Whoever or whatever it was, it wasn't trying to hide.

Slowly, she began stepping back. She did not want to be here anyway. She knew what was here, even if whatever was coming didn't. She'd told herself she'd find it, notify the police anonymously. She was never here.

But another twig cracked. No one was supposed to be off the trails! Then again, if she was, anyone could be.

Was it even human?

She was just wondering that when another twig snapped followed by a growl.

Fuck. Not good.

Anything growling would be able to find her no matter how

stealthy she thought she was being. Still, maybe she could get out of the way. Maybe it was not coming for her but going after the same thing that she was.

She could only hope.

Breathing in through her nose, she carefully placed another sneakered foot behind her and moved just a little bit back. The whole time her eyes scanned for the interloper as well as the signs she'd been looking for in the first place. She was close. She could feel it.

Then, just as she was a few more steps away, a voice.

"Gabe! Stop growling!" It was a male voice.

Gabe was probably a dog then. That made her less concerned about being torn limb from limb. Though that was a good thing, it made her *more* concerned about Gabe's human. A human would be able to recognize her face later.

Cindy did not want her face associated with any of this. The person might not know yet that she was here, but she did and she was willing to bet that Gabe knew, too.

Trying not to breathe, not to move too quickly, or let the man spot her movement, Cindy peered over. She could just see him, coming quickly through the trees. Closer. Too close. *Dammit.*

She stepped backwards and back again. Only, this time when the twig snapped, it was under her own foot.

"Hello!" The voice called out almost a bit excited.

No, she thought. *Don't be excited. This won't be good.*

"Is someone there? Gabe! Stop tugging!"

At any other time, she would have laughed. Whatever Gabe was doing it wasn't what he was supposed to be doing.

Instead, she stood still and held her breath, mad now that she'd worn the bright colors. She'd done it so that she could be found if she passed out on the forest floor again . . . like a dumbass. Now it would work against her.

"Hello?" The voice was searching, but then it found her.

"Hi, I'm sorry about Gabe. He's not coming for you. He's on the scent of something."

"Hi," she called back but turned her face away. "No worries. I was just heading out and . . . I wasn't supposed to be out this long. Nice to meet you, Gabe." She said it as though she were the kind of person who greeted dogs before people.

She waited for the man to call back, but he only said, "Gabe!" then "Gabe! What did you find?"

Cindy knew what Gabe had found.

She couldn't help looking. She searched the man out for the first time. His bright blue t-shirt and shorts left his limbs exposed, probably getting scratched up. Just like she had yesterday.

Were the two off trail on purpose? Or had the dog brought him here?

She didn't have an answer and she needed to not ever get one. She should leave.

Still Cindy was mesmerized as Gabe shoved his muzzle down into the leaves and the brush that had grown up under a fallen tree.

Of course, she thought and almost cried at the idea. She'd looked right at it, but when she looked at it now, it was green, lush. The forest had patches of underbrush, pops of bold greens. It would make sense that one of those patches would be what she had been looking for. She hadn't seen it because it had grown over.

"What are you doing, Gabe?" the man said again then he turned back toward her.

Damnit.

"He's not usually like this. I don't know what he has the scent of!"

"No worries!" But there were worries. Gabe was on it and Cindy knew it was not going to be pretty. She should be leaving.

But this was what she had come for.

And here was Gabe, digging it up for her.

She should leave! But she couldn't bring herself to turn and flee like she should.

"Gabe!" the man said again. But the dog still strained at the end of his leash. Gabe made it a few more feet, the man stumbling behind as he fought a losing battle with the dog's determination.

"Hi! I'm Gary," the man offered.

"Susan," Cindy called back, spitting out the first name that came to mind that wasn't her own.

He shouldn't look at her, she thought and she turned away. Too late? "I really— I really should leave."

"He won't hurt you."

That wasn't the problem.

Finally, Gabe moved backward. First, he shimmied out of the underbrush. The growling had stopped.

"What did you get, boy?" Gary was leaning forward to see.

No, Cindy thought. *No, don't look.*

Gabe was proud of himself. He was a big dog, beefy, probably German Shepherd. Maybe some Rottweiler thrown into a mix she couldn't quite identify.

She needed to keep Gary from getting a good look at her face. Gabe couldn't identify her to the police later, but Gary could.

Her car was in the lot. They would identify her license plate! There had to be cameras. No. It was too late, she'd already fucked it up just by being here. And Gary and Gabe were here. It was going to be found anyway! *No.*

Fighting the tears that pushed at the corners of her eyes, Cindy turned. She couldn't see the trail well enough to run. *Shit. Shit. Shit.*

"Holy crap!" Gary yelled out behind her.

Telling herself to turn and walk away wasn't enough.

It had been found! Gary would report it to the police.

"Oh, hell no!" Gary yelled, a deep guttural sound of terror.

Cindy turned back around and watched as Gabe trotted up to him a large ashy object clamped firmly in his mouth.

She couldn't look.

She wouldn't.

But it was too late. It was already seared in her memory. Almost as if the dog were smiling. It didn't look real.

"Holy fuck!" Gary called out as if the universe would help him.

Cindy knew what Gabe was trotting proudly to his human. It was a bare human leg that had once belonged to a dark-skinned woman.

"What the fuck is that?" Each yell was louder. "Do you see this?"

He was calling to her. The only other person there to share his horror. But Cindy didn't answer. She'd already turned and fled because she had seen it. She would see it for the rest of her life.

32

By evening, Georgia was exhausted. Though they'd gone back to the motel after lunch for a nap, it hadn't quite worked for her.

She wasn't much of a midday sleeper, but hoped the heat and her heavy thoughts would knock her out. Instead, she was hyperaware of everything. Cars squealed their tires in the lot. People had conversations seemingly right next to their motel window. Several times someone honked, and she tried to calculate exactly how many steps it was from the door of their room across the parking lot to the road.

The same road that was dead last night when Jesse went walking, now seemed to be a major thoroughfare—complete with road rage at four in the afternoon. Jesse had suggested that they sleep on the idea of Hannalyn being taken by a serial killer and also just sleep through the hottest part of the day.

It sounded like a great idea, and Jesse had crawled into her bed, pulled up the fluffy comforter, and immediately passed out. Georgia had only pretended.

By the time the investigator woke up, Georgia was cross legged on the bed with her laptop open and her brain fully on.

She'd climbed into the cool covers in just a t-shirt and her underwear. Though the motel room window air conditioning unit was chugging and doing a decent job, she couldn't quite bring herself to put on more clothing.

"Hey," Jesse said groggily. She rolled over to look at Georgia, her eyes hooded, clearly rested. "Did you get any sleep?"

Georgia lied. "Some."

"I was thinking we should spend the rest of the day looking for your mother."

The idea made Georgia smile. She was already doing that, of course. But it was nice to know that Jesse didn't have to be badgered into keeping her end of the agreement.

In a few moments, Jesse was up, dressed and working at the table as though she'd never been asleep at all. They talked a bit back and forth about what to search for, what would help or not, and anything they found.

Once again nothing turned up despite hours of searching. They found two different articles that sounded like they might link back to Sin. But after they peeled back the layers of the first one, the MO didn't work at all.

"Are you sure?" Jesse asked.

"I'm sure. Her kills are creative, and she would never let someone like that get off without any pain or suffering." It felt weird to say that out loud.

"But it's exactly the right kind of kill for her."

It was. Georgia only shrugged. "My birth parents met over a hit. She wasn't the only one taking these people out. If the two of them showed up to take out the same guy at the same time —" She watched as Jesse's eyebrows rose. It sure wasn't a standard love story. "—then it stands to reason that there could be others."

She tried not to think about the fact that her mother was doing the same work now that she'd done several decades earlier. The one time they'd really talked—when Georgia finally got the truth—her real mother, Annika, had told her that she thought Sin kept going because she just wasn't going to let them win. That she cut off the head of the beast multiple times, but a new one always grew back.

The very idea that there would be no rest for Sin sat heavy in Georgia's heart. Or worse, someone else had already put her mother to rest.

Forcing her focus back to the searches, they input everything they could think of. They checked different engines, looked at different databases, and so on. Jesse even had access to a few police archives. But only one other story popped. Very soon it was clear that one also was not Sin.

Eventually, Jesse looked up. "It's well past time for food. If we don't get some now everything will close." She waved her hand around the room as if to indicate the entire town.

Though she was still looking at her own laptop, Georgia could see in her peripheral vision that Jesse hadn't moved. There was something she wanted to say, and Georgia didn't have to wait long.

"I think it's time to look at NamUs."

Georgia felt the pressure at the back of her jaw, the cramp forming in the back of her neck. She'd been putting that off. NamUs was a national site for unidentified bodies—FBI agent's daughters knew these things. Morgues and districts took photographs, collected information, and gave them to the NamUs site. Families could send in their own information on their missing person. They could even send them copies of dental X rays or DNA swabs.

The site had forensic experts and volunteers that would match the families with unidentified or unclaimed bodies. It was not a place that Georgia wanted to go. The idea that Sin would not have someone to claim her simply didn't sit well.

Though Georgia's heart was holding back, her brain tried to be logical. "Maybe."

"Do you have dental records for her or know where to get them?" Jesse asked and Georgia shook her head *no*.

"You can give a DNA sample." Jesse suggested it as if it were a reasonable idea.

Georgia froze, but the other woman didn't seem to notice. "You're her genetic daughter. They can do a familial match."

The hope on Jesse's face was more than Georgia could handle. Her throat was closing, her thoughts scrambling as her fingers clenched into fists. She tried to say it in anything resembling a normal tone. "No."

Jesse frowned. "It's a valid way of determining if you match. I know that you don't want to think about the possibility that she's gone, but . . ." she paused and looked away. As seemingly cold and logical as Jesse could be about the case in front of them, she certainly seemed to understand Georgia's reluctance to set foot in certain directions.

She'd always believed, between what Aunt Sin said, the way she showed up randomly, and the clues her mother had dropped, that there was far more to the woman than met the eye. As a child she'd been told Aunt Sin ran her own business and that it was difficult a lot of times for her to get away. Sin had treated all three girls equally, but seventh grade biology class had sent Georgia to her mother asking some questions.

Her teacher had explained that it was common for children to look like a relative rather than the parent, and that it still meant they belonged to the family genetically. So finding out that Aunt Sin wasn't a blood relative had made Georgia even more suspicious that maybe she actually was.

Georgia scrambled quickly to cover. "Because of the work she does, just looking for her may alert the kinds of people that she takes out."

It was the best and most simple explanation for why she didn't want to put her DNA into a database to help search for her mother. And it wasn't the truth.

33

Giving up on the search for Sin, Jesse had finally gotten dressed and driven them into Shreveport for something different. She'd been getting a bit squirrely from eating at the same two places repeatedly.

Unfortunately, as she predicted, things were starting to close down. So, while it was different, the food was still the same—another drive thru joint. As she heard the wrapper crinkle, she felt as if she was hardening her arteries and clogging her own veins.

She normally loved a good fast food burger, but she had definitely hit her max. The one she held in one hand now tasted salty and fatty and she was about ready for a damn carrot. But she'd eaten all the ones she'd brought and she didn't have a kitchen in that little box of a cheap motel room.

There wasn't much she could do about that right now.

When she'd been drinking, she hadn't felt the effects of a crappy diet quite as much. Now that she'd sobered up, though, she could feel what she was doing and how badly she was doing it.

Next to her, Georgia dug into the food happily. Whether she

didn't know what she was doing to her system, or she simply didn't care because she was notably younger, Jesse couldn't tell. She took another hit of Diet Coke and tried not to think about it.

"Let's go to Magnolia," she said. Because she'd slept too long, she was by no means ready to go back to bed now.

Looking sideways at her partner and her happiness at the burger and fries, it was still clear that, whether Georgia had slept or not, she wasn't rested. She likely wasn't up for trekking around in the dark and looking for evidence in fields and with dogs. Not that Jesse had any dogs.

"What are we looking for when we get there?" Georgia asked from the other side of the car. She dunked two fries into a makeshift puddle of ketchup on a precarious piece of wax paper on her lap.

Jesse told herself she didn't like this car that much. "I just want to drive around and get a feel for the place. I realize it's ten years different but anything we see, anyone we see out and about—"

"Any parks where we can buy drugs?" Georgia suggested with a grin but then immediately the grin shut down.

It took Jesse a moment to realize that Georgia might equate her inclination for her husband's expensive bourbon to buying heroin in a rundown back corner of a small town in Arkansas.

Jesse tried to ignore the pain that brought. She told herself it didn't matter if Georgia believed in her or not. Georgia wasn't a friend; she was a partner and a temporary one at that.

Deciding to simply ignore all of it, Jesse told Georgia to pull up a map.

"Are we going to retrace Becky's path home from the club?"

"Should we go a different way?" Jesse asked, still trying to shake the irritation at Georgia's low opinion of her.

"No. Let's go the way Becky went," Georgia voted but she

was already pulling up the information they needed. "The club's not far from here."

It was the best place to start. They could follow her exact path. It took a few minutes and a couple of stoplights before Jesse pulled into the gas station next door and put the car in park.

"Have you seen it open?" she asked Georgia. She was starting to wonder.

"No, but it's a club."

"That's just it," Jesse said. She folded her hands across the steering wheel and leaned forward, head tilted as if that would make it clear. Ironically, sometimes it did. "I don't think I've seen anyone coming or going."

"It operates at night," Georgia replied as if that explained everything.

"It is night." Jesse was getting more curious.

"It's a Tuesday," Georgia instantly countered.

"Even so, we were here all weekend. I didn't see anything. No one was in the lot when we did come by on the weekend. Someone has to show up at four o'clock to cut the limes."

Didn't Jesse know that for herself? She'd supported herself as best she could through college—deciding first to become a doctor, and then a lawyer, and then to go to business school. Last she'd settled on journalism. By then she'd needed a fifth year. She'd worked just about every odd job a college student could have.

She knew about walking in the back door of the club in the middle of the afternoon. How the lights would be on, and the place would look utterly bizarre. She knew about cutting a whole crate of limes into wedges and how to check the levels on the liquor and restock the bar.

So why was no one ever here?

Had it fully closed? If so, when? "Add checking out the

hours to our list. I'm curious about this club. They already changed names once since Hannalyn disappeared."

In her peripheral vision, she watched as Georgia tapped out a note to herself while Jesse put the car in drive and circled the lot. There were no cars. "We'll come back and see what's here at other times."

They pulled out and Georgia talked her through a series of turns, getting them out onto the same state road Becky said she and Hannalyn had driven to get to the club. The phone records also confirmed she'd retraced that route at three in the morning when the club staff had finally talked her into believing her friend had simply left with someone else.

After getting them onto the state road, where they would drive for a while, Georgia stayed quiet. She looked out the window, absorbing all of it. Jesse wondered if the younger woman was picking it up from her, or if she simply had naturally good investigative talents.

It likely wasn't all from her. Most people who were good at this kind of work had a natural instinct. They were born curious and suspicious. Georgia definitely seemed to fall into that category.

"There's nothing out here." Georgia finally sighed into the open space. She'd been tapping on her phone the whole way. "I can't even get anything to download anymore. The signal had to be worse ten years ago."

"Agreed." Jesse wondered to herself how Becky had talked herself into driving back without her friend. She must have imagined some scenario where Hannalyn was okay, maybe even living it up without her. Being a bad friend . . . rather than a victim.

"Wow." Georgia leaned forward and began taking an interest as Jesse made the last few turns and paused at the stoplights. "There's not much here."

"It's fine." Jesse told her. "Just the way a small town is."

Maybe it was just that Georgia hadn't grown up in one of these flyover towns.

Jesse wasn't stupid. She hadn't simply let the woman push her way into the car and onto the trip. After she'd sent Georgia home the first morning, she'd done a fair amount of research. Professor Owen Dunham and his family had lived in Los Angeles for a while. They'd been places where he could teach and consult for the FBI, places with universities and Bureau branch offices. They'd not lived in tiny little towns like this. Or a place where the industry had fled and all that was left was the people.

It was exactly the opposite of what Georgia was used to.

They passed through another couple of lights and Georgia kept giving directions on how to get to Becky's house. They'd been up here before, but something about seeing it at night with everything shut down was giving Georgia a different opinion. "I understand now why they were willing to drive an hour to a club and meet up with friends they barely knew."

Jesse nodded.

"This is Becky's old house." Georgia pointed to a mid-sized house that now had blue and green trim.

Jesse pulled up in front and stopped. She turned off the engine and lights and just looked. She didn't have to say that Becky's parents no longer lived there. Georgia already knew they'd gotten mad about the *harassment* their daughter had received about the Burkhardts' case.

They'd moved within two years, even though Becky had come back. After graduating college—without her friend— she'd married a man she'd known in high school and settled down in the area. Where Becky lived now, the houses were newer and bigger, though on smaller lots.

After a few minutes with nothing moving, Jesse turned the car back on. "We should head over to the Burkhardts'."

"Sure thing," Georgia said. It barely took her a moment to

get the directions, for which Jesse was grateful. A small neighborhood like this would recognize a car that was out of place. If no one here knew that the Burkhardts had reopened the case the better that would be for all of them.

It was less than five minutes between Becky's old house and the Burkhardts.

"No wonder the girls were friends," Georgia mused. The high school was just past Becky's house. "They were close enough to walk to each other's places."

"But they weren't good friends back then," Jesse filled in. Wondering if Georgia had mis-remembered or she was simply trying to string together connections.

But as they got closer to the Burkhardts' home, Jesse began to frown. When they'd been here before the garage doors had been closed, cars neatly put away. Now, another car sat in the driveway and still another lingered at the curb out front.

"That's Harper's car," Georgia pointed out correctly for the one in the drive. "But the other looks like they're at the house at eleven at night and the house is dark. That means, whoever it is, they're staying over."

34

"The Rangers and the state Bureau of Investigation are scouring the area." Carter told her over the phone. He sounded as if he knew Cindy had come back to her room in the nice hotel, drawn all the curtains, and done her best to duplicate her cave at home.

It really hadn't worked. At home there wasn't an ice machine down the hallway. The one here was supposed to be quiet, but she could hear it. At home, clusters of people didn't walk by her door a couple of times a day. She'd been locked in the whole time since she'd gotten back.

She'd un-taped her pants while still out on the trail, barely remembering that running to her car, clothing taped shut and leaves in her hair, would only make her look suspicious. She'd straightened herself out, tied the long sleeved shirt around her waist and pulled her ponytail tie despite the heat. She desperately hoped she looked different than any description the hiker might give.

Then she'd calmly walked down the last bit of the trail and climbed into her car. She'd managed not to spin the tires and throw gravel. She could only hope no one noticed her.

At the hotel, she'd used her key on one of the back entrances and luckily ridden up in the elevator alone. She'd showered, then sealed every bit of light that she could.

"So you went hiking?" Carter asked it as though he were changing the subject.

He knew if he kept talking, if he kept asking questions, she would eventually say *something*. Cindy gave up early rather than waiting until he wore her down. "I did."

"Did you know what you were going for?"

"No . . . yes . . . *No.*"

Maybe Carter was just being himself. Or maybe he was the way he was because of the way she was. He said only, "Explain."

"I thought I was out for a nice hike the first day and my stupid ass went off trail."

"You stumbled into it?"

"Not that . . ." She let the words trail off. Even now she was mad that she hadn't been fully in control of herself. "But I stumbled into something."

Carter already understood the kinds of things she could *stumble* into. "So I went back the next day."

"Then, on the second day you knew what you were looking for . . ."

"I had an idea." She'd known, somewhere deep inside, though she hadn't even admitted it to herself.

"I'm sorry."

It shouldn't have surprised her, but it did. Just a little. Carter had always taken her abilities—and the massive shit that came with them—in stride.

He felt bad for what had happened to her when they were kids. He felt bad for being grateful that it hadn't happened to him. He had always supported her, felt that it was his duty to do so. Then later, when she had supported him, he became even more attached.

Though the hotel room was dark, she still closed her eyes.

Maybe it was time to send him off. To finally tell him to go live his own best life, whatever that might look like. She honestly didn't know. He'd been taking care of her for so long, while he always said it was both of them taking care of each other. At this point, she didn't even know what either of them could look like without the other.

But, about once a decade, she got this idea that it was *time to try.* Today, alone in a hotel room, with yesterday's memories pressing firmly at the back of her brain, no matter how she tried to scrub them out, she thought maybe this was the time not to think about it, *but to do it.*

"Do you want to hear what they're saying?" His voice cut through her heartbreaking thoughts. She could almost imagine him sitting on the couch with an ankle over the other knee, newspaper open in front of him, crinkling as he turned the page.

Except he wasn't reading a newspaper. He loved it, but that wasn't where this information would be. He had an idea where she was, and he would have been scouring the news in the area.

Then she wondered, *what if her visions were wrong?* What if the body was a hiker that had stumbled there, fallen, and hit her head? Nothing so nefarious as what Cindy imagined.

She'd certainly seen enough that her brain could make up its own wild, crazy, criminal stories by now. Though part of her absolutely did not want to know, the other part of her had to admit that she had left home not just to be away, but to hopefully end it.

Even Carter had urged her to push *through it* rather than sit and stew. So she asked, "What are they saying?"

"They're concerned," he told her, his voice lower than it needed to be. "That it's a serial."

35

It was almost evening and Georgia was twitchy, even though Jesse suggested they take the day off. Georgia found she didn't even know how. To Jesse it meant sleeping in, a leisurely brunch and nap, then going to see a movie in the afternoon.

Going along for all of it still hadn't stopped her brain. Even during the nap, Georgia dreamed of a house, of cars pulling in and out. She dreamed of Becky and the growing horror of realizing she had left her friend to a shitty fate.

Georgia had little memory of the film. She was pretty sure the good guys won in the end but, other than that, her brain had been elsewhere. The extra car at the Burkhardt's house still bothered her. It shouldn't have. People were allowed to have friends overnight.

But who was it?

To Georgia, maybe the issue was that the Burkhardts weren't just *people,* they were a broken family. They had a missing daughter and a second daughter who was managing to look exactly like the first daughter would have . . . had she survived.

How heartbreaking was that? Georgia kept wondering. To look at your surviving child and see the missing one every day. How bad must it be for Harper to know that her older sister was gone and to be all the evidence that remained of what could have been? She had to see it in her own face in the mirror every morning.

Then again, who was Georgia to analyze these other women? If she checked the numbers too tightly—and she tried not to—she was much closer to Hannalyn's final age than to Harper's. Or even Jesse's. She was much closer to being the victim than the resilient survivor.

Georgia liked to remind herself that she came from a long line of resilient survivors. How they chose to use that resilience had been questionable in many cases. But her direct line—her birth mother, and her birth father—well, she could only hope she had the genetics and education to keep from becoming a victim.

Though she managed a real nap earlier today, it had been brief, simple, and irritating. By the time Jesse had rolled over to see she was already awake, Georgia had input information into a system that Jesse had taught her.

It was easy enough to call up the cars' license plates from the pictures they'd snapped. Sure enough, the blue car parked in the driveway belong to Harper Burkhardt. The other car . . . that was where it got interesting.

Then Jesse had told her she hoped Georgia wasn't doing research and dragged her off to the movie. Now they were waiting on the Chinese food Jesse had ordered. Her partner was still not doing anything associated with the case, but Georgia was sitting criss cross on the bed, fingers flying, telling herself this was fine.

Research kept her from logging into her bank account to see her dwindling money. Jesse was paying her for the work by helping her search for Sin, not with cash. And Jesse was getting a lot more work out of Georgia than Georgia was out of Jesse. Simply because every time they'd looked into something for the Hannalyn case, it led five different ways.

Everything they looked into for Sin was a dead end. Complete. Final. Total. No leads. Nothing to see here. Move it along.

Georgia knew that was exactly how her birth mother engineered it. She'd long slept with the comfort that no one could find Sin. But now, when no one could find Sin, it was a problem. It plagued Georgia's thoughts at night and worried her deep in her bones.

There was no complaining about the imbalance of work because she was part of it. Right now, even she wasn't looking for her own mother. She was tapping away on the keys trying to figure out who that damn license plate was registered to.

"Couldn't let it go, could you?" Jesse asked from the other side of the room.

Georgia shook her head. While Jesse managed to take the day off, it crossed Georgia's mind that her mentor had also managed it without a bottle of booze. They'd been together nearly twenty-four-seven. Sneaking it would be difficult in the small room.

Hell, maybe she should get her own room. They weren't old friends on a road trip. At least neither of them seemed to have the innate drama to be good reality TV show fodder, but this situation wasn't Georgia's first choice.

"I couldn't," she admitted.

"It's okay. I've been there. In fact, I was so close to there, that's why I needed a day off. Sometimes I find if I let my brain rest I'm better when I come back." Jesse paused before asking, "What did you find?"

Georgia appreciated that Jesse simply assumed she'd been successful. "This second car at the Burkhardts'—"

"So it was actually at the Burkhardts' house?"

Georgia nodded. "It appears it belongs to Harper's boyfriend."

"Okay," Jesse said, "I'll bite. Who is Harper's boyfriend?"

"That's the part that you're not going to believe." Georgia grinned.

36

Jesse headed over to look at what Georgia had dug up. So much for her day off. Still, evidence was evidence. She couldn't ignore it. "Okay, spill. Who is he and what have you got on him?"

"Harper's boyfriend is Davis McNally." Georgia grinned like a cat with a canary, but Jesse wasn't connecting the dots.

Clearly, she didn't get it because Georgia quickly added, "He's a local boy who graduated Magnolia High School the year before Hannalyn. They dated in high school."

Jesse remembered. "They were on-again-off-again during the summers when she was home, right?"

"You've got it."

Jesse linked the name and the information now. The police had interviewed Davis extensively. They'd painted Becky badly, but Davis? They'd actually considered him a suspect.

After all, he was the only one with any sexual relationship with Hannalyn who was in the proximity of where she'd gone missing. They hadn't been able to find many other men in her life—Hannalyn was the quintessential good girl, after all. Her college friends had been in another state the night she'd gone missing. Even if they couldn't alibi out completely, there was almost no way they could have gotten to Shreveport and then back to wherever they were on the night of her murder with no one noticing.

"Davis was there? Overnight?" she asked Georgia now.

"Oh yes. Maybe they've accepted that Harper isn't quite the good girl they believed Hannalyn was." Her junior partner's words echoed her thoughts.

Jesse tucked that away. There had likely been plenty more men. Becky admitted that they'd hooked up whenever they wanted. Jesse turned her thoughts to now. "Are you sure they're dating?"

Georgia nodded. "According to her social media and his. Harper is dating a suspect in her sister's disappearance."

That did not look good.

The police had eventually let Davis go, though they'd never cleared him. While they didn't have any real evidence to pin the crime on him, he also didn't have enough to prove that he didn't do it. He and his friends had been high that night . . . so they hadn't been sober enough to say he'd been with them the whole time.

But he had been in Magnolia. That would have made it much harder to get there, get her, kill her, and get back without anyone noticing—high as a kite or not. The police hadn't felt they could put him in the 'no' column.

Georgia was saying as much. "They didn't have enough to pin it on him."

"Do you think he did it?" Jesse was asking before she even thought about it.

"No." Georgia's answer was swift and confident.

"Why not?"

"By all accounts he was genuinely surprised when he heard she was missing. He never tripped up anything or changed his story. And being high—which his friends do swear by—would have made it much harder to pull off killing his girlfriend and leaving no evidence at all."

Jesse fully agreed. "The problem is that they eventually let him go ten years ago. They didn't quite dismiss him, but he hasn't been living with the stain of being labeled a killer this whole time."

Georgia frowned, obviously not seeing why that was a problem.

Jesse elaborated. "We have all the interviews from when Hannalyn went missing. We have lots of information in these reports—" She reached over and tapped at the piles of paper she had filed in manila folders. "—about where he was that summer, and when he dated Hannalyn before, and all about his high school and college careers. But we have nothing between now and then."

This time Georgia caught on. Her eyes opened, her mouth widened and her head nodded along. "We need to fill in the missing time."

Jesse agreed, finding herself sliding into the uncomfortable chair at the little table. She wasn't supposed to work today. She was supposed to take a day off. If she'd been alone, she would have gone out to a museum this evening. Not ordered Chinese food in.

Or at least that's what she told herself.

A handful of minutes later, the food was ordered, and the smell of fried wontons and cashew chicken wafted up to her and pushed out the smell of a good bourbon. It bothered her that she didn't just want it—she didn't just think she *needed* it— but that she could catch a whiff of the smell, feel a trace of the cool heat sliding down the back of her throat.

Now, as she took the bag, she breathed in something else she wanted. "Come eat. Take a break from the work you were doing while you were supposed to take a break."

Though she rolled her eyes, Georgia unfolded herself and

put the laptop aside. Jesse remembered days when she could sit in that same position for hours on end—terrible posture, hunched over, not moving—and it wouldn't bother her at all. Now . . . well, now she tried to make sure her knees didn't crack when she had to squat down for something.

She moved aside all the materials on the table and she and Georgia dug into the food. Her diet on the road was not the best. Then again, it had been liquid for a while at home. So, this was at least better? She'd be better if she got Ciara back.

"You look upset," Georgia commented after a clearly enjoyed bite that took out half an eggroll.

"No." It wasn't quite a lie. She wasn't upset about the options, but more about the fact that they weren't hers to decide. Someone else was making her choices for her, and for Jesse that was maybe as bad as the choices.

Luckily, Georgia let it go. She didn't let go of the case though. She polished off the last of the food on her paper plate and stood up to throw it away. "So we need to fill in the last ten years on Davis McNally."

"I'll pull up available data on where he's lived, worked, and anything official he's associated with."

"I've got social media," Georgia said.

Jesse finished her own meal and got to work. It wasn't long before she had the basics and showed them to Georgia. She took a different platform and joined Georgia in the social media search.

She scrolled back through time, not that impressed with what she found. He'd been dating Harper for almost a year. Before that . . . not much. She told Georgia the same. "I don't see much, it's taking forever to load and his stuff is all over the place. It's not all who he dated."

Georgia talked her through a search for Hannalyn's name then suggested she move forward in time from those posts. Leave it to the college student to be better at this, too.

Jesse had gotten onto social media mostly as an investigator. She'd been taught how to sift it. Apparently nothing beat the well-worn paths of an actual user. She'd never had her own accounts to tell people about her life until she had Ciara. She'd wanted to show off her daughter to her family and friends, but she'd never developed the ease that Georgia displayed.

This worked better.

Davis had been all over socials with Hannalyn. Then, after she disappeared, so did he. That made sense. He'd likely had a lawyer explain to him that anything he posted could and would be used against him in court. So he hadn't.

Slowly, he'd come back online—several platforms even. Georgia had found profiles for him in multiple places including two dating sites. Then he'd posted his girlfriends or been tagged when they posted pictures with him.

Jesse made a list of all their names and saved the data for their profiles so she could get back to them easily. As she began to loop into the posts from about a year ago, when he started dating Harper, Jesse looked up at Georgia.

"Do you see the pattern?"

Georgia nodded. "It's hard to miss."

37

"If you look before ten years ago," Georgia led in, now animated.

Jesse tried to hide the twitch at her lips. She hadn't looked *before* ten years ago. She'd been trying to fill in the missing years.

But Georgia wasn't done. She pulled up one picture after another. "Look. They're different. I mean, it's clear that he likes the cheerleader types. He clearly dates what looks like the popular girls." Georgia was still rolling, as if she just couldn't stop herself. "If you pop over to their social media—the girl-friends—they are definitely the popular girls."

Damnit, Jesse thought, she hadn't done that either. Clearly, her training was lacking the actual *use* of the tool.

The thought derailed her. She thought of her own social media and how she was getting asked why there were no updates about Ciara. She'd let those comments sit, unan-swered. She'd never planned on being a mother. In fact, she had planned on *not* being a mother.

This, right now, she reminded herself, was exactly what she wanted to be doing. Maybe not a motel in Louisiana, but investigating, solving cases. Her path had veered sharply when she'd fallen for Eugene. It would be too easy to call it a mistake. But not only had she fallen for the man, she'd fallen for his daughter, too, and that definitely wasn't any kind of error.

She surreptitiously checked the calendar even though she already knew. Even though Georgia was still flipping through a thousand tabs of accounts she had open.

One more week. She could do one more week, Jesse told herself. Then she would know.

Between searching for Hannalyn and Cynthia Beller, she'd put Ciara's name into the engines. Multiple times. No obituaries had popped up. No mentions of the child. *Good news.* She just had to keep repeating it. She could not let the fears—very real fears—run away with her. There was nothing she could do to stop this. That had been made very clear to her.

When she'd become a wife to Eugene, and a mother to Ciara, her career track had twisted, knotted, and even come to a dead stop. Eugene had turned out to be a controlling asshole rather than a doting lover. And Jesse's options—and her world —had gotten smaller and smaller.

She wasn't sure where her life would be right now if things in her small Florida town hadn't suddenly gotten so twisted just a year ago.

It was still affecting her. Some of it in a good way. The notoriety from that case had landed her other bigger jobs. Eugene being gone had removed the impetus to give a polite "thank you, but no." She'd taken them.

The FBI agents had come back to her multiple times, giving her pieces of assignments if not the whole thing. She turned out reports and handed them in not knowing if the cases were solved or the information she'd given useful.

It made her pause. It was interesting that she hadn't realized before that she'd been the one under the glass in that case. *She* was the one they investigated for a while. *She* was the one whose husband had turned out to be far worse than anyone could imagine.

Yet, while that had helped her get ahead now, she was still way behind where she would have been had Eugene not derailed her on purpose. Had Ciara not derailed her simply by existing and being wonderful.

Pushing her focus back to the images Georgia had downloaded, Jesse watched as the young woman flipped through screen grabs going all the way back to when Davis McNally was a fourteen year old kid. *Damn.*

Georgia finally commented. "He's been a bit of a Casanova."

Jesse raised one eyebrow questioning that assessment.

"Okay," Georgia agreed with a head tip and a half grin. "A self-proclaimed Casanova. For a very long time. But look, here's all the dates—girls—up to Hannalyn. Well, Hannalyn and their brief fling that last summer."

Jesse looked at the images. They were just kids, middle school and then high school age. She saw what Georgia had seen: a variety of them different shapes, sizes, backgrounds, skin colors. The kid had no clear preference. Just "cheerleader type."

Then, Hannalyn.

When she looked at the timeline now, Hannalyn was just the next girl in his line. When she looked at the timeline after that summer, though, that was not what she and Georgia had both found.

"They all look like Hannalyn." Georgia's voice was solemn.

Jesse nodded. Blond hair, blue eyes, similar build. If she didn't know better, if she hadn't seen the names on some of the posts, she would have gotten several of them confused. She was generally good with faces.

"What does it mean?" Georgia asked.

"That's the problem. It could mean anything. It could mean he was completely traumatized by Hannalyn disappearing. It could mean that he took it hard because he and Hannalyn were tighter than what he said—maybe he was even in love with her."

"Just like Becky didn't tell the police everything. Trying not to get in trouble." Georgia filled in.

"He was close to the same age as her, just a year older. So there's every possibility that he knew more than he was saying. He closed up like a little clam when the police questioned him—"

Georgia interrupted again, "Indicating that he knew more than he was saying."

Jesse nodded. It might not be things pertaining to her disappearance. People often covered for the dead, making them seem loftier or kinder or more angelic than they had ever actually been.

Jesse went back to her original thread. "On the other hand, it might not be guilt. It might be . . ." she trailed off, looking for a word she couldn't find. So she made one up. "Trophy-ism."

"What's that?" Georgia was shaking her head even as the gears turned. "I think I understand but maybe I don't."

"Hannalyn might be the first one he killed," Jesse supplied. "So then, he may be dating other women who look just like her as reminders of his—" She raised her fingers for air quotes. "Glory."

Georgia shuddered at that. *Good.* She should.

"So there's absolutely no way to determine any assessment of guilt from these images and this behavior?"

"No." Jesse told her. She couldn't have the junior detective playing TV show psychoanalyst and jumping to conclusions with no hard evidence. "It could mean anything from he doesn't realize he's doing it to a carefully plotted plan. But it does give us one more question . . ."

Jesse liked this one. They should be able to figure it out reasonably quickly. "We have a lot of overlap in our lists of names." They'd each been keeping track of Davis' various girl-friends through the years—Jesse on paper, Georgia digitally. "But we have some separate names, too. We need to combine them into one master list. Then we find out if any of them has gone missing, too."

38

"Damn!" Georgia shoved her chair back and sailed a bit farther than she intended. It was too late. She'd already earned herself a harsh look from the librarian at the counter.

Smiling as cover, Georgia waved softly and slid back into her carrel. Maybe she wasn't cut out for library research. Ducking her head, she tried to disappear.

She'd talked Jesse into leaving the godforsaken motel and switching to a new place that was going to cost them extra. But it was going to be so much better. It almost had to be.

The motel was fine, but neither of them had really gotten a good night's sleep. They were cramped with two of them in the room and . . . the list went on long enough for Jesse to give in. The investigator had also admitted they would be here for a while. This case wasn't solving itself.

Georgia had done the research herself. Between a website selling off unrented rooms and an additional weekly rate discount it was only fifteen dollars extra to get them a suite. She wasn't even in it, and she was already breathing better at the thought of her own room and maybe a little kitchenette. My

God, she was going to eat some vegetables. Not that she would tell her mother. She would simply give her parents the new address and be done.

Because of the switch, though, they'd had to be out of the motel by ten. Not that Georgia thought anyone at the motel was going to enforce that. Still, they'd packed everything and loaded it in the car.

It was concerning just how difficult it was to put everything back in her little suitcase. Her things had managed to spread in twenty different directions despite the tiny confines of the room. For the midday hours now, they were homeless until three pm.

The library seemed a good option for the time between. In fact, Georgia had planned on telling Jesse they should come back here more often. Now she was glad she'd held her tongue. This librarian wasn't her biggest fan.

Also, they couldn't bring all the documents out. God forbid one of the young teenagers walking by—whom Georgia suspected was a homeschooler—caught a whiff of what they were doing. She didn't want to be there for an uptight parent getting mad that she had talked about murder around Precious.

This time she pushed herself back slowly, catching Jesse's eye from around the edge of the carrel. The questioning expression on Jesse's face matched her words. "Davis McNally?"

Jesse, of course, had a well-modulated library voice. She probably lived and breathed in libraries before. Georgia really only associated them with school.

She nodded. "Aside from the fact that he only dates women who look like Hannalyn Burkhardt, there's *nothing* on him. I can't find a single criminal arrest record. I can't even find a point where he's been pulled over for a speeding ticket. He's so squeaky clean, he's polished to a high shine."

"And?" Jesse prompted.

"And that's it!" Georgia tried not to huff like the teenager she'd just mentally dismissed. "I'm done. There's nothing here."

Jesse nodded slowly before saying, "That's exactly the problem."

Georgia agreed. It *was* the problem. They followed this lead, and it hadn't panned out. But Jesse was looking at her as though she should put the puzzle together.

Georgia waited a beat, and then another, before she caved. "What?"

"That is the problem." Jesse repeated. "He's too squeaky clean."

Georgia's features pulled into a frown. Jesse explained, "Put my name in the search bar."

Georgia figured it was maybe a rhetorical exercise, but the way her mentor was looking at her she started typing.

A bunch of different things came up. For starters, there were a concerning number of Jesse Nash's, many of them men. She filtered those out and just looked at the women.

"Okay, now narrow it down to just me." Jesse pointed at the screen. She'd discretely rolled her chair over to read over her shoulder. Georgia held her tongue.

Sure enough, as soon as Georgia had her search confined to information about the woman sitting next to her, things came up. There was a notice of an arrest for a DUI three weeks ago. That one made Georgia raise her eyebrows. Then, further back than that, Jesse was tied to a Eugene Nash suspected of being a serial killer in Florida.

"Your husband?" Georgia didn't even think before she asked. Not only was it rude—*good lord*—but maybe she'd been staying in a hotel room with a serial killer of her own.

"It wasn't him." Jesse brushed it off as though the headline meant nothing. "Keep scrolling."

She found numerous articles that Jesse had written, but also police reports on Eugene Nash getting called in for domestic assault. There were ties to Ciara Nash, an eight-year-old girl. And Georgia was beginning to catch Jesse's point.

Not squeaky clean.

"Put yourself in." Jesse pushed now.

Georgia almost protested. Though her mind said *Oh hell no*, she knew it was only fair. It took a very short time to populate with information about her. Too short. Georgia couldn't prepare herself for the machine to spit out all kinds of information about her.

"See?" Jesse pointed to the screen. "Even you've been arrested."

"What?" *How was that there?*

"Are you denying that you were arrested?" Jesse asked.

"Kind of! They cuffed a bunch of us, but I wasn't charged. They didn't even hold me." She'd been at the park late at night with her friends. Things had gone down. To this day she still wasn't even sure what had happened. Just that there was noise from a group on the other side of the park, probably a fight, screaming, then police.

"They basically booked everyone and let most of us go," she explained.

"But see?" Jesse said again as though this explained everything. "Most of us have some kind of record that shows up. Most of us who are relatively good, upstanding, decent citizens."

Georgia wasn't going to say anything about that DUI. But it might have explained why Jesse went out infrequently during the days when Georgia had first tried to contact her then had watched her before approaching. She might be a drunk, but after that first run in it looked like she wasn't going to drive that way.

"We've got something on our records." Jesse reiterated. "And we certainly aren't killers."

Georgia's eyes were still scanning the screen in front of her.

"This one isn't even true!" she huffed out, but Jesse didn't look. She just shrugged as if it were all inconsequential. Maybe that was the point.

"You're not very old." Jesse commented softly, "and you've got a record online. A bunch of your friends were there. They were arrested with you. They've got records. Do you really think Davis McNally is this squeaky clean?"

Suddenly, Georgia had something else to be upset about. Not that Davis was squeaky clean, but that he'd managed to keep his record somehow looking better than her own. "There's no way," she murmured.

"Exactly." Jesse commented. "What is he hiding?"

39

J esse ate yet another burger in silence. This time they'd gone inside and sat at one of the little built-in tables with the curved plastic chairs that didn't move.

She dipped fries in ketchup and mustard and chewed slowly. They still had another thirty minutes to kill before they could check in at the new hotel.

Georgia had worn her down. Though Jesse would have liked to save the money, her junior partner definitely had a law career in front of her. Jesse believed she was a good arguer, but Georgia had outmaneuvered her at every turn.

The younger woman had anticipated each protest and had a counter that clearly showed why her option was better not only for Jesse but for everyone. She'd even suggested they might be able to wrap the case sooner if they could get some damn decent sleep.

They were both a little irritable after last night. More than the usual door slams or occasional honking, last night, at 3a.m. a couple several doors down had gotten into a nasty argument. On the sidewalk. At high volume.

Eventually a car door slammed and tires squealed away.

Jesse had thought it was blessedly over, but almost immediately the remaining male voice began arguing with another male voice. Jesse and Georgia had spent part of the night awake against their will. Jesse had been easier to convince of the move after that.

While there was no guarantee the new hotel would be better, it definitely seemed to attract a better class of citizens— and she hated thinking that way. She'd been many different classes of citizen herself.

In her earliest memories, her mom was a struggling single mother. They had been dirt poor, barely keeping the rent paid. Sometimes her mother managed it only with late payments. Sometimes she hadn't managed it. They'd been evicted more than once, though Jesse remembered her mom making it a game.

She remembered the orange box macaroni and cheese that had been a treat—something expensive they'd barely been able to afford. Then her mother had married, and her stepfather had put them firmly into the middle class.

Her stepfather, Jedediah Rusch, had been a kind and wonderful man who treated Jesse as his own child, despite the fact that she was seven by the time her mother had met him. He'd even given her a baby brother with a *J* name: Jeremy to go with Jesse.

And Jesse had loved Jeremy with everything her little nine-year-old heart could hold. She tried not to think about it now.

In college, she'd been poor again. Then poorer still directly after graduating and telling her parents she was making her own way, scraping things together, and wanting to do it all on her own.

Looking back, she could see she'd been afforded the opportunity to take risks that she might otherwise not have been able to. Because she knew—unlike her mother when she'd been very young—if she couldn't pay her rent there was somewhere to go. Even though her mother and Jed had faded to former shells of themselves, they would still unfold the living room couch for her, give her sheets and pillows and feed her.

Then she'd met Eugene. When they first got together, he had money. He'd swept her off her feet in a blazing love she'd never had planned for her own life. It was the kind of thing she'd seen between her mother and Dr. Jed when they first met.

Jesse had sworn off it for herself. Still, Eugene convinced her the two of them could weather anything. That, no matter what happened, even the kind of tragedy that had struck her own family, the two of them were rocks. Even better, they were one rock together. Jesse had believed.

She'd been a fool.

Eugene Nash couldn't weather anything. As soon as times had turned just a little bit tough, he'd broken. His claim of being a rock proved him nothing more than loose gravel. They'd slipped and spun their tires. If not for Ciara, Jesse would have regretted every last minute of it.

Her focus now needed to turn back to Davis McNally.

She followed his path from town to town, out of Magnolia. Off to college, Harvard for Davis McNally. Then to grad school: Massachusetts this time and the Sloane School. Jesse had had to search that name, but found it was top five for MBAs.

Davis McNally was racking up points.

He day traded for a while, making himself a good amount of money and seeming to handle the stress. Jesse put that as a mark in the *con* column. The kind of person who could handle the stress of the New York Stock Exchange, the way Davis had, that was someone who could handle the stress of pulling a knife across someone else's jugular and then cleaning up the mess.

She'd even managed to find murders in most every town he'd lived in while he'd been there. But to her disappointment, she couldn't find evidence that Davis was the culprit. He'd often not even been in town at the time of those murders, nor could she find any real common threads between them. A handful of the cases had already been solved and closed. One was a man who'd killed his family and then himself. Another was a young child who disappeared and was found dismembered and stuffed into a hollow tree. While there was a young woman who went missing, several things told Jesse this wasn't tied to Hannalyn Burkhardt.

At least she didn't think it was. Even the family was convinced this girl had run away. Also, Davis McNally had been in a conference out of state that week. His social media was clear, he was in another part of the country.

As frustrated as Georgia had seemed when he turned up so squeaky clean, Jesse was now. She'd recognized that flag to keep digging and she had dug. But all she had gotten for the effort was fifteen puzzle pieces of a one-hundred piece puzzle and a deep confidence that something was off with Davis McNally.

She chewed on her burger now and tried to figure it all out. But eventually Georgia reached across the table, tapping the flat surface in front of her. "It's time."

Taking a sip of no-longer-fizzy soda, she made a face of regret and set it back down. "All right."

But even as she gathered her trash, her brain began to wander again.

She had Becky, who had finally broken and talked, but still seemed to be holding something back.

She had the Burkhardts, who clung to a patently false belief about their own daughter. They were unshakable.

She had a single shoe found in a field, the sole painted red in an attempt to make it look more expensive than it was.

And she had Davis McNally, the on-again/off-again boyfriend who somehow made it to his early thirties with a record that revealed absolutely nothing.

Jesse shoved the wax paper down into the can, listening to it crinkle as it hit the other remnants in the already overstuffed trash. Next to her, Georgia opened the door and the heat blasted in, making her want to shrink back when she knew she needed to go forward.

They were headed to a new hotel that cost more money. She had more pieces and still nothing that fit. Something was going to have to pop soon.

40

"It's time to come home," Carter told her, his voice soft, not pressing but certain.

Cindy didn't quite answer. She'd answered the phone knowing it was him and what he'd want. For today that seemed like maybe enough.

She had not been out of the room once since she locked herself in. The No Room Service sign hung on the knob as did the Do Not Disturb. She didn't even open the door for food deliveries, just left it prepaid sitting in the hall until she was sure they were gone.

"You know, I'm right." Carter's voice told her she did. "If you're going to sit someplace with the curtains drawn, you might as well do it at home." In the space they had worked to carve out for her. Where the curtains blocked all the light.

Damn him, she thought he was pulling out the stops.

"You might as well do it where you can have your favorite foods. In a place that's already paid for." He didn't let the tone of his irritation creep in. Like he wasn't considering what this hotel was going to cost him in their regular monthly budget.

"You need to get back to work, don't you?" She asked it as if she were capable of changing a subject on Carter. He was soft but immovable most days. Her being stuck here was her own damn fault. It hadn't worked.

"I am at work. I've got the next handful of days lined up."

"Then you don't need me at home, interrupting." She didn't actually want to stay, but she couldn't quite bring herself to leave either.

Carter worked freelance. The money they'd inherited from their parents gave them food, shelter, and clothing and not much else. Carter picked up jobs here and there and covered all the extra.

Fuck. She hadn't really put all the math together before, but if she did, it meant that Carter was covering this hotel room.

"I can do both," he offered up drolly. "I do live here when I work."

She was going to have to leave. She couldn't put him out any more than she already had.

"It's not yet eleven." His voice was again soft and firm. "Check out. Hop in your car and come back."

Yes. Of course. As if she could just hop in her car. Her car didn't have blackout shades. She had to see people so she could drive. She would have to pack her things and huff her heavy suitcase down the hall and into the trunk again. It had been easier when she was hopeful. Now she knew better.

Carter might have a warm dark room and food waiting for her, but the baby bird was going to have to get shoved out into the world for a good number of hours first.

She held her silence for a long moment, probably making him worry. In the end, she just didn't want to do it. It was going to churn everything to step foot outside where the sun was shining. She knew it.

So far, no one had come knocking on her door to see if she had been there when the body was found. No one seemed to have any reports—at least not any that Carter had found—of someone who looked like her being at the scene. The jogger had mentioned someone else but found himself patently unable to describe her. For that, Cindy was incredibly grateful.

She held her tongue for another long moment before saying, "Fine. I'll come home."

She had just over an hour to pack and steel herself for the trip ahead of her. *She could do it for Carter.*

She told herself she could do it just to get further away from where someone in the hotel might remember her. In fact, she wouldn't even check out in person. Just call the front desk, leave her key on the dresser, and go out the back door. She wouldn't give them another glimpse so that they could put two and two together.

If they even had two and two.

She hoped not.

"I'm on it," she told Carter, the reluctance and determination both bleeding into her words.

"Good." His voice turned to a very gentle soothing tone—the kind he used when he was directing her to go the way he wanted. He'd managed to hold it in until now. But the relief had let something else seep through, too.

Cindy was moving. She had only two speeds—full steam ahead and stuck. She was opening the drawers that she'd unpacked into as if she actually lived here. After lifting the lid on the suitcase, she was grabbing a stack of clothing from the drawer to nestle it in, but the signals from Carter were coming through very loud now. She stopped. "What is it?"

He huffed. His lips pressed together. She knew his expression even across the distance.

"The body?" It was almost a whisper out of her mouth though she'd wanted to say it strong and confident, she couldn't.

She could see Carter nodding. That damn twin connection. Interesting, though, it wasn't just his feelings, but something else. Or maybe his feelings had been so strong she'd been able to figure out exactly what he meant.

She pushed the stack of clothing into the open and empty suitcase. That was all she could manage before she stumbled backwards. The backs of her legs hit the wooden board at the end of the bed. She sat down roughly, half sitting, half standing, phone pressed to the side of her face as she waited. "Well, who was she?"

"Annabeth Green," Carter said, neutral tone. The name meant nothing to her.

"Me either," he said.

Had she spoken out loud? Or was the twin connection just getting a clearer. Odd. It had been going on a long time. And, for the past number of years, after she no longer had been able to hold a job, when things had gotten really bad, they'd been around each other almost all the time.

"They're pulling up reports from when she went missing."

"Not that long ago," Cindy said before she caught her tongue. She'd seen what the dog had, and she hated that she knew what that meant.

"No sign of foul play. Her purse was gone. Her phone was gone. A lot of people argued that she'd simply walked away."

"Well, that wasn't true." Cindy understood that deep in her heart, but anyone who had ever doubted, well, they knew now.

"Wait . . ." she said. She knew she wouldn't see a death unless it was traumatic. She knew about the man in the woods counting down. But what did they know?

She asked Carter, "They do know now that it's a *murder*, right? She didn't wander off or hit her head."

"Oh yeah. They know."

41

Georgia's eyes opened slowly into the dark. She breathed in one long, slow deep breath, then another.

Yes, she reveled in the quiet. The new hotel was already much better than where they'd been. She'd let Jesse pick the room that she wanted first. Of course, she chose the big room with the bathroom. But Georgia had her own bathroom now. Nothing to complain about. There was no one slamming car doors outside. No one honking on the busy road.

Jesse, not having caught up from the night before when some of their precious sleep had been stolen, had suggested that they nap again.

Georgia had slid, almost naked, between the cool sheets and instantly fallen off. Now she sighed and stretched. It was evening. They'd had a late lunch, but they would still need something tonight.

They might have a mini kitchenette. She could have a glass of milk before bed. Her parents had raised all three girls downing gallons of milk, and Georgia had never quite outgrown it.

She could have cereal! she thought. Eat in the morning when she got up and have a little tiny bit each night before she went to bed. But that wasn't the point right now. She looked at the time.

They'd checked in at three o'clock and it was now just past five-thirty. Flipping back the covers, she slid into a pair of shorts, then padded her way out into the small main room.

Jesse wasn't up yet, so Georgia pulled out the chair at the little table. The seat was padded this time, nicer. The floor was carpeted, and just beyond it was a tile that delineated the "kitchen area."

Still no signs of life from the other room. So, as quietly as she could, Georgia tapped at her keys to begin yet another search.

She looked for big red bows. She looked for dead mafia assassins. She looked for surprising disappearances of local monsters.

There was a story her father had told them once the three daughters knew what Aunt Sin really was. He had paper articles from well before Georgia was born. Aunt Sin had dressed in the exact style of the campus rapist's targeted victims. Then she'd wandered campus for days with a backpack, a distracted expression, and a ponytail he could grab. When he finally grabbed her, it was his last attempt.

Georgia was immensely proud of that. The story also gave her elements to look for now. But nothing showed up. There were certainly a handful of happenings, any of which could have been Sin, but only if she changed her method. Or only if the reporting carefully filtered out certain pieces of information.

Back when her mother had started on her own little spree, that had certainly been the case. There were lots of things about her crime scenes that only the FBI knew. But these days,

Georgia was honestly surprised there wasn't some online video channel dedicated to the Christmas Bow Killer.

Her father had told her he'd called her birth mother the "grudge ninja" for a while, which made Georgia laugh. Still, excellent martial arts skills were often a hallmark of Sin's kills. But Georgia still couldn't find anything.

Again, she reminded herself that a Sin that did not want to be found could not be found.

Aunt Sin had told Georgia's parents once that there was a cabin in Georgia where she lived almost completely off the grid. That was why Georgia was *Georgia*. She thought of it fondly now. It was not only a tribute to the parents who gave up everything for her, it was an excellent family name that would hide her with her sisters, Charlotte and Virginia.

Her mother Annika had taught all three girls Russian as well. For Charlotte and Virginia, it had been part of their family heritage. Georgia had been given the same line, but for different reasons.

The lies had been for all their safety. She didn't know it— they'd never said it and she'd only put it together herself recently—but she'd put her very brilliant and otherwise safe sisters in danger simply by existing.

Finding Sin was absolutely about knowing that someone that she loved was safe. But it was also about knowing herself. It would mean a chance to ask the woman where the edges were creeping in. Where the curtain around Georgia might first be breached. Where best to keep her eyes trained.

But as she scanned the information now, there was still nothing.

She let it go and tried not to scroll mindlessly through social media. But ten minutes later, Georgia found herself having done nothing. Sure enough, one of the crime junkies popped up and started spewing scary stories at her.

The algorithms had picked up on what she was doing or

who she was hanging out with. She had certainly seen a hell of a lot more of these in the past week. Probably it was directly due to the things she was searching to try to find her mother.

Her thought stopped her dead. It was a sharp reminder that she wasn't doing this in secret. If nothing else, the bots on the internet knew. She had to be careful about who else might be following along. There was no reason the people she worried about wouldn't be at least as tech savvy as she was. Was she pinning a target on her own back just by looking for Sin?

There was nothing she could do now. So maybe this crime-cast/murder junkie reel would prove interesting. The young woman with red hair in pigtails absolutely did not look the part of someone reporting a horrific murder. She was a little too gleeful, a little too interested in the gory details. She definitely had "white woman who watches murder shows in her spare time" vibes. Then she'd taken it up a notch in an attempt to monetize it.

Georgia was mostly just waiting for Jesse to wake up, but no sound came from the other room. So she continued to watch the redhead drone on. The more she listened, the more Georgia became concerningly interested. Then, at last, she was almost lifting out of her chair to tell Jesse what she'd seen when, behind her, the main door beeped then clicked. It whirred as the digital lock opened.

Someone was coming in.

42

G eorgia whirled around. Facing the door now, she stepped backward quickly, putting the table between her and the attacker.

She'd already checked the room for egress when they came in—disappointed to find that there were no alternate routes of escape. They were on the second floor, so technically she could go out the window and probably not hurt herself too badly.

Except hotel rooms had notoriously difficult windows to get out of—something else she'd learned from her father. They did it on purpose to keep people from doing exactly what she was planning. Or from sneaking away from their parents or, God forbid, committing suicide from one of the higher floors.

With the window not an option, her muscles tensed as she rolled up onto the balls of her feet. Her hands brushed at the sides of her thighs, as if she might find her weapons there. But no, those were only for training.

Now she looked around for weapons. There was a plain ball point pen on the table, next to the hotel notepad. The paper was worthless, but the pen was gold. Snatching it up quickly, she watched as the door swung open. Her fingers curled around the back, placing her thumb over the butt of the pen, ready to do real damage.

"*Holy shit!*" Jesse jolted and almost dropped the grocery bags she carried. "Please don't attack me!"

The look in her eyes showed that she clearly now believed Georgia capable of killing. Well, Georgia had had the same thought about Jesse, so maybe they were even.

Her partner managed to just hold onto everything and Georgia felt her mouth twist. In disappointment or irritation, she couldn't quite tell. Deciding not to investigate the feeling, she tossed the pen back at the table, watching as it rolled away. *Let it roll off the end,* she thought. She hadn't deserved that kind of scare either.

Jesse came in then, obviously trying to breathe evenly after her jump scare, and she set the groceries on the table.

"I got up before you."

Well, that explained why there was no noise. And now Georgia felt stupid. "You went grocery shopping without me."

"We can go again. I just had this idea." She turned around and looked at the kitchenette critically. There were two little electric burners on the stove. "I can do it." Her tone said she was also convincing herself.

She pulled out microwavable pots of rice and produced a flat of ground beef. A large jar of premixed spices, milk, even a small bag of flour. *Damn.*

"Look." Jesse grinned. "I got some cereals. I remember you mentioned this so I bought this one."

Damn, Georgia thought again. The girl was good. Well, she was a professional observer and cataloger of interests, ideas, and quirks. It shouldn't be surprising that she'd bought the right cereal.

"You were right," Jesse admitted as she began moving food into the fridge. Jesse watched oranges and apples go into a bowl on the counter. A lone, late summer peach followed and her mouth watered.

"Oh, go ahead." Jesse waved to her. "Eat some of this. It's going to be a little while before I have dinner ready. But yes, I am excited for real food. And I'm excited to cook something. And mostly I'm excited not to eat the same three places we've been eating all along."

"Amen," Georgia agreed.

"You okay?" Jesse asked, only now noticing the irritation.

Georgia didn't want to admit she'd had no idea her friend was gone. Though she'd pretty much already admitted it by assuming attack mode. Jesse already knew Georgia had breaking and entering skills, now she also knew about some ninja skills, which her father swore she came by naturally.

"Can I help?" Georgia offered instead of a confession.

"I would love that" Jesse said, but she turned again, her face animated and bright for once as she looked over her shoulder at the tiny kitchenette area. "But I don't think there's room."

Good point.

Jesse was still chattering. The woman had needed decent sleep more than either of them had realized. "You were up. Did you get anything done?"

Again, Jesse—the infinite observer—had already figured out that Georgia-awake was Georgia-in-action. "I looked for my mother again."

"Me too. I did half an hour of searching before I left."

Wow, had Jesse slept at all?

The nap had not been intended for Georgia. She'd simply been suckered into it and then lulled by the cool sheets and the quiet. But she didn't want to admit to that either. "I'm guessing by your tone that you didn't find anything."

"Yeah. You?"

"Not about my mother." She said *mother* for Sin. *Birth mother* seemed too much, and reserved for someone she'd never met, someone who donated only genetics. That wasn't the case with her Aunt Sin. Sin was someone she knew well, someone whose visits she anticipated. When Sin would pop up and take all three girls out for ice cream or to swim or teach them a few karate moves, it was always an exciting day.

Her *real mom* was Annika. She was the one who'd put her own family at risk to take an infant in. The woman who'd named her *Georgia* so she'd fit with her new sisters. The woman who had raised her as if she'd given birth to the child herself.

She'd snuck in a heritage that Georgia hadn't fully understood was different from her sisters. Annika had been there for every scrape and bruise and taught her how to make hot chocolate. The same cocoa that Georgia had eventually informed their grandmother, "Mom's is better."

She could see her mother, younger, amused, lips pressing together as Grammy Dunham had informed her Georgia had let her know that she needed lessons.

"So you found something *not* about your mother?"

"I did." Georgia turned around, tugging at the laptop so she could tap the screen and start the video. "Or maybe *it found me.*"

The raised eyebrow that Jesse offered let her know she had been doing it wrong. She was supposed to search incognito browsers, not letting her own search history interfere, not letting the algorithms find her.

"I was on my own social media. I tapped out for a few minutes and then this popped up."

"Ooh." Jesse leaned in, looking closer. "I know her. Rachel Lashley."

Jesse rattled off the erstwhile reporter's name easily. "She used to write for the Times."

"And now she podcasts and films internet videos?" That didn't sound like a solid career trajectory to Georgia.

"Apparently she's making a lot more money now."

"She's a lot—" Georgia couldn't find the word and Jesse simply agreed.

"She's always been a lot."

"Well, she was reporting on a case. There was a body found very recently up on the hiking trails . . ." Georgia offered up more information. "They identified her as Annabeth Green."

"So what's the sensation?" Jesse asked, having gone back to organizing the groceries. Green beans, coconut milk, and more tried to pull Georgia's focus from the question.

"The sensation is that a dog was out hiking with his person. The dog pulled the owner off trail and then went nosing around. When he came out, he had a lower leg clamped between his teeth."

"Suitably gross," Jesse agreed calmly. Even things like this didn't perturb her.

"So, Annabeth went missing three days ago. Lots of people insisted that she just *wandered off on her own*." Georgia had emphasized the last few words and Jesse's hands stilled.

Turning, she asked, "You think it's like Hannalyn ten years later?"

"Well, let me tell you—" Georgia started, "No, let me let *Rachel* tell you." She knew where the words were in the video. She'd been so stunned that she listened three times to be sure her brain wasn't acting up.

With Jesse watching over her shoulder, she started Rachel up at the point that was most interesting. Jesse leaned in closer, and together they listen to the words Georgia already knew.

"Annabeth disappeared late in the night. She'd gone out with a couple of friends, nothing major, nothing out of the ordinary for any of them." Rachel paused dramatically. "Then she went to the restroom *and never returned*."

Georgia watched as Jesse's eyes flicked toward her, the similarities a little too close. But she pointed again at the screen. "That wasn't even the big thing."

43

Jesse stood, hands planted on the table, staring at the screen. Rachel Lashley was telling a story that sounded far too similar to Hannalyn Burkhardt's.

Jesse's mouth was hanging open. Dinner forgotten.

"One shoe." She looked at Georgia, who reached up and tapped at the device to pause the video.

"Exactly. There was no sign of her. Everything went missing with her—her purse and wallet. Everything but her car, which was left in the parking lot. That was one clue in Annabeth's case that maybe she didn't just walk off, but there was no sign of foul play."

"Until now." Jesse couldn't help but grind out the words. They should have been more worried about Annabeth. "Now all signs are foul play."

"Yeah, and the body's in a state park almost fifty miles away from where she disappeared."

"Someone's spitting nails this morning," Jesse said calmly to herself, trying to both think about the person who would do this and not think about him.

She knew that she shouldn't jump to conclusions, *but how*

could she not? It had to be the same person who had taken Hannalyn. "How old is Annabeth?"

"Thirty-four." Georgia answered calmly, not reacting visibly to the bomb she'd just dropped. Jesse needed to get her breathing together.

"Notably older," she murmured.

"Actually, almost exactly the age Hannalyn would have been," Georgia pointed out, her words rolling smoothly and evenly, hitting Jesse almost like punches.

"Shit, shit, shit," Jesse stood up, hands on her hips. "Looks like you've arrived."

They had a real serial killer. Georgia almost grinned.

To a certain extent Jesse felt the validation of it all. But, at the same time the pride of being right was swelling in her and a pit was forming in her stomach.

A serial killer.

She'd been in the same town as one in Florida and that one had come far too close to home. Her fear now was because the thing she was right about was so awful. And it could be part pure visceral reaction—probably bordering on PTSD, if not firmly in the center of the bullseye.

She stepped back, purposefully dropping her hands and forcing her shoulders to relax. As if moving like a normal person and breathing a little better would be the thing that would make this all go away.

But it didn't.

"Jesse?" Georgia asked. When she looked up, the younger woman smiled. "This is good news."

In Jesse's brain, everything snapped together: Georgia's pleasure at finding an answer and her own petrified fear. "No, no it absolutely is not."

Georgia opened her mouth to ask why or counter her comment. She didn't give the younger woman the air to speak.

"Having a serial killer is never a good thing. Having one who's operated for ten years—"

"At least ten," Georgia interjected. This time her tone was more solemn, as she was catching on to why Jesse was so nervous.

"We're supposed to solve a *cold case*. We're supposed to find out about a young woman who maybe walked away, got involved with the wrong person. Someone who, if they're still alive today, doesn't want us to know. They might snap and try to hurt us. Or they might be on the verge of confessing and it'll be a relief to tell us everything they did—if we can just find them and tell them it's okay."

Jesse sucked in more air as the panic set in. "None of that applies now. None of what our case was supposed to be is *this*." She jammed her finger at the screen. "This is someone who hunts human beings like prey. And since we haven't even heard of him or his *work* yet—" She caught herself using *him* again. At least statistically, it was a damn good bet. "They haven't caught him yet. The authorities don't even know he exists. Just us."

She watched as Georgia's color faded with that hit of knowledge.

"And he killed someone *last week*." She watched as the last of it absorbed into Georgia's psyche.

Then her new junior partner—because that's how she really was beginning to think of her—nodded slowly. "Are we done then? Are we out?"

"Are *you* prepared to defend yourself from a serial killer coming after you?" Jesse meant it to be rhetorical. But she could tell from the expression that blinked across Georgia's face that the young woman liked to think that she was.

Jesse knew better.

Everyone had the fantasies. Everyone believed that if someone broke into their home, they would get to their gun, have perfect aim, and lay the intruder out. But that basically *never* happened.

Everyone believed that if they were grabbed from behind on the street, they would be the one who could fight and would know whatever the magic move was to break this particular chokehold. Everyone believed that when the time came, their adrenaline, their knowledge, and their sheer confidence would get them out of it. And Jesse knew far too well that it almost never worked that way.

Annabeth Green knew that now. It was becoming clear Hannalyn Burkhardt had learned that lesson ten years ago. Jesse had learned it for herself about fourteen months earlier— though she didn't say that part to Georgia. What she did say was, "We have to hand it over to the FBI."

Georgia nodded, already knowing that if you had a serial killer in different states, that was likely the agency to handle it.

"They can do things we just can't," Jesse rambled as though Georgia Dunham might need a lesson in what the FBI could do. Hell, she probably knew better than Jesse did. "They can set up a joint task force, get boots on the ground."

Georgia nodded along. Though it was clear the younger woman agreed with her, it was just as obvious she was disappointed at losing the case.

"If we try this ourselves," Jesse said, knowing she had already won the argument, but wanting to drive it home, wanting Georgia to sleep well with the decision. "And he killed someone else while we're looking for him . . .?"

She could almost hear Georgia suck in a breath. She watched the young woman visibly draw back several inches.

Exactly. She thought.

"We are not equipped to solve this. We do cold cases and this case just got very, very hot." She'd used *we*.

"All right." Georgia didn't sound reluctant, but she didn't like it.

"We strike while the story is still abuzz. We call the FBI and hand over what we know. Maybe there's a tip line." Then her brain clicked into gear. "No. I know two agents I can call. That would be better, although I'm sure this isn't their case."

Georgia frowned and looked at her as if maybe she were being dense. "My father's an FBI agent."

"He's retired," Jesse replied almost as quickly as Georgia offered it up.

"*Please*," Georgia drolled, "I don't think any of them ever really retire. I'll call him."

44

"What do you think, Dad?" Georgia asked, her eyes flicking to the little counter in the kitchenette as her stomach grumbled.

The food had been set out and left there. They'd both been distracted by the realization that the Annabeth Green case was connected.

It just figured. They'd just gotten into the nicer hotel and now, chances were they were going to hand this all over to her dad. They'd probably get some confirmation tomorrow that the FBI was on it. Then they would pack up and head off their separate ways.

How would she keep Jesse looking for Sin? Because that had been the arrangement.

There should be a handful more days looking for her birth mother, if they were truly going to even this out by hours or even just effort. But there was nothing to follow where her mother was concerned. Georgia was proud that Sin was so good at covering her tracks. But, after months of searching by herself, and even enlisting a professional, she was starting to hate the same thing she used to admire.

"All right." Her dad had been taking notes. "I'm going to call it in with all the information that you've given me. They'll run it through everything . . ." He paused.

"ViCAP?" Jesse asked and Georgia could hear the refusal from her father before the words even hit the phone line.

"Annabeth Green appears to be the only violent crime we know in this case. Hannalyn Burkhardt won't be in that system. Others probably aren't in there or we should have caught it already. We're going to be looking through missing persons from linked cases. And that's going to be a lot of work."

"*Fuck*," she heard Jesse mutter.

Her father must have heard it too, because he explained, "Missing persons don't always get uploaded into state systems, let alone national databases. Hopefully, cases like this are odd enough that we can find them. Maybe we can link enough to figure out what we're doing."

"Good. Thank you!" Jesse called out, inserting herself again into the conversation. Still, the words came out disjointedly, as if escaping from a machine whose gears all churned in different directions.

Georgia was telling her father goodbye and thank you and all the usual "yes she was still safe" things as she watched Jesse turn around and seem to catch sight of the food still on the counter.

"I'll cook!" she announced. Though Georgia had figured that out already.

Finding measuring cups, Jesse began to get to work. She had to figure out how to operate the stovetop, then make everything fit on the tiny counter. Then suddenly she stopped, as if someone had turned her off.

Slowly she turned around. "It was the right shoe in both cases." She repeated it, her eyes glazed over. Then she looked right at Georgia. "Tell your dad it was the right shoe."

Georgia nodded. Not another call. She tapped out a message to him only to have him reply quickly.

— Yes. Already got that.

Of course he had. What she said to Jesse was, "He's on it."

Someone else would tell the Burkhardts what they'd found. Not them.

Though as Georgia imagined how the case had shifted, how the same gory details would be even worse with a serial killer, she decided maybe it was better that she didn't have to be there for it.

Rachel Lashley had given up all kinds of details about Annabeth Green's death already. Georgia could now imagine telling Harriet and Jefferson that their daughter had been stabbed multiple times and left to die in a National Forest somewhere. Who even knew where Hannalyn would be? The cases were states apart with a full decade separating them.

He could be killing close to home and the cases followed him as he moved, or he could be traveling. It could be anything. But Georgia wouldn't be the one to find out. The very act of searching for this man could be dangerous. Following her mother was dangerous enough. They were off the case.

Trying to distract her brain, she sat down at the table and clicked out of Rachel Lashley's too-enthusiastic rundown of Annabeth Green's last hours. Logging into one account after another, she traded her laptop for her phone and scrolled mindlessly.

Faster than she liked, she was dead bored with tips on how to improve her love life. How had that gotten into her algorithms? She didn't even have one. At least she got videos of puppies, kittens, and dancers. And the occasional protests in a foreign war-torn country.

Stopping, she turned back to the computer. It would be okay. She could still look. Everyone was searching this exact topic right now, so it wouldn't put a target on her back. It alerted no one.

Typing in "Annabeth Green," she watched as hundreds of links popped up. Most of them were a repetitive spray of information—articles posted within the last twenty-four hours. They said that the missing woman had been found. Tons of click-bait titles liked to tell everyone just how she was found.

No one had been this concerned when Annabeth had simply been missing. It took a little bit of digging to get back to the early pieces. To the pleas from her family begging anyone who had seen her to call the hotline. They'd even made paper printouts and stuck them to the telephone poles around town.

Georgia clicked a few promising links and read how Annabeth had been out with friends. The friends became worried when she didn't return from the restroom. *Maybe Annabeth went out the back*, one of the friends had suggested in an interview. She and Jesse had considered that for Hannalyn, too.

She wasn't supposed to be looking, but Georgia didn't really acknowledge that she was. Until she turned around and said to Jesse. "The restroom is the perfect place to abduct people from."

"It is," Jesse agreed, but she didn't look up from where she was stirring something in the pan that was smelling increasingly better and better. Georgia's mouth watered.

"The restroom hallway is often dark, often empty," Jesse said still looking in her pan. Between sentences she grabbed a spoon and tasted it. Georgia was jealous. "The restroom hall often links to other things. Like into the back kitchen or offices. There's often a door that leads out the building."

"One that's not secured, covered by a bouncer or a hostess, or anyone who would notice the comings and goings." Georgia thought that through. She could tell her dad that, but he would already be on top of it.

He said he would call them back in a bit and let them know

what he found. He'd tell them who was taking the case, give them a name and contact info to turn over all their notes and images.

Georgia shouldn't be thinking about it anymore. Her stomach rumbled so she stood and cleared her things off the table. She found paper towels in the tiny kitchenette and folded them like napkins. The silverware didn't match, which seemed odd, given the other niceties of the place, but she set out forks as Jesse served them on plain white plates.

The rice—despite being microwaved—was fragrant. It all smelled amazing and Georgia shoveled the food into her mouth. "This is so good!"

"I made extra. It reheats really well," Jesse told her, not quite with a mouthful of food but close.

Georgia didn't fault her. It was the first real meal they'd had in . . . She decided not to count the days. They ate mostly in silence, which Georgia hoped Jesse took as a sign of a meal well prepared. Not what she'd expected from a woman who ate only whiskey in the days before they left.

Instead of saying that, she offered to handwash the dishes. Jesse covered the bowl with a paper towel. But what were they saving it for? They wouldn't be here tomorrow.

"We should watch a movie," Jesse announced when there was nothing left to do. "A romantic comedy, something the exact opposite of what we've been doing."

Hadn't they tried that before? Jesse still seemed nervous. Maybe she wouldn't be okay until Dr. Dunham called back and told them that all the boxes were checked, and the case was off their shoulders.

When the movie was finished and her Dad rang them with impeccable timing during the credits, it was almost midnight.

It wasn't good news.

45

J esse tossed and turned, damning the nice bed with the cool sheets. She damned the cool air from the thermostat that actually made the room the temperature she had punched into it. And the blessed quiet.

What she wouldn't give to hear an argument outside her door right now. She could not turn her brain off. She could not stop the worry and fear that crept in at the dark edges each time she closed her eyes.

Sleep came in fits and starts, her dreams concerning and odd. The first one she remembered involved her being a serial killer herself. In a later one she fostered baby otters and nearly drowned in the river with them. There were several in between she'd already forgotten.

In all of them she was fine, until something went horribly wrong. She woke up gasping, tossing and turning again, until she tried to force herself back into another fitful round of sleep.

At six she gave up, threw off the covers and sat up. The light seeping around the blackout curtains was enough to tell her she should quit trying.

Her feet hit the carpet, toes curling, not out of pleasure but anxiety. She brushed her teeth a little too quickly and showered off the fine layer of panic that had coated her while she slept.

This time she was the one sitting at the table when Georgia emerged still in her pajamas. A yawn broke her expression but then she returned to a reasonably peaceful look. Despite the bad news, Georgia, it appeared, had slept like a baby. *At least one of them had.*

However, the words out of her mouth told the truth. "That was not an easy night."

Georgia stilled and for a moment Jesse stopped, too, and just looked the younger woman up and down. Her own college days came back to her, times when she could do this kind of relentless and unforgiving work and still look halfway decent the next day.

"What do we do now?" Georgia asked.

"You can go home," Jesse offered. She didn't really think Georgia would take her up on it, but she had to offer. There was every chance Owen Dunham would force his daughter's decision. "You can pack up and get out of here and stay safe."

She didn't like the way the words were coming out of her mouth. Georgia didn't flinch or even look away. She wasn't the kind of liar that Jesse had initially thought she might be when she'd opened her eyes and seen Georgia Dunham sitting on her couch, her own vision blurry with good whiskey. That meant Georgia wasn't hiding a directive from her father to get the hell out of here.

If Georgia left, it would be up to Jesse. She sincerely doubted there was much she could say to persuade Georgia to go. "I'll take care of this. I'm the one who promised the Burkhardts that I would do everything I could to solve the case."

"I'm in." Georgia's lack of tone—either fear or conviction—surprised Jesse not one whit.

"I don't think you should. You have to apply for school. You need to . . . I don't know how long this will take."

"I think it'll go faster now." Georgia shrugged and Jesse laughed.

It was a high, shrill pitched sound with no humor. "No, it'll be worse. With one case, you do a spider map out from the original person, and you keep knocking on doors until someone feels bad enough to tell you what actually happened. Or they're stupid enough to slip up. So far, this is already two spider maps. We don't know where or how they link, just that they do. And I have a feeling it's going to be fifteen or twenty before—"

"You think he has twenty victims?" At least that got a reaction out of placid Georgia.

She shrugged. "The Grim Sleeper had *a hundred and eighty* photos of women—many still missing."

She watched as her young partner visibly swallowed. "The Grim Sleeper?"

"Los Angeles. Eighties, nineties? Look it up," Jesse said, dismissing the question, her gaze getting pulled back to her screen. Her fingers flew over the keyboard again, as she tried to accomplish something, *anything*. She needed something to make sense. Something that would tell her she was okay and she could calm down.

She could almost feel Georgia looking her up and down, assessing that she wasn't quite right. "Let's go get breakfast. Something nice. We'll sit down, somewhere we have to tip and we'll make a plan."

"I don't think you should." *Should what* . . . Jesse didn't define that.

"I'm staying," Georgia announced, brooking no argument. The irony, of course, was that she was walking away as she said it. She closed the bedroom door, the click punctuating her statement.

Jesse accepted that it probably wasn't worth her effort to

fight. Hell, between her breaking-and-entering skills, and clearly some underlying ninja, maybe she would be safer with Georgia.

Fuck, she thought again, pushing the lid down on her own laptop. As if closing it could make it all go away. She got dressed, grabbed her car keys, and met Georgia back in the small central space just a handful of minutes later.

Georgia's hand was held out. "Let me drive."

"I don't know," Jesse said.

"Come on. I'm safer. You're all wound up like a ball of yarn that has three kittens in it."

She had to laugh. She was *not* a ball of yarn with three kittens in it. That was a happy, joyful thing. She was a serial killer cold case.

"I'm a good driver," Georgia argued, "and you're not safe."

Still reluctant, though, to let go of her control, Jesse felt her fingers curl around the thick key fob. Georgia moved her hand one more time, indicating that Jesse should hand them over and when that didn't work, she said, "I don't have any DUIs."

Damn, the girl played hard. "I'm sober," Jesse said. "You've seen it."

"I know. But you're not good right now and I am a good driver. I was taught by an FBI agent."

Those words were said just as Jesse dropped the fob into Georgia's open palm. If she could have, she would have snatched the keys back. Jesus Christ, the last thing she needed was aggressive, car-chase driving. But Georgia was a calm and careful driver, seeming to be mindful that she was in a borrowed vehicle.

Jesse didn't know where they were going, but her junior partner had a plan and directions. She took them directly into Shreveport, quickly finding a brunch place.

Inside, once they were seated, Georgia started the conversation. "So, as Dad said, the FBI can't find anything. The cases that we have—where we're going to have to look, they're going to be in local databases."

"We're just going to have to start radiating outward from the locations we already have." Jesse added. She didn't like it. That was four places. Shreveport—where Hannalyn went missing. Magnolia—where she lived. And two places for Annabeth—the bar and the state park. "The problem is, if that doesn't pop anything, we don't have any idea where to look next."

Georgia's eyes narrowed. Water arrived at the table as did a plate of small pastries while they waited for an omelet for Jesse and a stack of French toast for Georgia. *Must be nice.*

"You know something . . ." Georgia accused her.

Yeah, she did. "NamUs. Remember them?"

"Right, the missing persons website. Oh, can we search them?"

"Not really. You have to have backend entry to get the kind of info we need. The average person can't just log in and find these details about missing persons. Only the very basics, only the things that the families have chosen to share publicly. NamUs also has physical files on a lot of the missing: dental X rays, jewelry, things that can be matched. A lot of its digital, too —pictures, tattoos, anything that can be used to ID a body, or a live person if they're lucky."

Georgia grinned up at the server and waited for him to leave the food before she grinned at Jesse. "So if we can't search it . . ."

Jesse watched the tables around her. She was used to doing this on her own. Coming out, getting a table, flipping through her info as she ate. Hiding the pictures when anyone walked by. She wasn't used to tempering her speech. And teaching Georgia what to do and what kind of access they could get and where, well, that was a whole new ball of wax.

"So you *can* search it." Georgia was grinning again.

"No," Jesse admitted, "but I have access to someone who

can."

"Great. So we get them to look for women—" She cut herself off, thinking. "Annabeth was thirty-four, so forty and under? Missing from a night out. Maybe ones who seemed like they might have just walked away?"

"Yes and no. I don't think we limit it to women, at least not at first." Jesse was still working through it. "Not the age either. Two cases isn't enough to make boundaries. I do suspect the search will eventually limit itself to women." It always did. She hated that. Okay, not *always*, but if she always bet on that, she'd be a hell of a lot richer. She took the first bite of her eggs and let the savory flavor hit her taste buds. Jesus, she'd needed this. Maybe she could make omelets in the little hotel. Because they sure as hell weren't leaving now.

Once she ate a few bites, she told Georgia, "Then, once we get some areas to search, we go to NamUs and the Doe Network and . . ." there were too many. "We should check the Bureau of Indian Affairs. DOJ."

"So, all of them," Georgia gestured with a fork full of thick bread dripping in syrup.

"At least we shouldn't have to search the missing kids network." Jesse offered a fake grimace for that. "Hopefully we'll get some hits."

She squeezed her eyes shut as if a prayer could make it all happen. As if any of her prayers held any weight. "Then we start searching anywhere we get a hit."

Across the table, Georgia looked happy. Glad to be back in the game. But Jesse had been pleased to have income. She'd been glad to be doing work that she liked. Happy to help a family find closure, even though she was confident it wouldn't be a happy ending. But now as she looked at her partner, she saw Georgia felt the way that she had when the case had started.

Georgia had no fucking clue what was coming.

46

Cindy hated every minute of it. She hated the sunshine. She hated the other drivers on the road. She hated that she suspected she was headed right into rush hour in a major city. She hated that she would sit in this traffic when she didn't have a job or a schedule or even live here.

Then again, here she was—out and about, on the road. Clearly, she sucked at being a recluse.

She was mad about the whole thing. She'd left home, thinking she would get away, thinking she would enjoy the sunshine and nature. Wasn't that how it was supposed to work? Go outside, commune with the leaves and the squirrels for your mental health. She thought she had done exactly that and her mental health had taken a big, hard hit.

But she'd felt the pull from the beginning. She'd just lied to herself about it.

She wondered if there was some kind of therapist for people who kept finding bodies. For someone who kept seeing death.

Cindy liked the idea that a reader lived a thousand lives, but she had died a thousand deaths and here she still was. *Why wasn't she dead?*

She had moments when she wished her kidnappers had succeeded. What would it have been like to have been tortured only once and have actually *died* from it? Whatever it was—and she had thought about it a lot over the years—she had theories.

It had unlocked something in her, being in the trunk. She could still feel the rough carpet in her darkest hours. She could still breathe in the terror. Smell the harsh cleaner in the fibers—had she been more together, that alone would have told her something bad had happened in that trunk before the bad thing that happened to her.

It had broken something inside her. Something had cracked and the crack wasn't where the light got in. It was *never* the light that got in. Her therapists had talked to her about letting go, about meditation techniques, about closing her eyes and breathing deeply. And then the woman had watched as Cindy had done exactly that.

Though she closed everything—her eyes, her hands, her thoughts—the crack remained. Her therapist had watched her freak out, as Cindy tried to talk through what she was seeing. Finally, the woman had the wherewithal to ask her to open her eyes. Cindy had *known* how it would go, but she'd gone along in the hopes that maybe the therapist would be right this time.

The therapist thought Cindy was crazy. Cindy thought her therapist was stupid, because honestly, all she had to do was wait a few days and check the news. It wasn't repetitive or intrusive thoughts. It was *real*.

Eventually the therapist had sent Cindy to a psychiatrist. There had been medications, side effects like upset stomach, dry mouth, and dizziness. The worst had been the brain fog. Then, when the crack let something in, she hadn't even had the mental wherewithal to be able to sort it out.

That had been a rough six months. That was how long it

had taken her to give up. She'd swept every expensive pill bottle out of the cabinet, letting them bounce and roll across the bathroom floor. She'd yanked the caps and chucked all the pills down the toilet.

Carter had caught her. She'd almost thrown two of the bottles down the toilet, too, she'd been so mad and frustrated. In her anger, the stupid childproof locks had thwarted her. She'd thought Carter was going to stop her but, one look at her face, and he'd known better.

He gently took the pill bottle from her hand, squeezed it in just the right way—and bless him, he'd handed it back to her. It had been satisfying hearing the little pills clink off the porcelain. They had sunk down slowly drifting out of her life.

One bottle held little yellow and green capsules. Those had floated. But Carter pointed to the handle, and they'd been sucked down with the flush. That had been the best she'd felt in the six months since she'd foolishly started thinking she could treat her condition.

Now, she was medication free. She was side effect free. And she'd come to terms with the fact that nothing could fix it.

Turning off the freeway, she took the next exit that looked like it had something that would help. If she was going to be stuck in traffic, she might as well have a snack and a restroom break.

She found what she needed and climbed back in with a soda and a bag of hot french fries. When she got back on the freeway, she felt her stomach clench at the idea of sitting again in rush hour traffic. But more than that, she felt her hands on the steering wheel, she watched as her own grip turned the car. She went left, not right.

What was she doing? Was her avoidance of rush hour just that deeply ingrained?

She realized quickly that wasn't it. Something else was

going on. She drove a full hour in the wrong direction, cold sweats keeping her from analyzing the choice she'd made.

She should have been much closer to home now. Then, when she passed an intersection that she'd already passed once from the other direction, she remembered the bold urge to turn the first time. This time she did it.

She was getting further and further away, the dread growing deep in her gut. She was headed entirely the wrong direction.

She was going to have to call Carter and confess. But soon enough he was going to realize that she wasn't there even if she didn't call. He might already know. Likely, he was feeling her panic—that twin connection went both ways.

She drove another thirty minutes, her breathing shallow, the voice in her head telling her repeatedly that she should turn around, that she should call her brother, let him know what had happened.

She didn't do any of it. None of it made sense until she saw the green sign, and the name of the town she was headed toward.

47

"Damnit," Jesse said, a little surprised that she'd said it out loud. Georgia looked up at her but didn't say anything. She seemed to already understand.

Once again, Jesse was grateful that Georgia had talked her into moving out of the tiny motel. The space here was already closing in. even with more than twice the square footage. She had her own room. There was a place she could go and close the door and right now she was really tempted.

Except it wouldn't work. She couldn't close out what she was seeing.

"Number three?" Georgia asked.

She sighed. It would have to suffice for *Yes*. Georgia nodded solemnly.

They'd settled in. At breakfast, they'd made a plan since the FBI wasn't taking the case. The analysts hadn't found what they needed to call it a serial killer.

They'd not found more—not murders. What Jesse and Georgia were searching out were cases more similar to Hannalyn than Annabeth. Missing persons weren't enough to put the FBI on it. Especially not when each case involved a legal adult who could have just walked away.

Now, if Georgia and Jesse could find more *bodies*, then the FBI would happily call the whole thing a serial and take it off their hands. Not unless they had more proof. Until right now, all Jesse had was two missing women a decade apart, one of whom had turned up stabbed repeatedly in a horrific way.

They'd procrastinated by shopping first. Having decided what they needed to do, Jesse made her driver for the day stop at an office store where she bought a pack of legal pads, nice pens, sticky notes and anything she could passably justify as 'for the case.' She told herself they were supplies and she could bill it all to the Burkhardts.

She had also put off making a decision about how to tell the family what they'd discovered. The Burkhardts might be able to deny what had happened to their daughter, but Jesse was confident—too confident—that she was right. She hated it.

Unable to procrastinate any longer, her stomach full of omelet, and nothing left to do but the work, she and Georgia had come back to the hotel room. She'd contacted her person at NamUs. She'd contacted her friend at the DOE network. She'd reached out to a generic email from the Bureau of Indian Affairs website.

Jesse hoped that the case didn't lead them to that direction, if only because jurisdiction would be so hard to prove, but she would be remiss if she didn't check. She hit send on the email and wondered if and when she would hear back, and what it might say if she did.

Lisette—her friend behind the scenes at NamUs—had already pinged her back to let them know she was on it. Jesse and Lisette went way back, and while that definitely worked in her favor for getting information, it worked against her because the information sometimes came in faster than she could deal with.

Lisette sent over two cases almost immediately, and she was still digging. Jesse was waiting in real time as Lisette checked the backlog searching for any kind of linking material and pulling up cases that had things that matched to Hannalyn and Annabeth.

The second one came with a note. Lisette thought it wasn't right, but she'd rather Jesse rule it out. Jesse did that right away, her breath huffing out as she realized how tense this was making her.

She didn't know what she would find, and she thought about the thing she'd told Georgia—the Grim Sleeper was credited with fifteen murders, but was plausible for ninety-six. Bundy confessed to thirty individual murders. Documentation suggested at least sixty-five. To this day, no one knew how many the Golden State Killer had killed, but he'd been known as the East Area Rapist first, then the Original Night Stalker. He'd done so much damage over so long, he'd gotten three monikers.

Her stomach rolled as her email pinged again.

Forcing herself to check, she felt her shoulders drop when she saw it was from Chuck. Jesse was forwarding all those emails—from the DOE Network—to Georgia.

Chuck had sent her six cases, and Jesse tried not to think about it. There had also been a few she and Georgia had found first. Those were added to the stack, too.

Georgia immediately stopped her pacing as she dove in to her assignments. "Can I rule out the ones that I don't think fit?"

That, too, had given Jesse pause. Her immediate gut reaction had been to say, *Yes, rule out anything that you have the slightest inclination to rule out.* But that came from her deep desire to take something else off this hideous plate that kept piling higher. But she'd had to stop and think that wasn't the way to solve the case. It wasn't the way to get justice for the missing and as much as she hated it, they had to leave everything in for now.

She sat there with her tongue feeling dry, craving the hot liquid feeling of a good bottle of whiskey that she couldn't afford. "Let's set very clear criteria. Because, yes, we need to rule some out, but we have to be doing it the same. And the information coming in from each case is going to be different."

They stepped aside from the work of combing through the cases to be sure that if they dismissed the case, they were both dismissing it for the same set of reasons. They quickly developed their own parameters—a disgusting little list that Jesse used to double check the ones they'd already chosen or dismissed.

At least this one still failed the basic test, but she felt more and more sick to her stomach each time she looked at it. Even the ones she was dismissing upset her. Someone had gone missing, and their family desperately wanted to find their loved one.

The vast majority of missing persons cases were resolved. But that usually happened in that "golden window"—twenty-four, forty-eight, or seventy-two hours, depending on who you asked. Once the cases went cold? Then the numbers plummeted. Jesse knew the odds of finding any of these missing were low. Very low.

She turned back to the second case. Next to her, Georgia was tapping away on her keyboard, sorting through the DOE Network cases, not seeming too bothered deep in her soul the way Jesse was.

The work of sorting them meant that Jesse and Georgia then had to go further than the information they were handed. They had to look for the original source material. The report would hand them the original location of the missing. They could then go to that location's police department and pull the original reports along with the police logs, which were public access.

They looked for news outlet articles that usually accompanied the early days when someone went missing. In a lot of cases, they could go onto the social media accounts of the missing person or family members and find updates. Using all of this, they stitched together a whole case, and they could apply their new criteria.

To her disappointment, the case Jesse was looking at fit. Her email pinged and she didn't get to rest. It took less than half an hour to see that this new case fit, too. Bringing her to two cases. Georgia had one, which meant they had a total of five with Hannalyn and Annabeth.

She had to assume that they were missing the vast majority of victims. Lisette and Chuck were still working, combing through data on their respective networks. More would roll in.

Jesse wanted a shot of tequila. She wanted a snack. She wanted to get up and walk away. She wanted to tell the Burkhardts that she wasn't the right person for the case.

But she didn't have the finances right now to turn down the work. Fighting Floyann and Betty in court had drained her savings and she'd still lost.

She stood up to pace a small circle. Maybe she could suggest a break. Even as she considered the idea, Georgia slapped down her pen and said, "Fuck."

Now there were six.

48

This part sucked. It had taken the better part of a day to get the Burkhardts together in one place. Then, when Jesse had pulled up with Georgia riding shotgun—back in her usual spot today—they'd seen the car.

"Is that okay?"

Jesse didn't need to see her partner's face, she could hear the frown. Even her own internal monologue was going, *Oh, hell no, no, no.* "It's absolutely not. We have to get him out of there."

"Does it matter?" Georgia asked her voice now shifting tone. "He stayed overnight. From all appearances, he and Harper are tight. He doesn't seem to be dating anyone else."

"That's a recipe for her telling him, if not *everything*, at least what we're about to tell her." Jesse couldn't agree more, but that didn't make it okay. "We still can't have him there."

This part sucked.

Davis McNally was a concern. In fact, he was the only person on their suspect list right now. She hadn't been able to find much more about him, though most of their time had been devoted to weeding cases.

They did find that Davis was within a hundred miles of two of the missing persons locations—not Hannalyn or Annabeth, though.

They had six total.

Each time she checked her email, Jesse felt the trepidation seeping in, afraid that something else had come in from Lisette or Chuck or from whoever decided to answer her at the Bureau of Indian Affairs, or the missing persons network. She was petrified there'd be another match.

The FBI generally liked to have three murderers with matching MOs to assign a team to finding a serial killer. Jesse had six. But the problem was five of them weren't classified as murders at all. And those five still had the option that the missing person had simply walked away.

That was why Owen told them the FBI wouldn't take it. He needed harder evidence. He couldn't turn missing persons cases into murders because Jesse and Georgia believed it.

Jesse had thought that terminology was a bit harsh, but she did understand the underlying factors. A manhunt would be a massive, costly effort. They had to be sure. She now saw it as her duty to convince the FBI of what they had.

She would do whatever was necessary to make that happen. Since it wasn't done yet—and just out of basic decency—she and Georgia had to tell the Burkhardts what was happening before the media did.

That meant right now.

She didn't know how long they had before someone else with a missing loved one caught wind of something similar. Annabeth wasn't supposed to be found. When the autopsy report came out, there would be even more evidence. The Burkhardts were in for a rude awakening. Jesse was trying to soften the blow.

"Okay." She announced it into the air of the car. They

couldn't sit out here like stalkers. "I think I have an idea and we're just going to have to make it work."

"I'm here to go along," Georgia said as if that were actually true. Georgia was contrary as much as she was helpful. At least when she was contrary she usually had good ideas.

Climbing out of the car, they walked carefully and with purpose to the front porch and rang the doorbell. A nervous Harriet answered. "You wanted to meet? Is it good news?"

Jesse couldn't make the poor woman wait, so she simply said, "I'm afraid it's not."

Georgia stood stoically by as Jesse watched Harriet's expression crumble, a brick wall under an explosive force. Her shoulders slumped. Her back lost the steel of hope that kept it straight. Then she saw Harriet pull herself together.

"I understand," the woman said, though, clearly she was forcing the words out. She understood it logically if she didn't believe it. Jesse knew that one. She felt the effort it took when Harriet said, "This is what we hired you for. We need the truth, even if it isn't pretty. Come in."

Jesse murmured a *thank you* and followed Harriet into the living room, where at least this time she was familiar with the path and what it would be like. On the left of two little couches facing each other across the coffee table sat Jefferson with an empty seat for Harriet. On the other couch, exactly as Jesse had feared, sat Harper, her hand folded neatly into Davis's.

Two chairs sat at the end, clearly pulled up and not part of the original arrangement, just waiting for Jesse and Georgia to take their places in this macabre little dance.

With as subtle of an eye as she could manage, Jesse motioned for Georgia to take her spot and then she looked at the four already seated. She spoke to Harriet and Jefferson first. "I'm very sorry, but we need this to be immediate family only."

"Of course." Davis immediately obliged, though he wasn't the one spoken to. *Good.*

Untangling his hand from Harper's, he turned it over and patted it, as if that would make any of this okay. He was standing up, but Harper tugged him back down. She protested, "Davis *is* family."

"I understand." Jesse tried to be as comforting as possible, while inside she recoiled. She did not like this man. She got no bizarre vibes off him standing this close and that made her even more squirrely.

Something was off about him. It was possible that the man who had stabbed Annabeth—and possibly Hannalyn—multiple times was sitting in the living room waiting to hear the news with the family. Jesse pushed. "I'm sorry, but if you weren't born into this family or married into it, then Georgia and I cannot give this information."

"It's fine," Davis said, seeming almost embarrassed. Jesse believed she could tell from the way he looked at Harper and smiled, as he once again extracted himself from her hold, that he believed she would simply tell him at some point soon.

The elder Burkhardts looked a little confused. But Davis this time hopped up and managed to make it out of the room without Harper protesting.

Jesse didn't say anything until she heard the front door click closed. Even then, she waited for the sound of the car starting and the tires moving out of the driveway. If he was as bad as she thought he might be, he could have bugged the place, but there was nothing she could do about that right now. They were just going to have to chance it.

"I'm sorry about that," she apologized again, finally taking her seat. She leaned forward, elbows resting slightly on her knees, noticing that Jefferson mimicked her position. Harriet and Harper leaned back, hands folded, nervously fidgeting.

This part sucked. "While we do not have definitive news about Hannalyn or a resolution of her case *yet*—" Jesse emphasized the *yet,* "—we have been speaking with the FBI."

She watched as Harriet visibly swallowed.

"There are now five other cases attached to Hannalyn's." She paused for emphasis. "You cannot tell anyone the information I'm about to give you."

She looked at each of the three of them in turn, making quick eye contact. Then she did it again. "Not anyone. You only have this information because you are the immediate family of Hannalyn Burkhardt." Then for even more emphasis, Jesse turned to Harper. "You absolutely cannot share this information with Davis McNally or anyone else."

She waited for Harper to verbally agree.

She could only hope it worked.

49

"I guess that went as well as it could." Georgia commented as she climbed into the passenger seat, still experiencing a disconcerting range of emotions. Beside her, Jesse answered only with a nod, a shrug, and a twitch of her head, indicating that even she didn't know.

That was okay. If Jesse didn't know, then she didn't have to know. The big question was Harper—whether or not she would keep her forced promise to withhold the information about a serial killer. "Do you think she'll tell him?"

"Fifty-fifty." Jesse sighed and started the engine, then she waved back at the house, though Georgia couldn't see anyone. They pulled away and Georgia figured the wave was just in case anyone was watching.

The Burkhardts had not taken the news well, though that was not a surprise. It had been easy to tell from the beginning that Jefferson and Harriet held out hope that Hannalyn would be found alive. She'd always wanted to say—but Jesse would not let her—that didn't they understand what that would mean? Something in their daughter's life had been so terrible that she had to flee from it. That she was in mortal danger. And that was the best case scenario. Others were that she was sex trafficked. Had a psychotic break. None of them were good options.

Still, they had been very surprised to hear that there was likely a serial killer involved.

Jesse had laid it on thick about how they couldn't tell anyone, even Davis. She didn't say "especially Davis" though she had told them that everyone associated with Hannalyn prior to or around the time of her disappearance was still a suspect.

Harper had laughed. The only laugh of the day—of the entire conversation—and she offered a wide grin. "It couldn't be Davis!"

Georgia was impressed that Jesse had snapped a glare at the woman and simply said, "You're not qualified to make that judgment. If you tell him, you will be breaking FBI protocol. You will be making it difficult for the Bureau to find your sister."

Good one! Georgia had thought at the time. Tie Harper's behavior to being able to do the job that they needed to do. Sure enough, Georgia, watching the conversation like a tennis match, had seen Harriet's eyes go wide. If nothing else, Jesse had gotten the elder Burkhardts on her side.

"Hope she doesn't tell," was all Jesse uttered now as they got farther and farther from the house and prayed that what they said stuck.

The morning job was done. She could tell that Jesse was disgruntled, but Georgia didn't want to jump in. What good would it do? She didn't think Jesse was mad at *her*. And what Jesse *was* mad about was nothing that she or anyone else could fix.

Unfortunately, they headed straight back to the hotel. Though it was a thousand times better than the small shabby motel, it had become a place to house the research of a serial killer.

Quietly, almost solemnly, but not with quite enough decorum for the context of the day, the women swiped the key at the back door of the building and rode up in the elevator. But at the door to the suite, Jesse started swearing.

It took Georgia a moment, but she caught on even as Jesse said it. "Where's the damn door tag?"

There was no Do Not Disturb sign swinging from the handle. *Shit*.

Georgia stepped back and watched as Jesse frantically ran the key again, pushed open the door and barged inside the room. They had left everything out. *The irony*, Georgia thought, was that while they had been out trying to be sure that the Burkhardts didn't share any information with someone who was at least affiliated with the case, *they* might have been here sharing information with the entire population of the hotel service of Shreveport, Louisiana.

"It doesn't look disturbed." Georgia said it quietly, knowing her own relief wouldn't be good enough for her senior partner. Jesse didn't respond. She was already at her now open bedroom door, turning around to face Georgia, arms crossed. She pointed to Georgia's own bedroom door with a glare.

So she opened it.

The bed was made. "Son of a bitch!"

Now she was as mad as Jesse, but she could hear that Jesse was already on the hotel phone. Her boss was letting someone at the front desk have it. She could hear the tone and quickly figured out the reply was, "We'll get another sign up on your door as soon as we can."

Jesse was grinding through her own words, the promise not enough. "Is there a way we can lock it when we leave? . . . No, I don't mean that it automatically locks. I mean enough to keep the maids out."

This, Georgia thought was the only upside to the fact that the FBI had not taken the case. They weren't actually sharing any kind of secret information. She had spent too many evenings at the dinner table with her father. She knew, despite all of Jesse's threats to the front desk that there was no violation.

But Jesse was mad. She was telling them how they had left the sign out because they had sensitive information and about how they had chosen this place because they believed it was secure.

Georgia had tried not to laugh. They had chosen this place because *she* had found it on a discount site. But the FBI had flat out rejected this case, at least at this point. Their best scenario would be to get enough information to make the case files sensitive information once they handed it over.

Rant aside, having done everything she could, Jesse slammed down the phone and headed to the fridge. Quickly she pulled out the makings of a sandwich. With a few sparse motions, she asked Georgia if she wanted one and Georgia nodded.

Then she headed out the door. Jesse needed a moment, maybe so did she. She should have said where she was going, but there wasn't really room for words in the angry, irritated space. She'd only passed three other room doors before she realized the room was a *scared* space.

Scared that they wouldn't find the killer. Scared that they wouldn't find enough to convince the Feds to take it. Scared that Hannalyn Burkhardt would forever remain "missing" but now her parents felt worse than they had before.

She put money in the machines and got little bags of chips and two sodas—diet for Jesse. She even knew which chips to get.

But Georgia, as the bottles were robot-armed into the opening, realized she had more determination than she'd thought.

She was in this until the end. They had to find Hannalyn or proof of what had happened. And she was going to be there when they locked this asshole up.

She took her goods and her grit back to the room where Jesse folded up the last of the sandwich fixings and put them back in the fridge. As she saw what Georgia brought, she offered a small smile and an explanation. "You should know, I got three more pings while we were in with the Burkhardts."

"Three more cases?" Georgia asked.

Jesse laughed, a raw, wry, steely sound. "Three *emails*. One from the Missing Persons Network, one from the Bureau of Indian Affairs. And one more from Lisette. She sent one case. Indian Affairs sent two. Missing Persons sent five."

Georgia understood now. Jesse's mood wasn't entirely constructed of Harper Burkhardt's desire to break instructions. It wasn't entirely composed of the fact that the FBI had turned down the case. Or the maids getting in.

It was that there were possibly eight more missing women attributed to this guy.

She tried to be chipper. She accepted the sandwich and popped open the top of her soda and made a space for herself and her laptop at the table. "Well then, let's get to work."

Like Jesse, she now desperately wanted to get away from this case. Wanted to hand it over to the FBI as soon as possible. She watched as the forwarded emails started populating her inbox.

Georgia was given four of the nine cases and, as she glanced through them, her stomach dropped.

50

J esse tried to breathe evenly. When that didn't work, she forced it—in through her nose and out through her mouth. She needed the sandwich for fuel, but now she regretted it. It wasn't sitting well.

"Nine," Georgia said.

"Nine," Jesse admitted, eyes falling closed. She'd never hated a number so much.

What was it that made people do this? She knew the statistics. She'd rattled a few of them off to Georgia. Each time she watched as Georgia was stunned.

People knew serial killers existed. Honestly, it was still highly unlikely that you'd run into one, but the bad ones were weeded out pretty early. They had low kill counts because they got caught. They left evidence, kills were matched to them, and they were put away a few murders into their career.

But the good ones . . . Jesse tried not to visibly shudder. Georgia would see and Jesse was trying so hard to keep it together. Whatever she was achieving outwardly, she was definitely failing inwardly. The good ones . . . they could operate for decades undetected. They were virtually unstoppable.

Knowing that the sooner they found what they needed, the sooner she could be rid of this, Jesse tried to get back to work. She needed the case to be finished. She could hand it to the FBI and tell the Burkhardts that they were in good hands. As of right now, she had told them the truth. She and Georgia were building the case for the FBI.

Thinking back to what she'd told them, she realized Harper might be able to put together that what Jesse and Georgia had wasn't actually sensitive FBI information . . . not yet. Definitely nothing they could do about that now.

Her plate was empty, the sandwich and chips gone. Georgia's small plate was bare as well. Their sodas nearing the end.

She noticed things about Georgia, things she might not have expected in one as young as her partner was. Georgia capped the soda so she didn't spill on her equipment. She followed through on her promises, even when they were made reluctantly.

In her own early twenties, Jesse had been a bit of a mess. Ambitious and clawing her way upward, she'd not been aware enough to be cautious of the people around her. She'd hurt others, played some office politics that she regretted now, made decisions thinking that the things that came to her were aimed straight at her and not that she was maybe sometimes a side effect in someone else's war. It hadn't occurred to her that she wasn't the center of the universe, that things weren't always going to be the way they were.

Still, things had mostly come easily enough that she assumed it was merit and not luck. Life had taught her otherwise before she hit thirty. Then she'd met Eugene, thinking that he was a stroke of luck. That had turned sour, too, and worse, it had the side effect of making her question her own judgment with people.

She didn't question her judgment about how to handle the cases, though. What kind of investigative work to do, or which cases she could solve, that still sat right. But she absolutely no longer felt she could just trust her gut about the people around her. It was where Davis McNally sat right now. She was convinced there was something off—something bad—about him. But she'd married the last man she'd had strong instincts about and look how wrong she'd been about him.

At least she hoped it made her a better reporter. Looking back, she realized when she'd interviewed someone or met them, she'd gotten a distinct impression of who they were or how they were. Then she found the evidence to support that. Not the most thorough method and honestly until somebody decided to pick her work apart, no one would really notice.

"What's next?" Georgia asked.

This was not the part she wanted to be doing, but the only way out was through. "The next thing that we have to do is find whatever information we can about each missing person and their cases—if there even is one."

She saw the look on Georgia's face and understood that the young woman was asking, *There's more?* But there was always more.

People's lives were whole stories. There would always be someone else who'd come into contact with them to interview, to ask how they felt, what their impression was. Find out what they'd seen and then push for the things that they thought maybe weren't important. Those things could crack a case wide open.

"There's more," she told her partner. "We need to requisition the police departments. Explain who we are, what we are investigating. Put in special requests."

Georgia nodded. These were all things they'd already done for Hannalyn's case, things Jesse had requested well before Georgia had pushed her way onto the case.

"But we need to make a plan."

"Okay?"

It was clear that this is one of those times that Georgia had no idea what was happening. And maybe, just maybe, she would go along. Georgia had done a good job of being a relatively silent partner during the discussion this morning. She'd only occasionally interjected enough to be clear that she was more than just a warm body. She showed she knew what she was doing as part of the investigation but let Jesse run the show.

"Next," Jesse sighed, because nothing lined up easily. "We have to go to some of these places and search on foot. The best thing that we could possibly do is find another body."

Georgia nodded. "Do you think he knows that we're looking?"

Jesse knew who *he* was. It was a question Jesse thought about each night before she went to bed. *Did whoever they were looking for know about them?*

She gave Georgia the answer she'd figured out. "If it's Davis, definitely."

"But he alibis out of some of these murders."

"That's true," Jesse conceded, but she hadn't ruled him out entirely yet. "It's possible he could still be it. Being in a different part of the country doesn't preclude getting somewhere, not in this day and age. And he's got the money to afford direct flights, fake IDs, things like that. We need to dig into him deeper."

"Absolutely." Georgia's agreement was fast and easy, but her next question wasn't. "Do you think it's possible that he killed Hannalyn and somebody else got this other woman? Annabeth."

It took a moment to suss out the pieces, but when Jesse answered, she was confident. "I don't think so. Hannalyn is definitely part of the bigger case. Given our search criteria, it's possible we weeded out a couple that should have been included. And it's possible that we included a couple that we should have weeded out. But the police searched the entire area around where Hannalyn's shoe was found and there was no evidence other than the shoe itself and two drops of her blood. They did a reasonable search around Annabeth's shoe, too. Those officers found no evidence in the area other than the shoe itself . . . And one drop of her blood that was on it."

"There was a drop of blood on it?" Georgia asked, a bit incredulous.

"Yeah," Jesse said. She'd only just found that out herself. "I started reaching out the other night when I couldn't sleep. I asked everyone I knew who might help for whatever inside scoop they had. Anyway, I have a friend who's on the police force in Denver—"

"Annabeth wasn't found in Denver."

"No," Jesse agreed, "but it's close enough and her case is big enough that she didn't go to the local ME. They sent her body to Denver." She watched as Georgia grinned.

Then, the grin fell away. "Davis was in Colorado last week."

"Yeah," Jesse nodded again. She hated that part.

51

Thoughts of heading off to look for bodies had been front and center, but Georgia understood why they were still here. They were waiting for police reports to come back from various precincts around the country. Whoever this guy was, he wasn't staying put.

Jesse had argued that Annabeth's body was the only information they had to go off where they might find someone else. None of the others on their list had turned up and the FBI didn't find any dead bodies from missing persons with one shoe and a drop of blood being the only indication that they hadn't walked away.

That meant this guy was good. No one had found any of his victims yet . . . except for Annabeth. Jesse had gone so far as to hit up the Burkhardt's for the money to hire someone with a cadaver dog.

She'd found someone close enough to drive in. Marjorie and Tinkerbell from Pacific Search and Rescue had just closed a case in Arkansas. Jesse had caught them right before they left town.

Jesse didn't know Marjorie, but she knew PSAR and liked their people. She'd been pleased at the find. The longer Georgia worked with her, the more she realized that Jesse could have turned her down that first day. She could have easily said no, that Georgia could not come along.

Jesse knew exactly what she was doing. She was the brains of the operation. And it wasn't that Georgia was stupid, but she was definitely the brawn.

So she readily followed along when Jesse took them to the store the night before for hiking gear, including small packs. This morning, they'd headed to the Loggy Bayou state managed land. Not quite a park, it was the closest place to stash a body without heading back toward Magnolia. They met Marjorie and Tinkerbell at the parking lot to the campground.

Tinkerbell, it turned out, was a huge pitbull-Rottweiler mix of a bruiser. Marjorie was a small blond woman with wild curls and the look of a seasoned . . . everything. She greeted them with "This is the perfect place to hide a body."

Jesse had agreed. Georgia asked why. She wanted to know.

"There are roads in and out. It's a wildlife management area, so if you get in with your body, most others aren't going to risk finding it. There's a campground here at the edge, so the roads are well enough traveled and no one will question someone coming or going with a good truck and a lumpy tarp in the back."

Well, that was bleak. But Georgia nodded and said thank you.

Marjorie invited them into her SUV and drove them further in, then the four of them—Tinkerbell included—had started to search in earnest. Georgia continued to ask questions, hoping she wasn't becoming obnoxious. Marjorie seemed happy to answer.

"Don't you use bloodhounds? Or purebred dogs?"

Marjorie, the first human in the line, was following Tinkerbell's lead and called back over her shoulder. "Statistically, certain breeds are better at it—like hounds. But it is always about the dog before it's about the breed."

She had turned and smiled back at Jesse and Georgia, her blonde hair bouncing in its frizzy ponytail. Her gear for hiking let them know that she was the professional and they were just the slobs following along.

"Anyone who tells you otherwise is an idiot," she said. She'd made Georgia smile with that.

They'd follow a trail for a while, until Tinkerbell would tug off path or Marjorie would decide this looked like a good place to hide a missing person.

The dog seemed to very much enjoy the work. Georgia was more concerned about not getting blisters. Jesse had hired Marjorie and Tink for three days. Of course, they hoped to find Hannalyn this first day, but that assumed they'd picked the right place to start. It was a total crapshoot.

To Tink's credit, she started tugging and barking at three that afternoon. Marjorie had let the dog off the leash and commanded, "Find."

The dog bulldozing her way through the woods made Georgia glad she was not on the receiving end. Then Tink waited for the trio to catch up to her. Sure enough she had a spot picked out.

Georgia—shocked as the dog sat and stared at a spot in the bushes and Marjorie had told her that yes, that meant there was a body there—had asked, "What if it's a deer or a bear or something?"

"It's not." Marjorie had called back over her shoulder.

For a fleeting moment, Georgia had wondered why Marjorie hadn't named her dog Elphaba, or maybe something a little more fitting for a blonde wood witch. Marjorie continued. "She's trained specifically not to alert on animal remains."

A quick look at Jesse, marching along mostly silently, revealed that she already knew this. And that she was trying not to get her hopes up for Tinkerbell's clear alert.

"If she did . . ." Marjorie talked while she helped them pick their way through what clearly wasn't a trail. "We'd be here all day digging up animal carcasses. Think about how many dead animals must be out here. What she's found is definitely human."

When they reached the dog, Marjorie reached into her pocket. First, she praised Tinkerbell effusively, even though they hadn't dug anything up yet. Then she pulled off her backpack and opened it. It was deceptively small, and Georgia's impression of her as a woods-witch was further solidified when she pulled out a piece of metal and unfolded it into a shovel. Then she pulled out another one and handed it to Georgia.

So they were digging.

Tinkerbell was back on her leash. Marjorie had looped the end over a branch and though it wouldn't hold the stout dog it did the trick of keeping her in place.

Georgia had been excited. Day one, they were out taking wild shots at where this killer might have hidden Hannalyn, and here they were.

She believed in their success already even as she stabbed at the earth with the shovel that was just a little too short. Even though they hadn't found any body yet, she believed in Tinkerbell.

She wondered why Jesse wasn't as excited as she was.

Though she was surviving on energy bars and energy drinks and the swamp was hot enough that she thought she might die, she was all in. She was in the woods digging up a body! She shoveled the heavy earth aside feeling the sweat roll down her spine. Over and over until Marjorie slapped a hand out to stop her. "Enough!"

Georgia pulled back and she saw then what Marjorie had been watching for. The bones were not white. The small space only revealed a few pieces. Getting down on her knees, Marjorie cleared out a space around what they'd revealed and then slowly poured a bottle of water over it, revealing even more.

"It's human."

"You can tell?" Georgia asked, feeling the muscles starting to pull tight across her back as she finally stood up straight.

"I think so, but I know Tink can tell."

Marjorie immediately pulled out a satellite phone, alerted the authorities, and rattled off their coordinates. Then she got yellow tape out of that magic backpack and cordoned off the area.

Though Georgia offered to do more digging, Marjorie forbade it. So they all sat back and tried to stay hydrated as they waited for a park ranger to show up. They quickly handed off the case to local authorities.

Jesse started gathering all the information of every ranger and detective and sheriff's deputy that passed through. She had printed copies of one-page full of information on Hannalyn. She handed one to each person with any kind of badge.

That, and her license helped explain why they were out with a cadaver dog searching for human remains. But this also let everyone know about the Burkhardt case.

It was hours later before they were back at the hotel. Georgia lingered in the hot shower, glad she didn't have to worry about her dad telling her she was running up the bill. Her muscles were tight, and she reminded herself to stretch later, but she didn't do it then.

It was dark before they ate a real dinner and waited for information to roll in about the body they'd found. She asked Jesse why they'd left everything behind and weren't doing anything else. "You don't want to be helpful?"

"We can't do this kind of work. It requires a medical examiner and a forensic examiner or it's not going to be right. We don't want to interfere." She paused then looked less than thrilled. "But it's not Hannalyn."

"How do you know?" Georgia was genuinely curious. She didn't really doubt Jesse's assessment, but what told her that?

"We don't even know the sex of the person they found."

Georgia nodded. She'd already found herself adopting some of the words that Marjorie used. Not *gender*, but *sex*. *Long bone*. *Skeletal remains*.

"Because," Jesse said, "he didn't bury Annabeth. He tucked her up under a log. So he shouldn't have varied the way he handled the bodies. It doesn't match."

"Does it have to?" The cases were ten years apart. His methods could have changed. Still, that wasn't enough to convince Jesse to be hopeful. Georgia pushed a little further.

"They are a decade apart," Jesse reiterated, her face still containing that deep, thoughtful look of someone embroiled in something that they didn't like. "Burying the body means you want to get rid of it and you don't want anyone to find it. That makes sense."

Georgia nodded. She agreed with all of that—as if her agreement mattered. But that didn't explain why Jesse was convinced this wasn't Hannalyn.

Jesse kept going. "Annabeth was ten years *after* Hannalyn. If it's the same guy, he should be getting *better* at this. Hannalyn's should have been the body in the open and Annabeth should have been the body he buried."

Oh hell. Yeah. That meant that Hannalyn likely was not buried, but under a log or something. *Interesting.* "So is this just an errant hiker?"

"It could be . . ." then Jesse shook her head at her own answer. "No, it couldn't. Errant hikers sit on logs and fall asleep and die of exposure or hypothermia. They hit their heads or get bit by snakes and don't get back up. They don't bury themselves."

It took another person to bury a body. "So we found another killer, just not the one we want."

"Probably," Jesse said, "and we'll be going out again tomorrow. Because we have to keep looking for Hannalyn."

52

"Tink and I have to be done," Marjorie announced, much to Jesse's dismay.

She'd explained the expense of the search dog to the Burkhardts. Though they disliked the idea that they were searching for a body, after a brief discussion they understood that finding Hannalyn could mean the case would go to the FBI. That they could arrest her killer and protect other women in the future.

The Burkhardts weren't the kind of wealthy that had private jets and yachts. But they were definitely the kind that could afford a cadaver dog. They'd ponied up the expense and Jesse's disappointment now was not that the money wasn't there, it was, as Marjorie explained, simply that Tinkerbell had to stop.

They'd searched Loggy Bayou a second day and this morning they'd voted to try the Red River National Wildlife Refuge. It was Jesse's second choice. Closer to town, it didn't get the body as far away, but it would have been an easier dumping ground.

It didn't matter though. They hadn't found Hannalyn.

"We can come back in a week. Tinkerbell will need the rest

and there are travel days on either side." Marjorie looked at her as if to ask if that was okay.

Jesse just said, "I'll get back in touch, if that's okay? I have to talk to the family."

Still, she considered hiring another cadaver dog, but they weren't an easy resource to come by. She'd found one in Mississippi before landing Marjorie and Tink. Though the handler was available, the dog did not have the hit record that Tinkerbell had.

But what else could she say? Logically she understood. Marjorie had told them up front that Tinkerbell was coming off another run where they found another body—that was why the pair had been free to come here.

Given that they'd found a body on the first day at Loggy Bayou, Tinkerbell was putting in her time. They'd searched the entire second day at Jesse's request—on her conviction that the body they'd found was not Hannalyn. Now, they'd searched most of an entire third day.

Neither of these last two days had yielded anything. Which meant Tinkerbell was on her feet all day, nose in the air, or to the ground, or stuck in the passing bushes.

Jesse had been right. She'd just gotten an email from the medical examiner. "The body we found? It wasn't her."

In fact, it wasn't even someone related to the case in any way, shape or form. "A man who went missing three years ago."

Georgia nodded at her, unhappy with the results, but not surprised. Marjorie and Tinkerbell took it all in stride.

Jesse could not express how disturbing it was to be trying to solve one murder case, then run into eight more associated murder cases. Then, while working that probable serial killer case, find *another* body of an entirely unrelated murder. There were too many damn killings in the world. Maybe she needed to start reporting on dog shows.

But she hated dog shows. And catching someone was far

too satisfying to leave it behind. So she was in the damn muggy woods—the bayou, actually—with two women and a dog, looking for dead bodies. Her own body was considering dying. She almost couldn't drink her water fast enough.

The heat was enough to make her rethink the job again. Maybe she could find the job satisfaction, but without all the murder. She needed to find somebody's missing jewelry or trade back some swapped-at-birth babies or help an adoptee find their genetic relatives.

"It'll get dark soon," Marjorie announced. Though it still looked bright to Jesse, she admitted they had to find their way back before the sun set, not just stop then.

The words filled the space between Jesse's acceptance and Georgia's clear desire to plead for one more day. Georgia also seemed to war with her unwillingness to ask more of an animal she adored. While Jesse appreciated Tinkerbell's ability, the broad head and staunch body scared her more than a little. Whatever Tinkerbell decided to do, Tinkerbell could accomplish.

Georgia, on the other hand, referred to Tinkerbell as *puppy* at every turn, scratched her head, and even had difficulty keeping her hands off the dog. Marjorie had been clear at times that Tinkerbell was working and that she was not to be interfered with.

Now with the hunt declared off, and all that was left was to leave the woods for the day, Marjorie surreptitiously handed treats to Georgia. The younger woman fed them one by one to Tinkerbell while scratching behind her ears and in between her shoulder blades and telling her what a good girl she was. Tinkerbell loved every second of it.

At least the dog was happy, Jesse thought. The three women turned around and began their trek back quietly. Marjorie and Tinkerbell led the way. Though this wasn't their home territory, they were clearly the more seasoned hikers.

"It's hard to find bodies out here," Marjorie commiserated. "A place like this, you don't need much to make a body disappear. Just a big cat to wander through at the right time. Or a pack of coyotes, wolves, and the body parts get scattered."

"That doesn't seem like a very good murder scenario." Georgia had input from the rear of their little hiking line. "I mean, burying the body seems more likely to keep it hidden."

"It does," Marjorie readily agreed. "But look at the body you found already. It wasn't left out."

Jesse had to concede to that—though Tinkerbell had been the finder. The body they'd found was three years old and it was skeletal. Most of the evidence was gone. But it had been buried, preserved as best it could. What Jesse was thinking though was interrupted by Marjorie's next words.

"We haven't even found any random long bones. I've had it happen before. Where Tinkerbell alerts and when we get there all it is is a long bone abandoned by some other animal that carried it through the woods. We have no way of identifying it unless it's got an implant—"

"An implant?" Georgia interrupted.

"Major implants—unlike something like dental implants—will always have a serial number on them. Sometimes there's no serial number, but there's a particular kind of work and we can match that to a missing person. Pins, something like that." Marjorie talked animatedly as if the dog at the end of her leash hadn't been trained to the scent of decaying human flesh. "Animals can scatter the body parts for miles. It can definitely make them harder to find."

Jesse had to think about that for a moment. Annabeth seemed to have been stashed almost as if her killer was simply done with her. As if she were trash. That it was easier for him to hide her than to make the effort to strip any evidence.

That, she thought, *was confidence*. She had to hope that that confidence would mean that eventually he would slip up. The other possibility was that the science could catch up. Evidence could come in ways that no one predicted, so he wouldn't even think to hide or cover it now.

The group was still over an hour out from the parking lot, at least by Jesse's estimates. It had been a long, slow day. They had not simply followed the trails but ducked off in between them, using Marjorie's navigation skills to keep them from disappearing into the woods and being lost forever themselves.

As they got nearer to the exit, the sky did begin to darken. Marjorie had been right. When Jesse looked up again, time had passed without her realizing. Night was starting to fall around them as they'd been out a little longer than planned, trying to still stretch Tinkerbell's last day to the last minute.

They'd been quiet though, and Jesse's thoughts had turned to what they would possibly do next. They still had to find evidence for the FBI. Her ultimate goal was to get this case off her hands. They needed to find evidence of—

Tinkerbell, barking twice, tugged at her leash.

"Are you serious, girl?" Marjorie asked. But Tinkerbell's sudden snap to attention was all that Marjorie needed to reach down and release the clip on the leash.

Tinkerbell, hot on the trail, dashed into the underbrush, barking as she went.

53

Georgia wanted to ask, "Now what?" but that would require her getting out of bed.

A move would be exciting, but she didn't have the energy to start. It was excitement that she could enjoy more if she just rolled over and went back to sleep.

But the light was coming in around the edges of the curtains. It was well into Wednesday, and she hadn't had to get up to trek through the woods and smell of bug spray and her own sweat. She was clean and she damn well intended to stay that way.

There was nothing they could do yet about the skull Tinkerbell had found yesterday, anyway.

The dog had alerted, the three of them had followed, and by the time they arrived where Tink waited, they were all pushing through with LED high beams their only light in the dark woods.

Had she not been in a group, Georgia would have been petrified by the pitch darkness of the night. Only the slightest hints of moon peeked through the trees; it wasn't enough to keep the shadows at bay. Strange noises came from all around.

She simply recited to herself that Jesse and certainly Marjorie would not be out here if the three of them weren't relatively safe. It was Tinkerbell herself who made Georgia feel a hell of a lot better. If nothing else, the dog would growl and warn them that something was coming.

So they picked their way along, following as the big dog jumped agilely ahead, and then waited, then jumped ahead again, before eventually leading them to a fallen log half covered in overgrown bushes.

The light leached out from around the edges of the high beams. Georgia could see how Jesse tensed when she saw the fallen log. *It couldn't be the same, could it?*

It was Marjorie who carefully peeled back the layers. "I'm no forensic anthropologist or crime scene tech—" She talked as she headed toward Tink and knelt down to inspect the point the dog stared at. She worked deliberately, asking them to direct the light, "—but I'm good enough that I feel relatively confident that I'm not destroying evidence."

She pulled blue gloves from her pockets again and then carefully held back the branches, often making Jesse and Georgia step up to help so she could get deeper and deeper into the space. Each time she peeled back another layer Tinkerbell let out another small yip.

They were getting closer.

Eventually, they found a handful of small bones which Marjorie declared human. "They're hand and foot bones, ankle and wrist bones."

Jesse nodded along and Georgia, as a law student, simply had to understand that Marjorie and Jesse's agreement was going to be enough. Then, when Tinkerbell kept barking at the other end of the log, they picked their way through the overgrown brush.

There, they found the skull.

Georgia had woken up three times last night, dreams of that

skull jolting her from sleep. She talked of nothing else while they'd waited hours for the police to arrive, Marjorie once again calling in on her satellite phone and giving them exact coordinates.

They'd been told to wait while the police put out yellow crime scene tape. They waited while the two officers who arrived first immediately called in other help. The three had been questioned about what they were doing out in the woods after dark with a cadaver dog.

Luckily, Jesse had a PI license and Marjorie had her paperwork on her, too. That went a long way. The cloak of professionalism seemed to be large enough to wrap Georgia as well, though she felt she was only along for the ride.

Still, Jesse had introduced her as "my partner in training" and for a moment in the middle of the happiness of the success in the horror of the find, she felt the brief swell of pride.

They'd answered all the questions, gotten permission to eat the last of their energy bars and sports drinks, and been told not to go far. It had been well past midnight when they'd been released. Georgia was grateful that the Red River Wildlife reserve was closer to Shreveport than Loggy Bayou had been. At least the drive was short.

She'd convinced Jesse she wouldn't make it to the hotel though, and they'd driven through the one open place for hamburgers. Despite putting a cold and fizzy soda into her body, she passed out immediately, only to be jolted awake by evil dreams.

Now, she rolled over again, the sunlight winning the battle. She heard Jesse out in the main room. The clock told her it was almost noon. They'd gone past their checkout time.

They had more than a full day of driving ahead of them. She had to get up.

Convincing herself that she was a real grownup and she

could do this, Georgia brushed her teeth and her hair, washed her face and managed to open the door feeling almost human.

As she stepped into the main room, she found that Jesse had cleared the place out.

"Get dressed," her partner issued the statement—not cheerfully, not flat, but somewhere in between. "We'll see if they can give us a late checkout. I'll tell them we'll come back."

Georgia nodded and Jesse kept going, no longer looking at her, but into the fridge, as if to decide what to do with the remaining food. "We'll hit the road ASAP. Spend the night in the middle somewhere. Then get up to Rockford, hopefully by midday tomorrow."

Georgia nodded again, though Jesse wasn't even looking.

They'd chosen Rockford because of the case and the information they had on it. Very similar to Hannalyn, this young woman was in her mid-twenties and had disappeared during a night out with her friends.

She had gone out to her car to retrieve something and never come back. The car was still there. Her purse, phone, wallet, and personal items were all missing with her. All that had ever been found was a single high-heeled shoe with a drop of blood on it.

There had been another case that had been just as compelling. But Jesse had voted against it. The victim had been a young man, and Jesse had wanted to put it off. The possibility of investigating it and having it not turn out to match their killer was higher given the difference in victims.

But if Rockford didn't pan out, that was where they would go next.

Georgia looked around the room, out the open central window, thinking that she might not come back to Shreveport at all. "Any word on the skull?"

Jesse shook her head. "Too soon. It could be weeks. The

only thing that gives the case any priority is Hannalyn's parents pushing for it. But they don't live in Shreveport."

They'd learned by listening to the talk among the officers and crime scene techs that the skull, the hand and foot bones, and anything else they might have discovered after the three of them were dismissed, would go to the Shreveport forensic center. But that was once the team excavated everything in the area and found whatever they could.

"Did they find any more bones?" Georgia just assumed Jesse would know everything.

"I don't know if they even finished the excavation yet." Jesse at least looked at her this time, and Georgia could tell that her erstwhile boss was resigned to waiting again.

Marjorie said the skull would be the most important thing for identification.

Jesse added a little more. "So far, they haven't found anything identifying." Then she changed the subject. "We need to get going."

"Will this possibly take weeks to ID?" Georgia asked.

"Unfortunately, yes."

"Can they do dental identification?" The skull had a handful of front teeth. Georgia had been hopeful.

"Not enough teeth." Jesse burst that bubble quickly. "And the teeth that it did have were not molars, which are usually better, *and* they were dentist-straight."

Georgia twitched her shoulders and shook her head, not understanding what that meant.

"People with unusual teeth can often get at least a preliminary match when a skull is found with matching unusual teeth. That happened a lot in Katrina where the dental records were lost, too."

Georgia shuddered, but Jesse left no room for her reactions.

"But once somebody's had braces, particularly at a young

age where the teeth grow into that position, they all look the same."

Georgia nodded this time, recalling pictures of Hannalyn. The girl did have what Jesse called "dentist straight teeth."

"Go." Jesse prodded politely. Georgia headed back into her room. There wasn't much to pack. Once again, though, as she put everything in the suitcase, she was reminded that she had packed for Florida, naively believing she would spend a few days. She would find out about the investigative journalist who had not gotten back to her, then swiftly and stunningly convince Jesse to take Sin's case.

Georgia had thought she'd be home studying for her LSAT and waiting to hear news of her mother. That was beyond laughable now. Instead, she was in Shreveport on her way to Rockport, Illinois.

And another murder.

54

Cindy headed out into the woods, hating every minute of it. Same story, different park.

It wasn't that she hated hiking, in fact, the woods were gorgeous. The weather was beautiful today. It was still awful. She hated the compulsion to be out here. She hated why.

She would have liked to have said she couldn't identify the impulse that brought her here, but she absolutely could and that made it worse. She knew what was in these woods.

Cindy had seen enough of it the night before. Her dreams had been plagued with disturbing visions she couldn't ignore. She came out today, partly because of the urge and partly because she still—probably falsely—believed that if she could just see it for herself, she could lay it to rest. That at least some if it would go away.

She put one foot in front of the other on the hiking trail, moving farther along with a level of determination that allowed her to enjoy almost nothing of what was around her. She'd passed someone a little while back and she was reminded of the time. She would need a break soon.

But she didn't want to stop. She just wanted to power

through, find what she needed, and figure out how to make it look like she hadn't even been here. Then she would leave and know that things were taken care of. Annabeth Green's family would get closure now, even if Annabeth's own closure had been horrific.

Cindy was still pretty sure she was the only one who knew exactly what had happened. Now she knew there was another one here.

She didn't know all the physics or details of how what she did worked. She only knew that it did. And that she hated it.

As she pushed forward, the hill got steeper but the path stayed wide and relatively rock and root free. She replayed the words from her conversation with Carter last night.

"You were supposed to be home two hours ago. Where are you?"

"Not home," she'd admitted, immediately getting waves of emotion off her brother—anger, irritation, but mostly concern. She'd added, "I'm safe."

"What happened?" He knew to ask *what,* because ultimately, he couldn't ask her *why* she'd done it. These days that answer was always the same.

"I was on my way home. I was halfway there and then I just took a turn."

"Is there another one?" he asked softly.

"There always is."

Sometimes she got a respite for a couple of months. Sometimes the things she saw were so horrific that she stayed home and didn't function. That was when she closed the curtains and blocked out the light. It helped, but only a little. In those times sometimes she could only wait for it to pass.

But not this. This was strong. It ran deep.

She'd only felt the urge at this level a handful of times before in her life. Again, it was why Carter had suggested she come out in the first place. She didn't bother assigning blame, none of it was either of their faults. They both were old hands at this game by now.

So instead, he had asked her, "How do you intend to stay out of the limelight on this one?"

They both knew if anyone figured out what she could do, it would be trouble. And that wasn't speculation. She'd had trouble before. Police Departments, investigators she'd been trying to help, had turned on her. It had not turned out well. There were places that still recognized her name and told people not to listen. Which she thought was odd because she was always right. Always.

"Same as last time?" she had suggested, the question mark at the end deliberate. Cindy honestly didn't know how she would do it. She just knew it was important enough that she achieve it.

This was her faith. It was hard fact that something was at the end of the line once she saw it. The faith was the idea that there would be a way out.

Her stomach grumbled but she could feel it in her bones that she was getting close. People were coming the other direction on the trail. The path was a loop around the entire Shanks Conservation Area. There were connecting offshoots to various parking lots on different sides of the park. The river bordered one long side.

The dog saw her first.

Another dog, she thought. But this one barked and, as she got closer, it tugged at its leash. *Damn*. It wasn't just barking, the dog was barking *at her*.

"Felony, no." The voice came, male and sturdy.

Cindy stopped. The dog looked like it had a mission. The long leash it was on was taut, though she didn't tug. Her little red jacket had writing on it. If this was a service dog, Cindy had no idea what she was serving.

Cindy approached slowly. She needed to stay on the trail.

The dog was on leash, so it should all be fine even if it was acting a little odd. She would just walk around it, duck her head, offer a soft *Hello* out of sheer politeness to the people with the dog, then pass on by.

They would barely remember she even existed. She looked down the trail behind the dog to get a better idea of what and who was coming.

First, she saw the man. Tall, with his dark brown hair pulled back, he had shocking blue eyes and a wide full mouth. The concern on his face focused entirely on the dog, not on her. He held the leash and seemed to be in full control of the reasonably large animal. *Good.*

Behind him, two women followed along—one tall and lean, brown hair pulled back in a ponytail, the other rocking a short almost jet-black bob. The second one was looking around, so Cindy ducked her face to the side. She offered a small wave and stepped to the side of the trail. Proper etiquette. *Forgettable etiquette.*

Still, the dog came right up, within a few feet of her. Then it sat down sharply, stared and barked three short yips.

"Well, that's unusual," the man said.

"Your dog doesn't normally bark at people?" she asked, breaking her rule and having a conversation. She didn't look at the man though. She looked at the dog, it couldn't ID her to the police. But the dog was staring.

"Ian Carello," he said, holding his hand out. What could she do but shake it? She did not want to touch this man. She did not want to touch anyone, but it would be memorable if she didn't.

With no other real options, she took his hand, "Cathy," she lied. "Cathy Bass."

It had the same initials as her name, but no one should be able to find her. As her hand grasped his, she almost jolted. Memories shot through her system—not her own. She tried to hide the physical reaction of seeing what he saw. There were girlfriends, dates, parties, and bones. Dug up human skeletons, dead bodies, and more. There were injured people, some sad, some screaming, some happy too be rescued. Too many memories like that to be coincidental—all of them had dogs in them.

Felony, he'd said. *What an unusual name,* but she didn't say it out loud, just yanked her hand back, hoping the connection would be broken. She nodded to the two women, thinking again she would sidestep the trail and be gone, but the dog continued to stare at her.

Long and lean, it was brindle with floppy ears and a face that defied breed. As she stepped around, it moved to the side, planting its butt and blocking her. Then it barked again. The same three short yips.

"That's so weird," Ian said, "She's alerting on you."

"Why would a dog alert on her?" the younger woman with the ponytail asked from the back of the small group.

Cindy tried to shrug it off and step to the side. Once again, the dog blocked her, barking three times. Ian looked back to his two companions, before looking at Cindy, aka Cathy, once again.

Then he said words that chilled her to the bone. "She's a cadaver dog."

55

J esse's heart raced. The cadaver dog was alerting on the woman—a woman who was clearly alive and standing right in front of them.

Had hiring Ian and Felony been a mistake? Marjorie had highly recommended them. But this?

Jesse looked the woman up and down, taking in the reddish hair, round curves, and brightly colored clothing. She did not look like a seasoned hiker. Jesse recognized the look because it was her own.

Ian was trained for searching and so far, he and Felony seemed to have done their jobs just fine. But he clearly didn't quite have the delicate touch needed to let somebody know that a cadaver dog thought they were a dead person walking.

"I know this is weird," she said, her hands loose at her side as she tried to look non-threatening and calm. "We're out today trying to solve a— a missing persons case."

She'd almost stuttered over the words. She'd almost said *Murder*. A missing person would be much easier for someone else to digest. Surely, Cathy would put it together, that the missing person must be suspected to be dead if they had the cadaver dog out.

"I hate to say this but if the dog is alerting on you, you must have passed by what we're looking for." Again, she carefully avoided the terms *dead body*, *decaying corpse* or anything of the like. Cathy looked skittish enough already. "Can you tell us where you went today?"

Cathy shrugged, her face turning away oddly, as if she didn't want any human contact. Jesse wondered for a moment if the woman was on the spectrum, or mentally ill, or possibly just very shy.

Cathy waved one hand back behind her, indicating the walkway. "I've only been on the trail today."

That was all she offered before she tried to step aside again. Jesse would have liked to have let her go. Right now, she was grateful that Felony was stopping her. The woman smelled like a cadaver, so she must have gotten close enough for the dog to pick up the smell. "There wasn't anything unusual on the trail?"

"No, ma'am," Cathy answered, still looking aside.

Good, she would miss that Jesse almost flinched at the response. She would have thought Cathy was older than she was, not the kind of person to *ma'am* her.

"I hate to bother you, but if we can find this person, it will help their family tremendously." Jesse could see the war in Cathy's eyes.

She waited out the debate for a few moments until Cathy made a decision. "I don't know why your dog is alerting on me." She continued to look at the ground. "I haven't touched or been near any cadavers today."

"All right then." Ian had said "cadaver dog." He'd introduced the odd word into the conversation and Cathy had picked it up. Jesse wished he hadn't, but it was too late now. She tried again. "Maybe you did, and you don't know."

"I would know." Something in Cathy's tone was confident, despite the fact that she was speaking to the tree on her right.

"People don't always," Jesse pushed but she didn't finish the sentence.

Cathy's sharp gaze snapped to her, letting her see the pink, round cheeks and mouth, firm chin. Hazel eyes glared now. "*I would know.*"

What an odd statement, Jesse thought, but she saw the moment that Cathy realized what she'd done. Whether she figured it out for herself, or read it from Jesse's own uncontrolled reaction, Jesse couldn't tell.

Beside her a small cough and shuffle told her Georgia was stepping into the conversation.

"We're really hoping that you can help," Georgia laid it on thick and Jesse recognized her own training in the words. *Introduce yourself.* "I'm Georgia Dunham, one of the missing people we're looking for is my mother."

Oooh, good one, Jesse thought. Not false, but not true either. Georgia's mother was absolutely not part of this case, but they were looking for her. *Points to Georgia.*

Next, let the person know that you're in trouble and they can be the hero. "I really need to find her. I need to know where she is. That's why we're out with the search dog today."

Yes, Georgia played that one well, too, Jesse thought. Whether the young woman had picked up on it or done it naturally, she also avoided words like *cadaver, corpse, murder,* and *death*. The kinds of terms that really put people off these conversations.

"I don't know why, but the dog seems to think that you know something that can help."

More points to Georgia. Because honestly, the dog thought Cathy Bass smelled like death. But the woman was skittish, and Jesse was glad that no one was quite willing to say that to her.

Except maybe Ian. Ian was incredibly forthright. Though she liked that about him, it was not the play for this situation.

"Please help us," Georgia begged again.

Jesse had to admit that perhaps the student had become the master on this one, though Georgia did have a card that Jesse could not have played. They were looking for Georgia's own mother, and that personal connection was an ace.

This time when Cindy looked up, she glanced back and forth at the three of them. "There are no cadavers back there on the trail."

She said it softly, but with a confidence that startled Jesse. Cathy talked as if she knew about cadavers, as if she were speaking from a point of education, and not just the average arrogance that people had.

People always believed they would know what they had encountered and what they hadn't. Lord knew, some of the things that Jesse had encountered working with the FBI agents in Florida were things her brain hadn't even been able to process. But Cathy spoke now with an affirmation that said she knew of what she spoke. Jesse chose to believe her.

"Do you have any professional purpose for being out here?" Cathy asked, this time her eyes went to the dog.

Felony was wearing her bright red vest with the Pacific Search and Rescue logo emblazoned across it. It didn't say *cadaver dog*, which Ian had explained tended to put people off.

Quickly, Jesse reached into her pocket and produced the PI license she kept at the ready. Though it was issued from a different state, most people didn't flinch. Ian also reached for credentials. Only Georgia didn't have any.

Ian was coming back up in her estimation, even if she wasn't sure about Felony. There was still no explanation for why the dog alerted on a clearly live human.

Marjorie had recommended that—if Jesse and Georgia were going to a new search location that they could call Pacific Search and Rescue for another cadaver dog. It had taken some fast talking, but Jesse had both managed to get the Burkhardts to pony up the money for a search for this missing woman on the idea that the FBI may very well pay them back if it became a serial killer case, and get Ian and Felony on a plane out here to meet them today.

Jesse tried not to let her mind wander. Cathy Bass was an enigma. Jesse was paying attention. The woman didn't touch either of them as she reached out. She carefully didn't touch the ID either, though she got close, her finger moving as if to trace the words.

Interesting. Jesse thought. She'd also flinched when she shook Ian's hand, after looking as if she really didn't want to. Cathy seemed very touch averse.

In the end, after inspecting the IDs in detail and doing everything except pulling out her cell phone and calling it in and checking their numbers, she took a step back, dropped her hand, and nodded shortly.

"My name is Cathy Bass," she repeated, and, for the first time, Jesse thought maybe she didn't believe her.

"There are no cadavers behind us on the trail. I'll help you out."

How could she even help? If she wasn't going back the way she came, what was there? Jesse wondered, but the dog thought the woman smelled like cadaver, so she listened.

Then Cathy's whole demeanor shifted. Her back straightened, her chin came up, breath filled her lungs and she suddenly looked taller, almost imposing. "I'll help you, but first you have to agree that I was never here."

56

Georgia followed along, as usual, bringing up the end of the line. The line was now one person longer.

While she and Jesse were dressed in lighter khaki colors that tended to blend into the woods a little bit, Cathy was dressed in multicolored leggings and a bright t shirt. She talked about cadavers as if it were her usual conversation.

It sure hadn't been Georgia's until recently, though she reckoned she had more than the usual exposure to it given her father's job.

Cathy's offhand use of all the terminology and her conviction that she was leading them the right way—backtracking their steps a bit—gave Georgia pause. *Was Cathy the killer?*

She sure didn't look it, but how would she know where the bodies were buried unless she had buried them?

Georgia was left trusting Jesse, who had placed Cathy at the front of the line, in front of even Felony. Cathy could be leading them to certain death, but they were three on one—four if she counted Felony, and Felony looked like she would take a bitch if prompted. It also allowed them to keep a solid eye out. Cathy could not sneak up on them from the front.

The woman wasn't the fastest hiker. She was deliberate though she grumbled a little. Georgia felt that. She'd been hiking a lot of days recently.

Ian grumbled a little, too. He was not here to follow others, just his dog. But Jesse had pointed out that, first off, he was right: He knew what he was doing and Felony was an excellent hunter. But also, that *she* had hired *him*. She kept her voice low, but said if she wanted to follow Cathy, then that was what they should do.

She soothed the irritated man by reminding him they would put Felony to use once Cathy had done her part.

Felony had seemed to like Cathy just fine once she started moving. The dog followed right behind, her movements spry and curious, her head occasionally twitching and tipping to the side as if trying to figure out what was up with the woman.

Georgia wished her own sense of smell was better because she was having crazy thoughts. Option one was exactly as Jesse had suggested: Cathy had come into contact with a cadaver and Felony was smelling it on her. That one made the most sense.

The next option was that Cathy was a ghost. If Georgia hadn't seen the pictures of the missing woman, then she might have guessed that Cathy was actually Kyla Kasher—and the ghost was leading them to her own body. But Cathy was absolutely not in her mid-twenties with brown hair and a wide, beaming smile, earrings dangling almost to her shoulders, and lipstick bright enough to be a lighthouse signal.

Option three: Cathy was a zombie. Georgia almost liked this explanation best, because Felony was not trained to alert on ghosts but on decaying human flesh. *Zombie* would absolutely fit the bill. So Cathy was yet another dead body from somewhere in the woods who'd gotten up and was now helping to avenge other victims.

Georgia had to admit she'd checked out the woman surreptitiously. But there were no stab marks on Cathy's body.

No bruising around her neck. No obvious signs of murder. It was most likely the first option, but Cathy sure seemed convinced that she had not come in contact with any dead bodies.

Another thing that caught Georgia was that Cathy had startled Jesse. Who did that? Who managed to get a reaction from the ever-vigilant Jesse Nash? It made Georgia wonder why a person would be so sure of that.

Georgia understood that basic human confidence was way out of whack. People tended to be very confident about things that they had no business being confident about. They firmly believed in the false memories they carried. She'd taken a whole class in it, getting ready for law school, thinking she might want to be a trial lawyer.

But she'd taken her classes in interrogation through the FBI. Access she had via her father. Most lawyers were not trained by FBI investigators. But Georgia knew the stats and Cathy's confidence wasn't really the thing that got her.

It was the fact that she sounded *right*.

She was so lost in her thoughts about who and what Cathy might be that she almost bumped into Jesse who trailed Ian who trailed Felony. Cathy had stopped.

"Here," she said and motioned to her right.

"Off the trail?" Ian asked. Then he turned to Jesse and kept his voice low, but not low enough. "This is weird."

Jesse only shrugged, stepped around him, and then in front of Felony. Maybe working with Tinkerbell for several days had helped, because Jesse no longer seemed so skittish around the dogs.

Taking a spot next to Cathy, she motioned into the space Cathy had pointed to. "If you're willing, go ahead."

Georgia watched as Cathy stepped off the trail, ducking down under a branch. The arc was thin and green and cut across where they were needing to go.

Cathy handled it gingerly and said only, "Thorns," as though she had already known it was there.

Ian hung back, motioning each of the other two to go ahead of him. This time he and Felony would bring up the rear. Their pace slowed considerably. Being off trail was a lot more work than just following a well-worn path.

They stayed quiet, Cathy didn't seem to want to talk, and Georgia had nothing to add other than her zombie theory, and that was probably best kept to herself.

It wasn't too long before they reached a small clearing. She watched as Cathy paused, still in the trees, looking into the space in front of her. Though she couldn't see Cathy's face, only her back, somehow Georgia could tell this wasn't easy. Cathy was taking deep breaths, closing her eyes, and steeling herself for something, but there was nothing in the space.

Still when Cathy finally stepped into it, she visibly shuddered.

Something racked her body, though she obviously tried to fight it. Everyone saw it.

"Are you okay?" Jesse asked. Stepping forward, she put her hand on Cathy's shoulder.

Even as she saw Jesse reach out, Georgia thought *No!* That was not the right reaction. *Cathy doesn't like to be touched.*

But she couldn't even get the whole thought through her head, before Cathy had swung her arm back almost violently shaking Jesse away.

Jesse stumbled back but recognized the issue. "I'm so sorry," she said.

Cathy turned around, wide eyed, looking between the three of them as if she'd just seen a ghost. As if she'd forgotten they were there. Again, Georgia thought of her three theories of why Felony might have alerted on this woman.

They all watched as Cathy turned back to face the clearing. She sucked in a deep breath through her nose before stepping into the clearing. Whatever had made her react before was under control now. "Follow me."

She led them along a little almost-path. Something the animals used, Georgia guessed. Quickly, Cathy stopped and turned, and looked each of them in the eyes before saying, "I was never here."

She emphasized each word oddly and Georgia waited until Jesse nodded. Going along with her boss, Georgia nodded, too. If Jesse would deny the woman's existence, so would she.

When Cathy still stared, Jesse replied quickly and easily. "Of course. I will keep my word."

Georgia, when Cathy looked at her, nodded again in turn. Then Cathy looked to Ian, who still seemed confused and irritated. But his focus was on Felony who was now tugging at her leash, ready to run off.

He agreed quickly, as if he simply wanted to do what it took to get back to working with his dog.

With all three agreements in place, Cathy tipped her head in what Georgia took as a *thank you*, then visibly swallowed. Waving her hand in the same direction that Felony was trying to go, she offered, "Your dog is right. The body's over there. Just past those two trees. There's a fallen log. Felony looks like she can smell it already. It's overgrown with green vines, and one of the bushes has pink flowers."

Georgia felt her eyes go wide. What a concerning array of details Cathy had. Something about the description of the bushes nagged at her, but she couldn't put her finger on it and there wasn't time to suss it out.

"Thank you," Jesse said.

She seemed to be opening her mouth to say something more, but Felony barked. Ian made the executive decision to let the dog off the leash. It was clear he trusted Felony to stop when he told her, return when he told her, and not just go crazy.

Georgia believed him because Tinkerbell had been so obviously well trained. He was recommended by Marjorie, and Georgia trusted that. He was just not used to trusting a random hiker more than his dog.

"Felony." Ian was using his command voice, Georgia could tell now. "Find."

Georgia watched as he headed off after the dog and Jesse quickly stepped in to follow him. Georgia was falling into place at the back of the line again, this time moving as quickly as she could. They were all trying to keep up with Felony.

They were excited now, almost as pleased as the dog. Possibly at the end of their hunt. Georgia felt a rush of adrenaline that they might have found a body on their first day. What insane luck.

Though, was it really? They'd spent so long searching for any evidence of Hannalyn to only ever find a single wallet— that they knew. So maybe this wasn't luck, but more like Jesse said. They had a direction, and they could think like the killer.

She turned around to tell Cathy Bass *Thank you.*

But she stopped. Jesse and Ian were getting farther in front of her, but Georgia didn't move.

There was no one there to tell *Thank you* to. Cathy Bass was gone.

57

"It's three, Dad. It's enough." This was her father, she wanted to ask rather than demand. But she also didn't want to be on this case for a moment longer than she had to.

Jesse had let Georgia make the call—or maybe she had nudged Georgia into it. The phone was on speaker on the table in front of them, and Jesse had her case files out ready to refer to them as needed.

It had taken three days since they'd found the last body. Jesse had pushed and pushed and pushed and it wasn't official yet. But she'd done what she could, and they needed to hand off to the FBI.

"Is it official?" Owen Dunham asked.

Georgia hated to admit it. "No dad. Not yet. They sent the body to Chicago. The ME is backed up, but we did get a preliminary from the Forensic Odontologist."

"He says it's Kyla Kasher?"

"She," Georgia corrected. "Hannalyn Burkhardt has been positively identified too." Hannalyn's ID had come through just the day before. Then Jesse called last night and pushed the

Chicago odontologist to reveal the results before the full write up was turned in. Jesse was very convincing.

They'd almost been cooling their heels in the meantime, but not quite.

They did start by taking a whole day off after finding the body they believed was Kyla. Ian and Felony had hung out for half of the day, already paid for their work, but then Jesse had sent them home. They were on a plane and back in Washington already.

Jesse and Georgia had gone to a movie, eaten a nice dinner out and then hit a bookstore. Georgia had bought more books than she could possibly read here. But she'd opened a romance and started in. About halfway through she succumbed to sleep. Then she'd slept well past ten.

Just yesterday, Harriet Burkhardt had called. Georgia could hear the tears streaming down the woman's face as she had let them know that the body they'd found was in fact her daughter. Harriet had sniffled and her voice had cracked as she told the two women "Thank you. Thank you for finding my baby."

She'd gushed as if they'd brought back Hannalyn alive and whole. Georgia had not expected to be so heartbroken. Though she'd never been convinced Hannalyn was alive, she knew that Harriet had. The mother might not have fully believed it, or maybe she understood that the odds were not good. But she'd clearly clung to that last hope so tight.

This was not the outcome that she had prayed for.

Harriet was too emotional and hadn't told them anything other than that the medical examiner and the forensic anthropologist had identified the body as Hannalyn. She'd at least added, "I'll have the report sent over to you."

It had shown up by courier the next morning. The woman was heartbroken, but she got shit done. She was the one who'd found and hired Jesse in the first place.

Jesse had signed for and opened the report the previous

morning before Georgia had realized what was going on. Jesse had just pulled out the prints and said, "Oh, hell."

It hadn't taken much for Jesse to share. But she hadn't spoken the words, just silently handed over the papers. Hannalyn had been stabbed at least seven times in her torso. The nick marks on the ribs the team had eventually found indicated various points similar to the wounds suffered by Annabeth Green.

Jesse had used her reporter skills getting the Chicago ME to give them information about Kyla Kasher. But even with all that information, it didn't take up a lot of their time. Given that their days were freed up—they were no longer out in the woods searching—Jesse had turned her attention to finding the surviving Kashers.

Georgia, who'd been mostly wearing hiking gear and stretch pants for riding in the car had once again had to pull out her nicest clothes. It was the exact same outfit that she'd worn to visit the Burkhardt family. The Kashers wouldn't know that, and she didn't have alternatives.

As soon as Jesse told the mother that she had information about Kyla, they'd been given an address and met up within the hour. Invited into the home quickly and graciously, they'd been seated in the living room. Georgia realized that this could be a great scam to get people to let her into their house. The Kashers had opened their doors, no questions asked, their grief and worry at the wheel.

Jesse had led the conversation. Mrs. Kasher had raised her children alone. Kara, the oldest of the four kids—whose names all started with K—sat beside her mother. Both women were very nervous. Georgia understood. Their daughter and sister had been missing for a handful of years.

Kyla had vanished into thin air. She'd been with friends—not even alone or in any kind of dangerous place. She'd gone out to the car, and no one had heard from her again. There had been no evidence except the one shoe with the lone drop of blood.

"You don't know me," Jesse started softly. "But I'm a private investigator."

She was repeating things she'd said over the phone. Georgia wondered if the repetition was intended to soothe. Though it might make this discussion just a little bit easier, nothing was easy here. In fact, Jesse had even planned to let Georgia do part of the announcement.

It was her turn. Georgia tried to talk calmly and with confidence. "We were working on the case of another missing young woman . . ." She told them about Hannalyn, and it was clear that they had no idea who that was. But when she said how Hannalyn had gone to the bathroom one night and not come back, the women's spines had stiffened.

They didn't have to be investigators to understand. When Georgia added, "All they ever found was one of her shoes with two drops of her blood on it," it was clear that things had shifted.

Initially the Kasher women were curious, concerned if she and Jesse were going to ask them for their help. If they were going to try and conduct an interview of some kind. But they had clearly not expected that there would be another case so similar to Kyla's.

Georgia watched as the words sunk in and the women had frozen in their spots.

It was Kara who whispered into the now silent air, "You think it's the same person? That he's done this before?"

Georgia had felt her eyes fall closed now. Just like she had when Kara had asked the worst possible question. The one they had to say yes to.

Talking to her father, she had to convince him to take the case to the FBI. She had to convince him so he could convince them.

"Yes, Dad. It's three. We have your evidence for a serial."

"I want cold confirmation on Kyla Kasher," he said, and she almost laughed at the alliteration of it all.

"We'll have that in just a day or two, Dad. But here's the thing, when you and the analysts looked, you didn't find any cases that matched because you were looking at *murders*. I realize a string of missing persons—adults—isn't likely the FBI purview especially given that there was no real evidence of foul play." She sucked in a breath. "But we've been doing that legwork, Dad. We have these three murders, but we also have a series of cold cases that we think are connected."

"How many?" he asked.

"Six more," Georgia told him.

On the other end of the line, she heard her father utter a soft *fuck*. He'd been pretty good about not swearing when they were kids. Not brilliant at it, but pretty good. Now though, she understood the need.

He said, "Send me all the information again. With those new pieces and tied to proof of murder—Is there proof of *murder*?"

She almost rolled her eyes even though he couldn't see her. He had taught her better than that—there was rarely *proof* of anything. But he needed to know the deaths weren't accidents, or even just random homicides. "Jesse got the preliminary ID on Kyla, and there are also nick marks on her ribs consistent with stab wounds into the torso. So yeah, not only was she found in a way she almost could not have put herself before dying, it's got to be murder."

"All right. Send it over, I'll see who I can get interested."

Georgia breathed a sigh of relief. This had been the goal, maybe not from the beginning but certainly once they'd realized how big and horrible the case was. *They'd really stepped in it, hadn't they?*

With a massive sigh of relief, she told her father goodbye and that she loved him.

Jesse had raised one eyebrow, but it was her *father,* Georgia thought. It certainly couldn't be the usual sign off for handing over a serial killer to the FBI.

She looked to Jesse. "So, we get this together, and then we focus on finding Sin."

"Sure," Jesse answered.

Georgia could tell from the way she said the word that that wasn't what Jesse had intended.

58

They *could relax now,* or so Jesse told herself. It was, at least, the image she tried to project to Georgia, but she was pretty sure she wasn't fooling anyone.

They'd spent the morning doing the usual: trying to pull up any stories or find any evidence of the continued existence of one Cynthia Beller, the assassin known as Sin. As usual, they'd turned up nothing—nothing that bore anything more than passing relation to Sin's MO. Nothing that showed proof of life. Nothing they could use.

Georgia was frustrated. "We have to do something different!"

Jesse agreed but didn't know what that was. She'd simply said, "What? We're doing all the searches that we can. Do you have a better idea of where to start?"

Georgia opened her mouth as if to say, *maybe there was a place*—

But then she'd shut it just as quickly as she opened it. Jesse felt the twinge and pull that made her work the way she did. *There was something there.* Something Georgia wasn't telling her.

"*You're* supposed to have a better place to start," Georgia had countered instead. "I hired you to think of things I couldn't."

Jesse had played her card. "Unless you want to tell me whatever information you're holding back, Georgia, there's not much else I can do. You're asking me to find a person who has very, very few public records, and almost none of them past the age of seventeen."

She had seen Georgia's mouth snap shut when Jesse had accused her of holding back. But now the young woman's head tipped like she didn't understand. Jesse leaned forward. "What do you know of your mother's story?"

It was a loaded question, but she was curious. Not only what bits and pieces Georgia understood of Sin's past, but how she would tell the story. The things that people chose to reveal were often as telling as what they chose not to.

Georgia started slowly, her eyes glazed, telling a story from far somewhere in her memory. "She was ten. Her sister was twelve. Her parents were married, and they had a normal life. Then her parents were killed during a home invasion one night."

Not the whole story. Jesse already knew.

"My mother and her sister went into foster care in separate places," Georgia continued. Though her voice was steady, her hands fidgeted with various things around her. She played with the hem of her shirt and picked up one of the tchotchkes that the hotel left on the table as decoration. She turned it over as she added, "My mother's sister Wendy died in foster care at age sixteen."

Also, not the whole story. Jesse wondered where this was going. She didn't have any of the family gossip, just had the papers that she dug up on Cynthia and Gwendolyn Beller. But Georgia had to know that there was more to it than that. One did not simply just "become" Sin.

Georgia quit speaking after that, so Jesse filled in what she'd found. "Like you said, when you can't go forward, you go backward. Your mother bounced from foster home to foster home. She was considered violent, even then."

The younger woman nodded slowly, taking it in as if she hadn't heard it that way before. But that couldn't be news to her either.

"There are a couple of reports that survived." The documents were old, Jesse knew. It had taken a while to get clerks and archives curators to dig them up. Then they'd photocopied paper reports and sent that. Jesse probably should have told Georgia that she'd requested them.

A lot of them read about a thirteen- to fifteen-year-old girl who showed up to school with bruises. In a lot of cases, that was the thing that got her pulled from a foster home and pushed to the next one. There was plenty of evidence of abuse, even if it couldn't be connected to any particular abuser—for both girls. But no one had seen Cynthia Beller getting in fights at school for the most part. Except for one time.

Georgia just wanted to know where her mother was *now*. But where Sin had been was maybe just as important. Jesse hoped she could use that to get a better idea of where Sin might go if she were hiding. But the information had stopped abruptly a long time ago.

But just before that . . . "Gwendolyn's foster father died. He was the victim of a home invasion."

Jesse had chosen those words carefully, making the connection for Georgia, who tilted her head and said, "My mother would have been what? Just a teenager. Are you suggesting . . .?"

"I'm not suggesting anything," Jesse said, hands open wide, though surely by now, Georgia knew most—if not all—of her tricks. Because she *was* suggesting something.

"Maybe," Georgia said. "We know she's more than capable of that now. Was there a bow?"

"No. But she would have been young."

It was clear Georgia was struggling to put those pieces together. She clearly had intense feelings for the woman who gave birth to her. A woman she knew but hadn't grown up with. She had a sideline view into how the woman ran her life—which was more than just about anyone else.

Jesse found it interesting that she had known something Georgia Dunham didn't.

"How does that help us find her now?" Georgia pressed. "I need to know if she's alive. I mean—" Georgia cut herself off.

Once again, she was withholding something. To a very real extent, Jesse wanted to push to say, "I can't help if you don't tell me everything." But, on the other hand, she understood.

She and Georgia Dunham had just worked a case together. She liked Georgia and she wasn't quite willing to turn the screws on that yet. "Well, I don't have anything else right now on where she is. That's why I went backward," Jesse said. "If I can find a trajectory, maybe we can follow it."

"So what now?" Georgia asked again. "Do we each go home and keep looking or what?" She sucked in a breath, looking uncertain. "As far as our work is concerned, this case is closed, right? I mean, we have to send everything to my dad but—"

"But *one*," Jesse interrupted. "We don't go home yet. The FBI hasn't officially accepted the case. I'm not quite willing to close out until they do. I'll feel much better when there's an agent that I can talk to. I want to hand the files to someone specific along with all my suspicions."

Georgia nodded.

Then Jesse dropped something else. "And, *two*, while we wait for the FBI to get their ducks in a row, I think you and I need to figure out who the hell this Cathy Bass is."

59

C indy had squealed the tires as she turned into the driveway. She'd hit the brakes too hard, jolting herself to a stop. She'd barely turned the car off before she was out. Her feet pounded up the walkway and she threw open the front door.

She hadn't even closed it behind her. She had simply run down the hallway, toward Carter coming the other direction. As she flung herself into his arms, she let go of all the tension, or at least enough of it to breathe again. If the twin connection was enough to let her know how he was feeling when they were a thousand miles apart, then this was too much.

Now, as her brother held her tightly, she felt everything flooding him. All the worry and the concern and even a bit of pride. *God, she needed that.* She breathed in and out, in and out, and tried to let it all go.

"You did it," he said, the pride creeping into the tone. "I know you went out and I know you didn't want to go. And I know I pushed," he admitted. She could almost hear the *I'm sorry* lingering at the tip of his tongue, but he didn't let it escape.

Maybe he wasn't sorry.

"I know," he said next, "that you're stuck with this. There's nothing you can do about what you see."

To a certain extent, she understood what he meant. But to a certain extent, it wasn't true. There were things she *could do*. She could sit very quietly and not touch anything. She could turn off the news and remove all the triggers.

She must have been rambling because he said to her, "Even with all of that, even though you did all of that, it still got through this time. So maybe the strongest of it is going to get in anyway. You can't stop it, but you went out and you did something good with it."

Wow, she thought, stepping back and taking a good full deep breath. It was good to be home. It was good to hold her brother. It was good to breathe her own air and smell the scent of home even though she couldn't name it. Cindy could feel herself sink into the familiarity of it all.

"*Did* I do something good?" she asked. "These women were dead before now, but at least their families had hope—"

"They also had terror," Carter told her. He said it as if he were a therapist and he knew these things in no uncertain terms.

To an extent he *was* a therapist. He was certainly hers. He didn't stop. "They had the terror of the unknowing. And now they *know*."

"But what they know is awful. They know that their daughters suffered," Cindy said. Even though the families didn't know the extent of it, they now knew that their daughter's end was on the harshest end of the spectrum.

Cindy wasn't sure that she might not be the only one who did know the extent of what happened.

Well, her and the person who did it.

Carter was shaking his head at her. "Yeah," he said, but his head went side to side saying *no*. "It's bad, but knowing is good.

Now they can finally grieve. They've lived in limbo, some of them for a very long time, and now they can finally begin to get on with their lives."

Cindy understood. Families of the missing were stuck. They often wouldn't move from their home, regardless of lost jobs, dropped wages, even damage to the home. They wanted to stay in the same place in case their loved one returned.

Now, they could move, she thought. Maybe that should be meant a little more metaphorically than physically. Still, it seemed to all be various shades of bad.

"It was awful." She sighed out the words as if the rush of her breath would push the memories away.

"I know." But then he shifted the subject. "Do you want me to get your luggage?"

Another deep breath, she was thinking but not saying *I'm a big girl.* But her brother still followed her out to the car. He grabbed the suitcase while she picked out the wrappers and empty bottles to bring into the trash.

Carter, being the organized and efficient wizard that he was, pulled her suitcase straight to the laundry room and began sorting the pieces. He put most of it directly into the laundry for her. "Is there anything particular you want for dinner?"

She could tell from the waves coming off him that he was thinking maybe he would buy her takeout, something nice. But she said, "I want soup from the crock pot or rice and beans. Something like that."

He grinned, a smile that he could have used on many, many people well beyond this laundry room, beyond the borders of this house.

Carter was truly stunningly good looking. And it pissed her off. She had the same genes that he did, and it was not playing nearly as well on her. But he'd worked hard for every bit of it. Despite how wonderful that smile was he, too, was to a certain extent stuck within a radius of this house.

"I love you Carter," she said. "I can't thank you enough for everything."

He just grinned softly and offered up a line that he'd used on her a number of times before. "You really need to start charging for these services."

She laughed, knowing that it was a bit of a joke and also wondering for a brief flash of time, if she could. But how? She couldn't hold the job. She couldn't be counted on to show up regularly. What should she do? Get a private investigators license like Jesse Nash?

Cindy likely wouldn't qualify. There were a number of states where her name was recognized by the local officers. She was grateful that the economy and technology also allowed them not to have to work with the locals. But even here, she was afraid a police officer might recognize her name from a few cases when she was a teenager, before she understood that if she didn't police what she said, they would.

Carter pulled homemade soup from the freezer. Maybe he was psychic in ways she hadn't yet figured out. But she was grateful again. Cindy hadn't realized how hungry she was.

He had everything. He set up trays in front of the TV, brought out steaming bowls and they watched a comedy involving New York apartments that couldn't be afforded. It had ridiculously zany happenings with one liners and a laugh track.

Two episodes later, her bowl was empty, and she was suddenly so tired that Carter waved her to bed, saying only, "I'm so glad you're finally home. I'll take care of this."

She had stumbled into the room, falling into her own bed. Smelling her own sheets and feeling her own mattress hug her had knocked her out almost instantly. But then, somewhere around the middle of the night, one eye had slowly, groggily peeked open.

She'd smelled the rich dirt and felt the sticks, rocks, and roots under her hands. Her fingers were already raw, fingernails torn, several of them bloody. She smelled something odd when she breathed in, something that tingled in her mouth and wafted faintly into her lungs. She couldn't quite place it. But she knew it wasn't the most important thing . . .

Then she heard the voice.

"I see you're coming awake."

60

Georgia had continued searching for her mother while Jesse seemed to be on a tear to find Cathy Bass. They had promised that *she was never there.*

"Aren't you breaking your promise?" Georgia asked, sitting on the couch, her laptop open.

Jesse was up at the table, working separately. But she didn't agree. "No. I've told no one that she was there. I've talked to the ME. I've talked to police, and I told them all a big, hairy lie that it was just the three of us. When they asked if there was anybody else there, I said *Felony.* So, no. I have not broken our promise." Jesse paused. "She didn't say we couldn't find her."

That was true. "She was weird."

"The whole thing was weird," Jesse immediately agreed, though she hadn't taken her eyes off her screen and her fingers hadn't stopped flying. However she was trying to find Cathy, Georgia didn't know.

"Do you think she's the killer?" Georgia pushed next.

"I don't." The confidence of Jesse's tone was almost alarming.

Although Georgia's instinct agreed, she wasn't quite ready to go on her gut feelings alone. "Why don't you?"

"Physiology. Demeanor. Word choice." Jesse listed all her reasons.

"But all of that can change with surprising swiftness," Georgia responded, only then realizing that she'd just told Jesse she had knowledge of such things.

"You're right." Jesse either didn't catch or chose to ignore the reveal. "Demeanor can absolutely change. Even physiology can appear one way when it's actually another. But I'm still putting my money on it not being her. There was something to her tone and her words that said she didn't want to be there."

Jesse finally set her pen down, leaned back in her chair, and folded her arms, as if she were only just now thinking it all through.

"Why would she feel that way?" Georgia pushed. It was all here, whatever Jesse had concluded, but she wasn't putting it together herself. "Would a killer lead to evidence of their own crime?"

"Well, there's absolutely the issue of believing that they can't get caught, that they're ordained by some kind of God or higher power to do this work."

Georgia didn't like the idea of serial killings being referred to as "work."

Jesse continued. "But it's not a smart move. Cathy Bass did not strike me as a dumb woman. Secondly, killers tend to have one of two reactions to killing. Either complete shame that they've been compelled to do something so horrible—and maybe that they enjoyed it at the time—or pride. Cathy Bass wasn't close to either of those."

Georgia could acknowledge that, but . . . "It's not possible for a serial killer to have another reaction?"

"I'm sure it is. But the researchers don't see it. We have to admit that not seeing it doesn't mean it doesn't exist. It's possible there are other reactions and the killers who have those don't get caught."

That added up, Georgia thought. Either pride or shame could bring a person down, but another emotion might keep them safer. Still, it didn't fully support the gut reaction that Cathy Bass wasn't the killer.

Georgia tried again. "There was something that really bothered me that she said."

This time, Jesse leaned forward, finally interested in what it was that Georgia was wondering.

"It was just before she disappeared. She didn't even go see the body." Georgia realized now that that was true. "She directed us the last handful of feet and turned around and left and she told us exactly what we were looking for. And I can't figure out why that bothers me."

"Oh," Jesse said, the tone letting Georgia know that Jesse thought *that one's easy*, as if it were. "She described the way the body looks *now*. Not only now, but *right now*. Maybe only for a couple of weeks."

Georgia felt her features pull together as she frowned. *What was Jesse even saying?*

Jesse tried again. "She described the plant life over the body and how one of the plants was blooming pink."

Georgia caught it. *Yes.* That had been what bothered her. If she had been the killer—the one to put the body there in the first place—Cathy would have known what it looked like *a handful of years ago* when Kyla Kasher went missing. "She knew what it looked like right now. So she'd been back?"

Jesse didn't quite answer. "She seemed almost like she didn't know where she was going."

"But she's the one who led us there."

"Yes." Jesse sounded like she was still working her way through it all herself. "But she did it almost as if she had been *told* about it. Not as if she'd been there before."

"Some of it seemed she'd been there before," Georgia countered. It was hard to get a good grip on Cathy Bass. "There was a place where she stepped off of the trail and acted like she knew the spot."

Jesse agreed. "It was all very odd, which may be why I think it's not her. If it was you trying to cover up the murder, but you were also leading people to the body you stashed somewhere, would you act like that? I can't imagine putting together that particular group of tics and twitches."

That one Georgia could agree on. "But if Cathy Bass isn't the killer, then how does she know where the body is?"

"Maybe someone told her," Jesse declared. "Maybe she brushed up against the killer somewhere in time and they talked—"

"About murder?"

"Or it's someone she knows. Like maybe her brother." Jesse shrugged but oddly, as if that wasn't really the answer either.

"She has a brother?" Georgia asked, a grin on her face. Now Jesse was just making leaps.

"Yes, she does," Jesse grinned back. But her grin said she was right. "A twin brother."

That was oddly specific, so Georgia stood up and crossed the short distance to look at Jesse's screen, almost incredulous. *"You found her?"*

61

Georgia had been pestering her the whole way, but Jesse's mind was made up.

"We promised we wouldn't do this," Georgia said.

"No, we didn't," Jesse countered for the umpteenth time. It was almost like riding with a small kid asking, *Are we there yet? Are we there yet?*

Suddenly, Jesse missed Ciara more than she could even believe. That first road trip with Eugene they'd wound up with Ciara in the backseat. Not what Jesse had planned. Ciara had kept asking rambling, ridiculous questions the whole way. Not letting Jesse catch a single one of her own thoughts. It had driven her crazy, but by then she'd already loved the girl and it had been too late to shake the feeling.

Her day with Ciara was getting close, so she ignored the simultaneous damp and dry feeling at the back of her tongue. She ignored the twist in her chest, the pulling ache that wanted a whiskey or bourbon.

"We're violating her privacy," Georgia pointed out, thankfully pulling Jesse away from her sad thoughts and concerning urges.

"We violate everyone's right to privacy," Jesse said. It seemed like a rote enough answer, but it made Georgia throw her head back and laugh uproariously.

"I guess we do."

Wow. She had actually found the right answer to make Georgia stop protesting. She'd never found the right answer with Ciara.

When Georgia remained quiet for a while, Jesse found herself wishing that the younger woman might just keep asking questions. It was a bit of a drive. It appeared Cathy Bass, a.k.a Cindy Baker, had come a good distance to find that body.

There wasn't enough information on her to know if she was traveling for something else or not. Though Jesse had found no work records. Even very little about filing with the IRS.

Though Miss Cindy and her brother Carter Baker had filed their taxes on a very regular schedule, the money seemed to come and go in fits and starts. Jesse couldn't get more detail than that, but they didn't have bad credit or fail to pay their bills.

Jesse was very much looking forward to unraveling this mystery. She just had to get through these last few days. Then she had to get through whatever it was she might learn about Ciara. She sucked in a breath and held it for a moment.

"Okay," Georgia broke the silence again and this time Jesse was grateful. "How did you find her?"

Jesse faltered for a second.

"Because seriously, that wasn't even her name, which we suspected. We didn't know where she lived. All we had was our own memory of her face. We didn't even have a picture for any kind of facial recognition software. So, what did you do?"

Jesse had evaded some things in the past when Georgia had

asked, but now she needed the conversation. So she divulged some of her secrets.

"Search engines are wonderful. You just need to know what to put in."

"Yeah." Georgia clearly scoffed at the thought. "I put in Cathy Bass—with a C and a K. I put in blonde hair, Hazel eyes—"

"Yeah, none of that works." Jesse waved her away.

"Obviously," Georgia replied. "Because I'm sitting over here on exactly jack shit, while you've got her name, address, work history, and the fact that she has a twin brother."

That at least made Jesse grin. Georgia was smart for someone as young as she was. The "junior partner" had brought her A-game. Jesse had met a lot of full-fledged adults who didn't have Georgia's ability to connect pieces together or even to just stay on task and fulfill the work. It might be because Georgia was driven by her own set of demons.

"I first searched *local woman finds dead body.*"

"But it's so generic."

Jesse agreed. "There was a lot to sort through."

"And she's not local." Georgia added.

"How did you know that?" Jesse asked and waited for Georgia's nod that said they hadn't known that. Not until Jesse found her.

Georgia sounded defeated. "I looked up everything about Kyla Kasher. No one mentioned another woman, hiker, anyone who fit Cathy's description."

"Exactly." Then Jesse added. "My search yielded a whole bunch of articles and links. There were a lot I could weed out and some I couldn't. Some of them didn't have photographs of the person who found the body. A lot of them were nothing related."

Jesse kept her eyes on the road, one hand on the steering wheel, but the other was gesturing as though that made her words fit together better. "Like someone went out in the back-yard and there was a body in the swimming pool. That's not it. Or they were out for a jog. Or the body was an elderly person with dementia who died out in the elements."

"So you then narrow it down to *hiker finds dead body*."

"Bingo." Jesse put her finger on her nose. A gesture she used to do to Ciara that would make the girl smile. Quickly she pulled it away. Even that made her think about a shot of amber liquid and the warm burn down her throat.

She was lucky, she guessed. Some people had these thoughts and urges to drink all day, every day. Some people had them stronger than her. She could swallow hers. Wait them out.

Still, she could probably use a meeting. A sponsor wouldn't hurt either.

"What did you find with the hiker search?"

"I put hiker *woman*," Jesse said, as if to correct Georgia for a ridiculous mistake.

Georgia grinned, taking it the way it was intended.

"But again, it was so many links and articles and . . . So I did something a little off the beaten path."

"What?" Georgia asked, humor and trepidation warring in her tone.

"I looked up the guy who found Annabeth Green. I called him—"

"You *called* him? To ask what? If there was a curvy, blonde woman dressed in bright hiking gear who led him to the body?"

"Pretty much."

She could see Georgia shaking her head. It might be stupid and a long shot. But it had worked. "There was not that. However, there was a woman of *exactly* that description who was there when he found the body. She seemed very upset at where his dog was going before his dog got there. Then, I described Cathy the best I could—"

"And everything matched?" Georgia sounded incredulous.

"It did. She used a different name with him, but for us she even used the same initials. It's her. So we're going to go see Cindy Baker. I'm pretty sure she doesn't want to be found, but she showed up at two bodies on this case so far."

"And that's way too much," Georgia added.

Jesse couldn't help but feel a burning curiosity as to how Cindy Baker might have done it. She pointed to the map on the GPS. "We're only twenty minutes away. Time to get your game face on."

"But how did you find her real name?" Georgia was not putting her game face on.

But it was fun to watch the young woman's jaw drop when Jesse told her.

62

A knock came at the front door—a couple of sharp sounds.

Each rap made Cindy's anxiety spike. Even though she told herself it was probably Girl Scouts selling cookies or someone wanting to know if they could redo the roof or fix the gutters. She attempted to force some calm over her body and only partially succeeded.

In a moment, she heard Carter's footsteps, then the door click open. She stayed in the back room. The curtains were open. The days had been better since she'd come home, and Carter had fed her soup and she'd gotten to sleep in her own bed.

In fact, she even had a sense of pride. This fucker was going to go down. Enough of these women were found now. The articles said the local police were working with the federal authorities—though it didn't say who—to build a case between states.

Cindy had been reading up. The second body had belonged to Kyla Kasher. Her mother and sister had no compulsion against telling the local papers anything they believed would help them. First, they'd spilled everything needed to find Kyla.

Now they were gushing with everything that might lead to Kyla's killer.

Trying to ignore the voices at the front door wasn't working. Carter's came through clearly, the others not so much.

He'd first asked, "Can I help you?" Then there was pause.

She wasn't sure she heard the reply, but it sure sounded like, "We came to see Cindy Baker."

Oh hell no. There was something in the tone that seemed a little off.

"She's not available right now." Cindy could hear the forced smile in Carter's voice as he kept the hounds at bay. There were more things said, things she couldn't make out. She sat very still, focus straining.

She figured from the tone that this was important and they would probably leave their business card. Cindy knew she would look at it and not recognize the name because she rarely recognized names. *Oh, the irony.* She would throw it away. And if she was lucky, they would never come back.

But the conversation didn't seem to dwindle down to anything like that. She found herself standing and slowly sneaking out of the back room. Heading toward the hallway, she told herself not to, knowing that if she showed her face, they would know that Cindy Baker was, in fact, home.

Was there an angle where she could see them? Could she get into the living room and peek out the window? Wouldn't they spot her there?

She was going to try it anyway. Some burning desire, one she wasn't familiar with, drove her to do it. Usually, she had no curiosity. She could sit in her room and let Carter handle or mediate any or all details without her.

So why did she need to know this now?

In the dining room, she snuck around the table and through to the living area, up to the couch. She climbed on it like she had when she was a child pushing her face up to the window and trying to see through the sheers. Only this time she moved slowly and tried not to bump the window dressings. She didn't want to give herself away.

Two dark haired women stood on the porch. All Cindy could see was their backs, but it was enough to grab her curiosity. Enough to step forward, out into the hall.

Bless Carter, he never lied. He hadn't said she wasn't home. He had simply said she wasn't available right now. They were being pushy, she told herself. She could make them go away. But the drive was some weird, twisted, urge to *know*. One that she wasn't familiar with.

She never needed to know. She'd always had knowledge forced upon her. She needed it to go away.

Still, Cindy followed her urge once again. Pasting on a smile, she stepped behind her brother, thinking to say, "what can I help you with?" But she only got the first two words out before she pulled up short. Her back stiffened and her eyes flew wide.

These two.

She recognized them instantly. Even not in their hiking gear. There was no third with them. No tall, handsome, lanky, coffee-haired man with the dog that would have scared her if she didn't get such good vibes off it.

"Hello," the shorter one said, the same sleek black bob swinging in perfectly straight lines that made Cindy think it took a lot of work. "Jesse Nash, you might remember me. And this is my associate, Georgia Dunham."

Oh, Cindy remembered. "Why are you here?" she asked, unable to hide the desperation in her voice. She wished she could stay calm. She wished she could pretend that it wasn't her, that she could have been smart enough to say, "You must be looking for someone else who looks like me. My name is *Cindy Baker.*"

But from the look on Jesse Nash's face, she was taking none

of it. Georgia, on the other hand, looked as if she were surprised that Cindy was actually Cindy.

"Can we come in?" Jesse asked and then very quickly altered it. "Maybe you can come out. I just have a few questions."

Fuck, Cindy thought. The first guy had been a hiker out with his dog having a good day. But this woman, she was a private investigator, Cindy remembered. They'd been out with a *cadaver dog.* At the time she'd thought that was great. Less work for her.

Only now did it occur to her that Jesse Nash might be able to find *her,* too.

"No," Cindy said. "I don't want to talk."

She refused calmly and evenly, stepping back away, using Carter as a shield. As if his tall lean form could cover her. She likely looked like a bear thinking it was hiding behind a light post. And she didn't care. She needed this to go away.

They promised! she thought, feeling her mouth turn down, feeling the old hurts creep back in.

Georgia took a half step forward before realizing her mistake and how much that made Cindy visibly flinch.

Georgia stepped back.

Small graces, Cindy thought, still petrified of the two women.

Jesse spoke next, making Cindy's thoughts swirl as she tried to follow the conversation through the web of cold fear that had descended. "We've told no one."

Georgia agreed. "We promised and we haven't."

"In fact," Jesse added, the conversation pinging like a prize match of a game she didn't understand. "We've covered for you being there."

Cindy didn't know whether to be grateful or irritated. Grateful that they'd done as they said, or irritated—petrified— that they were here.

"Why are you here?" She blurted it, the words pushing out almost combatively.

"We're here because we hope you can help," Jesse said. Then the woman paused for a moment and the next words that came out of Jesse's mouth stunned her to her bones.

63

I know, Cindy thought. Everything inside her rebelled against her own very existence.

There were many things she'd been afraid of happening, but this hadn't been one of them, because it had never even occurred to her that *this* could really happen. She dreamed of the police coming after her with warrants and handcuffs. She dreamed of neighbors with pitchforks. She dreamed any number of scary scenarios, but a private investigator sitting in her own living room, telling her that she knew everything was not one that Cindy had expected.

She knew what the police had accused her of. They suspected she was part of the murders she told them about, involved in the cases somehow. At the very least, they figured she was harboring fugitives, that she knew exactly who these people were, what they were doing, and how they were committing their crimes. And that she was withholding evidence.

Jesus. That was the one thing she would never do!

While she might have a face or a voice, she rarely knew anything else about the perpetrator. Over the years, as all the technology had progressed, it hadn't been good enough for her to say, "I heard him say this" or "No, his voice is lower. His nose is longer" and have that be anything that the police could use to find anything or save anyone.

Everything she could do, even at her best, had never really quite been enough. Then to get accused of being part of the problem was too much. She'd just quit helping.

She was afraid of public knowledge because people had already written articles about her. She'd been on the suspect list. The police had come and staked out her home, making sure she wasn't sneaking out at night, committing more crimes. The irony, of course, was that she'd never committed any crime, only had one of the most heinous ones committed against her.

Psychologists had weighed in on some of the articles—without ever talking to *her,* of course. They suggested that her own trauma had pushed her to do this to other people.

Cindy had suffered a wide variety of scenarios where people came for her and accused her of all kinds of things. But she had not in her wildest dreams been ready for Jesse Nash to say, "I know what you can do," and then to have her basically nail it on the head.

Fucking private investigator, she thought.

Carter had invited them in! Her brother had said, let's hear them out. That made it even worse. But she couldn't fight them *and* Carter, so she sat on the couch, fingers twisting, brain screaming loud enough that she almost couldn't hear what anybody said.

She watched them talk, not really processing anything except for Georgia Dunham reaching out her hand, touching Jesse's arm. Then she leaned toward Cindy.

"Are you scared, Cindy?" she asked.

"Of course I am!" Cindy snapped back. It was a practically stupid question.

Practically, because honestly, anyone who hadn't lived her life couldn't possibly understand how bad it could get. When Georgia had asked the obvious follow up question, "Why?" it became clear to Cindy that no one understood. No one except Carter.

Her voice faltered and she was beyond grateful when Carter picked up the thread and explained the things that had happened in the past. But why was he trusting these two women with that information at all? It wasn't like him. Usually, he protected her, put himself in between her and whatever might be coming.

This time, he didn't. Instead, he'd invited the threat inside and offered it drinks and cookies. She couldn't process anything, including her own brother. She was stuck in her own maelstrom of emotions.

At least Georgia and Jesse sat quietly, listened to what Carter had to say about how they'd dealt with retaliation in the past. Whether they understood or not, they both nodded their heads like they did.

Cindy tried to breathe just a little bit. She wasn't certain she succeeded, but she had to go by the fact that she hadn't passed out yet.

Jesse turned her gaze directly to Cindy. "I have no intention of telling anyone what you can do."

Cindy almost barked a laugh. She managed to hold it in because she had heard that one before. Once again, it was Carter who stepped in. While he was explaining—and while Cindy appreciated that she didn't have to—she only thought about how the more Jesse Nash and Georgia Dunham knew, the more they would know what would hurt her and Carter the most.

What they decided now and what they decided to employ in the future could be radically different. She'd learned that hard lesson in the past, too. Carter was hopeful, he was being nice, but he was also handing these women weapons that they could use against her.

She didn't trust them not to, she couldn't.

Her own judgment in the past had been less than stellar. She'd had a boyfriend once, a man she'd loved and believed in. After one fight he'd been mad enough to sell her out to the press. He'd begged forgiveness afterwards, but it didn't matter. He could do it again the next time. As if trust hadn't been difficult before that, it was virtually impossible afterwards.

She put her hand out, reaching for her brother, her touch begging him to *just stop talking*. But he looked back at her as if he knew something she didn't.

Fuuuuck. She depended on him so much that, even if he didn't know anything, even if he just believed something and it turned out to be completely wrong, she needed to go along with this. She needed to give Carter his due.

"There's a serial killer out there," Jesse said solemnly. "But I think you already know that." She didn't wait for Cindy to say anything. "We've handed the case over to the FBI, finally giving them enough information to convince them it's actually a serial and not just an odd series of missing people with far too similar evidence."

Cindy just nodded. *What was she supposed to say to that?*

Then Jesse added, "Some of the evidence that we gave them is because you found Annabeth Green's body."

"I didn't—"

"Yes, you did," Jesse interrupted. "You were there. I talked to the hiker."

Cindy felt her body go rigid. How did Jesse know? Trying to swallow only showed that she couldn't. Whoever this Jesse was, she was good. Whatever this Jesse was, she could ruin Cindy's life.

Cindy quit listening. She began making plans. She could sell the house. She and Carter could move. But that wasn't good for Carter. Carter couldn't stay by himself though. If Cindy was outed, they would come to the house. And when they found out about Carter, they'd come after him, too. To think they would *bother* him would be far too slight for the things he'd already endured.

There was a pause and they all looked at her. Cindy had no idea what they'd asked, what they were waiting for. So she just said, "There's nothing I can do."

Jesse shook her head as if to say that wasn't true. Georgia looked to her partner, *Was it for guidance?*

"I think you can do everything," Jesse said. "I've read the articles and even the police reports."

Damn her. Cindy had figured that because no one had read them in a long time, no one would. Stupid mistake.

"I need you to do everything," Jesse leaned forward now. "Because Georgia here did some math, and the numbers are scary. If we don't move now, we might be finding someone else far too soon."

The whole room paused at the gravity of Jesse's words.

But then she added, "And we'll be finding a body, because I have no idea how to get in front of him."

64

W hatever nerves Cindy had had—and Georgia had seen a lot of them—the woman had transferred some of them into her and Jesse.

The two had left the small home, hopped back in their car, then driven only as far as a nearby parking lot and tried to figure out where to stay. Jesse hadn't wanted to sit in front of the house while they looked up nearby hotels and rates.

Georgia had asked how long they'd stay in town and Jesse only shrugged. "How long will it take Cindy Baker to decide to help us or not?"

It was clear Jesse was damned determined to make it happen, though Georgia wasn't confident it was the right thing to do. Cindy Baker seemed immoveable. Her fear controlled everything. Given the things Carter had told them, Georgia was relatively confident that the fear was well founded.

Cindy didn't play as irrational, not when Carter was there backing her up. He was clear all these things had actually happened, and they had happened because of Cindy's "talent." They had happened because Cindy had shared her talent and tried to help others. If there was one thing Georgia had learned from Jesse—and there was certainly more than one—right now she was taking away the point that people were always the heroes of their own stories.

Maybe that's what was happening with Cindy. Or not . . .

As they drove away, Georgia asked, "What if it's not perceived? What if it is real? People don't like people who are different. People don't even like when others tell the truth about something, especially if it's a truth they don't want to hear. In general, *people need therapy.*"

Her father had taught her that a long, long time ago. He could show up with evidence that the youth pastor was molesting children and oftentimes, even the parents of the children who'd been hurt didn't want to believe it. The amount of effort required to overcome the belief in a hero was massive.

Jesse hadn't had a ready answer.

They found a nearby hotel. This time, they rented a suite without question even though there had been no deals, no discounts. Jesse seemed tired of fighting to save the money.

Initially, Georgia could see it had been a case to her. But over time, it had turned into much more. This was where Jesse had excelled as an investigative reporter. Georgia had seen the old articles.

Now, not unpacked but with her bags placed in her own room, Georgia came back into the center space and asked, "What if Cindy has warped her story? What if she's not the hero?"

"Well, she's not a killer," Jesse said in response. "And that's why I want her."

"How do you know she's not a killer? How do you know the people who accused her all those years and all those times weren't right?"

"Because she was twelve when it started." Jesse answered casually, but with a confidence that told Georgia Jesse didn't just think this, she'd done the research. "Twelve-year-olds aren't out there abducting multiple people."

While Georgia agreed for the most part, she wouldn't say never. But Jesse was still going to do the research.

"Because when she initially started telling people what she saw, she was in middle school. She showed up to school every day. A lot of the crimes were committed away from where she was, and they were committed during times when lots of people saw her in another location. So 99.99% chance she's not the killer and that means . . ." Jesse added, looking Georgia dead in the eyes, "that she can actually do what it looks like she can do. It doesn't matter if she's built herself into a hero or not. We need her."

That math added up. "And it explains maybe why Felony alerted on her." Georgia asked the next question. "What if *I'm* wrong?"

"You're not."

Georgia pushed. Jesse had more faith in her numbers than she did. "But what if I am? We're browbeating this petrified woman into doing work that she says terrifies the shit out of her."

This time Jesse looked away. "I don't like it either. *I don't.* But what can you sleep with at night? Pushing Cindy Baker to help us or reading the article about the next woman he's killed?"

Georgia involuntarily sucked in a deep breath through her nose. *Fuck,* because Jesse was right. But Jesse wasn't done.

"Or," Jesse offered, "In a month from now, when you have a really good idea that he's done it again, but there are no articles and you don't know where to look for the next missing person . . . Can you just go to bed every night, knowing that he's done it and no one else knows?"

That knocked the air out of her lungs. "Let me do my math again."

"You don't have to," Jesse said. "It'll show the same thing."

Georgia turned away. She had to do it again. She laid out all the cases, wrote down all the dates by hand, even though she already had it digital. Maybe coming at it from another angle would catch anything she missed the first time.

There were two men included in the list now. Georgia believed they belonged there—there were too many similarities. And the dead bodies—Hannalyn, Annabeth, and Kyla—gave them the evidence that they were right. The lone shoe with the drop of blood was a calling card.

This killer wasn't limiting himself to women. Whatever the rubric was for his victims they hadn't figured it out yet. But if she accounted for multiple gaps in time, and figured that they missed more than just one, he was killing roughly every eighteen months. That conclusion depended on the assumption that they weren't missing *a lot* of people, which was entirely possible. Putting her finger on one of the cases had her reading the name again: Hiro Mizuki. If Hiro was the last one that he had taken, that was seventeen months ago.

Back out into the main room, Georgia looked at Jesse, who immediately replied, "It adds up the same, doesn't it?"

Of course it did, because Jesse already knew that.

"And that means," Jesse sighed heavily, the sound of a burden, "The next one's in a month. Unless, like you said, you're wrong and we've already missed it."

65

"They're doing something no one's ever done before," Carter argued. It was so rare for Carter to actually argue with vehemence that Cindy felt compelled to at least listen.

She had tried to listen when the two women were here, but the static and roaring in her head had blocked most of it out. Carter, ever vigilant, had seen, so when he told them to leave—that Cindy would make her decision and get back to them—he closed the door firmly behind them and left Cindy to herself.

But only for a while.

Without asking, he'd brought her a cheeseburger from her favorite restaurant and then he'd stepped away, letting her sit and stew in her own thoughts and fears. When he came back later, she realized he'd been plying her, and it had worked. She was calm enough to talk, though she still didn't like it.

"Even if they mean well," Cindy told him, "They can change their minds at any time. They can get mad at me. When they do, they will have everything they need to bring me down."

Carter had simply shrugged. "It's not like it hasn't happened before. We can survive it."

"Can we, though?" Cindy had looked him dead in the eyes. *She* might survive. It would be awful, but she wasn't quite so confident about Carter.

The problem was, as he liked to tell her, none of it was her decision. Him staying here with her. How he chose to live his life. That he helped her where he could. Those were his choices.

"What do you want?" she asked, trying to recognize his massive contribution to her wellbeing.

"I want you to do it." He was calm and steadfast.

Her eyes went wide. They'd spent so much time cloistered away in this house, just the two of them. They'd built a safe haven finally. "I want to stay here where it's safe."

"But it's not safe," he countered.

The doors were locked. There were blackout curtains. She had a TV she could turn on or off. It was the best control they could muster. He'd settled into the community and, to an extent, the people were letting him be himself.

He sat down now in her favorite chair, something he never did, always leaving it for her. He put his hands flat on his knees, his back a little too straight, head up but eyes down. "It's not safe," he said, "Things can go wrong at any time." He sucked in a breath as if to brace himself for a hard truth. "It's only safe for the moment that it's safe."

She didn't say anything.

Carter spoke again, this time the words gushed out. "It's not safe. You just left. You just went out and found two dead bodies because you are compelled to do so. And you will be compelled to do so again whether you're here or out there. You'll *have* to do it. Because, like you said the ghosts are going to haunt you until you set them free."

"But not you, Carter," she told him. "What about *you*?"

"It's the same. The ghosts that haunt me are different. Mostly, I'm just a ship at harbor."

She knew the old quote. Though he'd never said it to her before, she'd felt it brewing for a while.

"A ship at harbor is safe, but that is not what ships are for."

She felt the pressure at the back of her eyes as her lids dropped shut and the tears squeezed out the sides. Carter was here helping her, but it was hurting him.

"But ships at harbor *are* safe." She whispered the words into the otherwise stillness of the dark back room.

Beyond the window, the sun lit the grass in a startling shade of green. Birds played, probably chirping, though the walls and the glass kept the sound out. They stopped at the bird feeder that Carter had set up and somehow managed to let the seed get low. So unlike him.

Cindy tried to imagine the idyllic world of the backyard. The birds, the fountain, the squirrels fighting for space and food. The occasional lizard that wandered in and scuttled up the wooden fence.

Carter's voice broke through her little fantasy about existing in a non-human world. "But ships at Harbor aren't safe either. They're *safer* but they're not safe even there."

She felt it. The collapse inside her chest. The wilt of her shoulders. Her spine sagging in defeat. She had known this day was coming. For all that she saw and witnessed and lived, this had only been a looming sense of dread. She'd expected that it would happen to her, not that Carter would bring it and place it at her feet and tell her she had to do it.

She whispered once again. "You think I should go?"

"I think you have to."

66

J esse jolted from the knock at the hotel door. After a moment, and a small burst of adrenaline, she huffed out. "We don't want any housekeeping!"

Ridiculous, she thought. They should know not to work in here.

"It's me."

Jesse stood up so fast her laptop almost clattered to the ground. *That was Cindy Baker's voice.* Even as she caught her breath, Georgia's head popped out of the bedroom, where she'd disappeared earlier suggesting she could just take a nap for a while. Jesse had almost laughed at that but hadn't wanted to stop her from believing.

Georgia managed to get to the door before her and throw it open.

Cindy stood, almost unmoving. She looked much like she had the day before—black leggings, long t shirt. This time she wore a little makeup, and her hair was pulled back. Not in the utilitarian ponytail from the woods, but more to say she had tried.

Jesse waited while Georgia went through the formalities of

welcoming the woman inside and thanking her for coming. It sounded like a done deal, but there was every possibility—Jesse knew—that Cindy had come to refuse in no uncertain terms. That she was here to hammer her point home and make sure that Jesse—always willing to push when she felt the need for it—did not show up at her door again.

Cindy didn't speak. Georgia led her inside, closed the door behind them and pulled out one of the padded chairs for her. Cindy took it, but still said nothing. She made no gestures, as if she was waiting for something to happen.

When Georgia took the seat beside her, Jesse finally found her legs and moved. Only when she was seated, did Cindy begin to speak.

"I don't want to do this," she said.

Fuck, Jesse thought, though she wanted to push more, Georgia was right. As much as Jesse did not want to go to bed at night, thinking that this man was out there and he was about to do it again, neither could she build her own peace on Cindy Baker's obvious terror.

Silence hung around the table for a moment. Jesse was opening her mouth to say, "I understand," to let Cindy know that she would stop hounding the woman. But Cindy beat her to the words.

"But I'm going to do it anyway."

Jesse felt her eyes fly wide and hoped she did a better job of covering it than Georgia did.

She could see Georgia's immediate intention to grab Cindy's hand and say, "that's wonderful. We're so excited to have you." But Jesse was grateful that Cindy was looking down at the surface of the table, and she cut her eyes sharply to Georgia, telling her *no*.

Luckily, the younger woman caught the gesture and restrained herself, because Cindy saying yes wasn't quite enough.

"What made you change your mind?" Jesse asked softly.

This time Cindy looked up. She waved her hands palm up as if to say she didn't know but what she said was, "Carter."

"Your brother?"

"He's the one who talked me into it. But I'm not doing it because he wants me to, I'm doing it because he made valid points."

Needing Cindy to be here for the right reasons, Jesse let the declaration settle before she asked, "And what are those?"

Jesse was pretty convinced Cindy could just drop them some information and leave and still be a help. But right now, she wanted to take this opportunity to make sure that Cindy was grounded. The more Jesse knew about why she had done it, the better she might be able to help later . . . or steer.

She didn't like to think about manipulating people that way. But she had to play to the end game. That was what she had to stay focused on, even if Cindy was delicate.

"You ran into me, and so did the other hiker, because I've been seeing this . . ." She waved her hand to indicate whatever she saw. "I had to follow it."

Jesse listened, still motioning subtly for Georgia to hang back as Cindy explained how she stayed locked in her house most days, how she was unable to hold a job because of the things she saw, and how she was compelled to find the two bodies—the women who turned out to be Annabeth Green and Kyla Kasher.

"It's a good system," Jesse said, then explained when both Georgia and Cindy looked confused. "You lead people to the bodies and then you disappear."

Cindy looked her dead in the eyes, a new woman in her place, no longer the timid soul plagued by visions. "You said it yourself. You found me. You figured out what I can do, and you've read about what happens when I'm identified."

That was true, Jesse thought, the articles had been cruel.

She couldn't imagine what things had been said to Cindy's or Carter's faces. Things that didn't get recorded.

"I have this . . ." Cindy reached into the large bag that had been slung almost unobtrusively over her shoulder when she came in. She pulled out two stacks of papers, bound with clips. "Carter and I whipped this up. He has enough training in business contracts that it will hold up in court. And I will sue the ever loving fuck out of either or both of you if you ever reveal me."

Jesse was surprised by the vehemence, but it told her this had happened before. It wasn't just the reporters and angry citizens that had come after her, but a bone deep betrayal by someone she had trusted.

Cindy looked at her again and then looked at Georgia. "Carter convinced me that I should do this. But this—" She tapped the stapled stack of papers in front of her, each several pages deep. "This is what made me believe that I could."

"You've had people turn on you before." Georgia's voice came just before Jesse could reassure Cindy that it wouldn't be them. *But could she speak for Georgia?*

Cindy replied, "I'm hoping that this will make you think twice, if you ever decide that you're mad at me, or don't like how a case came out, or think that my information was false."

"Do you give false information?" Jesse asked too quickly. She shouldn't have asked it. It was too harsh.

Cindy in the woods had seemed a delicate creature, but fragile Cindy was gone. This woman looked her square in the face and said, "No, I don't."

67

Georgia tried not to squirm in the silence of the car. This wasn't the comfortable silence that she and Jesse had developed. Now Cindy Baker sat in the backseat, staring out the window and not only not contributing to the conversation but somehow managing to shut it down with her very presence.

Georgia wasn't sure she felt like talking herself. Somehow the three of them had wound up on their way to a town just outside of Louisville, across the state line in Indiana.

In her wildest dreams, Georgia imagined that Cindy could name this person and point her finger at him. In Georgia's more realistic dreams, Cindy gave them enough information that Jesse could find him. Jesse had, after all, found Cathy Bass, aka Cindy Baker—who was basically a needle in a haystack. And she'd done it without even a proper name and no photograph.

But, as Jesse had pointed out—after they'd signed the papers and Cindy had gone home to pack for the trip—there was no good search for "man murders woman." It brought up enough articles and police reports to keep your stomach from turning. There was no way to sort it all.

Georgia thought she might be clever and searched for "local man suspected of weird behavior." She'd been typing it even as she jokingly said it. But Jesse almost leapt out of her chair, like she was stopping a child searching something that would turn out pornographic.

She'd even yelled, "Don't!"

But it was too late. Georgia's head had snapped back at the quantity of information pouring in. Even just the headlines made her lips curl back. She clicked the button to erase it all. "Apologies," she breathed out to Jesse.

"You only did it to yourself." After a heartbeat, she added, "I think we all have done it to ourselves at one point or another."

That at least made Georgia feel better. Maybe she wasn't the only idiot.

Though Georgia had begun to think her boss/partner could find anyone anytime, Jesse explained. "I could find Cindy Baker because she spent a good portion of her life not knowing she should cover her tracks. In fact, I found a couple of women like her around the US. Then, I pulled associated images. That one looked like her."

That made sense, though it hadn't occurred to Georgia before that Cindy wasn't the only one Jesse had found. "Are you amassing an army of psychics to go to in future cases?"

Jesse shook her head. "Three years ago, I would have told you that psychics don't exist. And I never would have called Cindy Baker. I would have been on the team calling the cops to have her arrested for knowing too much."

"What changed?"

"A wild and crazy case in Florida. It came to my back door, and I have to tell you of all the things I *saw* on that case, I only believe a third of it. And I'm confident I didn't see the half of it."

Georgia had smiled and laughed. And Cindy Baker had come back the next morning, bag in hand, telling them they were aiming toward northern Kentucky.

Before they were even in the car, Jesse had asked Cindy, "Any luck?"

They'd agreed before Cindy left the night before that she would spend her evening trying to see his face. To do more than hear his voice. See if she could get a name.

Cindy shook her head and, aside from a few comments about logistics, the conversation had stopped dead. Georgia felt she understood better today than yesterday the kinds of things Cindy went through. No wonder she was so reluctant. The information that she'd given them had gushed out as soon as they'd signed the papers, which Georgia and Jesse had both done willingly.

They heard about him drugging his victims and transporting them into the woods. About stealing their shoes, holding onto the pair as a trophy while the victim was still alive. He stripped them of any useful clothing or weapons, and then let them run until he could kill them.

They were always at a disadvantage, coming off being drugged. As far as Cindy knew, no one had ever gotten away. Apparently, he considered this something to do on a reasonably regular basis. Kind of the same way that hunters waited for hunting season to open.

"He likes spring and fall for the weather. He likes the nights to be a little colder so it's less likely they'll run into anyone on the trails." Then Cindy paused. "He did murder one couple out on a trail, because they caught him in action."

Georgia absorbed that, but it still hadn't sunk fully in. It moved into her system like a bad drug, hitting her organs in fits and starts.

The couple had been found just after Jasper Covington had gone missing. Jasper was on Jesse and Georgia's list, having disappeared from a Louisville nightclub, and the couple had died while hiking in Harrison-Crawford State Forest in Indiana. No one had made the connection.

That's where they were headed. Several hours into the ride, the conversation long since cold, her thoughts having grown stagnant, Georgia looked to Jesse with a legitimate question. "Why are we here?"

Jesse looked at her oddly. "Do you mean philosophically?"

Georgia fought the wry grin. "*No*. I thought we had decided that we were done with the case when we handed it over to the FBI. The whole point was that this is a serial killer. We did we hand it over, soo why are we still working it?"

Jesse's eyes changed as she caught Georgia's meaning. There was something small and tight that made Georgia realize she had stepped into something—maybe something Jesse didn't want to say with Cindy here. It seemed Cindy was the crux of why they were going.

"Because you did the math," Jesse said clearly.

Lovely, Georgia thought. It was somehow on her.

"Because you realized he's going to hit again in another month and the FBI doesn't know that."

"They *do* know. I told my father."

"No," Jesse countered, conviction clear. "The FBI knows *you* believe it. Until they pull all the cases for themselves and do all the math and come to a similar conclusion, they don't know it."

Fuck. Georgia knew about early days in a case like this with no imminent threat. It likely wasn't a priority for anyone, not yet. It wouldn't be until maybe they found another body and whether that was a fresh one.

"Also, I found Cindy," Jesse added. "Those two things, they tell me something very important: We can do what the FBI can't."

While Georgia fully agreed, the very thought made her blood run cold.

68

J esse stood at the edge of the parking lot where the gravel met the grass, as they headed into yet another State Park. *Definitely a pattern.* One that they had identified before Cindy Baker said so, but Cindy had led them to this park. This place with its early morning fog that had yet to burn off.

Cindy had said, in no uncertain terms, that she didn't give false information. She had occasionally mixed things up, because everything she spoke had to get filtered through her own beliefs. At one point, she had said one victim was one thing and they were a different victim. Something like that.

Jesse took that at face value. She had to admit her own experience with Cindy Baker had been unnerving, and bullseye sharp. She was hoping Cindy could repeat her success here and that would be enough to convince the FBI of the ticking clock.

It had taken a full day to get here. They knew there would be another murder soon. At least, she believed that. That had come from Georgia's math, and not Cindy. It was an ugly kind of thing that would keep her from sleeping.

"Shouldn't we have a cadaver dog?" Georgia asked.

"I wish," Jesse replied, "but I can't hit the Burkhardts for any more. They've already given enough, and we told them we handed the case over."

True, but it hurt.

"Ouch." Georgia clearly agreed.

This was now coming entirely out of her own pocket. But when she'd asked Georgia the question of what she could sleep with, she'd suspected Georgia's answer. More importantly, she'd already known her own.

Her daughter had lost her father in a brutal way. Jesse had been there for it. That was well after Ciara's mother had been hauled away multiple times, and finally declared unfit, given her rampant drug use. Which had sometimes happened in front of Ciara.

Jesse, used to a deep and burning need to solve the puzzle, was now completely unable to set this down—to let one more family lose. Not if she could help it.

"You don't need a cadaver dog." Cindy's voice came from behind them. She joined the conversations so infrequently that it was always a surprise when she did. In fact, this might be the first time she'd truly spoken up, not just answered a direct question.

The night before, Jesse had insisted that they carboload for the hike today. They ordered in and looked over the maps, figured out where they were going. Even though her own gut told her that speed was of the essence, She'd insisted they all take it easy for the evening and just make plans. They needed the rest.

"Here," Cindy had pointed on a paper map that she made Jesse provide. "This is where he lived. This is where he disappeared from. Somewhere like right here—" she pointed to a third spot. "That's where we'll find him."

Jesse had leaned back and looked at Georgia. Something in

the younger woman's expression said she understood the weight of trusting Cindy. Cindy who—if it came down to it—was never here.

They all knew Jasper Covington had spent his last evening at a very busy restaurant with friends. There was a long wait out the front door, but they'd eventually gotten a table and made it all the way to dessert before Jasper said he needed to take a call.

The three looked at the map as if it might tell them more. Georgia put her finger down, touching and moving, tracing the places that Cindy had pointed out. "Does he always operate across state lines?"

Jesse had felt her eyes fly wide.

"He does," Cindy said, seeming surprised at her own answer. As if Georgia's words had knocked something loose off the bookshelf in her brain.

"Big cities," Georgia murmured then corrected herself, "Well, big enough. And the people he takes actually live on the other side of the state line."

Jesse had leaned back, her mouth open, only then realizing the implications. "It's a smart move. It makes him that much harder to track. There's no local jurisdiction where the police report is filed—where the person went missing—and also where the family reports it. They're not even in the same *state*. It's a guarantee that the jurisdictions are going to have difficulty speaking to each other. They may never connect to having the same person."

Georgia had frowned at her. "But the person was reported missing."

"Usually by the family, and often—like Hannalyn—it looks like they just walked away. There's no need to search past state lines."

Jesse looked into the woods now, a calm dread settling into her bones. This case was already seven years old.

What Cindy said now, as they lined up, ready to begin was, "A seven year old case means the body is skeletonized. It'll likely be the same way I found Kyla."

"The same way we found Hannalyn," Georgia murmured. Cindy nodded though they never looked at each other.

"It's how he does it. He's confident that the bodies won't be found. Even if they are, they won't lead back to him."

"What does finding a skeleton get us, though? Don't we need a fresher body?" Georgia asked as if they might just turn around and go back. She'd signed on for research. To find her birth mother. She wanted to go to law school, not hunt murder victims in the woods.

"That would be great," Cindy acknowledged, "more evidence, more detail. But I don't know where that fresher body is." She turned immediately, as if to check the parking lot, be sure no one had overheard.

The fog was just pulling back through the trees and if Jesse believed in fiction, she would have called it foreshadowing. It was only as she looked at Cindy then, and took in the woman's resolve, that she realized Cindy had no formal training in any of this. Only what she'd picked up along the way, things that she'd been unlucky enough to bear witness to.

"But this is the one that we have," Cindy declared. "This is the one that I saw."

"We find it, we hand it over to the FBI," Jesse said, "it will speed up the case if nothing else. It will give us more information."

"Yes." Cindy looked back and forth between the other two. "This time, before we call anyone to remove the body. I need to touch it."

69

Georgia couldn't think of anything more horrifying than Cindy needing to touch the body. She hoped it would be enough though. Enough to see the killer's face, to get any kind of information that would tell them where he was. Or who.

But they trekked deeper into the woods and Cindy didn't talk. Georgia drank her energy drink and ate her granola bars, wishing she could feel more of the bowl of pasta Jesse had insisted on last night.

She was used to being a college student, and while she would consider herself reasonably active, she wasn't on any athletic team. She didn't regularly work out or canoe or run steps, though she did it once in a while, and sometimes she played beach volleyball down in the little sand pits at a school that definitively did not have a beach.

Mostly, she studied and she kept up her A's. She made sure that everything stuck with her. In their house, it wasn't enough to learn it for the exam. She'd watched over the years as her father, working a case, would pull out some random fact he'd learned a decade earlier. She knew the value of things sticking could mean life and death for others.

She'd agreed with everything Jesse said, but she hadn't asked yet about the hole in Jesse's plan. The gaping, concerning hole when they handed this case over to the FBI.

They were in the middle of the woods. Not much to do. Cindy wasn't talking, just leading the way and Georgia needed the answer. "How do we tell the FBI that we just found this body in a different state? A missing person from a different timeframe than the murders we were already looking at?"

Jasper Covington had been one of the cases they set aside as "maybe." Not one they'd handed over. That information had needed to be airtight.

Jesse turned around and looked at her. "I was hoping they would just believe it was our stunning investigative prowess."

"It kind of seemed, when we were talking to my dad, that when we handed the case over we were done."

"We *are* done," Jesse countered, though this looked a hell of a lot different than *done*. "The Burkhardts are no longer paying us."

Georgia felt the flinch under her tone though Jesse had tossed it off as if it were of no consequence. Georgia knew it wasn't.

Cindy stopped then and turned around. Georgia raised her hands, palm out to the woman as if to say *stop*. "We won't tell them about you. We promised."

Cindy nodded. "What do you tell them, then?"

"This isn't a case that we had already handed over to them," Jesse said. But it was clear from the tone in her voice that she was spitballing. This wasn't a problem she had already solved.

"Georgia figured out about the state lines thing," Cindy prompted. "You had the missing persons report. It's a legitimate claim that this is your discovery."

Georgia nodded, but . . . "Finding the body . . . it's a needle in a haystack."

But Cindy was the compass pulled directly toward the needle.

The conversation lagged then with no good solution. They walked a little further, each of their brains churning for what was the best way to tell the police that they had not simply stumbled upon *another* body, going directly to it, but without a psychic guiding them.

When they shared that information, Georgia knew the FBI would use it to go find the other bodies. To look at other cases that might now match. As Jesse had said, it would take them a while to get rolling. She didn't know yet if her father had even managed to get the case assigned to an agent or maybe an analyst yet. Jesse had not gotten her wish of putting it into a particular set of hands.

Ahead of her, Cindy walked with determination. She shook her head occasionally as if trying to shake off a bug Georgia couldn't see.

The third or fourth time she did it in a row, Georgia realized it was seriously irritating only Cindy. There weren't any bugs around. The women were all doused in repellent.

"Cindy?" she asked softly.

But the other woman didn't answer. Just kept walking forward, which Georgia now realized was occurring more mechanically than naturally.

She tapped Jesse on the arm and waited until Jesse looked back. She mouthed the words, "Do we touch her? Or is that bad?"

They were out here with a woman who suffered visions and they didn't know what to do. Once again things they should have decided before they came out.

Jesse didn't get to answer.

Cindy jolted. Her shoulders arched back, arms flailed, head

tipped straight up. This time when she shook her head it was more like she was coming back to herself.

"Are you okay?" Georgia asked at full volume, still not willing to reach out and touch. Cindy hadn't reacted well in the first place and now it might be actually dangerous.

"I am," Cindy said. She turned around, eyes wide. Whatever the spell was, it was broken. "I know what to tell the FBI about how you found the body."

70

"It's not here!" Cindy declared in surprise.

Georgia stopped dead a few feet away. Even she felt Cindy's distress.

Cindy focused on the spot in front of her, the fallen log, covered in brush, much of which had died here. She pulled back naked branches and looked again.

Odd, Georgia thought. *Weren't bodies supposed to fertilize the land and make it green and lush?* Her mind had been going fifty other directions, thinking about what they were going to do when they found Jasper Covington.

Instead, they weren't finding him.

She looked to Jesse, but Jesse didn't look back. She stared at Cindy, crouched down along the log, searching frantically, seeming to forget all her concern for not leaving her own evidence behind.

Georgia could see it on Jesse's face, she was rethinking Cindy's conviction. *Was Cindy just wrong this time?*

"It's here," Cindy declared.

"You see something?" Georgia asked, stepping forward as hope filtered slowly back in.

"No, I don't." *Crap.* "But I *know* it's here. This is the place." She stood up, turned slowly around, looking everywhere.

If Georgia hadn't understood the gravity of the situation, she could have laughed. Cindy was wearing neon-colored leggings and a tie dyed shirt along with what looked like a high school backpack. She and Jesse had things that looked more like workout gear, but clearly no one here was a seasoned hiker.

Her own clothing was shades of pink and gray, while Jesse had on a red top. Both of them operated under what Georgia assumed was the same fear: that should they fall and hit their head, they had to be bright enough to be found.

After two full rotations, Cindy squatted back down and huffed out her breath. At least she had her gloves on. She duck-walked to one end, peeling back the branches as she went, peering underneath, getting down on her hands and knees.

Georgia moved forward, her thoughts leading her body to say something. Jesse, reading her cleanly, reached out to stop her.

Georgia wanted to blurt out, "Hey, you're leaving evidence all over the place!" It might not be fingerprints. But she was leaving knee prints in the dirt, clear handprints where she'd knelt down and put her head close to the dirt to look up under the log. It was evidence that they hadn't just 'found' the body but that someone knew *exactly* where to look.

But Jesse grabbed Georgia's upper arm as if to pull her back, but more likely to stop her mouth from running. So Georgia just watched as Cindy scrambled to the other end of the log. Then she crawled the last few paces, lifted the branch and looked. She then pulled out her phone and used the flashlight on it.

Though Georgia could only see the back of her head, the frown on her face was obvious. This time, Jesse did look to Georgia and mouthed the words, "Give her a minute."

"It's here," Cindy said. Only this time Georgia didn't try to ask, didn't hope. It might just be the conviction speaking again.

Reaching in, Cindy blindly felt around, which Georgia thought was a supremely bad idea. Spiders, snakes? Even just thorns. But the tightening of Jesse's fingers into her upper arm told her again to stay silent.

At last, Cindy pulled something out and awkwardly rose to her feet as she held the piece in both of her hands. Dirt was piled on it. It was scoop shaped, smaller than a saucer. Cindy gazed down at it, examining what she held as if unsure of it.

Then she looked up at Georgia and Jesse. "Animals got to it."

Just like he wanted, Georgia thought. Either the bodies weren't found, or they were discovered by animals. Either of which was acceptable to him.

Cindy nodded. "This is it."

What *it* was, Georgia wasn't sure, but Jesse nodded at Cindy, saying *go ahead.*

Skull, Georgia realized and recoiled a little, the only thing she could think for something that size and shape. It was hard to tell with all the dirt on it.

She and Jesse stood still, barely breathing, only watching as Cindy peeled one of her gloves.

71

I t had been difficult to watch Cindy as she had touched the piece of skull. Though Jesse had doubted what it was, the moment Cindy's fingers contacted it, the doubt fled.

If the woman was acting, she deserved an Oscar. In fact, she deserved for a lot of the current Oscar winners to simply hand over their trophies to her. Her entire body tensed, her mouth fell open, her eyes glazed, as if she were no longer seeing things around her but some entirely different world.

Then she'd stood still. So still, with one blue-gloved hand holding the piece. Only her bare fingertips moved, slowly tracing whatever internal grooves she could feel. Her mouth started moving slowly, but no words came. As if she were unable to put human voice to what she saw.

Jesse's heart ached. Cindy had been clear from the start that she did not like what she could do. It was not something she had chosen, but something thrust on her. Something she would have gotten rid of if she could. It was clear that she didn't want to come along on the trip, but she was here because she felt she needed to be.

Jesse couldn't imagine seeing horror like this and only

being able to clear it with more horror—which seemed to be what had to happen. Cindy could have stayed home, sat in her room with the door closed and the curtains pulled, not even looking at the birds and the bird feeder in the backyard. Cindy had been almost poetic about the view she and her brother had built and fenced in, shutting out the world.

But even with every possible trigger shot away, it always still found her. Because once the first thread attached, she was part of the web.

Jesse could believe there was some kind of invisible web connecting people. She'd thought all along there were rare instances of unexplainable human connection, like when mothers knew—*just knew*—their child was in danger.

At the time, she'd written off Agent Eleri Eames' ability to be in the right place at the right time as good detective work. But later, Jesse suspected she'd been willfully ignoring the agents' alternative skills. Even so, she always figured one day science would find the connection.

As of right now, it was a theory at best. At worst, straight up woo. With Cindy here, she was much more ready to believe that those threads existed.

They had to be more like what Cindy suggested: that the threads were *forged*. Jesse thought whoever this killer was he was the connection between all his victims. The center of a web most people couldn't see at all. But Cindy could *read* it.

Eventually, Georgia jolted forward, reaching out and touching Cindy. Just as quickly she pulled her hand back. The spell was broken. Jesse had wanted to yell, *no, don't do it!* Though she agreed that maybe it was time to break whatever was holding Cindy so tightly.

Cindy looked at them, finally in the real world and said, "I'll tell you what I saw, later. After the police clear the scene. It'll make your lies easier to manage."

Jesse agreed. She already knew things she shouldn't. It would be hard enough to explain why she was here.

Cindy set the skull down with as much reverence as could be granted in the off-trail clearing where they stood. Then she walked Jesse and Georgia through the steps. "Put on a pair of gloves. Now, get down and look under the log like I did."

"I wondered," Georgia said even as she got down on her hands and knees, checking around the dirt. "I thought you were leaving a lot of signs behind."

Cindy even had Jesse pick up the skull. A bolt of fear lanced her chest before she even touched it, petrified that maybe she would see what Cindy had. It struck her then how much she did believe in Cindy Baker and what she could do.

So far, Cindy had not given them false information. But she was petrified that she might touch Jasper Covington's skull and experience the terror of it for herself.

No, thank you. She was more than content being her own dull, normal person.

Reverently, she set the skull aside for the police. Then she and Georgia pulled off the dirty gloves and set them aside, too. Lastly, Jesse fished out her car keys and handed them to Cindy, telling her they would call for a pickup or get the police to drive them.

Jesse knew that was likely hours away.

After Cindy disappeared from sight, they pulled out their phones and tried to get a signal. Of course, it wasn't much, and the calls kept dropping. They headed back toward the main trail until, at last, Georgia managed to get through.

Hopefully, they'd left no evidence of Cindy behind. Then, it was time to wait and see if they'd pulled it off.

"Eat and drink a whole bottle of water," Jesse had practically commanded it.

"I'm not hungry." Georgia brushed her off. Understandable. Jesse wasn't either. If there was anything that would make her not be hungry, finding human bodies was definitely on the list. "It doesn't matter. The police are going to be here for quite a while. We're going to plausibly go a long time without eating."

Georgia nodded and ate while they waited. They had minor conversations, keeping an ear out, until eventually two officers showed up. The way they were chatting and hiking up the trail in their street shoes and police uniforms let Jesse know they didn't take any of this seriously.

On the one hand, it made her mad and on the other she did understand it. How many times did they get a call that someone had found human bones and they were probably from a deer?

She and Georgia waited while the officer snapped pictures and sent his report in. He casually brushed the dirt from the skull, turning it over and handling it without the respect Jasper Covington deserved. These officers had not seen what that piece of bone had done to Cindy Baker.

Eventually they decided that it was, in fact, human and it was time to call in a forensic team. The older officer, a squat man with salt and pepper hair, looked at both of them, pointing as if there was anyone else around. "You two, don't go anywhere."

Jesse had only looked at him, shaking her head, as if to say *Where would she go?* They were, after all, the ones who had called it in. But they'd been pushed to the side and eventually sat down at the edge of the trail.

She played a game on her phone, watching as the battery slowly drained and thinking it would be difficult to reach Cindy if she didn't have a working phone. Then her arm was bumped and bumped again quickly. Georgia, still looking down at her own phone, tried not to draw attention.

Slowly, she turned the screen so Jesse could see the message.

72

T he floating sensation was odd—not tingly, not zingy, but the cells in her body seemed to vibrate at a different rate than normal.

She floated above the sidewalk, the people coming and going around her fuzzy. She startled at a chill and realized one of them had walked through her. He didn't seem to notice, and she resumed staring across the street.

The building had no markings. Anyone walking down this very touristy strip wouldn't pay any attention, not during the day. On either side of it were shops with windows and ads. But there, just an empty space. No logos, no glass, just a single door painted red.

A man stood outside, a velvet rope around him as he checked IDs, sending the people inside in pairs or small clusters.

She knew what she was seeing, but she couldn't pull out faces or read the words on the signs. *Where was she? She'd never been here before. Not in reality.*

Then a cold hand reached into her very being, grabbing at her and twisting. Did he know she was here? Watching, like she watched? Her chest froze, cells going cold. She would have stopped breathing, but she already wasn't breathing.

Slowly, she turned. Her feet didn't move, she wasn't even sure she had feet. She was just a consciousness on the street, watching, scanning, waiting.

He was here.

He was looking at the same door she was. The line wasn't very long. It was a weeknight. But he understood something. She could hear the ideas he worked with.

That was okay. In the city, the weeknights didn't matter as much. So many people had jobs that didn't depend on weeknights.

Monday nights were dark.

Monday? Did it mean something? Then it was gone, as if it were too nebulous for her filmy being to hold on to.

She turned again. Where was he? Could she see him?

She could *feel* him. She felt that he didn't know she was here. He didn't have that ability. Hell, who did?

It seemed it was only her and Carter, in the whole world, who understood . . . and not even Carter, really.

Then whatever tethered her to herself suddenly yanked. She was jolted back into her bed, the mattress bouncing as if she had dropped from a height. Coming awake, her lungs finally worked, breath flowing into her body. Eyes wide in the dark room as she stared upward.

Monday nights were dark.

What did that mean? She could hold the phrase now. But where was the street and the red door?

She jerked her body upright, feet hitting the floor. Before she thought about it, she had her laptop out. She'd brought it along not thinking to use it, maybe just to check emails. Carter would text her, but who else was there to communicate with?

It had struck her as she had climbed into Jesse's car to leave, how very sad that was and how very necessary.

The computer took forever to whir to life. She so rarely used it but she was glad now she had it. She pulled up maps and street views, checking everything she could.

Sometime later, she saw it. The door was blue in the picture, older, out of date. But that was the place! She knew where it was now. And *Monday nights were dark.*

It was Monday now, but very early hours. She could make it! *They* could make it.

Closing the lid without thinking, she ran out into the main room, realizing only then that she was dressed to pick up Georgia and Jesse. But their bedroom door was closed.

She'd been asleep. They must have gotten a ride. Bolting across the main room, excited with her information, she pounded on the door. Even as she did, she heard noise behind her.

Someone was knocking on the main door.

Confused, she whirled, heading the other direction and putting her eye to the peephole. Someone in a polyester suit jacket was at their door. She should have thought it through first, but she flung it wide.

"We're sorry to bother you, but we needed to check in." The woman sounded apologetic, very professional for the middle of the night. "Two different neighbors of yours reported a scream."

73

"It was me." She hoped she said it with an appropriate apologetic tone. But her mind was racing, her cells still humming. "It was a nightmare. I woke myself up, too."

When the manager didn't respond, she added. "I'm so sorry. Please let them know that I'm okay. I'm awake now. It won't happen again."

Though the woman finally nodded, she didn't seem to take Cindy's explanation at face value. Not subtly, she looked over Cindy's shoulder into the room. Nothing was out of the ordinary. The table not overturned. Papers not strewn everywhere. It was fine.

Cindy smiled as if she could convince this woman. Then watched as the woman's eyes roved up and down her exposed skin. She was grateful she was dressed—it was just past the dead middle of the night. Her short sleeves revealed that she had no bruises on her face, or neck or arms. Hopefully, that would be enough.

Though it didn't seem to fully appease her, the woman finally turned away, she said, "Okay. Sleep better next time."

As Cindy closed the door, she couldn't tell if it was a wish or a warning.

She didn't have time to care. Bolting back across the room, she knocked again on Georgia and Jesse's door. Only as her knuckles hit the wood she thought, *Why had they not come out when she'd knocked before?* Why had they not been worried about the woman at the door?

Grabbing the knob, she opened the door without thinking. She should have called out first, but she was in the suite alone.

Cold knowledge sank into her in a disturbing way. She had not known that she was the only one here. Shouldn't she have felt that? Or had she grown so disconnected from everyone except Carter, that she couldn't even feel a human presence anymore?

But there wasn't time to think about the misses, to dwell on shortcomings. She bolted back across the small space, into her bedroom, grabbing her phone off the charger and frantically tapping at the screen.

The only message she had was from Georgia.

- been detained. more later.

Oh hell, she thought. Still, they'd expected it and prepared the best they could. The two women would have to convince the police that somehow they had walked directly to the dead body and yet they weren't the killers and didn't know the killer.

But she did.

She knew now, not really enough but maybe enough to find him.

If Georgia and Jesse were detained, then there was nothing she could do. Cindy looked frantically around the room taking stock of everything she had. Then she bolted once again into the center of the suite where she saw what she needed lying on the table.

74

Georgia should have modulated her voice better, walking down the hallway of a hotel at this odd hour. It was practically 5a.m. She should be getting breakfast. Instead, she was getting in the elevator.

Jesse pushed the button and made the box whir to life. Georgia still felt revved, but her bones were starting to disagree.

The only police officer in the entire district who had any sympathy for them had driven them to the hotel. The two hadn't spoken on the ride home—what could they say with an officer listening?

Georgia hadn't had to feign exhaustion as her head lolled against the back seat. But now Jesse asked, "What did you tell them to get us out of there?"

Georgia couldn't help it. She was too tired to monitor her reactions and she snorted before she could stop it. "I played the *do you know who my father is?* card."

"Did they know who your father was?" Jesse asked incredulously.

"Of course not," Georgia replied. "But he is FBI."

"Former FBI." Jesse pointed out.

"I know," Georgia whined. "And that was what took so long. I gave them his number so he could tell them that we were working on a serial killer case." She saw Jesse's expression as the ding signaled the doors opening. "Yeah, they didn't believe that either."

Her senior partner led the way down the hall and added, "They were really unhappy when I said I thought I knew the name of the person that skull belonged to."

The hallway seemed to last forever and have twice as many turns as before. Then Jesse was swiping her key in the door. "You didn't tell them Cindy's theory on finding the body, did you?"

"Didn't have to." Georgia shook her head. They'd been separated and interrogated like criminals. To which Georgia had quickly pointed out, "We found a piece of the human skull and the first thing we did was we called you. Hardly what a killer would do." She realized after she said it, of course, that it was the wrong thing to say.

Why was she out there? Looking under logs? Why would she even think that the skull she found was human? What an odd assumption to make, and so on. She readily admitted that they were on a case looking for Jasper Covington. Something she and Jesse had decided to share before the police even showed up.

"It was all to be expected," Jesse sighed then closed the door behind Georgia before sagging against it. "I just didn't think it would take that long."

"Well, they did not want to call the FBI." Georgia wandered into the middle of the room and stopped. What was she even doing? "I gave them my father's number. But they pointed out that was how you set up a fake system."

"That's true." Jesse breathed deeply as if she, too, were getting her bearings and not doing it well.

"I know. So, they had to call the actual FBI and the actual

FBI had to hunt down my father. Then my father had to tell them which agent was taking over the case of our serial killer. And then I got to talk to him—"

"*You got to talk to the agent?*" Jesse asked, suddenly seeming to come just a little more awake.

"Hold your little horses. It was not that exciting."

That didn't seem to surprise Jesse either.

"What now?" Georgia asked as a yawn took over her body. She'd been yawning for hours, just fighting to stay awake. Falling asleep in the interrogation room hadn't seemed like a good idea. Over the course of her time there, they'd been gracious enough to bring her several bags of chips and a couple of sodas.

Even so, she was now both hungry and exhausted, struggling to figure out what to do first. Shove food in her face, or plant herself in the bed? She no longer cared that she was now sharing a room with Jesse so that Cindy could have her own space.

Opting for food first, she grabbed a box of crackers and dug her hand down in the plastic bag. Already, Jesse was holding her hand out. Georgia passed the box and glanced at Cindy's door.

Closed. At least one of them was getting some sleep.

Jesse, after eating her own handful of crackers, picked the conversation back up. "What we do now is get some sleep. Then we talk to Cindy tomorrow and figure out what to do next."

"That's right," Georgia remembered. Cindy had seen something when she had touched Jasper's skull, and she hadn't told them so that they couldn't slip and tell the police. That seemed so long ago.

Georgia had, of course, not even mentioned Cindy's existence the whole time she was in. She didn't ask Jesse if she'd held to their promise; it would likely have been the first thing out of her mouth if she screwed it up. She ate another handful of crackers, hoping that it was enough to keep her asleep for long enough to get rested, and then she watched as Jesse yawned again, too.

Looking around the room, Jesse frowned and paused, her handful of crackers paused halfway to her mouth. The move was so odd that Georgia froze.

"What?"

"Something's not right." Jesse looked around again.

Everything looked perfectly normal to Georgia—or at least normal for being stuck in a hotel room with Jesse. Then again, she was not operating on all cylinders right now. Probably not even half of her cylinders.

Jesse held her hand out, asking Georgia to stop as if she weren't already standing perfectly still. Then she headed over to the closed door to Cindy's room but stopped and looked back across the suite.

"Our door's open," she said, before pointing out, "We left it closed."

"Maybe Cindy needed something." It seemed perfectly reasonable, but Jesse already had her hand on the closed bedroom doorknob, slowly twisting it open and peeking inside. Then, in a flurry of movement, she flung the door wide and turned around and looked at Georgia.

"She's gone."

J esse felt her muscles constrict. Her eyes were as wide as
saucers. She didn't have to look in the mirror to know
that. She wasn't the type to panic, but she panicked
now.

"Cindy's gone," she said to Georgia as though Georgia
couldn't see for herself.

Georgia had immediately asked, "How did you know before
you looked?"

Jesse still wasn't quite able to put it together. Maybe it had
just been a sense that she couldn't hear anything from the
other room or . . . "Car keys."

Jesse pointed at the clean table. That was what it had been.
"She said she'd leave them on the table."

"So she took the car, too?"

"What the fuck?" Jesse hadn't put that together yet.

"Check your messages," Georgia offered calmly, as though
messages would solve everything, and it wasn't a crisis.

While she was outwardly speaking in sentences, Jesse knew
she wasn't operating at full capacity. Georgia at least seemed

calm, so Jesse did as instructed. Their phones had been confiscated for quite some time, so it was more than possible they'd missed a message—or twelve—from Cindy.

In that moment, she remembered the police telling her they'd seen someone named Cindy in her messages. Jesse had simply said, "A friend of mine coming over to say hello while we were in town."

Turning again, she scanned the room, checking one more time and still seeing no suitcase. No laptop bag. No lotions or toothpaste at the sink.

If it weren't for her car keys being missing—and likely her car—she might have believed she hadn't lied to the police at all. That maybe Cindy Baker didn't really exist. She'd seen weirder things in her life.

"Maybe the car is still here," Georgia posed it as if that would once again solve everything. "Do you have a backup key?"

"Just the one that manually unlocks the door."

Georgia sighed slowly at her. "So we can't click the button and see if it's out there. Let's go downstairs and look. Be sure the car is gone."

It was stupid, but it was reasonable, Jesse thought. "Why would Cindy take the keys but not the car?"

She hadn't realized she said it out loud until Georgia answered her. "Maybe to trap us here."

Why would she trap them? For a moment Jesse thought that would be ridiculous. What would the reasoning even be? But then again, why had Cindy taken her car?

Jesse and Georgia rode back down the elevator in silence and Jesse watched as Georgia patted her back pocket, double checking for the room key. As exhausted as both of them had been just moments before, this had shot them full of adrenaline. Jesse was wide awake now.

The cool morning air here was so different from Shreveport. So different from Rockford. Still warm enough to be a summer morning, and still getting bright already because the sun came up at such an odd hour right now.

Jesse was grateful that she wasn't looking for her car in the pitch dark with only the few weak parking lot lights to protect them from whatever might be out. The sun wasn't up yet, but the light was starting to show.

The back lot was a bust, so they headed around to the front. At last, Georgia turned and looked at her, shaking her head. "Do you have a tracking system on your car?"

Of course she didn't. Jesse shook her head.

"Do we have a tracking system on Cindy?" Georgia asked, somehow managing to make is sound reasonable. She was calm. Then again, it wasn't her car that was stolen.

She was about to push the door open to the hotel but, realizing they didn't want to have this conversation in the lobby, Jesse turned to look at Georgia.

"She told us she had seen something." Georgia was still being logical, her own hand poised on the other door handle. "She didn't leave us a text. I didn't see any notes around the room. So I'm assuming that either means she left in a massive hurry or she didn't want to tell us where she was going."

Jesse still didn't get it. They stood there, each with one hand on the door as if they were a team ready to greet new members to the hotel. No one was coming, so they stood and had their conversation here. Jesse still not quite comprehending everything.

Georgia looked as if maybe she had figured it out.

"But why would she want to not tell us? She took my car."

Georgia tipped her head. Something in her expression reminded Jesse of the case that they were working, reminded her the things that Cindy Baker could do. Things that were not claims Cindy made, but things Jesse believed based on evidence that she herself had dug up.

She felt it then, the knowledge sinking into the middle of her chest. Cindy was trying to protect them.

J esse headed back into the main room and checked the time.

5:13am

"We need a car."

"How would we even find one right now?" Georgia paused. "What if we need a flight?"

Good point, Jesse looked around the room. They could fly. If they flew, they might beat Cindy to wherever she was going, but ... "We don't know where to go. That's a problem."

"So, how do we find Cindy?" Georgia shot back.

For the first time, Jesse settled into her skin again. The panic retreated as Georgia's questions calmed her. Jesse had worked with partners in the past and even one she'd liked. Mostly she'd simply disliked having someone else insert their ideas into the investigation, someone questioning what she did. Maybe it was because Georgia wasn't a trained PI. Georgia didn't notice when Jesse bent the rules or flat out broke them, which was a lot of the time.

The questions she asked, Jesse could admit, often made her feel like a mentor. Right now, it felt like a good spot. Georgia was the one holding it together, so Jesse attached herself for the ride.

"Okay, first, we have to figure out where Cindy's going. How do we track her?"

"We should at least call her," Georgia suggested as if it were the most obvious thing in the world.

How had she missed that? *Damn.* Jesse pulled her phone out of her pocket and Georgia held her hand out. "How about I do it?"

Jesse wasn't one to argue with obvious reason. What she did do was start cataloging what they needed while Georgia waited for Cindy to pick up. Neither of them was surprised when she didn't, but they'd done due diligence at least.

"She's not answering. She's either not alive or she's unable to answer," Georgia said, to which Jesse had almost replied, "Duh."

Instead, she realized she was still a bit frazzled—no sleep, shock that Cindy was gone, her damn car stolen—and asked, "How else can we find her?"

Georgia frowned then snapped her fingers. "Carter! Carter might know. Maybe she called him."

Though Jesse was considering making this call herself, Georgia was already dialing.

This time, a voice answered, but he opened with, "What's wrong?" because it was after all very, very early in the morning there.

Georgia didn't beat around the bush. "Cindy's missing. She packed her things and took the car keys. She went of her own volition."

"She goes of her own volition a lot," Carter said. If he'd panicked at Georgia's first words, he had gotten himself together quickly. Jesse got the impression this wasn't the first time for him. "Where'd she go?"

"We have no idea. That's why we're calling you." Jesse

fought the urge to sigh the words.

"Is there any chance you have a tracking app on your sister?" Georgia was holding the phone in front of her so Jesse could listen in. They both heard as Carter let loose a maniacal laugh.

"Oh yes! Yes, I do."

Jesse watched as Georgia's face relayed her shock and pleasure. Surely her own face mirrored it.

Carter was still laughing. "After the last time when she just didn't come home, I put a tracking device in her purse. I just didn't expect to use it so damn soon."

"Does she know this?"

"Probably?" His voice rose, indicating he wasn't sure. "I don't know. I got one of those ultra thin ones and put it in her wallet behind her driver's license. She doesn't take it out much, so I was hoping it would be a while before she found it. I was hoping we could have that fight later."

"All right then," Georgia sounded upbeat, but they could both hear keys clicking in the background. Carter was on top of it. Jesse liked him.

"Where is she?" Jesse didn't need to know how or why Carter was tracking his sister, she just needed to know where Cindy was.

"Well," he said "looks like she's on highway seventy, heading northeast. You started in Kentucky, right?"

"Uh-huh," Jesse said, "along the border with Indiana."

"Okay." She could hear the heavier breathing in Carter's voice. He'd managed to stay calm but now he, too, was starting to panic. "She has my car, and she packed all her things."

Jesse hoped to calm him down and then she realized they were all better off if they all knew everything. Finding Cindy was becoming a necessity at this point.

"She didn't tell you why she left? No note, no text, no direction?" Carter's voice ratcheted up.

"Nothing."

The noises from his end of the line stopped. As if he'd quit breathing. "That means she's protecting you from something."

Oh, hell.

If Cindy was protecting them, then they were walking into some serious shit. Jesse told Cindy's brother, "She peeled off her glove and touched the skull. And—"

"It's hard to watch, isn't it?" Jesse figured he knew most everything about his sister.

"It was awful. It didn't look like the TV shows. It looks painful."

"I'm pretty sure that it is. What did she see? Did she say?"

That was the kicker right there, Jesse had to acknowledge the problem. "We sent Cindy on her way back to the hotel and we called the police. We need the bones on record as being found in that location and identified as Jasper Covington to make sure that this case gets cataloged as part of our serial killer case."

Jesse paused, wondering if she'd been duped. "She also told us that she would tell us what she saw when we got back to the hotel. That none of us wanted to hide any more information from the police than we already were doing."

Wow, Jesse thought. *She just said that. Out Loud.*

It didn't faze Carter, but she had to only hope no one was listening in on her conversation. The local police might have bugged the phones; they'd been in police custody for hours.

Fuck! It had been so late when they'd gotten out. She still didn't have enough sleep or functioning brain cells for this.

"I don't know where she's going. I don't know where you guys have cases," Carter told them, "But I'd guess she's aimed towards Pittsburgh, New York City. Some place on that line."

Jesse opened her laptop, grateful for the larger screen, and tapped at it, quickly pulling up maps. She listed a handful of places along the route that Carter had described.

"She left three hours ago, and she's already past Cincinnati and just past Columbus. When she drives, she doesn't stop and she's not slow."

Jesse started thinking out loud. "So if we get in a car and chase her—"

"What car?" Georgia had said. "First we have to get a car and that will take a while."

More problems.

"You won't catch up," Carter told them. "She won't let you."

"So we fly." Jesse was thinking it might be time to hang up and then thinking once again that it was best if everyone had all the information. Then they could keep tabs on each other, even if they couldn't keep tabs on Cindy. "All right. We need to find a city at the edge of the state line."

Jesse was proud of herself for putting the pieces together and feeling like her brain was finally working. Georgia leaned over her shoulder, looking at the map.

"Pittsburg is what? An hour from the Ohio line? Seems too far for our guy."

Jesse agreed. "That leaves New York, New Jersey, there are a handful of state lines there."

"What state park is close?" Georgia asked, and this time Carter, who must have opened his own map was getting in on the game.

He rattled off a few in the area. "Anything else along the way?"

"It doesn't matter," Georgia announced. "New York is where we go. Hopefully, we can land before she gets there, and Carter gives us the details."

"What if it's Pittsburg? What if she's just going somewhere random, not the site of one of his kills?" Jesse had to ask.

"Cindy doesn't do random," Carter told them.

Then Georgia said, "We'll let the airport decide for us."

77

They'd flown into New York City and Georgia was grateful the hotel had called a shuttle. Despite the early hours, the clerk had been glad to help.

Or maybe just to get rid of them. She made an odd comment about a noise complaint and their roommate.

What had Cindy done?

Georgia and Jesse booked the first flight available that would hopefully have them landing before Cindy arrived. But there was still the matter of getting a car on the other end and that neither of them had slept in over twenty-four hours.

It was possible they would have to backtrack until they ran into Cindy. When they landed, Carter would be able to tell them where she was. New York was an eleven-plus hour drive without stops. So hopefully, they could beat Cindy. If that's where she was going.

By the time they landed, Georgia managed to call her mother and sleep a little on the flight, catching a very necessary couple of hours. She needed more but took what she could get.

When the tedium of it had almost broken her, Jesse brought her A game. She was calling Carter even as she rolled her bag down the long terminal. She leaned back to Georgia, who was barely keeping up, and said, "Cindy's still in route."

It would be good to be right. It was a good thing Carter had essentially tagged *her* and not her car or her purse. She could possibly go out without her wallet, but most people wouldn't.

Georgia tugged her small bag along, again reminded that she was traveling light because she'd thought she was popping into Florida and then leaving after a few days. None of this had been the trip that Georgia Dunham expected.

They hadn't even called the police to hunt down Jesse's car. Though Jesse hadn't taken that off the table, it was a matter of safety for Cindy. Now it was a game of wait and see.

Georgia had never seen Jesse as happy as when she said she'd called her mom and asked her to arrange a car for pickup. "No lines, no contract, just sign and go."

"That's amazing. I'll have to send her chocolates or something."

Georgia laughed.

In the car, they navigated the maze of streets to get out of the city. They had a full tank of gas and a psychic to track.

"I'm going to try calling her again," Georgia announced. "Maybe she just doesn't answer the phone while she's driving."

Jesse only raised one eyebrow. Of course, the line rang right through to nothing. Only this time they had a pretty good idea that the car was still moving.

Georgia asked then, "What are the chances that she's been kidnapped? That someone came into the hotel, made her pack her things and get the car keys and is forcing her to drive away?"

Jesse mulled that over for a while. "On another day, it might be reasonable, but I'd have to put the odds pretty low. Who would even know to come and kidnap her?"

"Do you think he's figured us out?" Georgia asked.

"How could he?" Jesse asked, as if the question were preposterous.

But maybe it wasn't. "Well, you told me killers keep track. So he's probably aware that four of his bodies have been found recently . . . in rapid succession."

She watched as that hit Jesse. "But he almost definitely doesn't know about Jasper Covington yet. We found him less than twenty-four hours ago. We're the only ones who actually believe that's Jasper. There's probably only a small story out if anything. It'll be a while before that piece of skull is positively identified."

Even so, it was obvious Jesse didn't like that reasoning. Because Georgia was right. They had been operating under the premise that there was some kind of cone of silence—that this man wouldn't know they were chasing him. But if he was keeping track . . .

"If it's Davis McNally," Georgia said softly, "then he's known for a while."

78

J esse didn't know where she was going, she just kept turning the wheel trying to aim toward where Carter told them Cindy was. He kept updating them, but they didn't have the information themselves.

Georgia was playing point person, taking calls and passing information. "We've gone past where she is . . . at least I think so. Carter says she's reaching the edge of the city. But we're outside already."

Damn, Jesse thought. "Can you load a tracking app to your phone and *track yourself*? So Carter can track us and Cindy at the same time?"

Why hadn't they thought of that before? There were too many answers to that question. The whole thing took a while. Then Georgia was giving Carter all the login information.

There was a moment when Georgia protested. "I don't know that I'm comfortable with someone tracking me."

"You can turn it off tomorrow," Jesse assured her. "Hell, take my phone and do it!" They had to find Cindy and Georgia had softly put the tracker on her own.

Jesse had begun the dance of changing directions on a

crowded freeway. "I didn't see her. I would have recognized my own car, right?"

Georgia had shrugged. But Jesse knew her black SUV looked a lot like other black SUVs.

Georgia's phone pinged so often that Jesse had begun to ignore it. Until Georgia said, "Oh hell!"

Jesse knew she didn't have to ask, Georgia would tell her. For a partnership that had begun with low grade blackmail, it was working out pretty well. But she couldn't keep her hands from white knuckling the steering wheel.

Cindy hadn't contacted Carter at all. Not even while Jesse and Georgia had been in the air. She wasn't answering the phone for anyone. Though Carter was used to her running off, he was also used to her picking up the phone for him and confessing what she'd done. The fact that wasn't happening this time was concerning.

Carter had apparently been leaving more and more frantic texts. Georgia had been leaving friendlier ones even trying email. And Jesse had left escalating demands via voicemail. Nothing had worked.

Maybe she *had* been kidnapped.

Georgia started talking. "My dad just messaged. They've ruled out Davis McNally."

"What?" Jesse asked.

"He's absolutely not the killer."

"How did they—"

"He was seen by multiple other people, several states away at the times when the kidnappings occurred."

"I guess that's good." It would mean that the killer didn't know their faces or Jesse's car or where to find them.

"Yeah, but it's also bad," Georgia sighed. "If it was Davis, we would know who to arrest. As is, we've got nothing."

"Well, the FBI is on it. They can find whoever were in all these places at the same time as the murders."

"Like who?" Georgia's tone was curious. "Vagrants? Traveling salesman?"

"No," Jesse said, glad to talk about something she understood. "Someone with a great reputation."

"Do I need to search 'doesn't act like a serial killer'?" Georgia was already tapping on her phone and Jesse laughed.

The research skills she'd been taught somehow had translated as magic to Georgia. It was truly just a matter of knowing what specifically to enter and where, but Georgia still eyed her as though she could pull things out of the internet like a rabbit out of a hat.

"No," Jesse told her. "You're looking for someone with a good name. Like Davis McNally."

"Oh, he's not going to have a good name for long." There was a grin in Georgia's voice. "They've handed him over to the Fraud Division. You were absolutely right about him hiding something."

"Fraud?"

"He's been running some kind of insider trading deal, and even possibly a Ponzi scheme."

"Well, well, well . . ." Jesse was proud. "We at least got one bad dude off the street."

Georgia immediately went back to checking her phone, as if she could just search anything from it. Although, Jesse thought, maybe she could. Georgia looked up. "I don't understand. What do you mean someone with a good name?"

"He's a community leader," Jesse said. On the one hand, she felt like she was pulling the information out of her ass, on the other, she'd worked enough cases to know what these predators were. "He maybe runs the youth group at his church or a Boy Scout troop. He never misses a meeting. The families all love him. Maybe he's a mayor or he sits on the school board."

Georgia was looking at her oddly.

"Think," Jesse added, "about how long he's been getting

away with this. He has to cultivate his cover as carefully as he cultivates his kills."

"A friend told me that once . . ." Georgia spoke slowly, the words cutting deep. "I told her how much I liked her uncle and how I thought he was a great guy. She said *Of course you do*. Abusers groom their advocates as carefully as they groom their victims."

Ouch. Jesse thought. *There was a dark story there.* But Georgia was right. "That's exactly it. The ones who don't culti-vate a good name get caught quickly, thrown in jail, at least made to register their address as a sex offender. This guy—he's been at it for a long time. So, it will be someone with a very good name."

79

She was *here*. She was standing opposite the club with the red door. Cindy watched as the people went in, and she had no idea which one he was after. The night before, when she'd seemed to be floating, there had been no ability to distinguish faces, only to know that he was nearby.

That had been bizarre. She'd never done anything like that before. She could only conclude that she'd developed some kind of disturbing connection to the him. And she prayed he couldn't sense the link back to her.

Monday night was dark. She looked around, trying to make sense of it. It didn't seem dark at all. Streetlights flooded the place, people passed by her on the street, and she guessed the good news was that this was New York, and no one would look at her oddly just for standing here on the street.

She'd walked back and forth, trying not to be too obvious. What if he saw her then she became a target? Lord knew, she was not cut out for running barefoot through the woods. Checking her shoes, she imagined someone finding one of her overly comfortable sneakers with a drop or two of her blood. What field would they be in?

She knew she would fight, but she knew the others had fought back, too. No one had ever won.

She moved again, unwilling to let herself become the oddball that people remembered. Unwilling to let him see her, not if she could avoid it. But she also knew if she didn't do this now, if she didn't find a way to interfere and stop him, someone else would be dead by morning.

Her hands were shaking. Her chest felt as if her lungs were filled with heavy fluid. She could hear the air each time it passed in and out through her nose as she tried to calm herself down . . . and failed miserably.

Someone would likely think she was high. Someone might offer her drugs. She didn't need anything to make her see more or feel more. She already couldn't control her life the way it was.

Looking back, she watched the bouncer letting people in the red door. None of them stuck out to Cindy.

Their killer didn't have a type aside from younger and out with their friends. Cindy had no idea if the people entering by themselves were safe, or if they were meeting up with others inside. Everyone at the door appeared within the right age range. Men and women. People dressed to the hilt, and a few dressed down.

The victims' shoes had been everything from sneakers to a pair of Birkenstocks to Hannalyn's high heels, painted red on the sole. So it wasn't even as if he had some specific kind of shoe fetish. That would have helped her rule people out.

Cindy checked up and down the street but didn't see anybody she thought would be him. Her phone vibrated again in her pocket. She'd turned off all the noises, but the vibration seemed just as disruptive. She worried people would hear it and look at her, but it was New York and they all ignored her completely.

She made the decision then: One thing his victims had in common is that they had gone off on their own. Most had gone out the back door, only one had gone out the front to the parking lot and then disappeared.

There was no parking lot here. She began moving, pulling out her phone and looking at it, just to blend in with everyone else on the street, half of whom were looking at their phones, too.

As if she could blend in anywhere. She'd never fit in. Never again, not since she'd been twelve. Not since she'd first learned what she could do.

Carter's voicemails were increasingly frantic. Georgia and Jesse were also trying to get her to call back. No one had said anything specific, but she had a feeling that the two women were chasing her.

Maybe it was time to make use of them.

She considered answering the phone but instead put it back in her pocket and tried to make her way around to the back of the club. She'd check this first.

The streets were a grid. It should be easy, but it was so damn difficult to find the back door. Then, when she did get to the back, it seemed far too late to make a better choice. The door opened onto a dark alleyway and she wasn't willing to just hang out alone here.

Maybe if she had Jesse and Georgia with her.

She had done this all wrong.

But, as she stood there, the back door opened, and a man and a young woman came out. Cindy ducked behind the corner of a brick building to watch.

80

Georgia tried to work backwards. "I called Cindy again, no answer."

And now the locator was dicked up.

They'd been afraid of that happening. Once Cindy had headed into the city, the tall buildings often blocked her signal. It was impossible to tell exactly which street she was on until she moved, then the signal would disappear and pick up somewhere entirely different.

There was no knowing if the place it pinged was where she still was, or simply the last place the GPS system was letting them know about.

"Central Park," Georgia said, "It's a state park. It's known for murders, too." She was trying to get ahead, find where a body might be stashed. That had to be why Cindy was here alone, right?

"I don't know," Jesse seemed to think about it.

When they'd gotten off the flight, Jesse told Georgia she'd only managed to sleep a little bit of it. That she'd checked Cindy's information about how to find the victims. It had held up.

Georgia still needed to pass that information along to her father. Jesse had given it to the local police inquiring about the case. They still hadn't confirmed it was Jasper Covington though.

According to Cindy, the location where the victim went missing, and the spot where the shoe eventually turned up, should be used as a line. Bisect that line and it would run into a state park—where the body would be.

So now, she was looking at the map, zooming in and out trying to read the names and the green patches. "You're right," she agreed. "Plus, Central Park is in the same state, and he likes to move them across state lines."

She moved the map. "Oh! Great Swamp National Wildlife Refuge!"

Jesse scared her by turning and looking directly at her. "Yes! That sounds exactly like where he would leave them. He's been using swamps whenever possible."

"Helps the bodies to disappear," Georgia said then added, "But maybe you could look at the road?"

Jesse nodded. Somehow she'd managed to keep the wheels perfectly within the lines. But Georgia wasn't quite ready to test that.

"Okay." She was still looking at the map on her phone. "If we follow some line from there, back across into New York City . . . then that's where Cindy is, and she must know something."

Damn. Georgia was making so many assumptions that, if any one of them didn't hold up, they would just be very wrong. "We need a field for the shoe to turn up in. They always turn up in an empty space."

Jesse nodded and Georgia began looking for fields, requiring a much more fine-tuned approach. But it was too much. "I can't see fields on the map unless he's going to leave the shoe in Central Park or..." she scrolled and slid the map under her fingertips, "Prospect Park."

"No, that doesn't sound right."

Georgia agreed and agreed again when Jesse added, "Then we go to where Cindy last was."

Georgia's phone pinged again and she did what she'd been doing since they landed: switched back and forth between maps, notes, texts and calls, listening to voicemails, and leaving more of her own.

Now she opened the wrong app twice before she found the one that had left her a message. Each time she closed one with nothing new in it, she blinked. She was tired and starting to wonder if her phone was setting off random notifications.

She and Jesse had simply not gotten enough sleep. Given when Carter told them Cindy left—and she had driven the whole distance—Cindy had certainly not slept enough either.

Tapping her phone again, Georgia checked the last app where a message might have come. She gasped. "It's from Cindy!"

81

This wasn't it. Cindy watched as the couple kissed and made out. The young woman was clearly a party goer while he was in black pants and an apron looking like he worked there. They came out, talked, smoked . . . and nothing.

Shit. She was either at the wrong back door or this was the wrong couple or . . . Cindy didn't know.

The woman ground out a cigarette under the toe of her high-heeled shoe, kissed the man one more time before they both ducked back inside. Safe.

What if this was the wrong place? What if it was the wrong night? What if her out-of-body experience hadn't been the future but it actually happened last night?

Even as she worried that, something gripped right down the center of her body telling her to stay put. She didn't want to do that either. This was not safe. If she was mugged or harmed and somebody asked her what she was doing in a dark alley at night in New York she'd have to say *I was being stupid*.

For all that their parents had trained her and Carter to make wise choices—stay out in the open, be obvious, stay with your friends—Cindy knew better than anyone that wasn't always enough. She'd been snatched off the street in broad daylight. Nothing stupid like letting her drink get drugged or going out the back door with a stranger.

In the trunk of that car when the memories had assailed her, and . . .

She shut it down. *Not now*. Reliving those memories was never good. In fact, she was certain some of them were buried so deep she might never get them back. Which was probably a good thing.

She checked the door again, hopeful that she was in the right place at the right time. It was the best that she could do.

But it wasn't.

She could do better.

Pulling out her phone, she checked the message she'd sent Georgia with her location. She would confess more when they got here. But she wasn't surprised that Georgia messaged back.

- be there in 15 minutes.

As usual, Cindy thought, she'd been right. The things she learned or knew or believed on her own, those things were wrong as often as anybody else was. But the things that came in through whatever channel had opened up that day, they were never wrong. She interpreted them oddly sometimes, or missed things, but they were never *wrong*.

She stayed put. Jesse and Georgia would come and find her. As long as what's his fuck didn't grab her as his next victim first.

Cindy stepped away. Though she wanted to see the door, she couldn't risk putting herself in line to be next or even just to be recognized. She couldn't let him see her, so she tucked herself quietly into the shadows.

It was thirty minutes, not fifteen, before Jesse and Georgia showed up. She'd heard a car door slam nearby and sank further back, not realizing it was her friends.

Friends, she wondered. *She had friends.*

As they ran up the alley toward her, she turned, hands out, finger to her lips, for them to slow down and stop making so much goddamn noise.

"It's here," she told them, "It's tonight."

"Have you seen him?"

"No." Cindy fought the urge to wail. She'd just told her friends to be quiet and now she was about to start crying. "I don't know!"

"You said you're never wrong," Georgia repeated.

She wasn't. But she wasn't right this time either.

Georgia was speaking again. "We're here because we believe you and we trust you."

"We can do some good tonight," Jesse added.

She'd never done any of this before. Cindy thought how she'd never put herself into a place where she could become a victim. She'd never called anyone for backup, even Carter.

A few times, she'd gone out and put things in strategic places so someone else would find a body or a clue, something that she knew was left behind. Every once in a while—when that didn't work—she would call in as an anonymous tipster.

But standing in an alley in New York City, waiting for a crime to happen with two other women at her side? All of it was new. It made her feel both more secure and more petrified. What if he got all three of them? What if Jesse and Georgia went down? And it was her fault?

"You should leave." She suddenly regretted her decision.

"No." Jesse protested immediately. Georgia, too, stood her ground.

"Please!" but then she caught the movement in the background. She'd been so busy being upset that she hadn't seen the man that came up behind them.

But they all heard the click of the safety coming off.

Cindy was standing still, watching as Jesse and Georgia both froze. Between them, facing her, was a man. His face was covered, and his stance was as bold as his shoulder width.

He pointed the gun at the back of Georgia's head.

82

Oh *hell no*, Georgia thought. She was not going to get murdered in the back alley of some New York club that she hadn't even gone to.

Her father would kill her first. She would not die before she took her LSAT. She would not die before she proved to her father that—despite the fact that she did not have his blood—she was his daughter.

She took a bold step backwards, and another, until she felt the gun at the base of her neck. Moving through the panic that threatened to engulf her, she breathed deep, unsure why she was so confident.

With only her eyes, she looked first to Jesse and then to Cindy. Cindy shrugged, saying that she didn't know what was happening. *This wasn't their guy.*

Was she really just getting mugged?

"Wallets," he demanded. "Jewelry."

Georgia wasn't having it. He was behind her. She looked again to Cindy, a pointed stare that moved right, the best signal she could make.

Damn, the woman was *psychic,* she should pick up on this.

But it took three or four tries, Georgia standing still, her heart beating loud enough to hear it in her ears over the sounds of traffic rushing by and honking at the ends of the alley. Sirens came from the other direction and disappeared. Not for them.

Eventually, Cindy seemed to catch on. Slowly she stepped to the side, putting herself in line with Jesse and not with Georgia and the barrel of the gun. It had been so hard to stand still and wait. Not what Georgia was used to.

She would have rolled up onto the balls of her feet but found she was already there.

"Wallet," he barked out again.

Jesse, seeming just mad at the whole thing was searching in her pocket. Cindy scrambled through the bag around her waist and, for a moment, Georgia had the fleeting thought of *was Cindy really wearing a fucking fanny pack?* But she was grabbing her wallet in it and her tracking card too.

Georgia didn't move. She wasn't giving this fucker a quarter. She felt the gun push harder against the back of her head.

"Wallet! Jewelry!"

Then it came, the explosion her father had warned her about. Uncontrollable. Once she started, it was all motor memory. She'd practiced so many times, but never like this.

Dropping low, fast, she harnessed the adrenaline in her system to catalogue both Cindy and Jesse's reactions as she spun around. Now facing the gunman, she looked at his knees and his waist as she burst upward, shooting her hands up underneath his arm, forcing the gun out of his control and hopefully into hers.

oly shit, Jesse thought as she watched Georgia fight back in a flurry of controlled moves.

She'd dropped down and popped up, somehow maneuvering the gunman's arm. She had her own arm wrapped around his. Had she snapped his wrist? Jesse couldn't tell. But he dropped the gun into Georgia's waiting hand.

She then spun around, slid back several steps and aimed the gun at him now.

Jesse, not quite knowing how to react, still held her wallet in her hand. She'd been prepared to hand it over, not willing to die for the handful of change and not having to cancel all her credit cards. But apparently, Georgia was taking no crap.

She stood, unmoving, two hands on the gun. Then Jesse remembered: Georgia was a black belt. Georgia's father was an FBI agent.

Finally finding her wits, Jesse grabbed Cindy by the wrist and dragged her over behind Georgia. The youngest was clearly the best of them in this situation, and Jesse was more than willing to use her as a bit of a shield. She looked around her junior partner at the gunman, who looked just as startled as Cindy did.

Jesse stared him down, though she did not have his attention. Georgia and the barrel of his own gun definitely did. Jesse said loudly, "Her father is an FBI agent. You fuck with her, and even if you win, the terror of the FBI is going to come down on you for all the other times that you have done this. Your fingerprints will be matched, and you will be convicted of every single crime you've ever committed."

He might not have been looking at her, but her words soaked in. Hell, she'd guessed right, and he was not new to this. His hands came up in surrender and he began to slowly move backwards.

Apparently, not quick enough for Georgia, who aimed the gun at his feet and fired a shot into the pavement.

Turning faster than humanly possible, he bolted. Only after he cleared the end of the alley, disappearing beyond the brick walls, did Georgia lower the gun.

Immediately, she began to shake. "Holy hell." Her words were soft and rattled. "Practice does not do that justice. My dad warned me but . . ."

Jesse knew. She'd been in those tight situations herself. She'd gone in high on her own adrenaline, her husband missing, location unknown . . . She had been on the trail of a serial killer then, too. Nothing could adequately prepare a body for the wild fisheye lens of the world and the hyperaware state that came with it.

"Holy shit," Cindy mimicked Georgia's own earlier words. Then, "You're my hero."

That was for Georgia. *Fair enough,* Jesse thought. She was used to being the one to take action, the one that people said was so good in a crisis. But Georgia had saved the day today.

They all needed a deep breath. For a long minute, the silence settled over them. Jesse waited for the police to show up, for someone to come out the back door of the club, for anyone to ask if they were okay.

Georgia had fired a fucking gun in the middle of the city! But no one came.

The young woman still held it in both hands. Though it was aimed at the ground now, she was in control.

Then she told them, "You two watch the door. I'll watch your backs."

Reluctantly, quietly, Jesse and Cindy turned back to the club. Only this time, Cindy slowly began walking forward. Jesse paced, leaving Georgia standing where she was, watching down the alley and the little dip that led into a nearby parking lot. She was ready if anyone should surprise them from there.

Cindy got closer and closer to the club's back door. Putting her hand on the wood, she stopped and then shook her head.

"No." The sound was sad. She closed her eyes, her body rolling as though a lightning bolt had slowly passed through. If Jesse didn't know better, she would have thought it was a seizure. Then Cindy settled back into her own skin and jerked her hand away as if it had been burned.

"It's too late," she said. "They're gone."

Georgia turned around then, the gun still in her hands. "Fuck."

She put the safety on and began wiping it on her shirt, removing her fingerprints from a weapon that might be associated with a damn lot of crime.

"Here," Cindy said looking down into her little pack. "I have Kleenex and a real handkerchief."

When she finished, Georgia slowly set it on the ground. "I'm just not going to be responsible for it, and it won't get tracked back to me unless . . ."

She stood up straight and looked up and around. Jesse caught on. She was looking for cameras. Grabbing Georgia by the waist of her shirt, Jesse hauled her back, and snapped her own head down. "There's a camera at the other end of the alley. It's aimed along here, but it's far enough away it can't see your face unless you turn around and *look directly at it*."

Georgia nodded, lowering her own gaze to the ground.

Time to go. Jesse grabbed each of them by a wrist and began pulling them away. Cindy might not know where their killer was going, but she and Georgia had a damn good idea.

D*amnit!* Georgia pulled her hand free from Jesse's hold and walked a few steps back down the alley. Picking up the gun she'd just wiped her fingerprints off felt wrong.

She wasn't really prepared to carry it, so she did her best. Checked the safety again and tucked it in the back of her pants. Her father would kill her if he knew, but it wasn't as if she could walk around with it in her hand. And putting a gun down the front of her pants was beyond stupid.

Turning back to the other two, she saw Jesse nodding at her. "We'll take my car. Cindy, where did you park it?"

Cindy unzipped her little fanny pack and, without looking, grabbed the keys and set them in Jesse's hand. Jesse looked back to Georgia. "I have a gun in my glove box. I know how to use it."

Neither of them expected Cindy to want a gun of her own. From the look on her face, she was perfectly glad not to have one.

This time Cindy led the way without quite the determined march that Jesse had. Though she was more subtle in her movements, she was just as fast. They all knew what was on the line.

They exited the alley into the flow of people passing by. Georgia watched as Cindy's head snapped up, her eyes scanning the crowd. "Would you recognize him?"

"Not by looks, but maybe by . . ." Cindy didn't finish the sentence.

But she didn't see anything, and they quickly headed to the car. Clicking her fob and hearing the car beep gave Jesse obvious relief.

"I didn't know there was a gun in the glove box." Cindy's tone was somehow both apologetic and chiding.

Georgia motioned her into the front seat as she climbed into the back, pulled the gun out, and set it on the seat beside her. This was a mess waiting to happen. This was a gun used in other crimes and here she was taking it away from the scene and using it for her own purpose. Probably taking it to a completely unrelated crime scene. Her father was going to kill her anyway.

"If you don't want a gun in your car, don't steal cars," Jesse deadpanned as she started the engine and carefully pulled out.

"I don't know where to go." Cindy sounded desperate.

"We do. Great Swamp Wildlife Refuge," Jesse told her. With a glance in the rearview mirror, she instructed Georgia to find their best route.

Georgia nodded back. "I'm on it."

Cindy turned partly in her seat, trying to look carefully at both of them. "He killed a couple who interfered with one of his other murders."

"I remember," Georgia said, but she didn't look up until she was ready to tell Jesse which turn to take. "That's why I kept the gun."

Georgia could see Cindy visibly swallow at that. Even if they didn't quite know what they were doing, they were doing this.

Now that she had the route to the Refuge, she looked up, eyes flashing between Cindy and the rearview mirror to catch Jesse's gaze. "What exactly are we going to do?"

She wasn't going in without a plan *and a backup plan.*

"He has a young man," Cindy said. "I can see *his* face though I'm not sure if that does us any good. His victim is drugged. Probably about twenty five years old. He's wrapped in a blanket in the back of the car . . . In the footwell of the back seat, covered with . . ." she paused and Georgia looked up.

Interesting. It was almost as if Cindy was flipping through memories in her mind looking for what she needed.

"Cloth grocery bags and a jacket or two thrown over. It looks like a mess."

"He picks them out ahead of time," Jesse said. "He has to. It's the only way it would always be someone who was crossing state lines. I don't know if it helps if we know who this kid is, but maybe. Do you have anything else, Cindy?"

"No. I just knew it was that club. I knew it was the red door. And that he was there last night . . . the killer." Her voice was strained, and Georgia was grateful for the information, but she didn't want to know what Cindy felt.

"Was the victim there last night?" Jesse pushed.

"I don't know. But I kept hearing—" Her voice caught on itself as she spoke. "—*Monday night is dark.* I don't know what that means. Isn't every night dark?"

Jesse shrugged.

Georgia shrugged and changed the topic. "The refuge is almost an hour away."

"Fuck," Jesse muttered. "We can't get anywhere quickly."

"But it's an hour away for him, too. He's only a little bit ahead of us." Cindy then muttered to herself, *"Monday night is dark.* I don't get it. It's *not* dark in New York. Aside from the alley we were in, and that's always dark, not just on a Monday."

"Shit," Georgia muttered. "It's not the Refuge."

"What?" Jesse almost turned around.

"The street view is . . . not good. Built up, populated. Jersey traffic. He wouldn't take anyone there."

"What's the backup?"

"Pine Barrens in Jersey and Water Gap in Delaware." Georgia showed it to Cindy.

"Water gap." Thank God for Cindy's conviction.

Georgia started typing it into the search bar and gave Jesse a new set of directions. Once they were turned, she tried another search and was given definitions of *dark* and *night,* instances about new moons, and more. But the last link said, *Tuesday night is dark.*

"Oh!" Georgia called out. "I don't know if this helps, but—"

85

J esse pulled into the park only to find the gate closed, a
chain lock keeping them out. Cindy had directed them
to this entrance. It had a few trails but also a lake
nearby. Jesse's nerves were already on edge, though she
tried not to show it.

"We have to go back." She threw the car in reverse and
looked for a place to hide it.

During the drive, she'd shoved a granola bar in her face,
handing one each to Cindy and Georgia and not asking, but
demanding, that they eat. They'd shared the two extra bottles of
water that Cindy had left. Normally Jesse would worry about
the heat and micro particles in the water or even just trading
germs, but illness was not her concern right now. Death was.

They were all operating on not enough sleep and not
enough food, but there was no alternative. She loved cold cases,
because she could stop work at the end of the day and walk
away. Coming back the next day usually only made positive
differences.

She was good at solving the unsolved. But this case wasn't
cold now. It was hot. It was a ticking time bomb.

Maybe it was too late. Maybe the young man was already dead.

"He's not dead," Cindy said as if she had read Jesse's thoughts—a concerning turn of events. But Jesse didn't have time to deal with it.

"How do you know?"

"I got too close to this guy." Cindy was starting to panic. Though Jesse didn't generally like touching the woman, she reached out and put one hand heavily on Cindy's shoulder, applying a small amount of pressure until the woman calmed. It was a trick she had learned for her stepdaughter and she was pleased to see it work for Cindy.

For a moment, Jesse flashed to the thought that she was three days away from hearing from Ciara. She swallowed hard. What if this didn't work? What if Ciara stayed with Floyanne and Betty? What if Ciara called Jesse and no one answered? Because who would find them if they died out here tonight?

She pulled off the road and aimed along some ruts. The car bounced in the grass and Jesse forced her original thoughts back, hating herself for thinking it but she had to check all the possibilities.

What if the young man died? What if there was nothing they could do to save him? If they could find his body quickly and gather the evidence to convict this fucker, maybe that would be good enough.

Pausing for a moment, Jesse reminded herself that Floyanne was sober now and that she had only recently begun to truly understand Ciara's mother's addiction. In that moment, her tongue swelled just a little, the taste buds at attention as she thought of a very smooth bourbon. *That would be nice right now.*

She could almost talk herself into it. It would steady her nerves, calm her hands, clear her thinking of the clutter. She had fifty different threads that were all vying for attention. *Bourbon would help.*

Maybe it was simply best that there wasn't any in the car. It wasn't a decision she had to make. If she didn't follow through tonight she would never be able to sleep again.

Georgia was already climbing out as Jesse parked, her motions showing that she was stuffing the gun down the back of her pants again. Jesse didn't have a spare holster for her, but she grabbed her own from the glove box even as Cindy climbed out. At least this time, she wasn't dressed in her bright gear. Jesse took a quick look at their shoes. Sneakers. They were not prepared for this. No packs, no food. All she had was bug spray in the trunk of the car.

She used it, handing it off to the others as if not getting bitten by mosquitoes was the thing that was most important tonight. But the normalcy of it seemed to calm them down and when at last there was nothing else to do, she looked to the others. "Are you ready?"

86

C indy led their little group through the woods, petrified that someone would jump out and stab her. She had been through it before. But, this time, there would not be the little spot at the back of her brain that kept saying *this isn't happening to you*. The first times she'd seen things, she'd told herself *it isn't real*. Unfortunately, she had quickly learned that everything she saw was real and the voice had changed.

This time though, if he jumped out it would be her getting stabbed.

For a moment, she welcomed the thought. It would hurt. It would be terrible. But it would be the last time she would have to live it. Her death would kill Carter though. As much as she needed Carter, Carter needed her.

Footsteps padded behind her as Jesse and Georgia kept pace. Cindy led, pulled forward as if something was connected inside and yanking her along.

"Is this the path he took?" Jesse asked quietly, as if the three of them crunching their way through the woods in the middle of the night wasn't noisy enough.

"No," Cindy said. "He drove around to another entrance. Taking a slightly longer road, but less hiking to . . ." She couldn't bring herself to say *to where he wants to kill the man* because he didn't just want to kill. He wanted the hunt, the victory.

He was prepared. He'd driven the car through mud earlier on purpose, Cindy knew, but she didn't share that.

When a jolt of information hit her, she froze. Jesse ran into her, but Georgia, bringing up the rear, managed to stop herself in time. It took a moment for the three women to regain their footing.

She didn't apologize. "What do we do when we find him? If you kill him, what evidence do we have?"

She could see from the look on Jesse's and Georgia's faces that it was sinking in that they were the ones with the guns. One of them would have to pull the trigger and neither of them had her innate sense of who he was. If there were two people running through the woods, who should they shoot? And what if it was the wrong one?

"Do we have handcuffs?" she asked.

"Zip ties," Jesse said and then, "Fuck. They're in the car."

"If we can't tie him up, can we just detain him? We have guns."

"Does he have a gun?" Jesse asked now. *A bit late.*

"I don't know." His kills were definitely with the knife—that was his preferred method. "Can we hold a gun on him until the police get here?"

Georgia shook her head. "It took almost an hour for the police to arrive last time and that was during day shift. I can't believe he would let us hold a gun on him for any length of time. He'll have every reason to try to escape."

"Monday nights are dark." The phrase grabbed Cindy, thinking again that Georgia's explanation was the right one. The young man was an actor on Broadway and his theater didn't perform Monday nights. The theater was dark which is why he was out tonight.

An easy target. The killer knew this.

"It doesn't matter if he lives or dies. The victim can identify him, right? We just have to find the victim." Georgia looked back and forth between them. "It won't be enough to let him escape. We actually have to find him, make sure that he goes to the police, and ID's the killer."

"Does he know the killer?" Jesse asked, ignoring Georgia's questions.

Cindy felt that information flow in, too. As if it were in a book she possessed and she just needed to look it up. "He bumps into them a couple of times, thinking that at the right time, they'll recognize his face and think he's friendly."

Knowing these things meant she was connected, and she did not like being connected, not like this. She was afraid it wouldn't end until he was dead, but she couldn't quite bring herself to tell the others to just kill him.

"Our primary goal is to keep the victim alive and get them to the police," Jesse reiterated. "If we have to kill the hunter in the process, then we do. We'll just have to believe that the evidence will prove us right."

If not, Cindy thought, *they would all spend the rest of their lives in jail for conspiracy to commit murder.*

87

S he was almost blind in the dark. They didn't carry flashlights, but she followed the tug in her gut until the trail forked. She had to stop, close her eyes, and let herself feel something.

Respectfully Jesse and Georgia waited behind her and, for once, the three of them were quiet. Cindy wished she wouldn't get an answer, but she did. Pointing to the right without saying anything, she began walking again.

They were getting close. Close enough that she turned and pointed at their feet, telling them to stay quiet. They all agreed, though, if they could do it, she didn't know.

It was night. Animals scurried. The occasional nut fell from a tree and bounced and cracked. Birds called and crickets chirped. Or maybe it was frogs. But the sounds of three adult women walking down a path was hard to mistake.

If she didn't break twigs and crunch pine needles, then surely the pounding of her heart was audible. Her breathing grew shallower. Her fingers curled at her sides when she knew she should have them at the ready should she stumble and need to catch herself or should someone jump out.

She could only hope that Georgia or Jesse would shoot this fucker if that happened. Her job would be to give them a clear line of sight, because her other options were fists, or any stick or rock she could pick up.

She went a few more feet, stopped, listened, then moved again. The fourth or fifth time, when she didn't hear anything, Cindy considered giving up.

Then she heard it. A voice, faint, but the terror carried through the still night air. Turning, she looked to Georgia and Jesse. They both motioned to her with their hands up, as if to ask, "What?"

Could they not hear it? Were her ears better or was it something else?

She beckoned them to follow again as she headed toward the voice—voices. She was petrified. Every leaf crunched, every twig cracked beneath her feet and sounded like a gunshot in the middle of the woods.

She heard feet pounding, branches breaking and she realized the young man was up, already running. Her breath sped up as his terror shot through her. He was barefoot, which would slow him down. Because even if he was fast, there would be cuts. He would trip. He could twist an ankle.

In that moment, she realized something else, too—they had to split up.

One of them needed to chase the young man and the other would need to come with her . . . toward the killer. This got worse every second she was still alive.

Turning, she pointed to Jesse and mouthed the word *victim*. Then she pointed along the trail. Jesse nodded and took off, though Georgia looked confused.

Cindy motioned to her to continue to creep along with her. If Georgia heard the taunting voice, she didn't give any indication. But Cindy could hear him.

"Four . . .
Three . . .
Two . . .
One."

88

Georgia watched as Jesse took off in the opposite direction. But then, as she turned, she heard it: the pounding of footsteps, the screaming.

"Help! Someone help!"

But she and Cindy were creeping the other direction. She could make out the last several numbers of a countdown, and her own blood chilled, even though she wasn't the target. She had a feeling she would be soon enough.

Georgia couldn't see him until he burst into action, and she knew then why Cindy had chosen her to go toward their killer: Cindy had watched her in action in the alley. *Fuck.* Georgia was not confident that she could repeat it, but it seemed she was going to have to.

This man, too, was crashing through the brush. But his steps were light, his voice singsongy as he called out, "Ready or not, here I come!"

Georgia's skin crawled, she would never hear that phrase again without it invoking terror. But she couldn't afford any of those thoughts. She had to stay focused if she was going to get out of this alive.

Cindy motioned for her quickly to follow. Now they gave chase, not worried about the noise they made.

Everyone was running. Jesse was running down their victim. Hopefully she'd be able to convince him that she was the help and not the harm.

She and Cindy were crashing through the underbrush, beelining for the voice. Branches and thorns scraped and pulled at her. They snagged her clothing and left raw stinging marks across her bare arms. Several cut at her cheeks, but she repeated to herself that she was not going to die out here tonight.

They ran, pushing forward, Georgia in the lead. She spotted a small clearing just ahead. The moon was high and finally there was light. Just before she could bound into the space, Cindy grabbed her shirt and held her back.

Catching on, she tried to slow her breath as they waited, but they were both breathing loud enough to wake the dead. She saw her gun was out and held firmly in both hands, though she didn't remember pulling it.

So many times her father had made her repeat skills. She'd been irritated, thought it was overkill. Now she silently thanked him. It might be the thing that saved their lives.

Cindy pointed toward the center of the clearing. Then she motioned to stop before showing three fingers, then two, then one.

She and Georgia both leaped, Cindy impressive in her sudden agility. She pointed again, as she whirled to the right, seeming to track where he would be.

As Georgia turned, he came out of the woods, knife in hand. But, spotting them, he stopped still at the edge of the clearing. His head tilted, and his mouth burst into a wide grin. "There you are."

Oh hell no.

Her skin crawled and her heart tried to escape out her

throat, but Georgia made herself assess him. It wasn't good. Though the hand with the blade dropped to his side—almost as if he were giving up—his looked morphed as if to taunt them with a sarcastic, "Oh no. I've been found." But the way his eyes widened as he saw them told her he'd heard them coming and he was excited at the interruption.

Walking slowly forward, he kept his hands down at his side. Georgia would have shot him right then if they had not had the conversation earlier about hoping to bring him in alive. His confession might mean the difference between spending the rest of their lives in prison or not. Evidence from his body could match the older crime scenes. All of it would make a difference.

She stood her ground, holding the gun steadily as she called out, "Don't come any closer."

But he did. She noticed how he held the blade—with his fist around the handle, thumb over the end, sharp edge outward. He wielded more power that way both for a swing and a stab.

"I'm just out playing a game with my friend," he called as though this were a friendly conversation.

"The park's closed," Cindy told him, her voice firm and solid, once again impressing Georgia. Cindy seemed timid but she handled a lot. Apparently, she could stand up to a lot, too, when necessary.

"Then why are *you* here?" He gestured at them with the blade.

"Drop the knife," Georgia demanded, not moving an inch. "Don't come any closer. I will shoot you."

She would. She was not going to let this asshole get a hit on her.

He kept walking—strolling really—until he got close enough that a well-aimed burst of speed could surprise her and have him taking the gun from her hands.

Georgia pulled the trigger.

89

"Stop!" Jesse called out. "Please stop!"

But the young man kept running. He was fast, still in his club clothes, though barefoot. He was frantic and seemed unable to process anything she was saying.

She heard Cindy and Georgia from the other direction, shouts and voices. She could only hope that they were okay, defending themselves and hopefully bringing down their perp.

Again she berated herself for not bringing the zip ties. It had been stupid, and she hoped it didn't get them all killed. She had to focus here. Pounding through the brush, she chased this young man who did not need to be chased. But she needed him.

"Please stop. My name is Jesse." She pushed out the words between harsh breaths. "I'm a private investigator. My friends are stopping him!"

Seeming to finally accept some of it, the young man turned to look over his shoulder, but he was still running. His foot caught and twisted as he went down harshly. She could hear the sharp grunt as he hit the ground.

Her gun was out and as she moved closer, his hands flew up to cover his face. "No, no no no!"

Only then did she realize what she was doing. Trusting that Cindy was right, she prayed this was the victim and not their killer. Even Cindy hadn't seen his face.

A quick scan told Jesse he didn't have anything on him, no weapons she could see. She trusted that his bare feet meant she was right. She moved the gun to the side, pointing it away, but not holstering it. She had to be ready if someone came at her.

They were still operating on the assumption that the killer was only one person. *What if they were wrong?*

"Don't shoot." He wasn't yelling anymore. There were tears behind his voice and Jesse's heart cracked for him.

"I won't. I'm here to help. My name is Jesse Nash. I'm a private investigator. And I've been hunting this man for . . ." *Shit. Two months?*

Not long enough for this kind of trouble. She wondered if the Burkhardt's would give her a bonus for bringing Hannalyn's killer in herself.

"I need you," Jesse told him. "This isn't the first time he did this and it won't be the last, even if you get away. My friends are trying to detain him, but you'll need to identify him to the police."

To her surprise, he immediately protested.

Damn. It was a form of victim self-preservation, she knew. If he never spoke about it, maybe it simply hadn't happened. But Jesse wasn't above threatening.

"If you don't, he'll kill other people. That will be on your head." *Awful,* she thought. But she was out here tonight because if she didn't it would be on *her* head.

In the distance, she heard noises and hoped that Jesse and Cindy were holding their own. "My friends are detaining him now. He can't get you."

She hoped she was right. As long as he didn't somehow get

through them and come after her and the young man. Again, she remembered Cindy saying that this man killed two hikers simply for seeing him in action.

She decided she would be okay. Though Jesse knew everyone felt that way—everyone believed until the very last moment that they would be the one to survive—she believed it now.

It should have been a sign just how close death was.

Right now, her advantage was that she knew what he was, she had come here specifically for this killer, and she was prepared.

"I need you to come with me." The man just looked at her like he wanted to say no. She pushed. "If you want me to keep you safe, you have to agree to go to the police."

Straight up *blackmail,* she knew. And he looked stupid enough to refuse. At last, he agreed and started to get up, only as he did, he yelped.

His ankle. He'd twisted it on the way down. Not a good time, but not much she could do about it.

"Get me out of here."

Jesse held out. "We have to get my friends first."

He protested again, seeming to realize that meant going back the way he had come, back toward the killer.

Jesse wondered then if any of the victims simply didn't run. If they decided it wasn't worth it, and their last act was to steal the bastard's satisfaction. But now was not the time for any of that.

"We're going back. I'm not leaving my friends."

Whatever he said, she was his only means of transportation, of survival. She motioned to him to give her his hand so she could help him up onto his one still good foot. Then she draped his arm over her shoulder, using only one hand to stabilize him. It was all she could afford.

It barely worked. She needed her other hand for the gun,

because she no longer heard Cindy and Georgia. No one yelled out that they were fine. The noises from the other direction were not promising.

With tearful and heavy weight across her shoulders, she led the young man back exactly in the direction he didn't want to go. And she prayed that she found her friends still alive.

90

Georgia felt all her blood and her self-respect drain to the soles of her feet as the gun merely clicked.

She pulled the trigger again, her shame only heightened as the man laughed and ran toward her.

Son of a bitch! Her father had told her to practice, and she hadn't! She hadn't gone shooting again, not since sophomore year, when he'd insisted she do another round of practice.

Here she was. She had picked up a gun that was not loaded and not noticed it was too light. *Fuck her.*

The bullet she'd shot at the asshole's feet in the alley had been one in the chamber. She pulled the trigger again, as if this time it would suddenly work. But it didn't.

It all went down lightning fast—her actions, her guilt, her shame.

He was running toward her now and he had the knife out and ready. The golucky expression had turned to rage as he leapt toward her.

All she had was the metal in her fist. Cindy was already running.

Georgia turned and bolted but quickly outpaced Cindy. She

considered calling out for Jesse. Jesse had a gun, too, and Jesse's gun would be *loaded*.

Georgia still gripped the other one tightly. Her brain going a thousand miles an hour, and she had the almost hysterically stupid thought that at least with no bullets, the rifling from this gun would not be associated with this crime.

Reaching back, she grabbed Cindy's hand. She pulled the other woman along, as if her own speed could be transferred. But Cindy could only move so fast. Though fear gave her some burst, she was no match for a man who spent his time hunting humans in the woods.

Cindy's fingers clenched in her own, tighter for a brief moment, before they were yanked away. As Georgia turned, she slowly watched as Cindy stumbled backwards. He had grasped her clothing, grabbed her away from Georgia, and pulled her back in the blink of an eye.

He had Cindy's back pressed against him, an arm tight around her, and the knife at her throat. A sick grin twisted his features.

Georgia stood stock still. What could she do? He might hold Cindy as a threat, but there was absolutely no reason for him not to kill her. He had killed enough before that one more would change nothing for him.

He might keep her alive as a means of manipulation and Georgia prayed that was what he was going to do.

She could see from the look on Cindy's face that similar thoughts must be going through her own head. Though he held her with one arm wrapped around her torso, he pinned her arms at her side.

Georgia could see Cindy didn't fight. If she twisted, twitched or dropped, the blade at her throat would surely slice something important.

"If you run," he said, his voice lilting again, the words sickly sweet, "I'm killing your friend."

Georgia nodded. It was exactly as she had expected.

She watched as Cindy slowly closed her eyes and took a deep breath. His arms tightened down, and Georgia stood motionless, her useless gun at her side.

Cindy's slow deep breathing made her wonder if the woman was going to do something. He seemed to sense it, too.

Leaning forward, he spoke into Cindy's ear.

Georgia couldn't hear it. In her own silence, the forest had gotten louder. A cacophony of crickets and frogs and other night noises drowned out what he said.

It didn't seem to affect Cindy, but she slowly leaned into his words, until his lips touched her cheek in a grotesque kiss. Only then did Georgia realize what Cindy was doing.

The psychic jolted.

Cindy's shirt was long-sleeved despite the warm night. She'd leaned in for skin contact with the man who'd haunted her for months.

Electricity seemed to shoot through her body, her head snapping back and cracking against his hard enough to make him slightly lose hold. But Cindy didn't take the opportunity to break free. She was in a trance of some kind. A place where she'd put herself.

Georgia didn't know why. Maybe simply so she wouldn't be in her own body for her death.

It looked like a seizure, but it was enough to make him step back and eye her oddly.

Cindy might not be in her own head, but Georgia was. She took advantage of the momentary distraction and rushed forward.

J esse heard the sounds of the scuffle—the yells and the fighting, screams of terror that seemed to come from Cindy.

She didn't even know the name of the young man whose arm she had slung over her shoulder, but Jesse made a split second decision. She threw him off, letting him fall to the ground and told him, "Don't go anywhere."

She was almost tempted to add "I will find you," because she would. But there wasn't time, and he didn't need the threat.

Bolting toward the sounds, she rechecked the gun, making sure she had a bullet chambered. She clutched it tightly like the savior she hoped it could be.

All she could do was head toward the sound until she got to the clearing where she found Georgia fighting for her life against a man with a knife, a man desperately trying to stab her.

Stopping, knowing a bullet was their best bet, Jesse planted her feet and raised the gun.

She was close enough.

But she couldn't get a clean shot.

Georgia moved to block his swing. The knife came at her, moonlight glinting, putting all her instincts on high alert.

Turning, she raised two fists, pounding her forearms against his, blocking. Hopefully she bruised him as bad as she bruised herself, but he didn't drop the knife.

Most of her defensive moves were for use against average everyday attackers, like the mugger in the alley. Not with someone hell bent on killing her. But she wasn't going to let him cut her.

Dropping low, she attempted to get out of range of the blade. She swept her foot, but he dodged easily.

He didn't move like a trained martial artist, but there was still something feral and wily about him. As if he sensed when she was coming at him and from where.

Her thoughts tested every possibility, but her instinct had her stepping back. She tried to get out of arm's reach, because one step forward, one swing of the blade, and he would slash her.

She hyper focused, aware of nothing else as she let him

rush at her, his face a snarl of tangled rage. She stepped aside, one foot out, grabbing his other arm as she spun him, slamming him to the ground.

But he popped up as if he had simply bounced, something preternaturally evil controlling him. Before she had time to prepare, she had to defend herself again. Only this time the tip of the blade found its way into her shoulder. The cut burned like fire, but maybe even hotter was her anger raging up inside her.

How dare he?

She still had the gun in her hand. Though it was useless as a firearm, it made a solid rock.

He pulled her in close, chest to chest—a hug that, on any other day would have made her vomit. Taking advantage of the fact that he was taller than her and lean, she clenched her fist around the gun. Then raised it up behind his shoulder and whacked him hard at the base of his head as he tried to bring the knife down into her back.

The hit jolted him enough that they both paused. She put another inch between them as she heard Jesse yelling, "Don't move. I'll shoot."

Thank God, Georgia thought, though she was just as concerned as she was relieved. There was every possibility that Jesse had shown up just in time to watch her die. He was still close enough to do it.

At least Jesse would be able to save herself and Cindy.

Georgia's thoughts flashed to Cindy, then. *Where was she?*

But he grabbed her, spinning her around and startling her. She hated that she didn't gain her feet as quickly as she would like. He was attempting to pull her back to him, to put the knife to her throat the way he'd done to Cindy earlier.

She did not have Cindy's visions. She would not be able to startle him with that move. But she had no idea if Cindy was still mid-seizure in the grass, or what.

His voice was loud, blasting past her ear. His breath churning every organ as he called out to Jesse, "Go ahead. Shoot me. But are you going to shoot your friend, too?"

He was using her as a shield. Jesse would have to put a bullet through her to get it into him. Georgia almost wished she would.

She could feel the blade pressing along the side of her throat as she tried to figure out what to do next. If she dropped, she'd lean right into the blade. If she tried to slide out the side, she would just make it cut her.

With no options left that didn't end up with her dead. She closed her eyes and waited.

93

J esse stood still, her gun aimed right at his forehead.

Her focus was laser-like, but was her *aim?*

Was she good enough to hit him cleanly between the eyes, missing Georgia entirely? Because if she missed by even just a few inches, she would execute her junior partner instead.

At the gun range, she was steady and sharp, but now everything was shaking. Though she fought for whatever composure she could drum up, she was confident she didn't have it.

She blustered again. "I'll shoot you!"

He just laughed, throwing his head back. The knife was still at Georgia's throat, he was entirely in control. Jesse could see it.

He had no doubt that he could take all three of them and still hunt the man he had abducted. It wouldn't be what he planned, but it appeared the interruption was simply part of the challenge.

She loosened her hands and resettled them on the grip, feeling the sweat now between her palms and the butt of the gun. Her finger slowly squeezed the trigger, but not quite all the way.

Could she do this? If she missed, if she watched Georgia go down with a red hole in her forehead, Jesse would simply put the barrel in her own mouth next.

She didn't squeeze. She stared at him, the two of them stuck in a horrific standoff. Or only horrific for her and Georgia. He seemed to enjoy it, which only made her stomach roll.

At least if he sliced Georgia's throat, she would drop, and Jesse could shoot him then. What a morbid thought. Jesse pushed it far away.

"Seems we're stuck," he said. Then he laughed again—a chuckle that seemed to taunt her, to prove that he had the upper hand here.

Her rage screamed to be let go, to lose control and go wild. But she didn't do it. She only caught a flash of light color behind him. There was no other warning before she watched him jerk, limbs suddenly going slack.

Georgia must have felt the change and whirled deftly away.

Jesse felt the relief flood her as she watched Georgia move clear, but when her eyes shot back to him, she saw Cindy standing there, a rock clenched in her hand covered in blood, her own rage clouding her eyes.

She didn't look up. She just kicked him and screamed, "Never again, motherfucker!"

94

I t was almost twenty-four hours later, and Jesse was still shaking from the encounter.

Cindy had dropped him. He was out cold, but not dead.

There was, however, an obvious dent in his skull. Though Jesse didn't want to admit it, the blood on the rock still gave her a feeling of satisfaction.

He was in the hospital getting the best of care. The EMTs had cleaned and stitched Georgia's shoulder wound before handing her over to the police. He hadn't hit anything major, though Georgia was clearly pissed off that he'd gotten her. But she was alive.

Jesse tried to remind her friend, "We got him." But the three of them were pulled in different directions. The local Sherriff's deputies were no stranger to murder. But until it was all sorted out, they held all five of them in custody.

They'd found a man down on the forest floor in a closed National Park, a knife near his fingers, with only the slightest amount of Georgia's blood on it. Jesse and Georgia both had guns.

There was the rock Cindy had set nearby that had clearly been used to bash his head. Another young man was alternately whimpering and screaming for help, no matter what Jesse told him. He'd laid there, with only a twisted ankle, just past the edge of the trees. The deputies had listened to everyone's story and hauled them all in, waiting for evidence.

Jesse liked to remind them that Georgia was the one who'd called the police. But that wasn't enough to get them off. There'd been a moment where they'd considered flinging the gun Georgia held away into the woods. But, if the crime scene team was any good, they would find it. It would have Georgia's fingerprints on it and probably evidence from other crime scenes.

Hell, they decided just to tell the whole story as it was. With one omission.

In their version Cindy was a PI in training. She'd come along on this case to shadow them and see if it was a job she was truly interested in. *It seemed things had simply gotten much more hairy than expected.*

Jesse knew that story wouldn't hold for too long. It had to stick just long enough for someone else to get them out of here. Because once they checked Cindy's history, if they looked her up any more than just running her name for priors, it would all come out.

It was possible, there was no chance of her getting out of this with her secret intact.

Jesse had stewed in her own interrogation room and answered the same questions three and four times. Putting her head down on the table, she'd finally fallen asleep. She ate chips covered in orange powdered flavoring and drank nothing but sodas until she finally asked for a water. She didn't need the sugar. She sure didn't need the caffeine.

Eventually, they'd woken her, pulled her out, and put her into a separate holding cell. Quickly, Cindy and Georgia had been led in. Jesse popped up and hugged each of them as the cell door had clanked heavily shut.

It was just the three of them, no one else nearby that she could tell. Maybe the deputies were watching, hoping they would say something incriminating now that they were together. Instead, Jesse just said she was glad to see them.

All three seemed to understand there might be recording devices or cameras. So they asked if each other was okay, if they'd eaten, how was the young man faring? Then Jesse watched as Carter showed up to see his sister.

Cindy jumped to her feet of her own accord and stepped into her brother's arms. She broke into sobs even as the deputy let him into the cell. Then Carter was taken back out front.

An hour later, Jesse got to meet former FBI agent Owen Dunham. His blonde hair was graying at the temples, he had small lines around his eyes, and a face that somehow looked a lot like Georgia's despite everything Jesse knew.

She watched as father and daughter embraced with the kind of soul crushing hug that happened when you realized you were still alive.

But Jesse realized no one was coming for her. There was no one willing to drive or fly across the country to hug her just because they were glad that she was safe.

It hadn't really occurred to her before that maybe this was why she had held on to Ciara so tightly. Her parents would likely pay the bail through a service once they got the message she'd left. Maybe. *Two more days*, she thought. She'd lived through the night. She could make the call to her stepdaughter to be sure that the child was okay. To see if maybe she wanted to come home.

Or—and Jesse had to accept this if it happened—if maybe Ciara felt that where she was now was home. Jesse pushed that fear aside, because things began to move once Owen Dunham released his daughter from the cell and began making demands.

Jesse and Cindy waited.

The young man was also in the hospital getting treated for a twisted ankle and likely interrogated to death. She'd learned his name was William Pollar.

She thought of him as the eighth victim, but Owen Dunham had done more than just fly across the country to hug his daughter. Somewhere in route, he'd pulled as many strings as he could.

The man in the hospital with his head bashed in—much to Cindy's pride—was Gareth Dean Wallensky.

Jesse had learned that from the deputies asking her how she knew him and why she was in the woods. The name meant nothing, but she figured out pretty quickly who it had to be.

Owen and Georgia had disappeared down the hallway, the same as Carter. Fifteen minutes later they were back, and Owen was instructing the local officers to release Jesse and Cindy.

Jesse hadn't been aware all her muscles were clenched until she passed through the cell door, finally free.

The five of them had stood in the lobby, Cindy and Carter leaning against each other. Still twins. Never having quite outgrown the bond, Jesse thought.

Owen kept an arm around his daughter, as if he needed to hold her close to know that she was still there. Jesse wanted to tell both men how brilliant their family members had been, but instead Owen opened his mouth.

"We have a team on Wallensky's house already."

He was starting to say more, but Georgia interrupted him. "What is Wallensky like?"

Her father shrugged as if it were an odd question. "He looks like your usual good guy." Georgia made him explain. "He's on his church council, volunteers at a youth shelter, and is the only person in upper management to have been Employee of the Month five times at his company."

Georgia's eyes flicked to her, and Jesse almost laughed. *A very good name.*

But not after this.

Owen didn't catch the interaction, but he told them, "The team has already uncovered enough evidence to put him away. They pulled his wife and teenage son out and tore the place up. The evidence wasn't even that hidden."

What had they found? But it clicked. Like a kid in class who couldn't contain that she knew the answer, she blurted out, "The other shoes."

Owen nodded. "In the bedroom closet in a box, several boxes actually."

Several. Her stomach churned.

Georgia sat up in the middle of the night sucking in air.

But she stilled herself and listened. No footsteps came down the hall. She'd not woken anyone with her nightmares this time. It was only her and the dark creeping in at the edge of her dreams.

Nothing specific tonight. No one chasing her with a knife. No Gareth Dean Wallensky with his face haunting her dreams. No being abducted away from her friends. She'd had them all over the past few weeks.

Tonight there was just the eerie sense of impending doom. She had to count that as an improvement. Listening again, she made sure the hallways were silent and her parents were not coming to check on her.

She'd said goodbye to Jesse and Cindy there in New Jersey. Cindy had left with Carter, saying she would gather her things later if that was okay. Georgia and her dad had ridden with Jesse back to the rental car, the drive long and quiet.

Georgia grabbed her bag from the rental, then they'd dropped Jesse at her own car. She and her dad had returned the rental to the airport. From there, he'd booked them flights home. Georgia had slept in her own bed for three weeks now.

She had been telling herself she was recuperating. That she would feel better soon, start studying for the LSAT. Or she would as soon as she started sleeping better. But it had been three weeks, time to get moving, better sleep or not.

She stood up, thinking she should feel safer here, but home didn't quite fit either now.

Her room was stuck in time—exactly the way that she had designed it as a freshman entering high school. Her mother had done that for each of the girls: a big shopping trip to redecorate however they wanted for their high school years. But in college, she hadn't lived here, changing it again would have been pointless. Charlotte and Virginia's rooms were already converted into guest rooms. Only hers still held the bright tinge of hopeful youth.

It wasn't the room, though. It was Georgia who didn't fit anymore.

Feeling that she was fully awake whether she'd slept well or not, she decided to do something. Resting seemed to work better during the day hours, but she tried not to acknowledge what that meant. That meant, if she was going to work, it should be now.

At her desk, she pulled out the old office chair in the bright shade of blue that she had been so excited to find at fifteen. She sat down, the white desk showing its scuffs and marks and occasional nicks. Opening the book she had, she began reading about the different sections on the law school entrance exam.

Five pages later, she found none of it had stuck. She opened her laptop and checked her email, deleting the spam and the advertisements that had piled up the last few days.

She stopped. There was one from Jesse.

It had been there for two days, and Georgia hadn't opened it, hadn't seen it.

It probably wrapped up the case, but the case was Jesse's baby, not hers. It was Jesse who went back to the Burkhardts and told them about Wallensky. How he was out of the hospital and healing nicely in prison while he awaited trial.

They were hoping he would confess and plead out soon. At least for the murders that they had found the bodies for. Maybe more. There had been so many more ...

Georgia couldn't help but think, as she looked at the subject line that she didn't want to click, that there had been twenty-six single shoes in the boxes in his closet.

She had been *wrong*. He wasn't on an eighteen-month cycle. He was on a six-month cycle. One every spring and every fall— so many more than she had imagined.

More than any of them had expected.

William would have been number twenty-seven.

Georgia followed Pollar on social media. His ankle had healed—not a break, just a sprain. By last week, he was back in the chorus singing his heart out on Broadway. Good for him, she thought.

Good for them.

Then, knowing she couldn't put it off, she clicked on the email from Jesse. She fought the urge to squeeze her eyes shut so she still couldn't see it.

Sooner or later she would need to look. She might need to respond, though she figured it was just the same things her father had already told her. She'd pushed him to keep her apprised of the evidence piling up against Wallensky.

Using Cindy's triangulation with the maps, they had already found three more bodies, and had an ID confirmed on two.

Opening her eyes, Georgia forced herself to read the email.

Blurry at first, it was blessedly short. She blinked twice and read.

· · ·

GEORGIA,

I WANTED to thank you for all your help with the Burkhardt case.
Your work was essential to cracking it. You helped save lives.
    As per our bargain, I've continued to search for your mother.
    I found something.
    Call me.

ABOUT THE AUTHOR

A.J.'s world is strange place where patterns jump out and catch the eye, little is missed, and most of it can be recalled with a deep breath. In this world, the smell of Florida takes three weeks to fully leave the senses and the air in Dallas is so thick that the planes "sink" to the runways rather than actually landing.

For A.J., reality is always a little bit off from the norm and something usually lurks right under the surface. As a story-teller, A.J. loves irony, the unexpected, and a puzzle where all the pieces fit and make sense. Originally a scientist and a teacher, the writer says research is always a key player in the stories. AJ's motto is "It could happen. It wouldn't. But it could."

A.J. has lived in Florida and Los Angeles among a handful of other places. Recent whims have brought the dark writer to Tennessee, where home is a deceptively normal-looking neighborhood just outside Nashville.

For more information:
www.ReadAJS.com
AJ@ReadAJS.com

 X

www.ingramcontent.com/pod-product-compliance
Lightning Source LLC
Chambersburg PA
CBHW021127260626
47169CB00005B/1493